Rape in Stieg Larsson's Millennium Trilogy and Beyond

Also by Berit Åström

THE POLITICS OF TRADITION: Examining the History of the Old English Poems the Wife's Lament and Wulf and Eadwacer

Also by Katarina Gregersdotter

WATCHING WOMEN, FALLING WOMEN: A Reading of Margaret Atwood's Friendship Trilogy

Also by Tanya Horeck

THE NEW EXTREMISM IN CINEMA: From France to Europe (*co-edited with Tina Kendall*)

PUBLIC RAPE: Representing Violation in Fiction and Film

Rape in Stieg Larsson's Millennium Trilogy and Beyond

Contemporary Scandinavian and Anglophone Crime Fiction

Edited by

Berit Åström
Senior Lecturer, Umeå University, Sweden

Katarina Gregersdotter
Senior Lecturer, Umeå University, Sweden

and

Tanya Horeck
Senior Lecturer, Anglia Ruskin University, UK

Introduction, selection and editorial matter © Berit Åström, Katarina Gregersdotter and Tanya Horeck 2013
Individual chapters © Contributors 2013

All rights reserved. No reproduction, copy or transmission of this publication may be made without written permission.

No portion of this publication may be reproduced, copied or transmitted save with written permission or in accordance with the provisions of the Copyright, Designs and Patents Act 1988, or under the terms of any licence permitting limited copying issued by the Copyright Licensing Agency, Saffron House, 6–10 Kirby Street, London EC1N 8TS.

Any person who does any unauthorized act in relation to this publication may be liable to criminal prosecution and civil claims for damages.

The authors have asserted their rights to be identified as the authors of this work in accordance with the Copyright, Designs and Patents Act 1988.

First published 2013 by
PALGRAVE MACMILLAN

Palgrave Macmillan in the UK is an imprint of Macmillan Publishers Limited, registered in England, company number 785998, of Houndmills, Basingstoke, Hampshire RG21 6XS.

Palgrave Macmillan in the US is a division of St Martin's Press LLC, 175 Fifth Avenue, New York, NY 10010.

Palgrave Macmillan is the global academic imprint of the above companies and has companies and representatives throughout the world.

Palgrave® and Macmillan® are registered trademarks in the United States, the United Kingdom, Europe and other countries

ISBN: 978–0–230–30840–4

This book is printed on paper suitable for recycling and made from fully managed and sustained forest sources. Logging, pulping and manufacturing processes are expected to conform to the environmental regulations of the country of origin.

A catalogue record for this book is available from the British Library.

A catalog record for this book is available from the Library of Congress.

10 9 8 7 6 5 4 3 2 1
22 21 20 19 18 17 16 15 14 13

Printed and bound in the United States of America

Contents

Acknowledgements	vii
Notes on Contributors	ix
Introduction Tanya Horeck, Katarina Gregersdotter, and Berit Åström	1

Part I Stieg Larsson's Millennium Trilogy: Opening up the Debate

1. 'The Girl Who Pays Our Salaries': Rape and the Bestselling Millennium Trilogy 21
Priscilla Walton

2. The Millennium Trilogy and the American Serial Killer Narrative: Investigating Protagonists of Men Who Write Women 34
Barbara Fister

3. Lisbeth Salander as a Melodramatic Heroine: Emotional Conflicts, Split Focalization, and Changing Roles in Scandinavian Crime Fiction 51
Yvonne Leffler

Part II Dismembered Bodies, Wounded States: Gender Politics in the Millennium Trilogy and Beyond

4. Rape and the Avenging Female in Stieg Larsson's Millennium Trilogy and Håkan Nesser's *Woman with Birthmark* and *The Inspector and Silence* 67
Marla Harris

5. The Body, Hopelessness, and Nostalgia: Representations of Rape and the Welfare State in Swedish Crime Fiction 81
Katarina Gregersdotter

6. Over Her Dismembered Body: The Crime Fiction of Mo Hayder and Jo Nesbø 97
Berit Åström

Part III Rewriting Scripts: Language, Gender, and Violence in Contemporary Crime Fiction

7 Disarticulated Figures: Language and Sexual Violence in Contemporary Crime Fiction   117
   Meghan A. Freeman

8 Male Fantasy, Sexual Exploitation, and the *Femme Fatale*: Reframing Scripts of Power and Gender in Neo-*noir* Novels by Sara Paretsky, Megan Abbott and Stieg Larsson   136
   Zoë Brigley Thompson

Part IV Ethics, Violence, and Adaptation

9 Rape and Replay in Stieg Larsson, Liza Marklund, and Val McDermid: On Affect, Ethics, and Feeling Bad   157
   Tanya Horeck

10 *The Girl with the Dragon Tattoo*: Rape, Revenge, and Victimhood in Cinematic Translation   175
    Claire Henry

11 'Hidden in the Snow': Female Violence against the Men Who Hate Women in the Millennium Adaptations   193
    Philippa Gates

Index   215

Acknowledgements

In a book that seeks to open up a dialogue between Scandinavian and Anglophone crime fiction, it seems important to acknowledge our own cultural location as authors. Two of us (Berit and Katarina) are Swedish and work at Umeå University, while the other (Tanya) is Canadian/British and works at Anglia Ruskin University in the UK. All three of us share an interest in contemporary crime fiction, and we came together for this project to see what kinds of questions we could open up about the status of violence in crime novels through a cross-cultural approach. Working across cultures – and languages – has thrown up a series of interesting challenges and has made each of us re-evaluate our views on violence in the crime novel and the ways in which we encounter it. The results have been more fascinating and engaging than we could have hoped for. We would first of all like to say a heartfelt thank you to our wonderful contributors, who come from Australia, Canada, the US, Sweden, and the UK. Each and every one of you rose to the challenge of exploring how your own research on sexual violence and crime novels relates to the intriguing cultural phenomenon that is Stieg Larsson's Millennium trilogy. We would also like to thank Palgrave Macmillan, and in particular Felicity Plester, for seeing the potential of this project in its early stages, and Catherine Mitchell for answering our questions so patiently. Thanks also to the anonymous reader of our original book proposal, whose suggestions on narrowing the focus proved to be very astute. We could not have completed this work without the support of our respective institutions: thanks to Anglia Ruskin University for providing Tanya with a sabbatical during which she was able to complete the project and to Umeå Centre for Gender Studies, and in particular Annelie Bränström Öhman, for providing Katarina and Berit with much appreciated research time. Many other people helped along the way: thanks to Tina Kendall, still the best 'reader' in the business, who gave critical input at a crucial stage; Milla Tiainen for offering her ever intellectually astute and perceptive thoughts; Lisa Coulthard, Mary Joannou, Joss Hands, and Sarah Barrow for their support; Peter Messent for valuable and clever comments on an early draft; and Heidi Hansson for reading and asking difficult questions. Special thanks to Barbara Fister for being such a fantastic font of information on all things to do with crime fiction, and to Philippa Gates and Zoë Brigley Thompson for their wonderfully incisive and helpful suggestions. Finally, for all their support through the long winter months of writing and editing, we would like to thank our families: Patrick and Michael Yates, Liv Enqvist and Nicklas Hållén, and Hugh, Grace, and Edward Perry.

Contributors

Berit Åström is Senior Lecturer in English at Umeå University, Sweden. Her work spans centuries and genres, from Old English love poetry, to contemporary crime and science fiction, to male pregnancy fan fiction. In 2011–2012 she was visiting scholar at Anglia Ruskin University, Cambridge, UK, where she held an Intra-European Fellowship from Marie Curie Actions, Seventh Framework Programme, for a project called 'Transhistorical Tropes of Female Subordination', which investigates the recurring trope of dead and absent mothers in Western literature, from antiquity to the present day.

Zoë Brigley Thompson is Lecturer in English and Creative Writing. She is a reader for the journal *Orbis Litterarum* and for the Routledge/Taylor and Francis database ABES (The Annotated Bibliography of English Studies). She has published the edited collection *Feminism, Literature and Rape Narratives: Violence and Violation* (2010), which also features her essays 'Introduction: Transnational Feminism(s) and Rape Scripts' and 'The Wound and the Mask: Rape, Recovery and Poetry'. She has also published a collection of poetry *The Secret* (2007).

Barbara Fister is an academic librarian at Gustavus Adolphus College in Minnesota and the author of a guide to women's literature from the third world as well as three mysteries, the most recent of which is *Through the Cracks* (2010). She maintains a website on Scandinavian crime fiction in English translation and writes about academic libraries for Library Journal and Inside Higher Ed.

Meghan A. Freeman received her doctorate in Victorian literature from Cornell University and is currently employed as an adjunct assistant professor in the Department of English at Tulane University in New Orleans, Louisiana. Her current project concerns the representation of aesthetic experience in the nineteenth-century novel, with a particular emphasis on how this experience is refracted through the lens of gender and sexuality. She has taught courses on Victorian literature and culture, mystery and crime writing, as well as women's literature.

Philippa Gates is Associate Professor in Film Studies at Wilfrid Laurier University in Canada. Her publications include *Detecting Women: Gender* *and the Hollywood Detective Film* (2011), *Detecting Men: Masculinity and the Hollywood Detective Film* (2006), and *The Devil Himself: Villainy in Detective Fiction and Film,* co-edited with Stacy Gillis, (2002). Her current book project is an edited collection titled *Transnational Asian Identities in Pan-Pacific Cinemas: The Reel Asian Exchange* (with Lisa Funnell; forthcoming).

Katarina Gregersdotter is Senior Lecturer at Umeå University, Sweden, and a literary critic. Her main area of research is Anglophone and Scandinavian contemporary crime fiction, but she works on a wide variety of subjects, including Margaret Atwood, zombies, gender, and emotions. Her latest article is 'Made Men and Constructed Masculinities: Viewing the Father-Son Relationship in *The Sopranos*', and she is currently co-editing, with Nicklas Hållén, an interdisciplinary anthology on masculinity and femininity in literature, media, politics, and social studies (forthcoming).

Marla Harris is an independent scholar with a PhD from Brandeis University, where she completed a dissertation on silence in eighteenth-century British women's fiction. She has published journal essays and book chapters on a variety of literary topics, including detective fiction, young adult literature, and graphic novels.

Claire Henry is a PhD candidate in the English, Film, and Media department at Anglia Ruskin University. Her current research examines the politics, ethics, and affects of contemporary rape-revenge cinema. She holds an MA in Screen Studies and a BA in Cinema Studies and Gender Studies from the University of Melbourne, Australia.

Tanya Horeck is Senior Lecturer in Film Studies at Anglia Ruskin University. She is the author of *Public Rape: Representing Violation in Fiction and Film* (2004) and co-editor, with Tina Kendall, of the anthology *The New Extremism in Cinema: From France to Europe* (2011). Her research interests include contemporary film and theory, documentary, violence, crime, affect, and spectatorship.

Yvonne Leffler is Professor of Comparative Literature at the University of Gothenburg, Sweden. She has published several books and articles about Gothic fiction, nineteenth-century novels, and popular fiction in postmodern society. She is currently leading an interdisciplinary research project, 'Fiction, Play, and Health', the aim of which is to explore how popular stories serve as modern myths that establish and reveal present ideas of happiness, success, and well-being.

Priscilla Walton is Professor of English at Carleton University in Canada. Her publications include *Our Cannibals, Ourselves: The Body Politic* (2004), *Patriarchal Desire and Victorian Discourse: A Lacanian Reading of Anthony Trollope's Palliser Novels* (1995) and, together with Manina Jones, *Detective Agency: Women Rewriting the Hardboiled Tradition* (1999). She is presently working with Sheryl Hamilton, Neil Gerlach, and Rebecca Sullivan on a new project called *Biotechnological Imaginings: From Science Fiction to Social Fact*.

Introduction

Tanya Horeck, Katarina Gregersdotter, and Berit Åström

A 'bleak and savage story'

The long-awaited Hollywood remake of *The Girl with the Dragon Tattoo* (2011), by director David Fincher, came with warnings from its lead actor, Daniel Craig, that it contained very violent material, and was for adult eyes only. The film's reviewers duly noted its graphic and 'slick' violence (Scott 2011; Phillips 2011) but it is rather surprising how the rape and revenge scenes – which are central to the film and to the Millennium trilogy as a whole – are elided in the film's critical reception in North America and the UK. Sexual violence is not seriously discussed, debated, or indeed in some cases even mentioned, in the film's reviews,[1] possibly because at this stage in the cultural retelling of the bestselling Millennium trilogy, the story is so familiar. As Kenneth Turan wrote in the *Los Angeles Times*:

> As readers of the Stieg Larsson novel and viewers of the recent Swedish film version know all too well, what's on offer is a bleak and savage story of crime and punishment that features generous portions of sadistic rape, twisted torture and murders that can charitably be called grotesque. (2011)

Of course, such a statement begs the question of what, exactly, is so fascinating about such 'grotesque violence' which, by now, has been replayed over and over for our cultural consumption, from novels to Swedish film versions to Hollywood blockbuster.

Taking as our starting point the 'bleak and savage story' of rape and revenge found in the Millennium franchise, this book sets out to explore the issue of rape and sexualized violence in contemporary

Scandinavian and Anglophone crime fiction. One of the main aims of this anthology is to contextualize Stieg Larsson's work by putting the Millennium trilogy into dialogue with, on the one hand, a selection of Scandinavian crime writers such as Jo Nesbø, Liza Marklund, and Håkan Nesser and, on the other hand, Anglophone crime writers including Sara Paretsky, Val McDermid, and Megan Abbott. While many commentators have noted the influence of Anglophone writers on Larsson's work, this source of inspiration has not yet been explored in any detail. At the same time, as publishers continue to eagerly capitalize on each new Scandinavian writer as 'the next Stieg Larsson', there has not been a sustained attempt to put the work of Larsson into dialogue with that of other Scandinavian writers. In comparing and contrasting the work of these different writers, and in exploring the productive exchange that occurs between Anglophone and Scandinavian crime fiction, we open up important questions about the 'bleak and savage' violence that Larsson's work has come to be both criticized and applauded for.[2]

It is necessary to keep in mind that the idea of a unified 'Scandinavian crime novel' is problematic (Nestingen and Arvas 2011: 9), as indeed is the idea of an 'Anglophone' one. While we recognize the necessity of respecting the cultural and historical specificity of individual novels, our concern is how reading crime novels from different geographical and cultural locations provides insights into how notions of sexual violence, victims, and vengeance are constructed across cultures. And, as many of the essays illustrate, there are close links and similarities (as well as intriguing disjunctions) between the approaches to sexual violence in the selection of Scandinavian and Anglophone crime novels (and films) explored in this volume.[3]

Violence towards women has a long and complicated history in crime fiction, dating back at least as far as the lurid penny dreadfuls of the nineteenth century, with their stories of sexual violation, murder, and mayhem. It should be noted, however, that this volume is not intended as a study of the history of sexual violence in crime writing;[4] rather, we are interested in exploring the ways rape is used to voice social and political criticism and to explore questions of victimization and agency. While rape and sexual violence is an integral part of crime fiction, this is the first book-length study to interrogate the role that it plays in the genre.[5] That rape is everywhere present in crime fiction yet surprisingly under-theorized in the critical literature on the genre attests to the curious way in which 'rape is at once present and absent, a given, but not quite there' (Russell 2010: 2). Though it is often overlooked as a mere plot device, or dismissed for its violent excess, sexualized violence is, as the contributors to this book demonstrate, fundamental to contemporary crime fiction and its attempts to raise critical questions regarding socio-political formations, the body politic, and the relationship between the individual and society.

In our engagement with debates over gender, sexual violence, and vengeance in contemporary crime fiction, we want to build on the (by now) substantive body of feminist theory on rape and representation in literary and visual culture,[6] at the same time as we are keen to open up a set of new questions regarding the issue of the affect and ethics of violence, and the entangled relationship between victimization and empowerment. As Sorcha Gunne and Zoë Brigley Thompson write, 'In the twenty-first century, the most urgent task for feminism is to build on the work of late twentieth-century feminism(s) by recognizing the subversive work that is being done by modern and contemporary writers on the subject of sexual violence' (2011: 4). In other words, it is critical to explore texts that attempt to 'challenge the stipulation of gender roles and myths in relation to sexual violence' and that seek to rewrite 'the roles of "victims" and perpetrators' (11). It is our contention that contemporary crime fiction is doing critical and challenging work on the subject of sexual violence, and one of the themes that runs throughout the chapters that follow concerns how the relationship between 'victims' and 'perpetrators' is undergoing complex revision in the work of a range of crime writers.

Contemporary crime fiction: a new violence?

To argue for the subversive potential of crime fiction is not without dispute, however, especially given the genre's reputation for conservatism. The retrograde aspects of crime fiction are visible in the resolutions of the stories and in the narratives' alignment with male authorities and institutions of law and order, and in particular in the genre's predilection for female victims, and extreme and brutal violence against women. For example, in 2009, a minor controversy broke out when British crime fiction writer and reviewer Jessica Mann declared that she would no longer review crime fiction featuring misogynistic violence. She wrote:

> Each psychopath is more sadistic than the last and his victims' sufferings are described in detail that becomes ever more explicit, as young women are imprisoned, bound, gagged, strung up or tied down, raped, sliced, burned, blinded, beaten, eaten, starved,

suffocated, stabbed, boiled or buried alive...Authors must be free to write and publishers to publish. But critics must be free to say they have had enough. So however many more outpourings of sadistic misogyny are crammed on to the bandwagon, no more of them will be reviewed by me. (2009)

This declaration struck a chord with many female crime writers and readers and led to much debate regarding the extent of violence against women in contemporary crime fiction. Echoing some of Mann's comments, feminist writer Melanie Newman brought Stieg Larsson's books into the discussion when she argued that, despite being labelled 'feminist', they were 'just the latest in a line of novels which aims to titillate readers with graphic depictions of men raping and murdering women' (2009). In other words, though Larsson so clearly disapproves of misogynist violence, it does not mean that his descriptions of such violence are any less problematic. As the contributors to this volume demonstrate, however, the violence found in Larsson's works cannot automatically and simply be dismissed as 'sadistic misogyny'. In the Millennium trilogy, and many of the other novels discussed within this volume, violence is used to carry out important cultural work, raising questions about society, gender, and politics, and forcing readers to question their attitudes towards vengeance and victimization. In this anthology, then, we want to explore how violence operates in a selection of contemporary crime novels and films, interrogating what makes scenes of sexual violation so compelling and disturbing.

What film scholar Linda Williams has written of the popular and much reviled film genres of horror, pornography, and melodrama is equally applicable to a consideration of the contemporary crime genre:

> To dismiss them as bad excess whether of explicit sex, violence, or emotion, or as bad perversions, whether of masochism, or sadism, is not to address their function as cultural problem-solving. Genres thrive, after all, on the persistence of the problems they address; but genres thrive also in their ability to recast the nature of these problems. (2000: 219)

In depicting sexual violence as a serious social problem, many of the crime novels examined in this anthology are concerned with recasting a dominant script that features women as passive victims of violence. Rather than merely decrying the excessive nature of sexualized violence in contemporary crime fiction, then, we explore the kind of work it performs and consider the complex ways in which we are called upon to engage with it as readers. For example, in her contribution to this book, which conducts a comparative analysis of British author Mo Hayder's *Birdman* (2008 [2000]) and Norwegian author Jo Nesbø's *The Snowman* (2010), Berit Åström argues that the disturbing violence of these works is 'central to their attempt to examine critically society's contempt for women and their bodies'. And, in her chapter in the final section of this book, Tanya Horeck analyses two popular crime series – Liza Marklund's Annika Bengtzon novels and Val McDermid's Tony Hill/Carol Jordan novels – in relation to the Millennium trilogy, to make a case for 'the productive potential of our engagement with violence'. The replay of sexually violent images in these works, Horeck suggests, functions as a space where difficult questions are raised about the uncertain relations between 'victim and agent, abused and abuser, self and other'.

The Girl with the Dragon Tattoo

Unsurprisingly, a central point of interest throughout this anthology is the figure of Lisbeth Salander, variously described by reviewers as: 'an outlaw fantasy feminist-heroine' (A. O. Scott 2011); 'a pitiless elfin avenger' (Hitchens 2009); a 'tattooed, pierced, vengeful, bisexual misfit' (France 2009); 'a feminist avenging angel'; 'an androgynous, bisexual, computer-hacking twenty-something' (Sandhu 2010); 'a vision of female empowerment – a kind of goth-geek Pippi Longstocking' (Gibbs 2008); and a 'feminist avatar for the Wikileaks era' (Hornaday 2011). *Entertainment Weekly* has recently gone so far as to call Salander the 'most interesting character of our time' (Harris 2011). What makes Salander so interesting, and so culturally relevant, is her blend of vulnerability and violence. As David Denby of *The New Yorker* writes, 'She is both a victim and an avenger, a woman damaged, abused, yet defiantly sexual – a woman prepared to hit back and to stay out in the danger zone, unwilling to change, ready for more' (2011). Victim *and* avenger: more than any other contemporary pop culture character, Salander brings these two categories together in ways that are both thrilling and troubling. To return to *Entertainment Weekly,* and a recent cover which featured American actress Rooney Mara dressed up in her *Girl with the Dragon Tattoo* garb, Lisbeth Salander is described as not only the most 'interesting' character of our time, but also the 'coolest'. Salander's 'coolness', of course, relates to her alternative appearance as a goth and her self-styled otherness as an individual who resists sexual and social conventions; as Philippa Gates suggests in her chapter on the Millennium film adaptations, her dramatic make-up and clothing is her superhero costume. This designation of Salander as 'cool' has gained great currency with the release of the Hollywood film and it is significant that the marketing of the American film version of *The Girl with the Dragon Tattoo* has brought out the more disturbing aspects of the sexual politics at the heart of Larsson's trilogy. In particular, the concern that, when all is said and done, the bestseller is nothing but 'a wish-fulfillment fantasy disguised as a thriller which, despite pretensions to "feminism," conceives of women as beguiling, dangerous, complex systems to be investigated by men (i.e. Larsson)' (Vishnevetsky 2011). Especially damning in this regard is a sexy and sensational promotional poster which has circulated for Fincher's film, which features a topless Rooney Mara as Salander, nipple ring exposed, with Daniel Craig embracing her from behind.

There is something uncomfortable too, about how this hyper-sexualization of Salander relates to the strong images of rape that are at the heart of her story, as was recently captured by the controversy that broke out when the Swedish-based international fashion chain, H&M, developed a line of clothing known as 'The Girl with the Dragon Tattoo collection'. The clothing line was designed to tie in with the release of the Hollywood remake and sought to draw on the 'edgy style' of Larsson's heroine (Dumas 2011). Such an appropriation of Salander's sexually abused heroine for the purposes of commercial high street fashion did not go without controversy. Rape survivor Natalie Karneef published an open letter to H&M on her blog, where she emphatically stated that they were 'putting a glossy, trendy finish on the face of sexual violence and the rage and fear it leaves behind' (Karneef 2011).

Karneef's complaint not only makes explicit the troubling undercurrents behind the sexualization of Salander as a global consumerist brand, it also raises the fascinating question of what happens when Larsson's heroine is re-imagined and reworked in different contexts and cultural locations. The question of cultural translation and adaptability is one of the themes of our book, as addressed by film scholars Claire Henry and Philippa Gates in their individual chapters, which investigate the translation from novel to film and the subsequent movement from Swedish film to Hollywood blockbuster. More broadly, though, all of our contributors, in one way or another, address the issue of cultural exchange and explore what happens when different crime novels (and films) are put into dialogue with one another.

In the first part of our book, 'Stieg Larsson's The Millennium Trilogy: Opening Up the Debate', the authors introduce the topic of sexual violence and contextualize Larsson's work in relation to feminist hard-boiled crime novels, American serial killer fiction, and Scandinavian and Anglophone avenger crime novels respectively. Priscilla Walton's opening chapter, '"The Girl Who Pays Our Salaries": Rape and the Bestselling Millennium Trilogy', considers the centrality of rape to Larsson's novels, exploring how he builds on the work of feminist crime writers of the 1980s and 1990s at the same time as he opens up important 'new questions about the politics of revenge, the individual and the state, and victimhood and justice'. While much emphasis has been placed on Lisbeth Salander as a lone wolf who battles against villains and institutional corruption on her own, Walton argues that Larsson shows how the struggle to achieve retribution and justice must be a communal undertaking. She writes that: 'Rape and violations of power can rarely if ever be solved by an individual. They require a systemic change, which the Millennium series in many ways significantly foregrounds, given the webs it weaves both to imprison and then to free Salander.'

Barbara Fister's chapter, 'The Millennium Trilogy and the American Serial Killer Narrative: Investigating Protagonists of Men Who Write Women', considers the success of Larsson's novels with American audiences. Exploring the Millennium trilogy in relation to American serial killer fiction, such as Thomas Harris' seminal novel *The Silence of the Lambs* (1988), and Cody McFadyen's Smoky Barrett series, Fister examines how Larsson draws on such material at the same time as he reworks it in powerful ways. Resisting the temptation to depict evil as the act of an aberrant psychopath, Larsson instead reveals that it is men in positions of social and economic power who 'hate' and abuse women. Fister comes to the intriguing conclusion that 'the enthusiasm with which American audiences have embraced Lisbeth Salander may signal a shifting perception of sexual violence in popular culture'.

Continuing the investigation into the use of rape as a motif in the Millennium trilogy is Yvonne Leffler's chapter, 'Lisbeth Salander as a Melodramatic Heroine: Emotional Conflicts, Split Focalization, and Changing Roles in Scandinavian Crime Fiction'. Leffler considers how Lisbeth Salander, Sweden's most 'famous avenging angel', relates to other female avengers in the work of Scandinavian authors Åsa Larsson and Camilla Läckberg and Anglophone authors Peter Robinson and Sara Paretsky. Leffler's particular focus is on the 'importance of expressive strategies and melodramatic structures in novels that present the female avenger as the point of identification'. As Leffler persuasively argues, Larsson uses expressive melodramatic techniques not to 'confirm but to challenge' the borders between good and evil, victim and perpetrator, and, in so doing, is in keeping with a strong tradition of politically engaged Scandinavian crime fiction.

Where does the misery come from?

Gloomy, pensive, dark, foreboding, and bleak:[7] these are the words that repeatedly surface in reviews and articles on crime fiction from the Nordic countries and, according to many, the climate and setting, with long dark winters and light summers, are ideal for creating extremely violent and sinister plots and characters. While there are many different theories as to the source of all the 'misery' of contemporary crime fiction, including, for example, the influence of television and the rise of forensic crime shows with their gory and explicit body horror, it is clear that the current trend for explicit violence in crime writing is very much bound up with the interest in Scandinavian crime fiction and what it has come to represent as a 'global brand' (Nestingen and Arvas 2011: 14). In focusing on the treatment of rape in Stieg Larsson's Millennium trilogy, and its relationship to other Scandinavian and Anglophone crime novels featuring sexualized violence, we are therefore situating ourselves in relation to a burgeoning field of research into the cultural phenomenon that is Scandinavian crime fiction (Nestingen and Arvas 2011: 14).

So far, however, violence as a subject of study has not made much of an encroachment upon that burgeoning field of research. It is absent as a category of analysis, for example, in Andrew Nestingen and Paula Arvas' introduction to their important book, *Scandinavian Crime Fiction*. This is particularly noteworthy when we consider the kind of grim violence that has come to be associated with the Nordic take on the genre.[8] Violent images are indeed central to the global exportability and commercialization of Scandinavian crime, for example in Stieg Larsson's work, and in the works of those that are hurriedly being translated in the wake of his success. This includes Jo Nesbø, who is marketed as 'the Norwegian Stieg Larsson', and whose books have been described as 'so-violent-you-shouldn't-read-them-before-dinner crime novels' (Coffey 2011).

While crime fiction has long been seen as a conservative genre where traditional ideologies are upheld and reaffirmed, it has also been taken up with great relish and success by writers who seek to re-appropriate it for more subversive ends, as a genre 'capable of carrying a complex social and political agenda while still attracting a mass audience' (Plain 2001: 5). Indeed, Scandinavian crime fiction has its roots in the 'socially critical police procedural' novels (Nestingen and Arvas 2011: 3) about detective Martin Beck by Maj Sjöwall and Per Wahlöö from the 1960s and 1970s, whose wide-reaching influence is underscored by just how many times they are mentioned throughout this volume. Given the strong presence of social criticism in the Scandinavian crime novel, perhaps it is not surprising to discover its suitability as a genre for exploring and engaging with rape as a serious social issue. In Scandinavian crime fiction there is a significant emphasis on the decaying welfare state, the trouble lurking just beneath the surface of democracy, and links between the individual body and the social body, as Katarina Gregersdotter discusses in her chapter. As a result, an important space opens up in the genre for a politically engaged analysis of rape and its relationship to the body politic; in particular, the question of who is included – and excluded – from dominant definitions of citizenship and human-hood.

The second part of this volume, 'Dismembered Bodies, Wounded States: Gender Politics in the Millennium Trilogy and Beyond', considers the rise of Scandinavian crime fiction through a close examination of sexually violent images and their relation to issues of the body and the body politic. In 'Rape and the Avenging Female in Stieg Larsson's Millennium Trilogy and Håkan Nesser's *Woman with Birthmark* and *The Inspector and Silence*', Marla Harris explores the differing treatments of rape found in the work of these two Swedish male writers. Harris argues that Nesser's work, which has its antecedents in pulp fiction by American writers such as Cornell Woolrich, ultimately shifts attention away from women as victims of violence, whereas Larsson's work, which is so strongly influenced by late twentieth-century Anglophone feminist crime writing, turns a powerful spotlight on systemic misogyny. What is especially interesting, writes Harris, are the different views of the rape victim found in the work of Nesser and Larsson; although Larsson's representation of women, violence, and vengeance is not without its flaws, it is still noteworthy how he, unlike Nesser, presents a more 'open-ended' construction of the rape survivor.

The chapter that follows, Katarina Gregersdotter's 'The Body, Hopelessness and Nostalgia: Representations of Rape and the Welfare State in Swedish Crime Fiction', is also a comparison of the Millennium trilogy and a male-authored Swedish crime novel, in this case Anders Roslund and Börge Hellström's novel *The Vault* (2008). Gregersdotter interrogates bodies as signifiers of the Swedish welfare state, as well as repositories of hopelessness and nostalgia and, like Harris, notes the optimism and hope for future social transformation underlying Larsson's work, which is in stark contrast with the distinctly darker and more pessimistic tone of *The Vault*. Yet, however different the novels are with regard to their deployment of nostalgia and hopelessness, Gregersdotter's reading suggests that these politically engaged crime novels point to the increasing significance in Sweden of crime fiction as a vehicle for critiquing the welfare state and the commodification of the body in a globalized economy.

In the final chapter of this part, 'Over Her Dismembered Body: The Crime Fiction of Mo Hayder and Jo Nesbø', Berit Åström argues that the disturbing violence found in Mo Hayder's *Birdman* and Jo Nesbø's *The Snowman* is central to the critique of how 'society reduces women to their sexual and reproductive functions'. Hayder and Nesbø have a very different approach to the presentation of violence, with Hayder, on the one hand, describing the bodies of dead women in disturbing detail and Nesbø, on the other, strategically withholding such detail from the reader. However, as Åström demonstrates through a close reading of their works, both authors manage to avoid eroticizing the female corpse. Indeed, Nesbø and Hayder both critically deploy a serial killer narrative, ultimately demonstrating that the horrific crimes of the psychopaths so chillingly described represent 'society's attitudes and concerns writ large, taken to their logical conclusion'. Like Stieg Larsson, Nesbø and Hayder are concerned with exposing the actions of a society that hates women.

Subverting the format

As noted earlier, crime fiction is often considered to be a conservative genre, and crime fiction authors who wish to present themselves as innovators or rejuvenators tend to stress the rigidity of the genre's format as deployed by earlier writers (Horsley 2005: 6–7). Although the genre has its formulae and stereotypes, and eagerly 'deploy[s] them at every available opportunity' (Plain 2001: 12), there is potential for subversion, particularly in the case of gender. As Plain notes, the detective, regardless of sex or sexual orientation, 'always exists in negotiation with a series of long-established masculine codes' (11), but there is 'implicit within the genre...a considerable degree of resistance to reductive gender categories' (6). This resistance to such categorizations, as well as dominant paradigms, is explored in the third part of this book.

Part III: 'Rewriting Scripts: Language, Gender, and Violence in Contemporary Crime Fiction', focuses on language, sexual violence, and the subversion of dominant paradigms in crime fiction. Working with the theories of Jean-François Lyotard, Meghan A. Freeman analyses the concept of voicelessness, and the notion of speaking to, and speaking for, the victims, in Larsson's trilogy, Val McDermid's *The Mermaids Singing* (1995), and Susanna Moore's *In the Cut* (1995). While many commentators have noted that Larsson borrows from McDermid's novel, Freeman goes several steps further and analyses the ways in which both Larsson's trilogy and McDermid's *The Mermaids Singing* 'reveal how victims of sexual violence are often created *prior* to their violation by the social institutions that are supposed to protect and serve them'. Turning to Moore's novel, which 'calls attention to the violence of language itself', Freeman argues that *In the Cut* 'can be read as a meta-analysis of the stakes involved when graphic scenes of sexualized torture and torment are put into words', thus subverting even further the stakes of the crime genre.

In the following chapter, Zoë Brigley Thompson investigates how Larsson's novels, together with Sara Paretsky's *Body Work* (2010) and Megan Abbott's *Bury Me Deep* (2009), 'subvert retrograde scripts of gender and sexual power' in their reworking of the *noir* genre. Challenging traditional notions of the *femme fatale*, all of these novels 'convey sympathetic narratives about sexual exploitation that offer possibilities of healing'. What is more, they 'emphasize that the explanation for sexual crimes does not lie in the survivor's behaviour; blame is placed solely on the rapist, who is framed as the *femme fatale*'s deadly opposite: the *homme fatale*.' Like Freeman, Brigley Thompson is concerned with language and the ways in which it can be used and manipulated to both confirm and subvert notions of rapability and victimhood.

Origin stories

One of the most sensational and disturbing stories told about the origins of the Millennium trilogy is that when Stieg Larsson was 15 years old he witnessed the brutal gang rape of a girl, allegedly called Lisbeth, committed by his friends. It was this event, and the subsequent guilt he felt over it, that has been cast as the 'dark secret behind *The Girl with the Dragon Tattoo*' (Baksi 2010). A friend of Larsson's, Kurdo Baksi, has described how Larsson, 'haunted by feelings of guilt', later asked the girl 'to forgive him his cowardice and passivity'. She, however, could not, and instead told him that she would never forgive him. According to

Baksi, this had a profound impact on Larsson: 'It was obvious, looking at him, that the girl's voice still echoed in his ears, even after he had written three novels about vulnerable, violated and raped women' (2010).

Apocryphal or not (and in fact Larsson's partner Eva Gabrielsson has confirmed the veracity of the story),[9] this tale is compelling as it traces the narrative of a young man who witnessed a gang rape and did nothing to stop it, but who went on, as an adult, to write a series of best-selling novels about sexual violence against women – selling over 62 million copies in 48 countries ("Millennium" 2011). It is of great significance that the origin of Larsson's feminism and his 'loathing of violence against women' (Cooke 2010) should be found in this primal scene of rape, which is dramatized as the beginning of a radical consciousness and the start of a lifelong struggle to eradicate violence against women. The narrative told about Larsson witnessing a gang rape operates as a powerful origin story and forcefully reminds us of how rape operates as a structuring event or scene in popular culture, through which various conflicts regarding sexual and social difference are laid bare. It is certainly remarkable how familiar this 'origin story' has become; for example, it strongly resembles the now classic Hollywood film *The Accused* (Kaplan, US, 1988), in which a young man stands by and watches (but does not intervene) as a woman is gang raped in a bar. *The Accused* provided audiences with a 'get out' clause, in the figure of a bystander who eventually made good on his failure to intervene by testifying on behalf of the raped woman. Recent European arthouse films, however, such as Gaspar Noé's *Irreversiblé* (France 2002), Lars von Trier's *Dogville* (Denmark 2003), and Catherine Breillat's *À Ma Soeur!* (France 2001), offer no such way out in their gruelling attempts to question our ethical involvement with gendered images of pain and suffering.

The question of the ethics of violence is central to a discussion of the differences in textual and visual representations of rape. As already noted, Salander's transition from textual to visual economies has opened her character up to greater exploitation. Yet simultaneously, the medium of cinema, and its affective address to the viewer, calls on embodied responses to violence in powerful ways that need to be explored. The final part of this book, 'Ethics, Violence, and Adaptation' pursues the topic of our ethical engagement with violent images and looks at what happens when rape is replayed across various crime series and film adaptations.

In 'Rape and Replay in Stieg Larsson, Liza Marklund, and Val McDermid: On Affect, Ethics, and Feeling Bad' Tanya Horeck considers the important – and neglected – issue of our affective responses to graphic violence in crime fiction. Drawing on the work of theorist Marco Abel on violence, ethics, and affect, Horeck argues that what is especially salient about the Millennium trilogy, and the crime series of Liza Marklund and Val McDermid, is that 'the subject of sexual violence and its aftermath is developed over the course of several novels, thus enabling a continual re-evaluation and reworking of the question of violence and its relationship to notions of victimhood'. Looking at how rape gets replayed and redeployed across several novels, Horeck concludes that such repetition plays a crucial role in 'opening up, and provoking questions around, the very status of victimhood and the relationship between passivity and agency'.

The next chapter in this part, '*The Girl with the Dragon Tattoo*: Rape, Revenge, and Victimhood in Cinematic Translation' by Claire Henry, also focuses on questions of violence and affect, but this time in relation to cinema, a medium known for its powerful affective charge. Putting Niels Orden Oplev's *The Girl with the Dragon Tattoo* (2009) in the wider context of rape-revenge cinema, Henry explores how the Swedish film adaptation of Larsson's novel solicits what she calls an 'ethical spectatorship', although, as she also cogently argues, the potential of our ethical engagement, in which we are made to recognize our own complicity in scenes of violence, is ultimately curtailed by the film's reliance on an overarching moral framework. Moreover, Henry argues that the affective drive of the film relates to the troubling strand of 'anti-victimism discourse' found in Larsson's novel, whereby the sexual abuse victim is made to take responsibility for her own violation. As Henry demonstrates, the Swedish film adaptation ultimately suggests that the abused woman needs to stop 'whimpering' and fight back, which she does in scenes that are all the more problematic for how satisfying audiences seem to find them.

Finally, our collection concludes with Philippa Gates and her analysis of what gets lost in translation from Larsson's novel to Swedish film adaptations, and finally, to a Hollywood blockbuster. Similarly to Henry, Gates is interested in what happens to the representations of sexual violence and vengeance in the shift from the novels to the film adaptations. In '"Hidden in the Snow": Female Violence Against the Men Who Hate Women in the Millennium Adaptations', Gates argues that 'while Larsson's novels and the Swedish films question Salander's vengeance, the American film channels Larsson's characters and themes into a recognizably Hollywood formula – hetero-normativizing Salander and presenting her as an American action hero'. Considering how Salander is represented as a violent avenger across the different film adaptations, Gates examines the question of how Salander is 're-imagined' for different audiences and how this reworking relates to our engagement with violence. We noted earlier in this introduction that Lisbeth Salander is a central point of interest in this anthology, and what emerges in the different responses to her is not simply a recognition of her status as a difficult, complicated character. Rather, there is an awareness of how the ambivalence felt towards this twenty-first century feminist heroine relates to her various cultural materializations from fiction to film, in which she embodies a series of difficult questions about sexualized violence, ethics, and accountability. The aim of this anthology is not to attempt any kind of definitive answer as to 'the meaning' of Lisbeth Salander (as if such a thing were possible). Indeed, it is important to note that different readings of Larsson's heroine emerge throughout this collection: thus, while Priscilla Walton suggests that the Millennium trilogy argues for a collective response to sexual violence, Claire Henry contends, just as persuasively, that, through the figure of Lisbeth Salander, it presents an individualist response to sexual violence, which 'forecloses broader social critique and the possibility of the type of collective response characteristic of second-wave feminisms'. This is the stuff that compelling academic arguments are made of, and what is most fascinating about the responses to the violence of the Millennium trilogy found in this book is the fundamental questions underlying them: how should feminists theorize rape in the twenty-first century? What is the relationship between female victimization and female empowerment? And what is the nature of our affective/ethical engagement with violence? The kind of thinking on rape and sexual violence found in this book is profoundly engaged with asking such probing questions and interrogating the very terms by which we understand and encounter violent images in contemporary popular fiction and film.

Notes

1. This observation is based on reviews of Fincher's film in major newspapers and publications in the UK and the US, including *The Guardian, The Independent, The Daily Telegraph* (in the UK) and the *Los Angeles Times*, the *Chicago Tribune*, and *Seattle Weekly* (in the US). There are of course exceptions, such as A.O. Scott's review (2011) in *The New York Times*, where he expresses unease about the 'prurient' nature of the rape scene. It is also interesting to note that in Sweden there was tremendous media furore over the rape scene in Fincher's film, which was much derided as sensational and voyeuristic. See, for example, Ullgren (2012) and Axelson (2012a; 2012b).

2. The savagery is reflected in the original title of the first novel *Män som hatar kvinnor* [Men Who Hate Women], a point made by several of the contributors to this volume. The subsequent titles were less provocative: *Flickan som lekte med elden* [The Girl Who Played With Fire] and *Luftslottet som sprängdes* [The Castle in the Air That Blew Up], which for the English publication was changed to *The Girl who Kicked the Hornets' Nest*.
3. It should be noted that the contributors in this volume work from translations. In such cases, publication dates refer to English-language publications, not original publication dates. For a discussion of linguistic issues regarding the translations of Larsson's texts, see John-Henri Holmberg's 'The Novels You Read Are Not Necessarily the Novels Stieg Larsson Wrote' (Burstein et al. 2012: 29–42).
4. As Gill Plain has noted in her influential study *Twentieth-Century Crime Fiction: Gender, Sexuality and the Body*: 'The gospel of crime history is paradoxically both definitive and nebulous: in the beginning there was Poe. Or should that be the Newgate Calendar? Or *Caleb Williams*, or Aesop's fables, or the Bible, or even the Jewish Apocrypha?' (2001: 5). The story of the origins of rape in crime fiction is similarly slippery and hard to pin down. Does it begin with the biblical story of the Levite of Ephraim and the gang rape of his concubine, or the Victorian penny dreadfuls, or the graphic crime novels of Jim Thompson in America in the 1950s? Following in the venerable footsteps of Plain, rather than supplying a developmental history, we are more interested in what she calls the '"corporeal landscape" of the genre' (2001: 5), with a special focus on the body and the treatment of sexualized violation and violence in the contemporary crime novel.
5. There are a number of significant historical surveys of crime fiction (Priestman 2003; Knight 2004, 2010; Rzepka and Horsley 2010; Nickerson 2010 and Worthington 2011), but because of the structure of the material and the wide scope, rape and sexual violence are rarely examined in depth. Important feminist analyses of crime fiction, focusing on the feminist crime novels published from the 1980s onwards, such as *Murder by the Book* (Munt 1994), Kathleen Gregory Klein's *The Woman Detective: Gender and Genre, Feminism in Women's Detective Fiction* (1988) and *Detective Agency: Women Rewriting the Hard-Boiled Tradition* (Walton and Jones 1999), do include interesting discussions of sexual violence but do not offer a sustained analysis of the subject.
6. See, for example, Lynn Higgins and Brenda Silver's highly influential *Rape and Representation* (1991), which set the stage for the productive work on sexual violence and literary and visual culture that has followed; Jacinda Read's *The New Avengers: Feminism, Femininity and the Rape-Revenge Cycle* (2000); Sarah Projansky's *Watching Rape: Film and Television in Postfeminist Culture* (2001); Sabine Sielke's *Reading Rape: The Rhetoric of Sexual Violence in American Literature and Culture, 1790–1990* (2002); Tanya Horeck's *Public Rape: Representing Violation in Fiction and Film* (2004); Sorcha Gunne and Zoë Brigley Thompson's edited collection *Feminism, Literature and Rape Narratives: Violence and Violation* (2010); Dominique Russell's anthology *Rape in Art Cinema* (2011); and Alexandra Heller-Nicholas' *Rape-Revenge Cinema: A Critical Study* (2011).
7. See, for example, John Crace (2009) who, in his article on the rise of Scandinavian crime fiction, writes that: 'the Scandinavians have consistently come up with great plotlines that are as cold and bleak as the locations

in which they are set'. In the introduction to *Scandinavian Crime Fiction*, Nestingen and Arvas observe that Scandinavian crime novels are 'frequently gloomy, pensive and pessimistic in tone' (2011: 2).
8. See, for example, Rich (2009).
9. See Cooke's interview with Gabrielsson (2010).

Works cited

Axelson, T. (2012a) 'Så objektifieras Lisbeth Salander i nya filmen' [This is how Lisbeth Salander is objectified in the new film], *Dagens Nyheter* Jan 10, http://www.dn.se/kultur-noje/debatt-essa/sa-objektifieras-lisbeth-salander-i-nya-filmen, accessed 24 Jan 2012.
Axelson, T. (2012b) 'David Fincher har klippt klorna på den vassa Lisbeth Salander' [David Fincher has cut the claws on the sharp Lisbeth Salander], *Dagens Nyheter* Jan 3, http://www.dn.se/kultur-noje/debatt-essa/david-fincher-har-klippt-klorna-pa-den-vassa-lisbeth-salander, accessed 24 Jan 2012.
Baksi, K. (2010) 'How a brutal rape and a lifelong burden of guilt fuelled Girl with the Dragon Tattoo writer Stieg Larsson', *The Daily Mail*, Aug 2, http://www.dailymail.co.uk/news/article-1299216/Stieg-Larsson-wrote-novel-The-Girl-Dragon-Tattoo-fuelled-brutal-rape.html, accessed 28 Feb 2012.
Coffey, E. (2011) 'Review – Crime: Headhunters by Jo Nesbo', *The Independent*, Sep 17, http://www.independent.ie/entertainment/books/review-crime-headhunters-by-jo-nesbo-2879628.html, accessed 4 March 2012.
Cooke, R. (2010) 'Stieg Larsson – by the woman who shared his life', *The Observer*, Feb 21, http://www.guardian.co.uk/books/2010/feb/21/stieg-larsson-eva-gabrielsson, accessed 3 March 2012.
Crace, J. (2009). 'Move over, Ian Rankin', *The Guardian*, Jan 23, http://www.guardian.co.uk/books/2009/jan/23/scandinavian-crime-fiction?INTCMP=SRCH, accessed 17 Jan 2012.
Denby, D. (2011) 'The Movies Have Never Had a Character Quite Like Her', *The New Yorker*, Dec 27, http://www.newyorker.com/online/blogs/culture/2011/12/lisbeth-salander-the-movies-have-never-had-a-heroine-quite-like-her.html, accessed 29 Feb 2012.
Dumas, D. (2011) 'H&M forced to defend Girl with The Dragon Tattoo fashion line after rape victim accuses chain of glamorising sex attacks', *The Daily Mail*, Dec 15, http://www.dailymail.co.uk/femail/article-2074188/Girl-With-The-Dragon-Tattoo-H-M-line-accused-glamorising-sex-attacks.html, accessed 29 Feb 2012.
France, L. (2009) 'Not your normal Swedish sleuth', *The Observer*, Feb 15, http://www.guardian.co.uk/books/2009/feb/15/crime-fiction-stieg-larsson-the-girl-who-played-with-fire, accessed 14 March 2012.
Gibbs, J. (2008) 'The Girl with the Dragon Tattoo, by Stieg Larsson', *The Independent*, Feb 24, http://www.independent.co.uk/arts-entertainment/books/reviews/the-girl-with-the-dragon-tattoo-by-stieg-larsson-785262.html, accessed 14 March 2012.
Gunne, S. and Z. B. Thompson (2011) (eds) *Feminism, Literature and Rape Narratives: Violence and Violation*. New York: Routledge.

Harris, M. (2011) 'This Week's Cover: Why we're so fascinated by Lisbeth Salander in 'The Girl With the Dragon Tattoo', *Entertainment Weekly*, Dec 30, http://popwatch.ew.com/2011/12/29/this-weeks-cover-the-girl-with-the-dragon-tattoo-lisbeth-salander-rooney-mara, accessed 29 Feb 2012.
Higgins, L. A. and B. R. Silver (1991) *Rape and Representation*. New York: Columbia University Press.
Hitchens, C. (2009) 'The Author Who Played with Fire', *Vanity Fair*, December, http://www.vanityfair.com/culture/features/2009/12/hitchens-200912, accessed 14 March 2012.
Holmberg, J. (2011) 'The Novels You Read Are Not Necessarily The Novels Stieg Larsson Wrote' in D. Burstein, A. de Keijzer and J. Holmberg (eds) *The Tattooed Girl: The Enigma of Stieg Larsson and the Secrets Behind The Most Compelling Thrillers of Our Time*. New York: St. Martin's Griffin. 29–41.
Horeck, T. (2004) *Public Rape: Representing Violation in Fiction and Film*. London: Routledge.
Hornaday, A. (2011) '"The Girl with the Dragon Tattoo" sparks controversy, but buzz may boost box office numbers', *The Washington Post*, Dec 21, http://www.washingtonpost.com/lifestyle/style/the-girl-with-the-dragon-tattoo-sparks-controversy-but-buzz-may-boost-box-office-numbers/2011/12/21/gIQA8GHr9O_story.html, accessed 29 Feb 2012.
Horsley, L. (2005) *Twentieth-Century Crime Fiction*. Oxford: Oxford University Press.
Karneef, N. (2011) 'An Open Letter to H & M from a Rape Survivor', Nov 25, http://nataliekarneef.blogspot.com/2011/11/open-letter-to-h-from-rape-survivor.html, accessed 29 Feb 2012.
Klein, K. G. (1988) *The Woman Detective: Gender and Genre*. Urbana and Chicago: University of Illinois Press.
Knight, S. (2010) *Crime Fiction since 1800: Detection, Death, Diversity*. 2nd edition. Basingstoke: Palgrave Macmillan.
Mann, J. (2009) 'Crimes Against Fiction', *Standpoint*, Sep 9, http://www.standpointmag.co.uk/crimes-against-fiction-counterpoints-september-09-crime-fiction, accessed 4 Feb 2012.
'"Millennium " publisher launchesSalander app' (2011), *The Local: Sweden's News in English*, Dec 13, http://www.thelocal.se/37920/20111213/, accessed 14 March 2012.
Munt, S. (1994) *Murder by the Book?: Feminism and the Crime Novel*. London: Routledge.
Nestingen, A. and P. Arvas (eds) (2011) *Scandinavian Crime Fiction*. Cardiff: University of Wales Press.
Newman, M. (2009) 'Feminist or Misogynist?', *The Fword: Contemporary UK Feminism*, Sep 4, http://www.thefword.org.uk/reviews/2009/09/larrson_review, accessed 13 Feb 2012.
Nickerson, C. R. (ed.) (2010) *The Cambridge Companion to American Crime Fiction*. Cambridge: Cambridge University Press.
Phillips, M. (2011) '"The Girl with the Dragon Tattoo", Craig, Mara, star in sleek, slick, sick adaptation', Dec 16, http://articles.chicagotribune.com/2011-12-16/entertainment/sc-mov-1216-girl-with-dragon-tattoo-20111216_1_rooney-mara-lisbeth-salander-zodiac, accessed 3 March 2012.

Plain, G. (2001) *Twentieth Century Crime Fiction: Gender, Sexuality and the Body*. Edinburgh: Edinburgh University Press.

Priestman, M. (2003) (ed.) *The Cambridge Companion to Crime Fiction*. Cambridge: Cambridge University Press.

Projansky, S. (2001) *Watching Rape: Film and Television in Postfeminist Culture*. New York/London: New York University Press.

Read, J. (2000) *The New Avengers: Feminism, Femininity and the Rape-Revenge Cycle*. Manchester: Manchester University Press.

Rich, N. (2009) 'Scandinavian Crime Wave: Why the most peaceful people on earth write the greatest homicide thrillers', *Slate*, July 8, http://www.slate.com/articles/arts/culturebox/2009/07/scandinavian_crime_wave.html, accessed 4 March 2012.

Rzepka, C. J. and L. Horsley (eds) (2010) *A Companion to Crime Fiction*. Chichester: Blackwell Publishing.

Russell, D. (2010) *Rape in Art Cinema*. New York: Continuum.

Sandhu, S. (2010) 'The Girl with the Dragon Tattoo, review', *The Telegraph*, Mar 11, http://www.telegraph.co.uk/culture/film/filmreviews/7421715/The-Girl-With-The-Dragon-Tattoo-review.html, accessed 14 March 2012.

Scott, A. O. (2011) 'Tattooed Girl Metes Out Slick, Punitive Violence', *The New York Times*, Dec 20, http://movies.nytimes.com/2011/12/20/movies/the-girl-w ith-dragon-tattoo-movie-review.htm, accessed 27 Dec 2011.

Sielke, S . (2002) *Reading Rape: The Rhetoric of Sexual Violence in American Literature and Culture, 1790-1990*. Princeton: Princeton University Press.

Turan, K. (2011) 'The Girl with the Dragon Tattoo is too frigid', *The Los Angeles Times*, Dec 20, http://www.latimes.com/entertainment/news/la-et-girl-with-the-dragon-tattoo-20111220,0,716278.story, accessed 14 March 2012.

Ullgren, Malin (2012) 'Våldtäktsskildringar är en självklar del av underhållningsvåldet' [Descriptions of rape are a self-evident part of entertainment violence], *Dagens Nyheter*, Jan 18, http://www.dn.se/kultur-noje/kronikor/m alin-ullgren-valdtaktsskildringar-ar-en-sjalvklar-del-av-underhallningsvaldet, accessed 24 Jan 2012.

Vishnevetsky, I . (2011) 'In the Process of the Investigation: David Fincher and "The Girl with the Dragon Tattoo"', http://mubi.com/notebook/posts/in-the-process-of-the-investigation-david-fincher-and-the-girl-with-the-drag on-tattoo, accessed 1 Feb 2012.

Walton, P. L. and M. Jones (1999) *Detective Agency: Women Rewriting the Hard-Boiled Tradition*. Berkeley: University of California Press.

Williams, L. (2000) 'Film Bodies: Gender, Genre, and Excess' in Robert Stam and Toby Miller (eds) *Film and Theory: An Anthology*. Oxford: Blackwell.

Worthington, H. (2011) *Key Concepts in Crime Fiction*. Basingstoke: Palgrave Macmillan.

Part I

Stieg Larsson's Millennium Trilogy: Opening up the Debate

1
'The Girl Who Pays Our Salaries': Rape and the Bestselling Millennium Trilogy

Priscilla Walton

In May 2011, Dominique Strauss-Kahn, President of the International Monetary Fund, and socialist hopeful for the upcoming French presidential elections, was arrested in New York City for sexually assaulting a chamber maid. Charged immediately, Strauss-Kahn was placed under strict house arrest in New York City, and the prosecution moved to protect the maid, their star witness. By the next month, while the reputation of 'DSK' (as he is often referred to) was in tatters and various women had turned up and spoken out about questionable dealings with him in the past, the prosecution began to challenge the chamber maid's reliability: she had lied on her immigration papers; she had a boyfriend who was a drug addict/peddler, as well as several large unexplained deposits of money in her bank account. Ultimately, the case was dismissed due to lack of evidence and DSK is free to pursue his political ambitions. The DSK affair presents what I consider to be a typical rape scenario: he said/she said, where the one with power and influence – usually the man – wins. Generally, it is cases like DSK's that receive media attention because of the celebrity of the male in question. Those that tend to attract media attention when they come to trial, such as the high profile American rape cases of William Kennedy Smith, Mike Tyson, and Kobe Bryant, are undoubtedly problematic, and most probably deter women from reporting rape, given the publicity, the character attacks, and the sheer trauma of the process.

The story of the rape victim, whose identity is protected, often gets obscured, overlooked, and distorted in the media's depiction of such cases.[1] Where, then, do we find the victims' stories? Popular culture has always proved a useful springboard for information on major social issues – for example, daytime drama and AIDS, large studio films and rape, and romance fiction and female sexuality. In similar fashion, crime fiction is an important site for exploring questions regarding sexual violence and victimization. In *Detective Agency: Women Rewriting the Hard-Boiled Tradition*, my co-author Manina Jones and I conducted interviews with the major bestselling female crime writers of the 1980s (the heyday of the female dick), and found that one of their primary purposes in writing fiction was to keep feminism alive and women informed through their characters and scenarios. While claims to authorial intentions are tenuous at best, it is clear that the feminist hard-boiled genre certainly did work to foreground the intricacies of being a woman in a man's world and the difficulties involved therein. However, with a few exceptions, the hard-boiled female PI is a woman of the past, although the issues she helped to raise remain alive to some extent in other media: for example, television series like *The Closer* and *Damages*. But what is current, amidst the few detective writers from that era who remain, and others who have since begun writing, is a focus on the horror of rape and its impact on the victim.

Most recently, it is Stieg Larsson's phenomenally successful Millennium trilogy – and the character of Lisbeth Salander in particular – which has opened up significant public debate regarding questions of rape and the sexual violation of women. While many have hailed Lisbeth Salander as a new feminist heroine for the twenty-first century, others, such as Melanie Newman, have 'difficulty squaring Larsson's proclaimed distress at misogyny with his explicit descriptions of sexual violence, his breast-obsessed heroine and babe-magnet hero' (2009). Regardless of where one stands in relation to this debate about Lisbeth Salander, it is extraordinary the extent to which Larsson makes the question of rape and the sexual abuse of women the focus of his blockbuster trilogy. In what follows, I want to explore how the Millennium trilogy, and its overt concern with the plight of women, builds on the work of feminist crime writers of the 1980s and 1990s, while at the same time raising important new questions about the politics of revenge, the individual and the state, and victimhood and justice.

In the beginning

It is important to note that it was the Anglophone feminist crime writers of the 1980s, several of whom were openly admired by Larsson, who first politicized sexual abuse in popular fiction. Barbara Wilson broke new ground in crime fiction in 1986 with *Sisters on the Road*, in which her lead female character, amateur detective Pam Nilsen, is raped during a case. The experience of the rape is described through the eyes of the female protagonist:

> He raped me. With a punishing violence that had nothing to do with sex and everything to do with rage and hatred. My vagina was as dry as my mouth and every pounding blow stabbed through my body like a sword dipped in fire…I almost blanked out; my whole being reduced to a tiny pinprick that cried out *no*. (Wilson 1994: 194)

Other feminist crime writers from this time also deal with the theme of violence and rape; Canadian writer Elizabeth Bowers' *Ladies Night* (1988), for example, features a female protagonist, Meg Lacey, who becomes a detective because she was raped in the past and now wants to help the victims of sex crimes. In the work of Wilson and Bowers and others such as Leah Stewart and Barbara Neely, rape is treated as a central event which has consequences for the victim and which often serves as the 'origin story' for her emerging sense of strength and empowerment (Horeck 2004: 125–130). As Tanya Horeck has argued in *Public Rape: Representing Violation in Fiction and Film*, the 'political and representational issues surrounding rape are…inextricably connected to the form of the thriller itself. In particular, that subgenre of the thriller Tzvetan Todorov has deemed "the story of the vulnerable detective"' (2004: 127). Rape appears time and again in feminist crime novels from this period, which take as their primary concern the thorny issue of the relationship between woman's victimization and woman's agency.

The relationship between victimhood and agency, endangerment and empowerment, is explored throughout the V.I. Warshawski series by American crime author Sara Paretsky, who is name-checked in *The Girl with the Dragon Tattoo* (2008: 356). While Warshawski is not subjected to sexual assault in these early novels, she is continually placed in risky situations in which she has to defend herself. The comparison to be made between the feisty Salander and the 'tough' and 'sassy' Warshawski has not gone unnoticed. As Jennifer McCord comments: 'Before Lisbeth Salander of Stieg Larsson's books entered the consciousness of readers who love edgy, strong women, there was V.I. Warshawski' (2010). In Warshawski we find a precursor for Salander and her retaliatory violence, although Paretsky's heroine is much more restrained by her moral conscience. In 1985, in *Killing Orders*, Warshawski notes, after shooting a man in the leg in the midst of mildly torturing him to get a confession: 'What kind of person kneels in the snow threatening to destroy the leg of an injured man? Not anyone I wanted to know' (237). And she continues to agonize about her inclinations even though the thug in question had tried to throw acid in her face: 'I didn't like to think too much. About Rosa, or my mother, or the ugliness I found in myself that night with Walter Novick in the snow' (75). While this level of violence may, by contemporary standards, seem positively tame, it nonetheless anticipates the kind of reworking of a standard script of male violence and female victimization that began to appear in women's crime writing during this time.

In the UK, for instance, Sarah Dunant's heroine, Elizabeth, dreams of a way of rewriting the script of sexual violence. In *Transgressions* (1998), Elizabeth, the victim of an attempted rape, wonders what would happen if authors started 'to fight fantasy with fantasy' (Horeck 2004: 105). In Elizabeth's fantasy, the passive female victim in the thriller she is translating would be transformed into 'a kind of avenging angel for women in trouble, whooping down on violent men and snapping their bodies between their dog-like teeth' (105). Elizabeth later revisits this idea of fighting fantasy with fantasy when she wonders how she would take her 'own revenge like the avenging angels of her fantasies' (130).

While Dunant's novel appeared in 1998, seven years before the publication of Larsson's novel about Lisbeth Salander, her appearance accords with the rise of female action heroes in wider popular culture, like Xena, Buffy, and Lara Croft. Certainly there is enjoyment to be had in watching Lara fly through the air in some amazing kickboxing feat, or in Buffy's clever quip to some large vampire before she stakes his heart, but I would argue, as does Susan Douglas, that at least partly due to their generally masculinist venues (originally comic books, action television, computer games, and so on), these texts are often contradictory in their depiction of women's issues and are simultaneously feminist and anti-feminist (2011). This cult of the (sexy) female super-heroine may be an important context within which to situate the figure of Lisbeth Salander, but it is not so easy to dismiss her on these grounds. As Jenny McPhee argues, Salander is 'no Lara Croft or Charlie's Angels who must pay the price for her physical prowess by titillating the phantom male reader/viewer with her 36–24–36 scantily clad body' (2011: 26). For the petite, but strong, and fiercely intelligent Salander, who 'triumph[s] over relentless male aggression in deeply satisfying ways' (McPhee 2011: 26), is also, significantly, moulded from the tradition of the hard-boiled female private investigator novel of the kind fashioned by Sara Paretsky, as discussed above. The emphasis on the victim of violence and the aftermath of rape found in the feminist crime novels of the 1980s and 1990s is something that is pursued in depth in the work of Stieg Larsson, where questions of revenge and victimhood are amplified and put centre stage.

Rape and reparation

Larsson makes rape the leitmotif of his three novels, *The Girl with the Dragon Tattoo* (2008), *The Girl Who Played with Fire* (2009a), and *The Girl Who Kicked the Hornet's Nest* (2009b), all of which comprise the Millennium trilogy. Larsson, who died suddenly after signing a contract for his trilogy, did not live to see booksellers call his novels 'The Girl Who's Paying Our Salaries for the Next Few Months' (Burstein 2011: xix) due to their overwhelming earning power. These are not just bestsellers, they are blockbusters, and, on every level, they are about rape. It is, in many ways, the *raison d'être* of the series and I would suggest that the Millennium trilogy, which Larsson called *Men Who Hate Women* in Swedish, can be described as nothing less than a feminist manifesto which argues that violence against women is at the root of all society's ills.

Larsson, like earlier feminist crime writers such as Barbara Wilson, depicts rape from the perspective of the rape victim; but he does not stop there, since the rape victim in his trilogy, Lisbeth Salander, exacts devastating vengeance on those who have violated her. These novels provide us with an image of the female protagonist as victim, avenger, and action hero, all at the same time, making their discussions of rape the most vivid in print to date. Setting out its theme in explicit terms from the very beginning, with the opening epigraph '18 percent of the women in Sweden have at one time been threatened by a man', the first novel, *The Girl with the Dragon Tattoo*, involves an investigation into a disappearance/rape/serial-murder case from the past. The novel opens with journalist Mikael Blomkvist, who is manipulated into a situation where he is accused, and convicted, of libel. Blomkvist is financially ruined, disgraced, and a professional pariah (he is both fined and sentenced to jail), but like all of Larsson's characters, he is not just a victim. He is down but he is not beaten, as he realizes when a potential client, Henrik Vanger, promises to give him the evidence he needs to help him out of his professional problems, thereby offering the possibility of revenge and the recuperation of Blomkvist's career.

It is through 'the girl' of the title, though, that Larsson most closely explores questions of victimhood. Although Lisbeth Salander herself vehemently rejects the designation, readers discover that she has been a victim of the system all of her life. First, as a witness to the violent abuse of her mother by her father, the Russian spy Zalachenko. Later, as a mental patient under the care of Dr Peter Teleborian, having been sectioned for her attempt at stopping her father's brutality. Finally, the serious illness of her first guardian, Holger Palmgren, places her in further jeopardy when she is appointed a new guardian, Nils Bjurman. Bjurman sexually abuses Salander, and when she attempts blackmail to protect herself it backfires, leading to one of the most talked about rape scenes in contemporary crime fiction (2008: 224).

Although the scene seemingly places her in the role of victim, Salander refuses to passively accept what has happened and, returning to Bjurman's abode in order to set another trap, she rapes him and leaves him scarred for life: 'Bjurman felt cold terror piercing his chest and lost his composure. He tugged at his handcuffs. *She had taken control. Impossible*' (231). Using a recording of the previous rape, Salander blackmails him into submission, and then tattoos him with the following message: 'I AM A SADISTIC PIG, A PERVERT, AND A RAPIST' (235).

Having thus controlled one sexual predator, Salander and Blomkvist confront another in their work on the Vanger case, which, it turns out, involves a serial rapist/killer who has been operative since at least 1949 (323, 402). As the two ultimately discover, Henrik Vanger's brother (and eventually, his son) comprise a team of serial killers; although, later, the son proudly announces: 'I'm more of a serial rapist than a serial murderer' (402). The son, Martin, had been sexually molested by his father and initiated into the family business at a young age. When he raped his sister, Harriet, she fled the island and her previous life in order to avoid him.

Crucial to the conceptualization of victimhood in *Dragon Tattoo* is Salander's outrage over the attempt to label Martin as a 'victim' of his father's madness and abuse. When Blomkvist expresses a degree of sympathy for the kind of childhood Martin had, and how that may have led to his violence, Salander retorts as follows: '"Bullshit," Salander said, her voice as hard as flint...There was not an ounce of sympathy in it. "Martin had exactly the same opportunity as anyone else to strike back. He killed and he raped because he liked doing it"' (424). While it is the male character, Blomkvist, who recognises the horror the Vanger children must have endured and who tries to understand how such violence might beget further violence, Salander, the female victim of male violence, strongly refuses any such theory of victimhood. For Salander, it is imperative that those who are subject to violence fight back. Even more revealing, in this regard, is Salander's attitude towards rape victim Harriet Vanger, whom she refers to as: 'Harriet Fucking Vanger. If she had done something in 1966, Martin Vanger couldn't have kept killing and raping for thirty-seven years' (448). For Salander, it is not just about defending oneself, it is about making sure that others cannot be harmed; it is about a sense of collective responsibility.

After solving the Vanger case, Blomkvist realizes that he will not be given the evidence he needs for his journalistic revenge. As he consequently considers the possibility of writing a book on Harriet's case, Salander is outraged:

> You're in a position where you can continue to harm innocent women – especially that Harriet whom you so warmly defended in the car on the way up here. So my question to you is which is worse – the fact that Martin Vanger raped her out in the cabin or that you're going to do it in print? You have a fine dilemma. (461)

Larsson here highlights the fact that the media treatment of rape often constitutes yet another violation of the victims, what feminist theorists have referred to as a 'second rape'. Salander requires more than a book to keep the story quiet, and blackmails the Vangers into doing more:

> Martin videotaped his victims. I want you to do your damnedest to identify as many as you can and see to it that their families receive suitable compensation. And then I want the Vanger Corporation to donate 2 million kroner annually and in perpetuity to the National Organization for Women's Crisis Centres and Girls Crisis Centres in Sweden. (461)

As she does throughout the trilogy, Salander thus insists on making reparation to the female victims of violence. *Dragon Tattoo* sets up a rape pattern that the Millennium series follows. It begins as a 'sort of locked-room mystery in island format' (85), which the discredited Blomkvist agrees to help solve. Blomkvist agrees to investigate because he needs time to regroup and heal, and his healing takes place ultimately with his revenge. Salander becomes involved when Blomkvist confronts her and asks for her help – and after she is raped by her guardian and revenges herself on him. Salander has been violated by the court, molested by her physicians, and raped by her legal guardian, but she fights back with incredible force. Other characters are recovering from symbolic and physical violations through this serial rape case, and, at Salander's insistence, the corpses of raped women are traced back to the source of the violence by the Vanger Corporation, as noted above. In the second and third novels, larger issues are confronted, again about rape, but about those 'serial rapes' that are called prostitution: the kidnapping or hoodwinking of desperate girls from the Eastern Bloc, forced to become prostitutes in Sweden, and about the treatment of rape victims by the media and the legal system.

Playing with fire and kicking a hornet's nest

Larsson's piercing critique of the corruption in the upper echelons of Swedish government and bureaucracy evinces a politically engaged awareness of the relationship between violability, citizenship, and the workings of the body politic. The rapes in the following two novels of the Millennium trilogy become more extensive, moving from the personal to the public. Or, in that rape can be argued to be about power, not sexual fulfilment, the violations become broader, moving more into the reign of public power, which includes violations of the self and the social. These novels also further interrogate what it means to be a 'victim'.

The Girl Who Played with Fire commences with an exposé on the sex trade in Sweden. In other words, the serial rape of young girls is about to be printed in a book that exposes rape in its many forms. The exposé within the exposé concentrates on:

> the girls [who] are so far down society's ladder that they're of no interest to the legal system. They don't vote. They can hardly speak Swedish except for the vocabulary they need to set up a trick. Of all crimes involving the sex trade, 99.99 percent are not reported to the police, and those that are hardly even lead to a charge. This has got to be the biggest iceberg of all in the Swedish criminal world. (2009a: 79)

The authors of the exposé, a reporter and a graduate student writing a dissertation on the sex trade with the intention of revealing the submerged parts of the sex-trade iceberg, are murdered, along with Salander's guardian, Bjurman. Salander is charged with the murders and 'raped in print' all over Sweden.

Although Salander is initially sought for Bjurman's murder in *Played with Fire*, the tape of her rape is not made public until *The Girl Who Kicked the Hornet's Nest*, when Salander's lawyer plays it in court, finally exposing Bjurman as a sex offender. Salander achieves her revenge through his public exposure; she is ultimately released from guardianship, meaning she now controls her own life and does not need to report to anyone. Yet this situation points to a problem which Larsson documents but does not acknowledge. Although Salander sees herself as needing no one – and indeed she is often perceived by reviewers as a fierce individualist, a 'lone wolf' (Johnson 2010) – it is clear that even this tough, fearless action heroine cannot absolve herself alone. In Salander's case, especially, given how high up in the Swedish government her case extends, it would be impossible for her to combat her situation on her own. In each area (financial, professional, media, psychiatric, and judicial) she has help, and she has expert help. To make a substantive difference, there needs to be a systemic change, which the Millennium series in many ways significantly foregrounds, given the webs it weaves both to imprison and then to free Salander. In each example, it dramatizes a violation, as well as the ways in which an individual alone cannot revenge the violation.

As already mentioned, Salander is consistently violated in print: first when she is sought for three murders, and later through her trial. Salander's treatment by the media is vicious: headlines range from 'Psychopath Sought for Triple Killing' (2009a: 311) to 'Police tracking Lesbian Satanist Cult' (334). In the depiction of the media representations of Salander and her treatment by the legal system, Larsson exposes the paradoxical way that 'on departing from the rape script of master and victim, the witness can no longer present a "convincing" truth because it is only her powerlessness and lack of autonomy that can make her story believable' (Gunne and Brigley Thompson 2010: 11). Because Salander is powerful and defiant, she cannot be thought of as a victim within the public domain. Salander herself is very aware of the role of the 'victim' she is expected to assume and wants to avoid playing into such a stereotype: when she writes out her account of her story for the trial, she is 'careful to express herself precisely' and leaves 'out all the details that could be used against her' (342). While the media eventually publishes her judicial revenge, nothing can erase the 'second violation' she has suffered. At the same time, few victims have the media support that Salander enjoys, and she is able to fight in ways that the unnamed sex workers cannot: *Millennium* (the magazine) publishes an issue devoted to Salander on the day of her trial, and Blomkvist (the reporter) threatens to expose irregularities in print.

Judicially, Salander is violated again in the same way she had been all her life, such as when her rights were taken away and she was relegated to an insane asylum under the care of the paedophile Dr Teleborian, whose treatment she suffered between the ages of 12 and 17:

> Teleborian was the most loathsome and disgusting sadist Salander had ever met in her life...Not a single one of his actions could ever be reported or criticized. *He had a state-endorsed mandate to tie down disobedient little girls with leather straps*...every time Salander lay shackled on her back and he tightened the straps and she met his gaze, she could read his excitement. She knew. And he knew that she knew. (2009b: 355–356)

During the trial, Teleborian's reputation is ruined when it is revealed that he has eight thousand pornographic photographs of children on his computer (2009b: 541). Not every victim of psychiatric abuse conveniently finds pornographic evidence on the abuser's computer; however, few victims face the conspiracy that kept Salander in an asylum. Yet, here, again, Salander could not have fought the psychiatric community on her own. She needed her lawyer and the help of the secret police to uncover the history that placed her in Teleborian's care in the first place.

The judicial system is shown to be completely flawed in its treatment of Salander, at the same time that various judicial investigations are launched as a result of her case. In effect, the democratic process was violated by a breakaway group of the Swedish Secret Police, a remnant of the cold war. Calling themselves the Section, the few left still have considerable power in subverting the law if they fear that it is against the interests of national security (as they define it). The Section is a secret unit that 'exists inside the government. Its mandate puts it outside regular operations, and no questions should be asked' (93). The Section endorsed several violations of the judicial process:

> Security Police officers in seniors position had looked the other way when a series of savage assaults were committed against a Swedish woman. Then her daughter was locked up in a mental institution on the basis of a fabricated diagnosis. Finally, they had given *carte blanche* to a former Soviet intelligence officer to commit crimes involving weapons, narcotics and sex trafficking...He did not even want to begin to estimate how many counts of illegal activity must have taken place. (235–236)

The revenge, when it comes in the conclusion of the third novel, is sweet: the Section is closed down, Salander is acquitted of all charges and regains her rights as a citizen, and governmental inquiries are generated to stop any such agency from similar acts in the future.

In each instance of Salander's rapes and violations, she is avenged, thus making the novel a gripping and satisfying read. Yet, not all victims are so privileged, and not all are avenged. For example, there are the sex workers who are discussed in the novel, who are kidnapped and enslaved for money:

> It's no secret. It's not even news. What's new is that we have met and talked with a dozen girls. Most of them are fifteen to twenty years old. They come from social misery in Eastern Europe and are lured to Sweden with a promise of some kind of job but end up in the clutches of an unscrupulous sex mafia. Those girls have experienced things that you can't even show in a movie. (2009a: 77)

These women are never avenged, although Zalachenko's organization is closed down and there is an inquiry into the problem; it is not resolved because the social disparities that lead to its continuation are not resolved.

Conclusion

Building on the work of North American hard-boiled feminist crime writers of the 1980s and 1990s, the Millennium trilogy has been described as 'one long female revenge fantasy' (McPhee 2011: 26). Andrea Rushing has described the pleasure and affirmation one reader experienced reading 'books about new-style U.S. women detectives' after she had been sexually assaulted:

> Week after week I gulp as if drowning desperate for air, their plainspoken stories about acid-tongues, fast-thinking, single and self-employed women who not only dare to live alone, but scoff, sneer, when men try to put them in their 'weaker sex' place. Parched and starved, I read and reread Sue Grafton's alphabet adventures, but Sara Paretsky books became my favorites because her Chicago-based private investigator is even more bodacious and sassy than my pre-raped self. And, in stark contrast to television and movie renditions of women as powerless victims of men, she both withstands and metes out physical violence in every single book.

Murder mysteries restore order to worlds thrown out of balance. (1993: 137)

Reading detective fiction, then, at least for some, provides a kind of therapy. The female 'sassy' heroine found in the works of Sara Paretsky and others can be seen to serve as the foundation for Lisbeth Salander, 'a magnificently feisty modern heroine' (French 2010). It is significant that within the Millennium trilogy, we are provided with images of Larsson's alter ego – Mikael Blomkvist – reading feminist crime writers as he goes about his investigation into the serial rape and murder of women. Val McDermid has observed how:

> Blomkvist's reading progress in the book is from Sue Grafton through Sara Paretsky to [her] own work – reflecting in some way, the darkening tone of the book – as might be seen in the progression of the work of these three best-selling women crime novelists. (Forshaw 2011: 298)

Paretsky and other women crime writers from the heyday of the female hard-boiled detective may afford pleasure for readers, just as the sheer toughness and relentlessness of Lisbeth Salander, who has been raped and violated in every way possible, also provides satisfaction. Salander's refusal of the term 'victim', when she so obviously is one, in many ways underscores how she denies her victimhood in order to survive. Indeed, while one *is* a victim of rape, one need not *stay* a victim. Salander is thoroughly avenged by the final novel of the trilogy, but the fact that she does not do it on her own highlights the need for a collective effort – carried out by various groups in society – to fight against systemic violence. Indeed, the character of Lisbeth Salander can be said to function on two levels. On the one hand, she is a victim who refuses to stay a victim and who, very competently, turns the tables on those individuals who have harmed her. On the other hand, and at the same time, she is helped by various forces to combat systemic violence in Swedish society, thus suggesting that there is hope that substantial changes may be accomplished and that other victims, less well-equipped to cast off their victim status, may be avenged.

Note

1. DSK's alleged victim, 32-year-old Nafissatou Diallo, from Guinea, did eventually reveal her identity in an attempt to tell her story, but the charges were still ultimately dismissed. See Rushe (2011).

Works cited

Burstein, D. (2011) 'Introduction' in D. Burstein, A. de Keijzer, and J. Holmberg (eds) *The Tattooed Girl: The Enigma of Stieg Larsson and the Secrets Behind the Most Compelling Thriller of Our Time*. New York: St. Martin's. xv-xxii.
Douglas, S. (2011) *The Rise of Enlightened Sexism*. New York: St. Martin's.
Forshaw, B. (2011) *The Man Who Left Too Soon: The Life and Works of Stieg Larsson*. London: John Blake.
French, P. (2010) 'The Girl Who Kicked the Hornet's Nest – Review', *The Guardian*, Nov 28, http://www.guardian.co.uk/film/2010/nov/28/girl-who-kicked-the-hornets-nest-review, accessed 13 Feb 2012.
Gunne, S. and Z. B. Thompson (2010) (eds) *Feminism, Literature and Rape Narratives: Violence and Violation*. New York: Routledge.
Horeck, T. (2004) *Public Rape: Representing Violation in Fiction and Film*. London: Routledge.
Johnson, B. (2010) 'Most seductive predator since Bond', *Maclean's.Ca*, April 15, http://www2.macleans.ca/tag/lisbeth-salander/, accessed 12 March 2012.
Larsson, S. (2008) *The Girl With the Dragon Tattoo*. Transl. R. Keeland. London: MacLehose/Quercus.
Larsson, S. (2009a) *The Girl Who Played with Fire*. Transl. R. Keeland. London: MacLehose/Quercus.
Larsson, S. (2009b) *The Girl Who Kicked the Hornet's Nest*. Transl. R. Keeland. London: MacLehose/Quercus.
McCord, J. (2010) 'Review: Body Work: A V.I. Warshawski Novel', *BookReporter*, Dec 22, http://www.bookreporter.com/reviews/body-work-a-v-i-warshawski-novel, accessed 13 Feb 2012.
McPhee, J. (2011) 'Lisbeth Salander, the Millennium Trilogy, and My Mother' in D. Burstein, A. de Keijzer, and J. Holmberg (eds) *The Tattooed Girl*. New York: St. Martin's. 25–27.
Newman, M. (2009) 'Feminist or Misogynist?', *the fword: contemporary uk feminism*, Sep 4, http://www.thefword.org.uk/reviews/2009/09/larrson_review, accessed 13 Feb 2012.
Paretsky, S. (1985) *Killing Orders*. New York: Ballantine.
Rushe, D. and K. Willsher (2011) 'Dominique Strauss-Kahn's accuser goes public as case nears collapse', *The Guardian*, July 25, http://www.guardian.co.uk/world/2011/jul/25/strauss-kahn-accuser-breaks-silence, accessed 6 March 2012.
Rushing, A. (1993) 'Surviving Rape' in S. M. James and A. P A. Busia (eds) *Theorizing Black Feminisms*. London: Routledge. 129–42.
Walton, P. L. and M. Jones (1999) *Detective Agency: Women Rewriting the Hard-Boiled Tradition*. Berkeley: University of California Press.
Wilson, B. (1994 [1986]) *Sisters on the Road*. London: Virago.

2
The Millennium Trilogy and the American Serial Killer Narrative: Investigating Protagonists of Men Who Write Women

Barbara Fister

Readers in the United States were the last among residents of developed nations to discover the Millennium trilogy. Even though the books were international bestsellers, publishers were reluctant to launch them in the American market, uncertain about their audience appeal. Sonny Mehta, legendary editor and publisher at Knopf, eventually acquired the books and gave them a significant marketing push, but he later confessed that he had had reservations, saying 'I had nightmares that we would be the only country where it didn't work' (McGrath 2010). American readers, who embrace the short chapters and fast-paced, reality-lite storylines of James Patterson and Dan Brown, seemed an unlikely consumer market for thrillers that take their time developing a story, express leftist political views, and are translations set in a foreign country. There was precedent for Mehta's concern: globally bestselling authors such as Ian Rankin and Henning Mankell had not found as receptive an audience in the United States as they had elsewhere. Yet the trilogy became phenomenally popular in the US, just as it had in countries around the world. Why did it succeed against the odds? When describing the appeal of the books, readers in online discussions, blog posts, and reviews repeatedly attribute its appeal to the girl of the title.

What is it about this character that so captivated an American audience? Are these books – ostensibly focused on condemning sexual violence against women – truly feminist, or are they part of a misogynistic tradition that exploits depictions of sexualized violence for entertainment?

How does Lisbeth Salander and her story of rape and retribution fit with trends in American crime fiction, particularly with the rise of the serial killer narrative? To approach these questions, it is worth examining the multiple sources in popular culture that contributed to this heroine whom so many find compellingly original, and to compare Salander to other influential female protagonists created by male American writers such as Cody McFadyen and Thomas Harris. Larsson's heroine has seized the public imagination just as Thomas Harris's iconic profiler Clarice Starling did in the 1990s, yet the Millennium trilogy departs from the trends in American crime fiction established by *The Silence of the Lambs*. Although the trilogy incorporates aspects of the serial killer narrative made popular by Harris and others, it strategically resituates the sources of violence. Rather than depicting evil as a pathology of monstrous actors who have chosen sides in a Manichean struggle between good and evil, the trilogy suggests that violence against women is a choice made by men who have achieved social and economic power and who act out that power by committing violent acts against women. Larsson has selected familiar material from the repertoire of popular culture and refashioned it for his purpose in a way that draws in the sizeable audience for thrillers while challenging the ideology underlying popular accounts of violence against women.

Violence, victimization and resistance

The depiction of violence against women in the crime genre has long been under debate, with authors such as Sara Paretsky arguing that this form of gendered violence reflects sexism in society (Fister 2011). As is discussed elsewhere in this volume, the controversy has recently been revived, with blame assigned particularly to women writers (Mann 2009). A related issue is the role of trauma in the backstory of female protagonists. J. T. Ellison, the American author of a series of thrillers featuring serial murder, asked in a 2009 blog post, 'why does a strong female lead have to have a tortured background? Can a female protagonist make it in the fiction world if she's not been broken first?' She speculates that many readers can only accept behaviour that is not 'ladylike' if the character has been given a traumatic excuse for her toughness and capacity for violence.

> If, and only if, she has been raped or beaten or otherwise horribly misused … will she be allowed to acknowledge her bloodlust … society has conditioned us to tamp down our feminine wiles, to stow away

our power, to hide behind our men and only emerge once we've been raked over the coals through some unspeakable violence. (2009)

Ellison argues that 'we're victimizing our heroines', a suggestion with which journalist Jess McCabe (2011) concurs, concluding that writers feel it would be too difficult for readers to accept female characters who are freakishly willing to undertake unpleasant and dangerous work for the same reasons men do; they must have 'some added vulnerability so we the audience can still think of the character as in need of a good rescuing'. While male detectives are equally saddled with traumatic backstories, they very rarely suffer from the emotional aftermath of violence they experienced as a victim. More typically, they suffer from guilt due to violence they failed to prevent, usually committed against female family members (as in the case of John Connolly's series hero Charlie Parker, whose wife and infant daughter were tortured and killed while he was out drinking). The trauma of male heroes is not that they have been raped, but that their wives, sisters, and daughters have been.

Though Salander is portrayed as triumphantly capable, refusing to be merely a victim, she and other women in Larsson's trilogy suffer so much abuse that many critics question whether it is truly feminist, or if it is part of a body of popular fiction that exploits violence against women as entertainment. An anonymous writer who blogs under the name 'the rejectionist' questions whether using the same images of extreme and sadistic violence against women that is standard fare for bestsellers can possibly be feminist:

> Packaging that nastiness up as feminist is icing on an ugly cake. There are men who hate women: I am aware of this. Anyone who has ever tried living as a woman is aware of this. I don't need a ten-page explicit rape scene to bring this point home; I need only to leave my house...Most of us will never be abducted by a sadistic serial killer, thankfully. But all of us will, at some point, be told we are less because we are female. The worst thing about [*The Girl with the Dragon Tattoo*] is that it seems to be saying the only violence against women that counts is the kind that ends up with us dead. The rest of us, I guess, are just complaining. (2010)

Interestingly, the rape scene in *The Girl with the Dragon Tattoo* actually occupies not ten pages, but less than two. The pages leading up to the rape are devoted to Salander weighing her options as she plans a strategy to put an end to her guardian's sexual harassment. Her evaluation of her circumstances is blunt and unemotional:

> By the time she was eighteen, Salander did not know a single girl who at some point had not been forced to perform some sort of sex act against her will... In her world, this was the natural order of things. As a girl she was legal prey, especially if she was dressed in a worn black leather jacket and had pierced eyebrows, tattoos, and zero social status. (2009: 249)

Still, though rape is commonplace, Salander has no intention of passively accepting her victimhood. After being forced to trade oral sex for access to her funds, she lays plans to break his hold over her: 'There was no question of Advokat Bjurman going unpunished. Salander never forgot an injustice, and by nature she was anything but forgiving' (249). As her next meeting with Bjurman approaches, we do not see her experiencing anxiety or dread, a foreshadowing device commonly used in thrillers to heighten suspense. Instead, she works through her options dispassionately, including the possibility of staging a fatal 'accident'. She settles on filming his abusive behaviour so that she can threaten him with exposure and gain the upper hand. But the ferocity of his second attack catches her by surprise.

At first, the assault is seen from Salander's point of view and is brief. Bjurman overpowers her, silences her, and begins to rape her. As soon as she feels 'excruciating pain' (2009: 274) the scene shifts to Hedeby Island where Blomkvist and Cecilia Vanger are enjoying their healthy and consensual sexual relationship, one in which Cecilia explicitly sets the rules, before the action returns to Bjurman's apartment after the assault is over. We are given the facts in a notably unemotional manner: 'Salander was allowed to put on her clothes. It was 4:00 on Saturday morning. She picked up her leather jacket and rucksack and hobbled to the front door, where he was waiting for her, showered and neatly dressed. He gave her a cheque for 2,500 kronor' (274–5). The contrast between these scenes is unsubtle and underscores the distinction Larsson is drawing between sex enjoyed by equal partners and sexual assault as an exercise of power and an economic transaction.

Significantly, we are not party to Salander's feelings immediately following the rape. After she leaves Bjurman's apartment, she looks back, and we see her from his perspective: 'Her body looked fragile and her face was swollen from crying, and he almost recoiled when he met her eyes. Never in his life had he seen such naked, smouldering hatred'. Bjurman recategorizes her, not as a broken reed or a formidable opponent but as being 'just as deranged as her casebook indicated' (275), interpreting her anger as a symptom of a previously diagnosed disability. Though Larsson makes use of the common thriller ingredient of a violent sexual assault against a helpless and seemingly fragile young woman, he forgoes the tantalizing build of suspense and the sexualized violent entertainment of a 'ten-page explicit rape scene' in order to do something different. He has stripped away from this pivotal scene all indicators that submission can be sexy and instead reveals rape as the violent exercise of authority over the disenfranchised.

Bestselling bricolage

Writing in the *Christian Science Monitor*, Sarah Seltzer argues that the trilogy uses popular materials in order to successfully smuggle a subversive message into millions of beach tote bags in a kind of 'bait and switch' move – using entertaining and familiar popular culture motifs to make a serious point (2010).

> In an action-story landscape where women are too often relegated to girlfriend, sidekick or prey in need of defending, Salander grabs the spotlight and refuses to let it go...Larsson's novels achieve something perhaps more difficult than advancing a social-justice cause: introducing an utterly original female character to the world, one who avoids the tired archetypes of helpless victim, lovelorn and needy single female, karate-kicking babe, ferocious tiger mother, or deranged scorned mistress. Lisbeth Salander is a fascinating mess, a real piece of work, but she's active and human. (2010)

In Seltzer's view, Larsson appeals to American readers by using the familiar materials of a popular genre, but then overcomes the limitations of the roles typically given to women in that genre by creating a complex and original heroine.

In *Dragon Tattoo,* Larsson fuses two storylines from what seem to be opposite ends of the crime fiction genre, beginning with a traditional locked room mystery, then detouring into a more contemporary and violent thriller involving the systematic rape, torture, and murder of women by a sadistic and depraved father and son team. In fact, the three volumes of the trilogy are a pastiche of nearly every convention one might encounter in the crime fiction genre, a set of adventures unified by a singular social message: that men who hate women act on that hatred in ways that are far too often tolerated by society. In the same way, Salander herself is constructed out of a wealth of pop culture references in a combination that seems original, but is actually a bricolage of clichés. Larsson has assembled and repurposed genre conventions in ways that draw readers in, but then forces them to reassess and interrogate their expectations. Salander takes the position of the violated female, acting out a role that young women are expected to play in thrillers, but then she refuses to behave according to expectations. Her story and her style breathe life and purpose into clichés in a way that makes readers care about this familiar yet original character – and think differently about the role in which thrillers typically cast women.

Larsson is said to have conceived of Salander by wondering what Pippi Longstocking would be like as an adult. In an interview with Lasse Winkler (2010) he said:

> What would [Pippi Longstocking] be like today? What would she be like as an adult? What would you call a person like that, a sociopath? Hyperactive? Wrong. She simply sees society in a different light. I'll make her 25 years old and an outcast. She has no friends and is deficient in social skills. That was my original thought. (2010)

Her more or less autobiographical male sidekick is also drawn from one of Astrid Lindgren's heroes, boy detective Kalle Blomkvist, reimagined as a 45-year-old journalist, 'an altruistic know-it-all who publishes a magazine called Millennium' (Winkler 2010). When Blomkvist goes to Gottfried Vanger's cabin he browses through the books there, finding Mickey Spillane, Enid Blyton, and three books by Astrid Lindgren: *The Children of Noisy Village, Kalle Blomkvist and Rasmus,* and *Pippi Longstocking* – books he recognizes from his own childhood. The shelf also includes books on astronomy, shortwave radio, and Harriet Vanger's Bible (2009: 291–2).

In a sense, the Millennium trilogy holds many hidden bookshelves, and they provide clues to how the stories work by simultaneously meeting and subverting our expectations. Not only does Larsson make overt references to a number of crime writers in the three books, this playful intertextuality is also at work in the way that Larsson has borrowed various heroic characters from popular culture, as John-Henri Holmberg has noted in 'The Man who Inhaled Crime Fiction' (2011: 99–105). In addition to Pippi Longstocking and Lindgren's darker stories about Kalle Blomkvist, Larsson grew up with Enid Blyton's adventure stories, which were to the rest of the world what Nancy Drew and the Hardy Boys were to Americans. He was also a fan of Modesty Blaise, a comic strip character from the 1960s, British in origin but quite popular in Sweden. The parallels with Salander are striking. Modesty Blaise is a bold, sexy young heroine whose origins are a mystery, having been found wandering as an orphan in post-war Eastern Europe. After running away from a displaced persons camp, she becomes the head of an underworld operation called 'the network' before retiring wealthy and taking on odd jobs for the British secret service. There are certainly echoes of Modesty Blaise's story in Lisbeth Salander's relationships with older men, her illicit wealth, and her extralegal network, the Hacker Republic.

Larsson was not just familiar with popular culture; he was a serious fan (Holmberg 2011: 99–105). At the age of 20, Larsson published an article in a science fiction fanzine critiquing the Swedish crime fiction scene, finding little of interest in a genre then dominated by Agatha Christie-style puzzle mysteries like those of Maria Lang and Stieg Trenter, excepting in his critique only the work of Maj Sjöwall and Per Wahlöö. Instead, he lauded Raymond Chandler, Dashiell Hammett, and Ross MacDonald of the hard-boiled American tradition. After taking a job with a Swedish news agency, Larsson had the opportunity to regularly review crime fiction. His favourite authors tended to be women, including the founders of the feminist PI genre – Liza Cody, Sue Grafton, and Sara Paretsky – as well as writers who came later, notably Carol O'Connell, whose own series heroine, Kathy Mallory, is an orphaned sociopathic genius whose violent tendencies are barely held in check by an older male mentor. In short, Larsson's tastes map closely to the 1980s feminist turn in the genre, as women took the social concerns of the American hard-boiled tradition, stripped away its sexist elements, and recreated the detective hero in a feminist mode.

From sexism to social criticism

This feminist turn has its roots in the gritty realism and social critique espoused by Raymond Chandler. In his classic essay 'The Simple Art of Murder', Chandler makes a case for the importance of both realism and idealism in the detective story, arguing that detective fiction should take on questions of power and social injustice (1944). He describes his famous 'mean streets' as being the site of corruption, the routine abuse of power, and the failure of social institutions to fulfil their obligations. The only way to write about the real world, he argues, is to acknowledge these problems – but there must also be a 'quality of redemption' (59) provided by the hero, an able, courageous, ordinary, yet honourable man.

One form of injustice is conspicuously missing from Chandler's catalogue: sexism. In the 1980s and 90s, women writers took Chandler's master plot and rewrote it, reinventing the hero as a woman who, by her very status in society, is in a position to view the world from the perspective of the disempowered. In Chandler's world, women were either innocents who needed protection or femmes fatales who led men to their doom through sexual seduction. By rewriting the genre, women were able to keep the focus on unmasking injustice, while adding empathy and insight into socio-economic problems to their portrayal of the detective. In many ways, Sjöwall and Wahlöö were appropriating genre conventions in a manner similar to Larsson when they wrote their ten-volume 'story of a crime'. In a 2009 interview, Sjöwall said that she and her partner admired Simenon and Hammett and realized that the popularity of crime fiction offered a vehicle for social commentary even if the heroes were agents of state power:

> We realised that people read crime and through the stories we could show the reader that under the official image of welfare-state Sweden there was another layer of poverty, criminality and brutality. We wanted to show where Sweden was heading: towards a capitalistic, cold and inhuman society, where the rich got richer, the poor got poorer. (France 2009)

Now, she confesses that it did not accomplish the change they had hoped for: 'Everything we feared happened, faster. People think of themselves not as human beings but consumers. The market rules and it was not that obvious in the 1960s, but you could see it coming' (2009). Yet, their Martin Beck series laid a foundation for the critical examination of the failures of society that gives Scandinavian crime fiction its reputation for dealing realistically with social issues.

That said, Larsson's trilogy is very different from the ironic documentary style of the Martin Beck series, and is equally distinct from the glum and introspective melodrama of Henning Mankell's Wallander series. In Larsson's trilogy, the sweeping social critique found in Sjöwall and Wahlöö's series is transported into a lively bricolage of international popular culture references, tied together with a serious thread: a focus on violence against women. Lisbeth Salander is not just Pippi Longstocking as an adult, she is the counter-cultural hacker chick of science fiction and a kick-boxing ninja babe straight out of comic-book culture, as well as the model of professionalism, independence, and resistance found in the first feminist private investigators.

Though Larsson's foray into serial killer territory borrows elements from the graphically violent fiction that British crime writer and reviewer Jessica Mann finds so objectionable (2009), it approaches the subject from a different angle. At first, Blomkvist investigates the long-ago disappearance of Harriet Vanger by assembling information about the past of the eccentric and wealthy Vanger family, but when he realizes her disappearance may be connected to the grisly unsolved murder of an unrelated young woman, he hires Salander as a researcher to help him decode the hints Harriet Vanger left in the form of Bible verses linked to women's names and initials.

At this point the locked room mystery is abruptly abandoned as the mechanics of a serial killer story are set in action. Salander links the names and initials to women who were horrifically murdered, most likely by a member of the Vanger family. Blomkvist is shocked and tells her that he finds such a possibility preposterous: 'The idea that an insanely sick sadistic serial killer was slaughtering women for at least seventeen years without anyone seeing a connection sounds utterly unbelievable to me' (2009: 414). Salander replies coolly with a numbered series of logical propositions to prove just how easily these murders could go unnoticed, prefacing her argument with an authoritative source:

> We have several dozen unsolved murders of women in Sweden during the twentieth century. That professor of criminology, Persson [crime fiction author Leif G. W. Persson, who is also a respected social scientist] said once on TV that serial killers are very rare in Sweden, but that probably we have had some that were never caught. (414)

She goes on to refute Blomkvist's doubts by pointing out that the murders were spread out over time and carried out in different jurisdictions and with varied MOs, making for a pattern of violence against women that would be hard to see if you weren't looking for it. Later she rejects Blomkvist's characterization of the perpetrator as an aberrant religious lunatic: 'It's not an insane serial killer who read his Bible wrong. It's just a common or garden bastard who hates women' (418). Though Larsson is playing with a familiar melodramatic storyline, Salander's corrections to Blomkvist's assumptions are an opportunity to reiterate that he is oblivious to an everyday pattern of sexist violence.

In this scene, Salander explicitly challenges common interpretations of the nature of violence and the workings of justice as portrayed in the American serial killer narratives popularized by Thomas Harris, James Patterson and others. In what follows, I will examine the rise of the serial killer narrative in America and consider the significant ways in which such a storyline is refigured in *Dragon Tattoo*.

Serial killer narratives

Larsson deliberately frames the sexual murders that Gottfried and Martin Vanger have secretly engaged in for years not merely as a moral aberration, but as an extension of their political and economic belief system, one that justifies exploitation and oppression of all kinds. This is fundamentally different to the standard American serial killer narrative, which depicts sexual violence as an expression of the spiritual battle between good and evil. In this widely popular fictional universe, crime itself is not a social problem, it is a psychological malaise and a sickness of the soul. When violent crime is situated in a field of Manichean struggle, there is no room for social inequality or economic injustice to play a role, so readers can safely enjoy the story without having to recognize and confront sources of injustice in society. This moral framework for crime fiction is not only popular with readers, it replicates itself on account of being taught in writing workshops and how-to books (such as Frey 2004) which advise writers to structure their fiction as a mythic hero's journey. This separation of crime from social causes is tightly bound up in a neoconservative view of morality and the role of the state.

Though serial murder has been the stuff of popular entertainment since at least the days of Elizabethan pamphlets recounting notorious crimes (Marshburn and Velie 1973), the phrase 'serial killer' only entered common usage in the post-Watergate era, when the Reagan administration was trying to restore funding and political authority to institutions of law enforcement after public criticism had led to legislation that restricted police practices. The public fascination with serial murderers was enlisted in the cause because the threat of violent criminals arising without social causes effectively shifted crime from being a social problem, and therefore requiring state-funded social policy solutions, to being a moral crisis, requiring scientific and judicial intervention. Eliminating poverty would not solve the problem; instead, police powers should be enhanced to combat moral degeneracy (Jenkins 1994).

At the same time that crime was being reconceptualized as a moral rather than a social problem, popular psychology was also undergoing rehabilitation. Individual psychological trauma was deemed responsible for any number of social problems previously attributed to economic and social inequality as therapists helped their patients recover memories of familial sexual abuse. Moreover, as funding was withdrawn from social programs supporting child welfare, child abuse as a heritable form of sexual deviance passed from parent to child replaced poverty and neglect as a matter of public concern (Hacking 1991). The role of the profiler in popular fiction embodies these concepts of the scientific probing of traumatic events, the generational transmission of deviance, and the concept of crime as a moral issue, giving rise to the contemporary American crime thriller with a victimized yet morally strong female protagonist.

Thomas Harris captured the zeitgeist with *Silence of the Lambs* (1988), a bestselling thriller with a female protagonist who satisfied both feminists and tough-on-crime moralists. Though Harris did not invent the serial killer storyline, Leonard Cassuto credits him with popularizing it, calling Harris 'the Henry Ford of the serial killer story, the man who enabled their mass production' (2003: 220). Critic Stephen Fuller notes that Jodie Foster's film depiction of the book's protagonist, Clarice Starling, made the character a 'feminist icon', satisfying women who were seeking strong heroines who could fight their way past institutionalized sexism. At the same time, her absolute moral conviction appealed to the rising tide of ideological conservatives. 'This combination transformed Starling into a national totem, blending continuity and discontinuity with the past and mobilizing a deep and diverse range of public sympathies' (2005: 821). The serial killer narrative that pits a detective who is trained in science and psychology against a monstrously evil killer became enormously popular. In Patrick Anderson's estimation, *The Silence of the Lambs* is 'the greatest of modern thrillers. It does not transcend the genre but defines it. More than any other single novel, it *is* the triumph of the thriller' (2007: 158). Making Clarice Starling the protagonist, he argues, was 'an inspired move' because it infused the relationship between the key players with a frisson of sexual tension, expressed in 'the strange mating dance between the charming cannibal and the seemingly virginal Clarice' (155).

Harris defines the genre not only because *The Silence of the Lambs* was extremely popular, but because it has been endlessly imitated. Perhaps the most successful of writers to franchise serial killers as entertainment is James Patterson, who marketed his breakout book, *Along Came a Spider*, with a television advertisement that announced 'you can stop waiting for the next "Silence of the Lambs"' (Mahler 2010). Though it lacks the polish of Harris's novel, it combines a simplified moral conflict with fast-paced suspense and titillating violence. In Anderson's words, Patterson's Alex Cross series is 'sick, sexist, sadistic, and subliterate' (2007: 246). Nevertheless, Patterson has sold more books than any other American author, and between 2006 and 2010 his name was on the cover of one of every seventeen hardcover books sold in the US (Mahler 2010). Like many other successful authors, Patterson has diversified his product line by introducing female protagonists in the Women's Murder Club series. The serial killer narrative has dominated the thriller genre for two decades, with women profilers taking their place alongside male heroes. Yet their role is fundamentally different from that of Lisbeth Salander.

Shortly after the publication of *Dragon Tattoo* in Sweden in 2005, US author Cody McFadyen published the first volume in a series that, while it did not achieve the commercial success of Patterson's and Larsson's books, illustrates the fork in the road that appeared in American crime fiction in the 1980s. One path was the feminist reinvention of the American private investigator genre which flourished during the 1990s but has since flagged in popularity, even though its first practitioners, Marcia Muller, Sue Grafton, and Sara Paretsky, continue to add volumes to their series featuring women detectives. The other path is the commercially successful serial killer narrative pioneered by Thomas Harris and successfully exploited by James Patterson. In 2006 McFadyen continued that tradition when he introduced his female protagonist, Smoky Barrett, in *Shadow Man*.

Barrett is an FBI profiler who (like Lisbeth Salander) is physically small (under five feet in height), unusually talented, intelligent, and physically and emotionally scarred by trauma. As the book opens, a police psychologist is trying to bring her back from the brink of suicide after she was victimized by a man who murdered her husband and child, raped her, tortured her, and forced her to mutilate her own face with a knife. Barrett is able to get inside the minds of the serial killers she hunts, hacking into their thoughts in the way that Salander is able to break into computer networks. But in this fictional universe, evil has no social vectors. It arises like a genetic mutation of morality. In the novel, the protagonist refers to serial killers as 'alien' and 'an aberration, a different species' (2006: 99), and while they have often been 'made by Frankenstein parents' who replicate themselves by maltreating their children, they cannot be rehabilitated: 'The monsters are, without exception, irredeemable' (101). Cassuto connects the rise of this kind of serial killer narrative and its monstrous villains with the defunding of mental health institutions and the deinstitutionalization of the mentally ill. The fictional serial killer becomes an example of the futility of mental health interventions. As Cassuto puts it, 'the transformation of the mentally ill to monstrous criminals is the story of sympathy withdrawn...We once felt sorry for our mentally ill, but now they disgust us – and because they disgust us, they're fair game for a collective effort at monstrous objectification. Serial killer stories take care of this objectification for us' (2003: 227). Fictional killers must be diagnosed as incurably insane, because readers must not feel sympathy toward them or any sense of social responsibility; the only cure for these monsters is to be slain.

Barrett hunts monstrous predators who hate women because women embody innocence and vulnerability. These monsters are particularly dangerous because they appear human. As one character says of a serial killer, 'It was like the opposite of Halloween. Instead of being a human wearing a monster mask, [he] was a monster wearing a human mask' (McFadyen 2006: 331). In the denouement, as Smoky confronts the monster, her dead daughter appears to her like a religious vision to guide her hand as she slays her opponent.

This combination of a pseudoscientific 'bad seed' theory of deviant behaviour, coupled with religious imagery, satisfies neoconservative longings for moral clarity and an understanding of good and evil that is uncomplicated by issues of public policy. Evil is not nurtured by social inequality, it is an act of spiritual allegiance to the devil. This personification of evil is in many ways a cultural indicator of the American zeitgeist of the late twentieth century. The percentage of Americans who believe in the literal existence of the devil began to rise in the 1970s at the same time that public belief in the importance of social welfare programs began to decline (Harris Interactive 2011). Distrust of secular accounts of natural phenomena in favour of literalist Christian beliefs has also grown. A poll taken shortly after *Shadow Man* was published found that more Americans believe in the existence of Satan than in Darwin's theory of evolution (Stoddard 2007).

Lisbeth Salander and Smoky Barrett share features that are staples of popular culture, yet deliver very different messages. In Barrett's world, evil is a moral choice made by genetically flawed monsters; Salander sees evil as the brutal exercise of power in a social system that favours wealth and privilege. As survivors of rape and torture, both Salander and Barrett do battle with serial killers who were raised by abusive parents and have gone on to rape, torture, and kill women in secret while appearing to be respectable pillars of society. Each of these tough but vulnerable heroines appeals to American audiences, even though they are operating in fictional universes with very different assumptions about the roots of evil. Salander offers readers a fresh narrative about women's experience that places responsibility upon the individual's choices and within the context of power relationships. When Blomkvist tells her that it is hard to believe that a killer has successfully murdered women for years without detection, she logically explains how entirely plausible it is once you see the pattern – a pattern she experiences in everyday life. The denouement of the serial killer part of the plot is another demonstration of Larsson's playful appropriation of conventions. When Blomkvist stupidly follows Martin Vanger into his lair and is tied up and tortured, he is playing the 'fem jep' (female in jeopardy) role typically held by those characters mystery fans encounter so often they label them with the scornful shorthand 'TSTL' – too stupid to live. Larsson has borrowed a common formula, but reversed the genders so that a man can be threatened and a woman can be the rescuer.

Later, as Blomkvist tries to understand what has happened, he ponders the psychological damage that Gottfried Vanger inflicted on his son and mouths the generational replication of evil theory that Ian Hacking (1991) has incisively unpacked. Salander disagrees with typical bluntness: 'Bullshit...He killed and raped because he liked doing it' (2009: 515). As Blomkvist presses the issue, she points out with ruthless logic, 'Gottfried isn't the only kid who was ever mistreated. That doesn't give him the right to murder women. He made that choice himself. And the same is true of Martin' (516). As the conversation progresses, they both realize that Harriet Vanger must have been incestuously raped. The reason she studied the Bible was not for spiritual guidance; she studied it as a key to her religiously fanatical father's murders. The sacred text has become a manual for the interpretation of the motives of a deranged serial killer. Larsson has successfully appropriated the moral, religious, and pseudoscientific trappings that made the serial killer narrative an exciting yet comforting metanarrative for American readers, but by reversing roles and reimagining key elements, he has given Salander the opportunity to challenge and defeat its underlying assumptions.

Conclusion: what we talk about when we talk about rape

Sabine Sielke urges us to reflect on 'what we talk about when we talk about rape' (2002: 1) and to consider the rhetorical meaning of rape in a particular historical and cultural context. Rape has its discursive uses and is often 'an insistent figure for other social, political, and economic concerns and conflicts' (2). In the United States, rape narratives historically have shaped, and have been shaped by, conflicts between colonists and Indians and between whites and blacks. Widespread and institutionalized fear of rape has been used to subjugate women seeking greater personal freedom and to remind them that, fundamentally, they are prey. In Sielke's words, 'the very discourses that establish gender differences as differences in sexuality also construct female sexuality as victimization' (2). Quite often, the rhetoric surrounding rape has little to do with women and their lives; rather, the depiction of violence against women participates in 'the making of a world that tends to care little about violated bodies' (3).

That being the case, the enthusiasm with which American audiences have embraced Lisbeth Salander may signal a shifting perception of sexual violence in popular culture. In the Millennium trilogy, rape is not about sex; it isn't even about violence. It is about the unjust exercise of power in a manner that undermines social institutions and offends collective morality. Audiences respond to the fact that, in response to rape, Salander takes power over her assailant and inscribes him with a shaming label using the same tools that mark her triumphantly as a wasp and a dragon. The women in the trilogy do not react to the threat of sexual violence with fear, and Larsson does not build suspense in his audience with the threat of sexualized violence as his instrument. The male perpetrators of violence are not mutant aliens, they are men who hold political and economic power and use it to oppress others. As Blomkvist says towards the end of *The Girl Who Kicked the Hornet's Nest*, in a pontifical moment to his sister who has just successfully defended Salander in court, 'I told you you'd be unbeatable. When it comes down to it, this story is not primarily about spies and secret government agencies; it's about violence against women and the men who enable it' (2010: 514). Although the story is, in fact, about spies and secret government agencies, about corrupt officials, cold war politics, economic injustice, and abuses of state power, Larsson has decided that what we talk about when we talk about those things is actually men who hate women.

In *The Girl with the Dragon Tattoo*, Larsson has borrowed and refashioned the American serial killer plot as just one of many crime fiction motifs used in the Millennium trilogy, along with the locked room mystery, the dysfunctional family saga, the spy thriller, the financial thriller, the police procedural, the political thriller, and the courtroom drama, creating a remix of popular culture motifs that becomes an imaginative landscape in which a heroine who is also assembled from clichés can become her own original and engaging self. Her character and her highly logical yet passionate outsider response to state-sanctioned violence is what it takes to rally moral people – journalists, police, physicians, lawyers, and perhaps readers – to call social institutions to account. Larsson's interest in situating evil within social structures in which powerful individuals routinely make self-serving choices leads him to recycle familiar fictional storylines that have previously identified evil as a monstrous Other, capturing our sympathy with a compelling heroine whose task is to expose and confront our assumptions. In the end Larsson has done what the female crime writers who reclaimed the American private investigator narrative once did: he has successfully refashioned a popular genre in a feminist mode.

Works cited

Anderson, P. (2007) *The Triumph of the Thriller*. New York: Random.
Cassuto, L. (2003) 'The Cultural Work of Serial Killers', *Minnesota Review* 58, 219–229.
Chandler, R. (1944) 'The Simple Art of Murder', *The Atlantic Monthly*, Dec, 53–59.
Ellison, J. T. (2009) 'What the F**k is Ladylike?', *Murderati*, 7 Aug, http://www.murderati.com/blog/2009/8/7/what-the-fk-is-ladylike.html, accessed 13 Feb 2012.
Fister, B. (2011) 'Sisters in Crime at the Quarter Century: Advocacy, Community, and Change'. Paper presented at the International Popular Culture Association Meeting, San Antonio, Texas, 23 April, http://homepages.gac.edu/~fister/SinCPCA.pdf, accessed 13 Feb 2012.
France, L. (2009) 'The Queen of Crime', *The Guardian*, 22 Nov, http://www.guardian.co.uk/books/2009/nov/22/crime-thriller-maj-sjowall-sweden, accessed 13 Feb 2012.
Frey, J. N. (2004) *How to Write a Damn Good Mystery: A Practical Step-by-Step Guide from Inspiration to Finished Manuscript*. New York: Macmillan.
Fuller, S. (2005) 'Deposing an American Cultural Totem: Clarice Starling and Postmodern Heroism in Thomas Harris's *Red Dragon, The Silence of the Lambs*, and *Hannibal*', *Journal of Popular Culture* 38. 5, 819–33.
Hacking, I. (1991) 'The Making and Molding of Child Abuse', *Critical Inquiry* 17. 2, 253–288.
Harris Interactive (2011) *Harris Vault*. http://www.harrisinteractive.com/Insights/HarrisVault.aspx, accessed 13 Feb 2012.
Harris, T. (1988) *The Silence of the Lambs*. New York: St. Martin's.
Holmberg, J. (2011) 'The Man who Inhaled Crime Fiction' in D. Burstein, A. de Keijzer, and J. Holmberg (eds) *The Tattooed Girl: The Enigma of Stieg Larsson and the Secrets Behind the Most Compelling Thriller of Our Time*. New York: St. Martin's Griffin. 99–105.

Jenkins, P. (1994) *Using Murder: The Social Construction of Serial Homicide*. New York: Aldene de Gruyter.
Larsson, S. (2009) *The Girl with the Dragon Tattoo*. Transl. R. Keeland. New York: Vintage.
Larsson, S. (2010) *The Girl Who Kicked the Hornets' Nest*. Transl. R. Keeland. New York: Knopf.
Mahler, J. (2010) 'James Patterson, Inc.', *The New York Times Magazine*, 24 Jan, http://www.nytimes.com/2010/01/24/magazine/24patterson-t.html, accessed 4 Feb 2012.
Mann, J. (2009) 'Crimes Against Fiction', *Standpoint*, 9 Sep, http://www.standpointmag.co.uk/crimes-against-fiction-counterpoints-september-09-crime-fiction, accessed 4 Feb 2012.
Marshburn, J. H. and A. R. Velie (1973) *Blood and Knavery: A Collection of English Renaissance Pamphlets and Ballads of Crime and Sin*. Rutherford: Farleigh Dickinson University Press.
McCabe, J. (2011) 'Murder, She Blogged: Detectives in Distress', *Bitchmedia*, http://bitchmagazine.org/post/murder-she-blogged-damsels-in-distress, accessed 4 Feb 2012.
McFadyen, C. (2006) *Shadow Man*. New York: Bantam.
McGrath, C. (2010) 'The Afterlife of Stieg Larsson', *The New York Times Magazine*, 23 May, http://www.nytimes.com/2010/05/23/magazine/23Larsson-t.html, accessed 4 Feb 2012.
Rejectionist (2010) 'The Girl with the Lots of Creepy Disturbing Torture that Pissed Me Off: On Stieg Larsson', *Tiger Beatdown*, 29 July, http://tiger-beatdown.com/2010/07/29/the-girl-with-the-lots-of-creepy-disturbing-torture-that-pissed-me-off-on-stieg-larsson/, accessed 4 Feb 2012.
Seltzer, S. (2010) 'The Girl with the Dragon Tattoo: Why We Should Cheer Lisbeth Salander', *Christian Science Monitor*, 28 July, http://www.csmonitor.com/Commentary/Opinion/2010/0728/The-Girl-with-the-Dragon-Tattoo-Why-we-should-cheer-Lisbeth-Salander, accessed 4 Feb 2012.
Sielke, S. (2002) *Reading Rape: The Rhetoric of Sexual Violence in American Literature and Culture, 1790–1990*. Princeton: Princeton University Press.
Stoddard, E. (2007) 'Poll Finds More Americans Believe in Devil than Darwin', *Reuters*, 29 Nov, http://www.reuters.com/article/2007/11/29/us-usa-religion-beliefs-idUSN2922875820071129, accessed 4 Feb 2012.
Winkler, L. (2010) 'Stieg Larsson: The Man who Created the Girl', *The Telegraph*, 3 Mar, http://www.telegraph.co.uk/culture/books/authorinterviews/7803012/Stieg-Larsson-the-man-who-created-the-girl.html, accessed 4 Feb 2012.

3
Lisbeth Salander as a Melodramatic Heroine: Emotional Conflicts, Split Focalization, and Changing Roles in Scandinavian Crime Fiction

Yvonne Leffler

The most famous vengeful heroine in contemporary crime fiction is Lisbeth Salander in Stieg Larsson's Millennium trilogy, but she has many avenging soulmates. This chapter explores the tradition of the post-feminist avenging angel in contemporary crime fiction, with a particular focus on Scandinavian crime fiction. While Carol Clover has argued that rape-revenge stories fit into the horror genre (1992: 3–59), they also play a central role in contemporary crime fiction. Taking Jacinda Read's investigation of the rape-revenge cycle as a starting point (2000: 241–248), and considering melodrama as a dramatic mode where the core function is to make the readers feel sympathy for the victim-heroine (Williams 2001: xiv, 24, 29–32 *et passim*), I want to investigate the dominance of female victim-avengers in Scandinavian crime fiction, and the importance of expressive strategies and melodramatic structures in novels that present the female avenger as the point of identification. To bring some features of the avenger into starker relief, I will also discuss her appearance in a few Anglo-American crime novels. I begin by demonstrating how crime fiction, through the incorporation of some of the features of melodrama, has come to blur the boundaries between investigators, victims, and perpetrators. Through an analysis of a representative sample of Scandinavian and Anglophone crime novels by Håkan Nesser, Unni Lindell, Peter Robinson, and Sara Paretsky, I examine how female protagonists and their traumatic involvement in a primal scene of sexual violence are used in these works to raise provocative questions about the relationship between the detective and the criminal, and between the culprit and the victim.

Moving to a focused study of Stieg Larsson's Millennium novels, I analyse his use of melodramatic strategies and structures in making the reader identify with Salander. Larsson's novels lend themselves well to a melodramatic reading, taking into consideration Ben Singer's claim that melodrama operates as a 'cluster concept': strong pathos, heightened emotionalism, moral polarization, and an episodic composition with an abundance of dramatic situations and spectacular effects (Singer 2001: 37–58, see also Brooks 1995). I also explore how certain generic strategies are used in Scandinavian crime fiction in general, and in Larsson's in particular, to focus on sexual abuse, gender issues, and moral questions in order to critique the concept of the Scandinavian welfare state (Brooks 1995: 11–20 *et passim*). By employing the heightened emotionalism of melodrama, crime fiction is able to challenge polarizations of good and evil, of victim and perpetrator, and negotiate the meanings of crimes committed by victim-heroines such as Lisbeth Salander.

The criminalized detective

In today's crime fiction, the focus is often on actions caused by emotions. The rational killer of Conan Doyle's and Agatha Christie's crime novels, as well as later Scandinavian writers such as Maj Sjöwall and Per Wahlöö, has largely been replaced by a mentally-disturbed psychopath. Every killing forms part of an elaborate but veiled morbid pattern or composition; it is a riddle or rebus without any established rules. To unveil and catch this alien creature requires a detective quite different from Sherlock Holmes, Hercule Poirot or Miss Marple, all of whom rely on their brains and hardly move outside of their parlours. It also requires someone different from Sjöwall and Wahlöö's Inspector Martin Beck, who is an active and professional investigator but who is not in touch with his emotions in his daily life. Contemporary crime fiction calls for a detective working out in the field, investigating hideous crime scenes and decaying bodies; someone who is not afraid of the darker side of society. The contemporary detective also has to explore repressed human desires to be able to solve the case. Where once the detective was an outsider, uncontaminated by the crimes of the community under investigation, he or she is now a potential killer, barely kept in check by socializing forces. The reason the detective eventually catches the criminal is their similarity. The investigation requires a detective almost as obsessed, guilty, and contaminated as the killer; that is, a detective who has experienced, or is emotionally involved in, something similar to what made the killer into a killer. Therefore, at times, the story is just as much about the detective's conflicts and emotional fragmentation as it is about the crime that is to be solved. A case in point is Elizabeth George's crime novels, where the cases investigated not only involve Detective Inspector Thomas Lynley's emotional life, with the investigation seemingly concerning his past more than that of the victim, but also where his personal involvement and vulnerability are what allow him to solve the case in the end.

Similarly, in many contemporary Scandinavian crime novels the crime and the criminal are also linked, in one way or another, to the investigator's own history. In novels by Åsa Larsson and Camilla Läckberg, the female protagonists return to the regions of their childhood, and the crimes committed are always related to the protagonists' pasts. In Åsa Larsson's *Sun Storm* (2003) the investigating Stockholm-based attorney Rebecka Martinsson is heading to her home town of Kiruna in northern Sweden to support an old friend whose brother has been murdered, and she has to dig deep into her own painful past in order to be able to solve the case and help her friend. In Läckberg's *The Ice Princess* (2003), one of protagonist Erica Falck's childhood friends is found murdered and she is drawn into a web of secrets connected to her own childhood in the small Swedish west coast community of Fjällbacka. In *The Hidden Child* (Läckberg 2007) the crime is even more closely linked to Falck's family, as her questions about her dead mother set in motion a chain of hideous events. It looks as if someone is prepared to kill to prevent old truths from coming out, truths that concern Falck's own origin and the identity of her biological parents. Although it is never spelled out, it is initially implied that Falck might be the offspring of sexual violence.

Thus, in contemporary crime fiction the investigators are far more emotionally involved in the case than they used to be, and they are reactive rather than pro-active characters. The murder stirs up the investigator's hidden memories, personal secrets, emotional traumas, and even questions concerning their own origins. This motif seems to be especially prevalent in crime stories with a female protagonist, as if it is possible to dig deeper into the consequences of crime, especially questions of victimhood and sexual violence, through a female investigator. In such stories, the emotional and psychological aspects of sexual violence are explored both from her external position as an investigator and from her internal emotional viewpoint as a woman and a potential victim of rape and sexual abuse. Right from the start, the female protagonist becomes part of the criminal's dark past in a way that dissolves the distinction between investigator and criminal. Through her connection to the crime, the consequences of crime and violence are exposed and explored. It is not the female investigator's rationality, scientific and methodological thinking, or detachment from the case that brings resolution: she has to be emotionally involved, to feel and think like the killer, in order to be able to solve the mystery. In Åsa Larsson's and Camilla Läckberg's novels, the investigations are just as much a device to uncover the origins and childhood of the female protagonist as to solve a well-planned murder. That is, during the work undertaken to solve the various murders and catch the criminals, the real object under examination is the investigating woman, her hidden history, and her connection to the criminal.

The victimized avenger

This change of perspective and the focus upon the detective's personal secrets have the effect that his or her professional role – as the protector against, or an investigator of, the threat of violence and crime – is reduced, while the depiction of emotions and psychology is much more thematically prominent and allowed to influence the plot. The brutal murders are there to expose the dark vice and extraordinary violence of seemingly ordinary and sympathetic people who turn out to be guilty of vicious crimes. The hidden criminal is often part of the investigator's own past or community, which links the latter to the crime and the criminal, as well as to the victim, in an uncanny way. A story that may start from the everyday does not stay within the norms of realism; instead, there is a melodramatic hyper-dramatization of forces in conflict and a dramaturgy of excess and overstatement. The mimetic account of the everyday soon turns into a melodramatic hyperbolic representation of vice and brutality, often combined with a Gothic, uncanny intensity which stresses the connection between crime and horror.

Because the detective, like the protagonist in horror stories, is emotionally involved, he or she is contaminated by both the crime and the investigation. In the Swedish writer Håkan Nesser's crime novels, the link between the detective and the criminal is constantly emphasized. In *Woman with Birthmark* (1996), detective Van Veeteren admits that if he had not become a policeman he would have been a murderer (90). The only difference between the detective and the killer is that a detective like Van Veeteren never crosses the line; he explores the mind of the assassin and comes close to the abyss of darkness but, however close he gets, he never gives in to his own obsession. Although the detective does not become a mentally-disturbed killer, he or she tries out how it would feel to be one. This split focus means that the expected neat conclusion is replaced by an exploration of the boundary between the human and the monstrous 'other' which is reminiscent of modern horror. Today's numerous crime stories about avenging serial killers – or 'list murderers' as Leonard Cassuto calls them, as the victim-avengers kill specific persons on their list of abusers – are good examples of this tendency (2009: 246). The transgression and power of the serial killer lies in their centrality in the narrative, in being complex figures with the capacity to marginalize the detectives' rational qualities, as well as the final solution. The British crime writer Peter Robinson is part of this trend, and he has sometimes reused the same murder cases and the same evasive female serial killers in different novels. In *Aftermath* (2001), there is a report of a domestic disturbance, but when police arrive at the address they stumble upon a truly horrific scene which leads to violence and sudden death, as well as to a ritual serial rapist and killer. What seems to be a simple case hides even more horrors. When Detective Inspector Alan Banks investigates the background of the victim, the beaten woman, he discovers a cruel backstory of child abuse and incest, and eventually learns that the once-victimized child has turned into a ruthless murderer. Behind the male rapist hides a female avenger, and what appeared to be a victim of domestic abuse turns out to be a cunning sexual monster. As the female avenger tries to kill herself at the end, the reader does not know if she will survive to be prosecuted, or if she has been punished by a violent death.

Thus, there is no tidy solution to this story, but Robinson's devoted readers will find out later, in *Friend of the Devil* (2007), what happened to the female killer in *Aftermath*. The cold-blooded killing of a woman in a wheelchair turns out to be the planned murder of the sexual offender and killer from the earlier novel; the victimized avenger is now the victim of another victimized female killer. In addition, the later novel is also connected to one of Robinson's earlier works, *Caedmon's Song* (1990). On the face of it, the two deaths in *Friend of the Devil* have nothing in common, but when Alan Banks and his colleague Annie Cabbot dig deeper, the two murders share something disturbingly familiar, reminding them of an unsolved case far back in time, the macabre case of *Caedmon's Song*. Most of the story of *Caedmon's Song* is about Kirsten, the victim of a vicious assault. Initially, she has no recollection of the brutal attack, but slowly and painfully begins to remember fragmented details from the assault. While she is recovering, the reader encounters another woman in cross-cutting sections of the novel: in another part of England, Martha Browne arrives at a village by the sea to do research for a book, but is gradually revealed to have another project in mind, namely to find the man who once attacked her. In parallel sections, the reader is brought closer to both the severely injured victim Kirsten and the victimized avenging killer Martha: two women yet, at the same time, one and the same, where past and present, victim and avenger, cause and effect, are intermixed.

In comparison, some Scandinavian writers have highlighted the female avenger and her reason to kill even more explicitly by using the episodic and dramatic structure of melodrama. The predominant story, the depiction of the crime investigation, tends to be broken up by one or two other narrations, and consequently the story of the female criminal is often told from her point of view. In many novels about sexually abused victims, the female avenger and her mission are introduced right from the beginning, as in Håkan Nesser's *Woman with Birthmark*. In the first chapter the reader gets to know the female avenger Maria Adler from her internal viewpoint. The question to be answered is not *who* the killer is, but *why* she kills. The latter question is not fully answered until the very end of the novel, when the reader, for the second time, shares the killer's internal focalization and when most of the questions about her sordid childhood are answered. As a concluding epilogue, her last hours in life are presented from her viewpoint in a written confession that reinstates her as the protagonist, and which also restores the former relationship between the killer and the reader of the novel.

The switch of focus from detective to female avenger is further elaborated in the Scandinavian crime fiction of the twenty-first century, in which the primal scene of violence and the affective impact of gendered abuse are played out repeatedly. One of the clearest examples of this, and of the narrative technique of double or split focalization, is found in the Norwegian writer Unni Lindell's *Little Red Riding Hood* (2004). The novel is about three sisters and a retired policeman, Holger Eliassen, who, as a hobby (or obsession), investigates unsolved murder cases connected to male victims in the past. All of his cases seem to be connected to the sisters, and when new victims are found during his investigation, he is convinced that the oldest sister, Judith, is the murderer, although he lacks conclusive evidence. At that point in the story, the reader knows that Judith is the victimized heroine, and also knows the reason why she kills the men she does. Through her diary, the reader learns how she once was attacked in the woods by an unknown man with a blue tattoo on his leg.

Through the constantly changing perspectives, the reader participates from both the point of view of the victimized killer and that of the pursuing investigator. The reader not only learns what drives the killer to kill, but is also made to explore the consequences of the killing from the viewpoint of the investigator and his investigation. In this way, the reader has to experience both what turns a woman into a serial killer and why she chooses certain male abuser-victims. In the end, both the killer and the reader find out that the primal abuser, the attacker in the woods, is the investigating policeman. His obsession with these cases stems from his wish to cover up his crime of paedophilia. That is, the female killer and the male investigator's obsession originate from the same event: the attack in the woods where the killer was the victim and the investigator the assailant. By depicting events from multiple viewpoints – the abused girl, the avenging woman, and the guilty investigator – Lindell invites the reader to understand, or to imagine, what makes the grown-up woman act as she does. By sharing the victim-killer Judith's perspective, both intellectually and emotionally, the reader imagines what it would be like to be a victim of sexual abuse, and is thus asked to identify with – or at least to pity and sympathize with – the vulnerable little girl, and hence indirectly with the grown-up killer also.

Accordingly, Lindell refers to a cluster of melodramatic conventions: an episodic composition with plenty of dramatic situations in order to make the reader feel sympathy for the victimized heroine. However, Lindell does not heighten the emotionalism in order to confirm the moral polarization of melodrama, but rather to explore and question it. The reader needs to be emotionally involved with the female victim-killer in order to realize what caused her to kill, to be expressively persuaded that she has a reason to kill her former tormentor and all those other men who have the potential to become abusers. Lindell problematizes questions of innocence and guilt, right and wrong, and, in the end, raises the very core question of what the real crime actually is, and who should be punished for it.

The vengeful investigator

Because of the focus on the underlying causality and the motives behind the murder, and its origin in sexual violence or rape, the female killer has become the main character in current crime fiction either on her own or via her double, the investigator or detective. The primal scene of gendered sexual abuse is explored either from the female avenger's viewpoint or via the detective's investigation of the case. For that reason, the conditions for the audience's emotional participation are altered. Many contemporary crime stories are characterized by an advanced focalization technique which encourages the audience to participate from a variety of positions. Thus, the reader is invited to explore different aspects of sexual abuse and its social consequences.

One of the most prominent examples is Stieg Larsson's Millennium trilogy, featuring Mikael Blomkvist and Lisbeth Salander. The novels of the trilogy can be described as a mixture of crime, thriller, and melodrama, as well as a parody of earlier crime fiction and action thrillers. In addition to the melodramatically exaggerated battle between good and evil, the novels are also linked to melodrama through the use of disguise and change of identity, hidden documents, *deus ex machina* resolutions and outrageous coincidences, and, finally, surprising revelations of family secrets and supernatural villains, such as Salander's half-brother Ronald Niedermann (Agger 2010: 101–3). The first novel, *The Girl with the Dragon Tattoo* (2008), is more or less composed as a traditional detective story or a 'whodunit', with the crime committed in the past, featuring journalist Blomkvist as the investigating detective and Salander as his gifted and useful researcher. Yet, Salander is far from a detached researcher. The second novel, *The Girl who Played with Fire* (2009a), is, to a greater degree than the first, constructed as a police story or action thriller, wherein Salander is hunted by a couple of hired killers while Blomkvist is involved in a political murder case. The third novel, *The Girl who Kicked the Hornets' Nest* (2009b), concentrates to an even greater degree on the political theme and what could be called a hidden wound in the Swedish welfare state. The focus is on political corruption within the police and security services, as well as the fact that the crime committed against Salander as a little girl is sanctioned by the child welfare system. However, although the novels reveal a systemic problem within Swedish society, the story about Salander comes down to a face-to-face fight with those evil male villains society is unable to punish. Finally, the long-abused victim Salander must administer justice in her own way. Not until all secrets are uncovered and all villains are defeated will she eventually get her revenge and resume her rightful citizenship. Therefore, the narrative constructs one of those satisfying, 'imaginary solutions' that are characteristic of melodramatic texts (Ang 1985: 135).

However, Salander is an ambiguously coded figure; she is both an avenging victim and an investigating detective transgressing all boundaries. On the one hand, she is the tough girl in a narrative of besieged femininity and love; on the other hand, she is the defenceless, exposed, and victimized woman. Unlike famous male detectives in the hard-boiled crime genre, such as Raymond Chandler's detective Philip Marlowe and James Ellroy's David Klein in *White Jazz* (1992), Salander's private life and past are not a secret; they are part of the plot and are repeatedly acted out. Her childhood haunts her constantly, and it is not long before her father and half-brother appear and interfere in her life, thus becoming the driving force of the plot. Furthermore, the most emotional and intimate situations in her private life are a prominent feature of the narrative. She is explicitly bisexual, and she destabilizes and challenges some of the dominant and polarized gender values and stereotypes of crime stories, even those in lesbian crime fiction such as Norwegian Anne Holt's crime novels about the police officer Hanne Wilhelmsen. Salander does not, like Wilhelmsen, live a monogamous lesbian family life, pursuing a successful career as a police officer within a settled Scandinavian society. Instead, she rejects all established relationships, social identities, and traditional contracts of employment. She is a fusion of incompatible gender roles, as she is an extremely clever researcher and a physically fit fighter at the same time as she is a tiny woman and a vulnerable social outcast. As a combination of threatened victim, revenging computer hacker, and feisty avenger she is paying back for her lost childhood, a theme introduced in the first novel when she takes revenge on her new guardian following his brutal rape of her. In her quest for justice she – like Sara Paretsky's V.I. Warshawski and the majority of hard-boiled female detectives – avoids close relationships and family ties. Like Warshawski, Salander suffers from a paranoid fear of betrayal and maternal loss, and consequently she constantly rejects those closest to her, keeping them at a distance so that she will not be subject to the pain of bereavement (Plain 2001: 159). During her investigation, Salander uncovers, and is affected by, corruption in the environment in which she moves. However, unlike Warshawski she does not serve the interests of the law, but the interests of herself, as she is both the victim and the avenger of the crimes committed against her in the past. Her fight is acting out the pure and polar concepts of right and wrong, the primal ethical forces of melodrama.

As is the case with many victimized female avengers, Salander's crime fighting methodology is hidden behind a mask of unthreatening anonymity as she is constantly acting under assumed names and fictitious identities. Salander is both vulnerable and powerful. She is a waif who never ceases to mourn for her mother, and in the way she fights from the bottom and rises to the top she represents the upwardly mobile characteristics of the Cinderella character and her success story. However, unlike Cinderella, she does not turn into a fairy-tale princess; instead she becomes a successful professional woman and action heroine. In her mission to confront patriarchy, as it is embodied by state, family, and modern finance, she operates outside society, partly in a virtual digitalized world as a hacker. In that role, she is also helping other women in danger or in need of information. When Blomkvist's lover Erika Berger is pestered by a stalker, Salander acts the role of fairy godmother, catching the culprit by hacking into his hidden e-mail identity. Throughout the Millennium trilogy, she also proves herself as a fighting superwoman, such as when, at the end of the first novel, she arrives at the very last minute to save Blomkvist from the serial killer, Martin Vanger. Similarly, in the second novel, she proves to be surprisingly physically strong as she fights off and escapes from two professional killers, despite being both alone and only half the size of her attackers. Fighting back from her physically and socially inferior position as a tiny girlish woman, she proves to be a tireless campaigner for what she considers to be justice and equality. Her feisty spirit and her mission to fight crime also seem to give her supernatural powers; she is a twenty-first century super-heroine.

The intense and excessive representations of life and death in the Millennium trilogy demolish the facade of manners to reveal the essential conflicts at work in contemporary Swedish society. Moral dilemmas are dramatized and all of a sudden everyday life appears very uncertain; current attitudes are challenged rather than confirmed. However, political conflicts, such as economic corruption, illegitimate use of authority, and deficiencies in the childcare system, gradually recede into the background. Instead, the personal drama of the emotionally disturbed Salander is the focus and, just as in traditional melodrama, there is a mythmaking of the individual and personal. As in many Gothic melodramas, Salander is concerned with investigating and establishing the guilt of a number of men: her psychiatrist Dr Teleborian, her male oppressor and guardian Advokat Bjurman, and her father Zalachenko. If, as Gill Plain suggests, Paretsky uses Warshawski to turn the hard-boiled crime story into a 'feminist fairy-tale' (2001: 142), Larsson moulds the genre into an adventurous fantasy, referencing children's books and well-known melodramatic superheroes. Right from the start, the investigating journalist Carl Mikael Blomkvist references Astrid Lindgren's famous child detective Kalle Blomkvist and Lisbeth Salander is compared to Lindgren's naughty super-girl Pippi Longstocking. References to well-known detective authors are frequent – for instance, Dorothy Sayers and Elizabeth George – and there are also references to James Bond and Superman. The depiction of Salander alludes to Jan Guillou's agent Carl Hamilton, a computer genius and distorted Swedish James Bond, who may be interpreted as Salander's male predecessor as a vehicle for social critique. Like Guillou, Larsson depicts recognizable historical events, persons and facts about Sweden, whilst simultaneously referring to well-known fictional superheroes. The trilogy is a combination of a documentary report on certain aspects of Swedish society and a thrilling, fantastic action novel – an intriguing genre parody that accentuates primal forces in conflict.

In this way, the trilogy illustrates what Jim Collins calls the third stage in the traditional three-stage model of generic progression and decline common in the nineties: consolidation, variation, and collapse into self-parody or reflexivity (1993: 242–63). To a Swedish audience, the ironic or meta-fictional references to children books and hard-boiled heroes, such as Pippi Longstocking, James Bond and Carl Hamilton, are obvious. Consequently, the mythic dimensions are apparent and Salander's struggles assert what Peter Brooks argues is the melodramatic way of resacralizing the personal (1995: 16–17). As a melodramatic heroine, Salander is made to embody the purest moral and emotional conflicts and issues of the story. Compared to the other characters, she speaks very little. The reader very seldom shares her point of view; instead she is often depicted by external focalization: she is focalized by the narrator or some other character. When she speaks it is not to confess or to take part in a conversation; her speech is reduced to the most necessary questions and answers. This is even more true of the Swedish film adaptations of the trilogy, where Salander very much plays the part of the silent woman of melodrama; she is presented as a woman of few words who does not expose herself verbally, but by expressionistic means or gestural semiotics, through actions, bodily postures, gestures, and facial expressions. She uses what can be seen as a non-verbal language of signs, more non-arbitrary or genuine than speech, and consequently she is depicted as a mythical heroine rather than a true character or human being. As in melodrama, the plot centres on her in order to dramatize her nightmare struggle for recognition and her escape from primal horror.

One reason why Salander has become such a popular victim-heroine is thus not because the reader understands her or learns all about her, but because she is an enigma: who is the emotionally complex Lisbeth Salander and why is she the way she is? She simultaneously represents modern society and emblematizes a gendered critique of it. In one way, she is the female victim who is forced to give in, but she also becomes the feminist avenging heroine who refuses to submit to men who hate women. Salander represents a common fantasy of being abused, mistreated and weak, but still strong and capable, an ideal transformation from being the object of violence to being its acting subject. She does not even give in to death. When she is almost killed and buried alive by her half-brother and father in the second novel, she is, against all odds, saved by Blomkvist, and she heals incredibly rapidly in order to return to her quest. Like the persecuted heroines in horror stories such as Stephen King's *Carrie*, she is resurrected to haunt and hunt down her former oppressors. To a greater degree than most victim-heroines in Scandinavian and Anglophone crime novels, Salander overcomes adversity and takes the opportunity to become the agent of her own story. She embodies the characteristics of a killer in serial-killer fiction or list murder stories: she is an 'especially skilled individual', defined by her exclusion from society. Like these killers, she is also a powerful and evasive outsider (Plain 2001: 221–23). Unlike most killers, however, she is a hybrid and an amalgamation of hero and victim, the 'female victim-hero' or 'final girl' (Clover 1992: 4, 39–53), who fights back and survives because she uses the same weapons as her antagonist, the villain or monster.

The female victim-avenger and the primal scene of rape

The characterization of Salander bears resemblance to that found in contemporary Anglophone crime fiction, and she might be seen as a development of the victimized avenger in fiction by Peter Robinson or Sara Paretsky's vengeful investigator V.I. Warshawski. But above all, as a sexually abused female avenger she is part of a long tradition in Scandinavian crime fiction, where the detective formula is used to expose the dark side of political and social life in the welfare state. The portrait of an active, courageous, and assertive female protagonist reflects a social reality and a well-known gender ideology in the Scandinavian countries in its critique of male hegemony in society.

Much more distinctly than earlier victim-avengers, such as Maria Adler in *Woman with Birthmark* or Judith in *Little Red Riding Hood*, Salander explores and transcends her role as a female victim-avenger. In the end, she has not only accomplished her mission – that is, to take vengeance against her rapist and obtain redress for her painful past and the wrongs done to her within the legal system of the welfare state – she has also assisted Blomkvist in solving several other cases and consequently has saved the world from various bad guys, such as her own father and his henchmen. The way she and her literary forerunners have to act under cover to establish law and order shows the failings of the legal system when it comes to sexual violence against women. This under-cover work points to a crisis of the gender order, while paradoxically exposing the degree to which traditional constraints still prevail when it comes to family structure, close relationships, and gender roles.

The dominance of female criminals or avengers in Scandinavian crime fiction does not tally with the actual crime statistics. According to the statistics, men are more often convicted of violent crimes than women are in Scandinavia. Very few women are found guilty of murder, and even fewer of serial murder. A female killer is a sensational exception, a rupture of the social order. Nevertheless, female killers are frequently used in Scandinavian crime fiction, and it is tempting to suggest that they represent a fantasy of female retaliation against domestic violence. As indicated by the statistics on violence against women in the Millennium trilogy, women are often the victims of different forms of domestic violence and sexual abuse, a taboo subject and a fact that undermines the received idea of a Scandinavian welfare society that prides itself on women's liberation and state-run day-care. Thus, Scandinavian crime fiction may produce a new kind of social awareness, as well as highlighting hidden socio-cultural processes, forbidden fantasies, and repressed truths. Acting out its darkest sides from the viewpoint of one of its most clear-cut victims – the sexually abused female – Scandinavian crime fiction tells a contradictory story about the welfare state, which on the surface cares for its citizens, but at the same time abandons them to violence and misery. This image of the welfare state is a sensational revelation made within the narrative form of the crime story combined with the expressive strategies of melodrama, such as focusing on strong emotional conflicts and the consequences of violence and abuse from the victim's viewpoint, which in Scandinavian crime fiction is often a sexually abused woman's perspective. At the same time it stresses, according to the melodramatic mode, the paradoxical location of strength in weakness and the triumph of the victimized female. However, in Scandinavian crime stories, the episodic, dramatic composition and the expressive techniques do not confirm, but instead challenge the melodramatic polarization of darkness and light, good and evil, victim and culprit by blurring the boundaries between investigator, perpetrator, and victim. This heightened emotionalism is used to explore criminal behaviour, its causes and effects, and to make sense of certain crimes, that is, rape-revenge murders committed by victim-heroines. In this way, crime stories featuring rape, such as the Millennium trilogy, may be read as the melodramatic fantasies of a murderous feminist uprising.

Works cited

Agger, G. (2010) 'Krimithriller, melodrama og bestseller. Stieg Larsson's Millennium-trilogi' in G. Agger and A.M. Waade (eds) *Den skandinaviske krimi. Bestseller og Blockbuster*. Göteborg: Nordicom.
Ang, I. (1985) *Watching Dallas: Soap Operas and the Melodramatic Imagination*. London: Methuen.
Brooks, P. (1995 [1976]) *The Melodramatic Imagination: Balzac, Henry James, Melodrama, and The Mode of Excess*. New Haven: Yale University Press.
Cassuto, L. (2009) *The Secret History of American Crime Stories*. New York: Columbia University Press.
Clover, C. (1992) *Men, Women, and Chain Saws: Gender in the Modern Horror Film*. London: Bfi Publishing, Princeton University Press.
Collins, J. (1993) 'Genericity in the Nineties: Eclectic Irony and the New Sincerity' in J. Collins, H. Radner, and A. P. Collins (eds) *Film Theory Goes to the Movies*. London: Routledge.
Läckberg, C. (2007) *The Ice Princess*. Transl. S. T. Murray. London: Harper Collins.
Läckberg, C. (2011) *The Hidden Child*. Transl. T. Nunally. London: Harper Collins.
Larsson, Å. (2007) *Sun Storm*. Transl. M. Delargy. New York: Delta Trade Paperbacks.
Larsson, S. (2008) *The Girl with the Dragon Tattoo*. Transl. R. Keeland. London: MacLehose.
Larsson, S . (2009a) *The Girl who Played with Fire*. Transl. R. Keeland. London: MacLehose.
Larsson, S. (2009b) *The Girl who Kicked the Hornets' Nest*. Transl. R. Keeland. London: MacLehose.
Lindell, U. (2004) *Rödluvan* [Little Red Riding-hood]. Stockholm: Piratförlaget.
Nesser, H. (1996) *Kvinna med födelsemärke* [Woman With a Birthmark]. Stockholm: Bonnier.
Plain, G. (2001) *Twentieth-Century Crime Fiction: Gender, Sexuality and the Body*. Edinburgh: Edinburgh University Press.
Read, J. (2000) *Feminism, Femininity and the Rape-Revenge Cycle*. Manchester: Manchester University Press.
Robinson, P. (1990) *Caedmon's Song*. Canada: Viking Press.
Robinson, P. (2001) *Aftermath*. London: Macmillan.
Robinson, P. (2007) *Friend of the Devil*. London: Hodder & Stoughton.
Singer, B. (2001) *Melodrama and Modernity: Early Sensational Cinema and Its Contexts*. New York: Columbia University Press.
Williams, L. (2001) *'Playing the Race Card': Melodramas of Black and White from Uncle Tom to O.J. Simpson*. Princeton and Oxford: Princeton University Press.

Part II

Dismembered Bodies, Wounded States: Gender Politics in the Millennium Trilogy and Beyond

4
Rape and the Avenging Female in Stieg Larsson's Millennium Trilogy and Håkan Nesser's *Woman with Birthmark* and *The Inspector and Silence*

Marla Harris

What the poet Moniza Alvi observes of poets writing about rape can also apply to crime novelists: 'We can be seduced into thinking that the material itself is so strong and fascinating that we don't have to engage with it deeply, or apply much in the way of craft; an outpouring of emotion, or an emphasis on graphic detail will suffice' (2010: xix). Perhaps no recent crime novelist has stirred up as much debate about the representation of rape in fiction as Swedish journalist-turned-novelist Stieg Larsson, author of the internationally bestselling Millennium trilogy, whose villains include Nazi sympathizers, serial killers, and Russian spies, and whose litany of crimes runs the gamut from incest and murder to political corruption and corporate fraud. The novels contain numerous accounts of disturbing sexual violence, but the most controversial episodes are the rapes of the heroine Lisbeth Salander by her legal guardian Nils Bjurman, and her revenge rape of him, in *The Girl with the Dragon Tattoo* (2005).

With wildly enthusiastic reviews, male and female readers alike hailed the trilogy as a 'celebration of retributive female violence against men', that holds up 'a mirror to modern society' (Bernhard, 2010; Macintyre, 2010). Goth-garbed computer hacker Salander, a petite, kickboxing super-heroine able to pass through (fire)walls, comes in for praise as an 'avenging angel' (Kakutani, 2010). Judith Lorber describes the tattooed, pierced, and bisexual Salander as a third-wave feminist who 'revels in sexual openness, outrageous gender self-presentations, and emotional coolness' (2011). Still, a vocal minority of readers have taken exception to Larsson's avowed feminism, complaining about *Dragon Tattoo*'s 'graphic and gratuitous violence against women' and arguing that 'Larsson seems to want it both ways: to condemn such savagery while simultaneously exploiting it in graphic detail for titillating storytelling purposes' (Newman, 2009; Schwartz, 2010). That readers have had such divergent and passionate responses is testimony to the ways in which fictional rape and violence inevitably serve as reminders of the dangers faced by real women. However, criticizing Larsson for sensationalizing the sexual abuse of women ignores the fact that some of the most memorably unpleasant violence directly witnessed by the reader actually involves attacks on men, not women; indeed, Larsson is remarkably reticent when it comes to the details of Salander's rapes by Bjurman.[1]

The Millennium trilogy has enjoyed extraordinarily high visibility, not only because of the popularity of the books themselves and their Swedish and American film adaptations, but also because of a steady stream of Larsson-related gossip circulating online as well as in newspaper and magazine articles. Undoubtedly some of the initial interest was piqued by Larsson's untimely death in 2004 prior to the publication of the novels. Within the past year alone several biographical works have been published.[2] His high profile, along with that of more established writers like Henning Mankell, author of the Kurt Wallander series (1991–2009), has brought increased international attention to Swedish crime fiction, spurring the belated translation of works by other writers.[3] As a result novelist Håkan Nesser's *Kvinna med födelsemärke* [*Woman with Birthmark*], a disquieting story of revenge, appeared in English translation in 2009, 13 years after its original publication (1996), when it received the Best Swedish Crime Novel Award.

At first glance, *Woman with Birthmark*, about a woman who tracks down and kills her mother's rapists, appears to have much in common with Larsson's trilogy, in which sexually abusive men (who are often fathers or father-figures) try to preserve their reputations and power at the expense of women, and women fight back. On the surface, Larsson and Nesser's novels pose 'a powerful challenge to the way the West traditionally conceptualizes rape through facile oppositions such as male agency and female victimization, power and passivity, resistance and complicity' (Mardorossian 2010: 35). However, drawing on radically different gendered traditions of crime fiction, Larsson and Nesser express contrasting attitudes towards rape and revenge, and towards women as victims and as perpetrators. Maria Adler is the antithesis of

Salander; Salander is falsely accused of being a whore, a murderess, a madwoman, and a patricide, but Adler is arguably all of these things, an anti-heroine who epitomizes male fears about the monstrous female, symbolically castrating her victims by 'shooting the[ir] willies off' (Nesser 2009: 141). If Larsson's novels are about 'men who hate women', *Woman with Birthmark* could be described as a novel about a woman who hates men. As Larsson encourages the reader's identification with Salander and other abused women in the novels, while demonizing male rapists, Nesser blurs the differences between victims and perpetrators, and invites the reader's complicity with the rapists. Consequently, as Larsson's reader cheers the violent retaliation of Salander and her vindication in the courtroom, Adler's revenge (which culminates in her suicide) feels like a tragedy for everyone involved. This ambivalence is also evident in Nesser's *Kommissarien och tystnaden* (1997), published in English as *The Inspector and Silence* (2011), which offers yet another variant on the rape-revenge plot.

Woman with Birthmark and *The Inspector and Silence*

The fourth in a series of ten novels (1993–2003) featuring Detective Chief Inspector Van Veeteren, *Woman with Birthmark* follows Maria Adler, a drug-addicted prostitute suffering from AIDS, as she methodically tracks down and murders four men. With no clue as to a motive and with no suspects, the police struggle to establish connections between the murdered men in order to warn potential victims. Eventually they discover that the men had been National Service classmates 30 years earlier. Before the police can find Adler (or prevent any murders), she commits suicide by drowning, leaving behind an explanatory letter for Van Veeteren. Only then are the sordid circumstances revealed: as a young schoolgirl, Adler's mother was savagely raped by the four victims; moreover, one of them was Adler's biological father.

Nesser's plot is heavily indebted to *The Bride Wore Black* (1940), a pulp fiction by the American writer Cornell Woolrich.[4] In Woolrich's novel an attractive woman, Julie Killeen, sets out to avenge her husband's murder by donning disguises and insinuating herself into the lives of his suspected murderers before killing them, one by one. In a final twist the protagonist learns that her victims were, in fact, innocent of the murder, a discovery that undercuts any moral justification for her killing spree and negates any sense of triumph, since the real murderer is still alive. Nesser changes the identity of the victim and the nature of the crime, but retains Woolrich's ambiguous representation of the female avenger; by insisting upon her culpability, to some extent he makes reading her as feminist heroine problematic.

Despite transplanting the story to 1990s Europe, Nesser's characterization of Adler owes much to the male-authored, male-centred, and often misogynistic pulp-fiction tradition of crime writing, popularized first in inexpensive magazines and later in mass-market paperbacks. According to Erin Smith, the hard-boiled detective genre of pulp fiction, which flourished from the 1920s through the 1940s, was 'aimed emphatically at men', especially those who were young and working class; its hostility towards strong women, frequently depicting them as dangerous and deadly, was, in part, a response to the phenomenon of the career woman, 'the increasing number of visible, wage-earning women in jobs once reserved for men' during that period (2000: 165).

Adler, whose masquerades serve to de-emphasize her femininity, is a distorted version of the pulp's femme fatale; at one point she disguises herself to appear as unattractive as possible: 'with no makeup and wearing round, metal-framed spectacles, she suddenly looked like a librarian or a bored handicrafts teacher' (Nesser 2009: 14). At another critical juncture she even poses as a man. Brought up by her mother on a steady diet of self-hatred as well as hatred of men, Adler perversely contemplates taking a male sex partner 'just for the pleasure of infecting him' with HIV (9). Instead of using rape as a means of establishing empathy with female rape victims, *Woman with Birthmark* uses it largely as a plot device; the revelation at the end functions like a punchline seemingly deployed for its shock value.

Nesser's decision not to set the novel in Sweden, but in the fictional northern European city of Maardam, suggests a wish to shed social, political, and historical baggage, to examine human nature rather than national stereotypes. Adler exists in a kind of vacuum, without name, family, or friends. Visually, too, she is a chameleon: 'she had the distinct feeling that she was somebody else. New features and a new name' (14). In a sense Adler's victims are right when they conclude, after looking for traces of her in official records, that 'she doesn't exist'; she eludes us not only physically, by vanishing into the sea, but also emotionally (165). This is a novel about female violence in which we never see violence inflicted, a story about rape in which characters avoid talking about rape. The effect of this silencing is to deny Adler's claims to both victimhood (until the end, when we learn about her past) and to agency, since we never witness her in a position of power.

While Adler's perspective, like her body, is largely absent, or is presented incoherently in fragments, Nesser increasingly narrates events from the point of view of the men who are being hunted down, as well as from the viewpoints of Van Veeteren and his officers, who are trying to save them. As if to support the initial police hypothesis that the men are being terrorized by a madwoman, Nesser raises the possibility that Adler is insane: 'I'm crazy, she thought. Completely and utterly mad' (15). As readers, then, we are disturbingly coerced into entertaining the notion that the men are innocent victims, in spite of the fact that they are highly unsympathetic characters who are, at the very least, guilty of being bullies. Ryszard Malik, the first victim, is psychologically abusive towards his wife, regarding her with ill-disguised contempt: 'There's something wrong with her. Pure paranoia. No wonder the hotel wanted to sack her' (23). The second victim, Rickard Maasleitner, is a teacher facing suspension for 'dragging a cheeky fifteen-year-old out into the corridor and telling him to go to hell. Or back to the country he came from, wherever that was' (76). Thus Nesser 'offer[s] a subject-position to the reader only to expose the problematics of donning it'; the reader can identify either with an unlikeable, possibly mentally ill woman who derives an orgasmic thrill from committing murder, or with arrogant men who find pleasure in casually mistreating the people around them (Tanner 1994: 15).

Any lingering doubt about the men's guilt – although the actual crime remains unknown at this point – is dispelled when Karel Innings and Werner Biedersen meet to discuss killing Adler. In light of what we discover later about their gang-rape of Adler's mother, their language is richly ironic: 'I just thought it would be beneficial if we collaborated a bit. Shared the responsibility' (Nesser 2009: 168). The second half of the novel is devoted to a grim cat-and-mouse game between Adler and Biedersen that blurs the distinction between victim and perpetrator. Biedersen not only reverses their positions by stalking Adler, he also unwittingly becomes more and more like her. Just as she has managed to appear so mousy that she is nearly invisible, he, too, adopts the disguise of a 'drifter, a natural if regrettable background figure in any town or any street scene anywhere in the world. The perfect camouflage' (181). And, just as she refers mysteriously to her mission on behalf of her dead mother, he, too, claims to be undertaking a mission: to avenge 'the friends she had murdered, the widows and children, and the lives she had destroyed in the course of her blood-stained campaign' (267). Through Biedersen's rhetoric, self-serving as it is, the text acknowledges the collateral damage of Adler's actions; in the process of avenging one female victim (her mother), she creates new female victims, notably Maasleitner's teenaged daughter and Innings's widow. Again, the effect is to diminish Adler's moral stature.

One of the many disconcerting aspects of the text is that in spite of the fact that Biedersen is a would-be murderer, as well as a sexist who refers to the barman's Thai girlfriend as 'a good-looking piece of skirt', Nesser creates in the reader an unsettling tension between wanting Adler to find Biedersen and wanting Biedersen to escape (314). Ironically, in his growing fear of being followed and of being alone outside after dark, he experiences what it is like to be a woman – that is, to be physically vulnerable. When he finds himself in a bar full of rowdy female customers on International Woman's Day, the comparison with Adler's mother, a girl alone on the street surrounded by drunken men, is unmistakable. In Biedersen's nightmarish vision every woman is a potential predator, a parodic reversal of the normal state of affairs, but one that is reinforced within the novel.

As Biedersen is increasingly feminized, Adler is masculinized, even invading the 'men's room', dressed like a man, to murder him. This image of Adler as a woman trespassing upon male space resonates through the text. Van Veeteren's male police officers repeatedly seem intimidated by strong women, whom they regard as unfeminine. The adjectives used to describe career women are remarkably similar to those employed to describe Adler. While Adler demonstrates 'coldness and decisiveness', Maasleitner's ex-wife, a secretary in an attorney's office, shows 'signs of ruthlessness', and Innings's widow, a travel agent, is 'a powerful-looking woman' (237, 102, 207). Van Veeteren's observation that 'There's nothing much to stop a woman doing anything at all' hints not so much at his admiration of such women as his fear of them (201). Indeed, the subtext of the novel might be the 'fear of independent women' (Söderlind 2011: 163). Sylvia Söderlind's claims for Nesser's social conservatism are pertinent here, as she finds evidence in his work 'of a backlash against the gains of feminism since the revolutionary 1960s' (162).

In *Woman with Birthmark* Nesser subtly shifts attention onto males as victims of violence. Van Veeteren himself is assaulted late one night by 'a gang of bellowing young men who had evidently been lying in wait for a suitable victim' (2009: 258). The resemblance of his situation – minus the rape – to that of Adler's mother actually serves to diminish rape as a special kind of crime; there is a sense that the text implicitly establishes an equivalence between Van Veeteren's mugging and Adler's mother's rape. The novel's anxiety about the vulnerability of men displaces the focus from women as the victims of violence.

This displacement of the female rape victim is even more pronounced in the fifth instalment in the Van Veeteren series, *The Inspector and Silence*, in which Van Veeteren investigates the rape-murders of two teenaged girls, members of an obscure religious sect led by the charismatic Oscar Yellinek. Surprisingly scant attention is given to the girls themselves as the victims of brutal rapes, as if the fact that they were raped is a trivial detail. Instead, Van Veeteren's preoccupation with his own sexuality and his dislike of his ex-wife, whom he compares to a predatory 'spider luring the unwary into her web', colour his attitude towards the crimes, provoking lurid fantasies about the female members of the sect and their possible participation in orgies with Yellinek – and in lesbian orgies without him (2011: 13). When Yellinek himself turns up dead, Van Veeteren becomes obsessed with determining the guilt of Yellinek's three female assistants, whom he labels as madwomen and witches, locking them up in a psychiatric hospital and interrogating them as if he has already found them guilty.

The real criminals, however, prove to be not members of the sect, but an ordinary family. Mirjam Fingher, who anonymously tips off the police about the dead girls, and who kills Yellinek, appears to be a female avenger figure, but in reality is acting to protect her son Wim, who is actually responsible for raping and murdering the girls. Ultimately, Mirjam's murder of Yellinek is treated more severely than Wim's rapes and murders. Paradoxically, Van Veeteren's personal sympathies in the affair seem to lie with Mirjam's naive husband: 'One might also ask who was worst affected by this horrible business. The poor girls and their families, of course, but I don't think we should forget Mathias Fingher' (282). In this novel, then, a similar double standard emerges to that in *Woman with Birthmark*, in which male victims are taken more seriously than female victims, and in which women's crimes are judged more harshly than those of men.

The Millennium trilogy

In contrast to Nesser's tightly structured novel, Larsson's trilogy is reminiscent of a sprawling Victorian triple-decker, with multiple plots and an expanding cast of characters.[5] The materiality of Larsson's Sweden is reinforced by an almost mystical incantation of place names and consumer products, statistics about domestic violence, and the incorporation of real-life personages (such as the boxer Paolo Roberto); Larsson conjures up not a generic European past and present, but a specifically Swedish one. At the centre is Salander, a computer hacker/detective whose past includes a lengthy stay in a mental hospital. After her court-appointed guardian Bjurman rapes her (on two different occasions), she takes revenge by raping and torturing him.

Kurdo Baksi, a friend and colleague of Larsson, advises readers that 'If you are looking for a focus in Stieg's writing, I would suggest it is the woman's point of view' (2010: 118). Where Nesser shows the influence of the male-authored, male-centred pulp-fiction tradition of crime writing, Larsson aligns himself with the feminist crime novel, weaving in allusions to detective fiction by Anglophone women writers, from Dorothy Sayers and Val McDermid, to Sara Paretsky and Elizabeth George. Like his heroine Salander and her sidekick Blomkvist, Larsson resembles Sally Munt's description of the feminist sleuth as 'a moral watchdog from the Other who paces the streets in order to expose sex/gender oppression' (1994: 197). That oppression is omnipresent, from Salander's being raped to the sexual harassment that Erika Berger suffers as a newspaper editor. Salander's rapes not only expose the pervasiveness of misogyny, but they also conform to a recurrent pattern in feminist detective fiction, in which 'sexual violence is a way of establishing the female heroine's vulnerability, but also, significantly, her determination and resistance' (Horeck 2004: 128).

A major difference from *Woman with Birthmark*, where the rape is related in the third person in a letter, long after the assault, is that we are witnesses to Salander's rapes by Bjurman. Ironically it is through these scenes – or, more accurately, her responses – that we first come to know Salander as a character, since our earlier encounters with her have been through the eyes of other (male) characters. Larsson, however, devotes less space to describing Bjurman's rapes of Salander than he does to the spectacle of her raping him. The first rape, when Bjurman coerces Salander into oral sex in his office, takes up less than a page. The second, more devastating rape is instigated by Salander, whose revenge plans 'required her to allow Bjurman to attack her again' (2009: 244). Larsson is sparing with his description: there is a narrative gap from 8:30 on Friday night when she feels 'excruciating pain as he forced something up her anus' to 4:00 on Saturday morning, when she 'was allowed to put on her clothes' and go home (250). The lack of detail here, which leaves the reader to imagine what may have taken place in those missing hours, adds to the horror.

What, then, can we make of Larsson's strategic abridgement? He is clearly less interested in titillating the reader by displaying Salander as passive and helpless than he is in representing her as empowered, guiding the reader to decipher the significance of small gestures and expressions, such as the look of 'naked, smouldering hatred' that Salander gives Bjurman as she leaves his flat, or even the significance of saying nothing (251). Following the first rape she does not go to the police, a woman's crisis centre, or to a friend. She is actually planning to film the next encounter for blackmail purposes, but we do not know that. The narrator invites the reader to judge her: 'An ordinary person might have felt that her lack of reaction had shifted the blame to her – it might have been another sign that she was so abnormal that even rape could evoke no adequate emotional response' (227). Yet the narrator's loaded terms suggest, instead, the impossibility of judging her. The point, Larsson seems to be saying, is that rape is outside the realm of normalcy, and that we should not be tempted to normalize it by demanding that every woman follow the same scripted response.

Salander's resistance is also evident in another important scene, the flashback to her incarceration as a girl in St. Stefan's Hospital under the care of the psychiatrist/torturer Dr. Teleborian. In a foreshadowing of her rape by Bjurman, she is firmly strapped to her bed in restraints and handcuffs in what appears to be a prison cell, apparently subdued and powerless. Yet, experiencing the scene through Salander's consciousness, we are made aware of the contrast between her physical constraints and her mental freedom as she focuses her mind on reliving the act of revenge – setting fire to her abusive, wife-battering father – that has brought her to St. Stefan's. Her refusal to speak to Dr. Teleborian, like her silence after the first rape, is not an acknowledgement of defeat, but 'a form of protest against dominant, oppressive and hegemonic voices' that want her to feel guilty, ashamed, and helpless when she does not (Gunne 2010: 166).

The most dramatic example of Salander's resistance is her rape of Bjurman. Where 'crimes of sexual violence such as rape are often trivialized in popular thrillers', rape in feminist crime fiction, as in Larsson's novels, is treated as an exceptional crime (Munt 1994: 198). For instance, Val McDermid's fictional police detective Carol Jordan observes that 'No other violation comes close except death, and nobody's reported back on that yet' (2004: 15). Consequently, the methods of revenge undertaken by female victims, no matter how extreme, are therefore justified, even when, as in the case of Salander, they mirror the methods of a male sadist. Straddling Bjurman and penetrating him with the tattoo needle, Salander grotesquely parodies intercourse, but she also uses words as a weapon against him, as he and his colleagues have used words, in the form of psychiatric evaluations, police reports, and court decrees, against her.

In the trilogy this revenge rape, which precedes Salander's teaming up with Blomkvist, is crucial in establishing her as a heroine. Salander moves from avenging wrongs committed against her mother and herself to becoming an avenger of wrongs against women she does not know, a transformation begun towards the end of *Dragon Tattoo*, with her advocacy for Martin Vanger's victims, and consolidated at the beginning of *The Girl Who Played with Fire*, when she intervenes to stop Richard Forbes, a complete stranger, from killing his wife Geraldine on a Grenada beach. Later in *Played with Fire* a taser-wielding Salander breaks into the home of Per-Åke Sandström, a journalist guilty of rape and sex trafficking. Her lengthy torture and interrogation of Sandström echoes her assault on Bjurman, although she denounces Sandström verbally as 'a sadistic pig, a pervert, and a rapist' instead of tattooing him (2010: 518). Her final act of revenge takes place in the courtroom. Using words – her autobiography – and pictures – the DVD of the rape – she breaks her silence. This time it is not a physical attack on one man, but the dismantling of another kind of male body, that of the government or, more accurately, the Swedish security service.

Conclusion

Larsson, then, implicitly rewrites Nesser's gender politics; while Nesser foregrounds what he sees as a crisis of masculinity, deploying sexual violence against women as a plot device to be kept in the background, Larsson treats the sexual abuse of women as an (inter)national crisis. In Larsson's trilogy and Nesser's pair of novels the plots are set in motion by the rape of a young girl, but the gendered traditions of crime writing on which these authors draw affect the ways that they portray men and women as victims and perpetrators of violence. Nesser, adapting a male-authored, male-centred pulp-fiction crime novel as his source for *Woman with Birthmark*, treats rape as an isolated incident that can be contained and resolved within the pages of the novel, as is also true of *The Inspector and Silence*. Both works, betraying an underlying anxiety about late-twentieth-century gender roles, ultimately shift attention from female victims to male victims, and from male criminals to female criminals.

Larsson, on the other hand, strongly influenced by the late-twentieth-century feminist crime novel, regards his fiction as a logical continuation of his social and political activism against the oppression of women. In what could be construed as a return to second-wave feminism, however, he downplays the impact of race, ethnicity, social class, religion, and nationality on shaping attitudes towards gender. He also rejects the idea of rape as an unusual crime, committed by strangers: the many raped and murdered women, whose stories are related throughout the trilogy and through the official statistics that punctuate Larsson's novels, serve as a chorus that amplifies and contextualizes Salander's experiences of rape, showing them not to be aberrant, but sickeningly commonplace. In *Woman with Birthmark* what threatens to become a national crisis – a serial killer murdering unrelated men – is revealed to be (only) a family matter. What begins as a family matter in Larsson's novels – Harriet's disappearance – reveals a systemic misogyny that extends far beyond the Vanger household to implicate almost every social institution in Sweden, including the national government.

Larsson's stance, however, is not without its difficulties. If Nesser is all too ready to suspect women of being guilty (of something), Larsson is in danger of falling into an essentialist trap by casting his female characters in too positive a light. Apart from shadowy figures like Harriet's mother or Salander's twin Camilla – rare examples of women who are arguably complicit with patriarchy – Larsson's women are attractive, strong, open-minded, and intelligent, and possess a moral code and sense of social justice. In addition, unlike the morally murky universe of Nesser's novels, Larsson neatly divides his male characters into heroes and villains. Because Larsson's villains – men who hurt women – are apparently without redeemable human qualities, it makes it easier for the reader to endorse the extreme violence that is levelled against them and to relieve Salander of any culpability. Female revenge in Larsson is satisfying because right and wrong, good and evil, are clearly defined.

Above all, Nesser and Larsson offer two opposing ways of understanding the female rape victim. Looking back to an earlier literary era, *Woman with Birthmark* links rape directly to death in a plot that punishes not only the rapists, but also the rape victims. The strong sense of guilt that Adler feels as a result of her mother's rape and her own illegitimacy mark her as an example of the sexually transgressive 'fallen woman', a familiar figure in Victorian literature and culture, who typically spiralled downward into prostitution and early death. Adler's conformity with this nineteenth-century type is part of what contributes to the novel feeling 'strangely anachronistic' (Söderlind 2011: 161).

In contrast to Adler, whose identity is inextricably bound up with her perception of herself as a victim, Salander, who 'had never regarded herself as a victim', is a survivor (2009: 237). There is, of course, a considerable irony in the fact that she has to present herself as a victim in order to counter the prosecution's hostile presentation of her as a perpetrator of violence against her father and other men. Sandra Walklate comments that 'the passivity and powerlessness associated with being a victim are also associated with being female. It is this link that is problematic for those working within the feminist movement who prefer to use the term 'survivor' to try to capture women's resistance to their structural powerlessness and consequent potential victimization' (2007: 27).

Although the trilogy circles back to her rape again and again, Salander moves beyond simply seeking justice for herself to advocating for other women. Compared to Adler's fatalistic belief that the stigma of rape is passed on like a mutated gene (or a disfiguring birthmark), Salander argues for the more appealing possibility that women who find themselves in the position of victim can change the plots of their lives. While Adler's suicide produces closure for the case and for the book, Salander's own plot is open-ended, as her final gesture of opening the door to let Blomkvist in also challenges the reader to look from the pages of the book to the world outside.

Notes

1. Although beyond the scope of this essay, the 2009 Swedish film *Män som hatar kvinnor* [*The Girl with the Dragon Tattoo*], directed by Niels Arden Oplev, treats the rape(s) of Salander quite differently, devoting substantial screen time to Bjurman's rape of Salander.
2. See, for example, B. Forshaw (2010) *The Man Who Left Too Soon: the Biography of Stieg Larsson*; E. Gabrielsson (2011) *There Are Things I Want You to Know about Stieg Larsson and Me*; and D. Burstein *et al.* (2011) *The Tattooed Girl: The Enigma of Stieg Larsson and the Secrets Behind the Most Compelling Thrillers of Our Time*.
3. Contemporary Swedish crime fiction is frequently considered as part of an emerging sub-genre with close ties to crime fiction produced by novelists in other Scandinavian countries. See Nestingen and Arvas (2011).
4. Woolrich's novel was adapted by François Truffaut as a film, *La Mariée était en noir* (*The Bride Wore Black*, 1968). Adler's surname is probably an allusion to Irene Adler, Sherlock Holmes's charming and formidable adversary in Arthur Conan Doyle's 'A Scandal in Bohemia' (1891); she disappears (on a trip with her husband), leaving a letter behind for Holmes.
5. In fact, Larsson's novels resemble the mid-nineteenth-century English sensation novel, a popular Victorian genre known for its fast-paced plotting, its interest in crime and detection (often inspired by real-life criminal cases and trials), and its subversive heroines.

Works cited

Alvi, M. (2010) 'Foreword: "An Unsafe Subject"' in S. Gunne and Z. B. Thompson (eds) *Feminism, Literature and Rape Narratives: Violence and Violation*. New York: Routledge. xi-xx.

Baksi, K. (2010) *Stieg Larsson: Our Days in Stockholm*. Transl. L. Thompson. New York: Pegasus Books.

Bernhard, B. (2010) 'Stieg Larsson's *The Girl Who Kicked the Hornet's Nest*', *The New York Sun*, 13 May, http://www.nysun.com/arts/stieg-larssons-millennium-final-volume-due-out/86955, accessed 13 Feb 2012.
Burstein, D., A. de Keijzer, and J. Holmberg (eds) (2011) *The Tattooed Girl: The Enigma of Stieg Larsson and the Secrets Behind the Most Compelling Thrillers of Our Time*. New York: St. Martin's Press.
Forshaw, B. (2010) *The Man Who Left Too Soon: the Biography of Stieg Larsson*. London: John Blake.
Gabrielsson, E. (2011) *'There Are Things I Want You to Know' about Stieg Larsson and Me*. New York: Seven Stories Press.
Gunne, S. (2010) 'Questioning Truth and Reconciliation: Writing Rape in Achmat Dangor's *Bitter Fruit* and Kagiso Lesego Molope's *Dancing in the Dust*' in S. Gunne and Z. B. Thompson (eds) *Feminism, Literature and Rape Narratives: Violence and Violation*. New York: Routledge. 164–80.
Horeck, T. (2004) *Public Rape: Representing Violation in Fiction and Film*. London: Routledge.
Larsson, S. (2009) *The Girl with the Dragon Tattoo*. Transl. R. Keeland. New York: Vintage.
Larsson, S. (2010) *The Girl Who Played with Fire*. Transl. R. Keeland. New York: Vintage.
Kakutani, M. (2010) 'A Punk Pixie's Ominous Past', *New York Times*, 21 May, http://www.nytimes.com/2010/05/21/books/21book.html, accessed 13 Feb 2012.
Lorber, J. (2011) 'The Gender Ambiguity of Lisbeth Salander: Third-Wave Feminist Hero?', *Dissent*, 7 July, http://www.dissentmagazine.org/online.php?id=477, accessed 7 March 2012.
Macintyre, B. (2010) 'The Girl Who Stormed On To the Bestsellers' List', *The Times*, 18 Feb, http:www.timesonline.co.uk/tol/comment/columnists/ben_macintyre/article7031243.ece, accessed 13 Feb 2012.
Mardorossian, C. M. (2010) 'Rape by Proxy in Contemporary Caribbean Women's Fiction' in S. Gunne and Z. B. Thompson (eds) *Feminism, Literature and Rape Narratives: Violence and Violation*. New York: Routledge. 23–37.
McDermid, V. (2004) *The Torment of Others*. New York: St. Martin's Press.
Munt, S. R. (1994) *Murder by the Book? Feminism and the Crime Novel*. London: Routledge.
Nesser, H. (2011 [1997]) *The Inspector and Silence*. Transl. L. Thompson. New York: Pantheon.
Nesser, H. (2009 [1996]) *Woman with Birthmark*. Transl. L. Thompson. New York: Vintage.
Nestingen, A. and P. Arvas (eds) (2011) *Scandinavian Crime Fiction*. Cardiff: University of Wales Press.
Newman, M. (2009) 'Feminist or Misogynist?', *The F Word*, 4 Sep, http://www.thefword.org.uk/reviews/2009/09/larrson_review, accessed Feb 13 2012.
Schwartz, M. (2010) 'The Girl with the Dragon Tattoo Trilogy: Did Stieg Larsson have a problem with women?', *Shelf Life*, 18 June, http://shelf-life.ew.com/2010/06/18/stieg-larsson-tattoo-book-women-characters, accessed 13 Feb 2012.
Smith, E.A. (2000) *Hard-Boiled: Working-Class Readers and Pulp Magazines*. Philadelphia: Temple University Press.

Söderlind, S. (2011) 'Håkan Nesser and the Third Way: of Loneliness, Alibis and Collateral Guilt' in A. Nestingen and P. Arvas (eds) *Scandinavian Crime Fiction*. Cardiff: University of Wales Press. 159–70.

Tanner, L. (1994) *Intimate Violence: Reading Rape and Torture in Twentieth-Century Fiction*. Bloomington: Indiana University Press.

Walklate, S. (2007) *Imagining the Victim of Crime*. Maidenhead: McGraw-Hill Open University Press.

5
The Body, Hopelessness, and Nostalgia: Representations of Rape and the Welfare State in Swedish Crime Fiction

Katarina Gregersdotter

The Swedish model of the welfare state, also known in Sweden as the 'People's Home', has come under criticism in Swedish crime fiction since Maj Sjöwall and Per Wahlöö's novels about policeman Martin Beck (1965–1975). The People's Home can be summed up by the notion that 'the state is a benign institution protecting and nurturing the nation' (Nestingen 2008: 11). However, as Andrew Nestingen and Paula Arvas write, Sjöwall and Wahlöö regarded the welfare state as an 'incrementalist compromise with capital' (2011: 3), which was moving further and further away from issues of class and justice. As they also maintain, the Scandinavian welfare states have 'been embracing neoliberalism and globalization since the 1980s' (8). Recently, many authors of crime fiction, in particular those writing in a Swedish context, have linked the transformation of the welfare state to both globalization and patriarchal structures. What might, then, be termed a global patriarchy has led to a growing sex industry where, for instance, sex trafficking can be viewed in the light of a globalized economy, and where free trade accordingly includes the commodification of human bodies. Stieg Larsson's Millennium trilogy (2005–2007) and Anders Roslund and Börge Hellström's novel *The Vault* (2008) launch sharp critiques of sex trafficking and are the most prominent examples of recent Swedish crime fiction which discusses rape as a form of systematic trade in, and commodification of, bodies. Similar to Stieg Larsson, Roslund and Hellström have an explicit political agenda within their novels, and it can be argued that they are amongst the most political authors in Swedish crime fiction today. In an interview, they state that they are 'pointing out problems [they] see in [their] society' (Burstein *et al*. 2011: 127–128), and thus far every novel has dealt with a very specific 'problem' such as homelessness, capital punishment, or child molestation. Indeed, social commentary is part of both plot and characterization in novels by Larsson and Roslund and Hellström, and their books share many themes and ideas about contemporary Sweden in an increasingly globalized world. However, what makes them different is their treatment of what I call the motif of nostalgia and hopelessness.

The motif of nostalgia and a sense of hopelessness can be found in many contemporary Swedish crime novels, including those by Roslund and Hellström. Interestingly, as I want to discuss further in this chapter, these concepts are completely missing in Larsson's trilogy, despite the pervasive existence of a characteristic 'Swedish disappointment' (Lundin 1981: 10) elsewhere in Swedish crime fiction, a disappointment which can be seen as the root of the motifs of nostalgia and hopelessness. A scene from Åke Edwardson's *Frozen Tracks* (2007), where the plot circles around the abductions and sexual abuse of young children, serves as an example of the hopelessness–nostalgia motif. In the novel, while standing in the middle of a square in Gothenburg called Doktor Fries Torg, one of the detectives, Halders, reflects that:

> Time had stood still here, in this square, which had been built during the period when the Social Democrats always formed the government, when Sweden's welfare state was strong, when everybody was cared for from the cradle to the grave and looked into the future with confidence, anticipating the fulfilment of their dreams. In this square I'm a little boy again, Halders thought. Everything here is genuine, this is what it looked like then. (91)

Here, the detective reverts emotionally into his safe childhood, and only then is the future bright. The idea behind the People's Home – that every person deserves a good, decent life, and that everybody should be cared for – is reflected in this quotation, which suggests that nothing will ever be as good and pure again. The main advocate of nostalgia is Henning Mankell's character Kurt Wallander, also called 'the melancholic policeman' (Tapper 2011b: 418). Throughout the series (1991–2009) Inspector Wallander observes contemporary Sweden, and the novels can be seen as a contemplation of the transformation of the welfare state. Wallander himself embodies a longing for a country that used to be. It is only in the final novel, which carries the appropriate title

The Troubled Man (2011), when Wallander is diagnosed with Alzheimer's disease, that he can no longer feel nostalgia.

Wallander's poor health and his physical body have always troubled him, but an emphasis on the body of the investigator is not limited to Henning Mankell's novels. There is a strong relationship between the body of the state and the body of the protagonist in many contemporary Swedish crime novels, and in this chapter I regard this as an integral part of the critique of the welfare state found in these books. In *The Vault* and the Millennium trilogy the bodies of the investigators are contrasted with the commodified bodies of the victims of rape and the trafficking industry. The globalized economy and the transformation of the welfare state are therefore seen to influence the bodies of those who solve the crimes, and those who are the victims of crimes.

In this chapter I want to examine how both *The Vault* and the Millennium trilogy forge links between the physical body and the social body as a means of criticizing the commodification of the body in the contemporary welfare state. Trafficking is a subject used by both Roslund and Hellström and Larsson to highlight the transformation of the welfare state; to discuss the fact that capital comes before people, and that a globalized economy can lead to the commodification of the body. Despite the explicit focus on trafficking found in both *The Vault* and the Millennium trilogy, they differ from one another when it comes to the concepts of nostalgia and hopelessness. *The Vault* has more in common with Henning Mankell's novels, where the protagonist longs for an undefined past where everything was better, whereas Larsson departs from the Swedish tradition with the exclusion of nostalgia; there is no inscribed feeling of hopelessness in the Millennium trilogy. Moreover, the powerfully made connection between society and Lisbeth Salander's body in the Millennium trilogy, as well as the focus on sex trafficking, reveals an outspoken feminist agenda, which is less present in *The Vault*.

Body, society and commodification

In the Swedish society of the 1960s and 1970s that Sjöwall and Wahlöö depict, there is a symbiotic connection between the health of the nation and that of the investigator. Michael Tapper suggests that the authors 'use the main characters' bodies as metaphors for the sick and decaying society: Melander is constantly on the toilet, Rönn always has a cold and Kollberg is fat and tired. Like Jensen, Beck is constantly plagued by stomach aches and nausea' (2011a: 23). This subgenre of Swedish crime fiction has appropriately been termed the 'Ulcer School' (Lundin 1981: 10), which basically suggests that the police investigators are physically and psychologically affected by society. In other words, a diseased People's Home produces a diseased people and vice versa. In more recent Swedish crime fiction, Sjöwall and Wahlöö's implied link between the social body and the physical body is advanced even further, a move which is perhaps inevitable given the impact of globalization and the increasing strain placed upon the concept of the People's Home: political decisions favour the free and global market, and the welfare system is not given the same financial support as before.

Henning Mankell's Kurt Wallander is one prominent member of the 'Ulcer School'. He is not an alcoholic, but he is often described as drinking too much, too often. Furthermore, he suffers from diabetes, and Barry Forshaw describes the character as 'one of the signal creations of contemporary crime fiction: out of condition, diabetes-suffering and with all the headaches of modern society leaving scars on his soul [...]'(2012:21). Instead of taking care of himself, Wallander continues to consume too much alcohol and too much fast food. He could be seen as a typical workaholic, but his never-ending internal monologue concerning the state (and health) of society taken together with his physique invites the interpretation that his body can be seen as a metaphor for the society in which he lives and works.

The female equivalent to Wallander is found in Swedish crime writer Mons Kallentoft's protagonist. Female police inspector Malin Fors' alcoholism and general emotional and physical self-abuse show her destructive reaction to society. This is seen in her almost Ahabic, monolithic obsession with finding the man behind the very brutal rape of social worker Maria Murvall. The rape has left many scars on the victim, but above all it has left her mute and institutionalized. The pondering of the viciousness of the rape and the problems of solving it add to Malin Fors' alcoholism, which increases with every novel (this is a crime that is not solved until the fifth novel in the series). There are hints of alcohol abuse given in the first novel, *Midwinter Sacrifice* (2011): Fors debates with herself whether she should reach for Tequila bottles, and becomes very defensive when her daughter reminds her of the time she had to help her to bed because she was too drunk to manage it on her own. She exclaims: 'That only happened once, Tove. You only had to do that once. ONCE' (2011: 44).

If it is not drug or alcohol problems, then it is general health problems and poor physical fitness that plague the characters of Swedish crime fiction. In *The Vault*, the protagonist Ewert Grens is very overweight and considers his wife to be in better shape than he is, something Michael Tapper has also noted (2011b: 655):

> It struck [Ewert] how bafflingly unchanged she really was, [how the twenty-five wheelchair-bound years] in the land of the unaware, had left so few traces. He had gained twenty kilos, lost a lot of hair, knew how furrowed his face had become. She was unmarked, as if you were allowed a more carefree spirit that kept you young to make up for not being able to participate in real life. (2006: 23)

At first the comparison between Ewert and his wife might seem like an exaggerated comparison to make, but it stresses the link between body and society since in reality his wife is worse off than he is, both physically and mentally. However, Ewert's daily confrontations with societal problems through his line of work add to the deterioration of his physique.

Stieg Larsson's novel can also be situated in the twenty-first century 'Ulcer School' of Swedish crime fiction, but although he still places emphasis on the link between the physical and social body, his novels develop a different, overtly feminist, version of the body politic. To a higher degree than any other of the protagonists and their fictional contexts, the representation of Lisbeth Salander's body in Stieg Larsson's Millennium trilogy illustrates the way that Swedish crime fiction depicts a metonymic relationship between the body of its central protagonists and the body of the state. In Lisbeth's body and the use of her body, we also find a strong response to the state. Although very petite, her body becomes a tool which she can use to her advantage. Lisbeth Salander is not part of the law enforcement agency – quite the contrary – but she nevertheless plays a substantial part in the criminal investigations of the trilogy. On the one hand, when she is a young girl she is institutionalized and tied to a bed by Dr Teleborian, who has complete control over her movements. On the other hand, after her release from the institution, she eventually recreates her physical body. Still figuratively tied down, on account of having a guardian and no right to her own money, she nonetheless begins to claim control over her body. Her appearance is described on many occasions in all three novels, both by the external narrator and by other characters. Lisbeth Salander's body cannot go unnoticed and it is only when she has a breast augmentation, covers the large tattoo on her neck, and wears a wig that she blends into the population. Her transformation into a more conventionally sexually attractive woman who buys into the norms of physical womanhood is a comment on society in two ways. Above all, in the context of the novel, it means that she can continue transgressing rules and laws in other ways. It should be noted that in no way does she change her goals of revenge and justice, nor does she compromise her personal morals. Furthermore, as 'Salander was the woman who hated men who hate women', (2009b: 596) she uses her own body as a sign of protest. She is well aware that she is looked upon as freakish, but she is also realistic about it, as the world is governed by men, and she 'didn't know a single girl who had not been forced to perform some sort of sexual act against her will' (2009a: 213). She also believes that 'this was the natural order of things. As a girl she was legal prey, especially if she was dressed in a worn leather jacket and had pierced eyebrows, tattoos, and zero social status' (213). She is a victim of violence, of sexual and governmental abuse, at the same time as she makes the closing of the cases in all three novels possible. Her tattoos symbolize every occasion on which she has been victimized, and when she enters the courtroom in the third and final novel she has exaggerated her appearance even further, removing all traces of the traditionally sexually attractive woman. Blomkvist thinks she looks like a 'vampire in some pop-art movie from the 60s' (2010: 612). As she knows she is 'legal prey' on account of her looks and status, her revenge on the people and institutions that have harmed her in the courtroom becomes emphasized when she herself exaggerates her low status through her clothes, hair, and make-up. Revenge and justice cleanse Salander's body, and all the malicious rumours regarding her morals, sexual preferences, and sexual history which have followed her character throughout the trilogy are dissolved.

In comparison to the victims of sex trafficking in the novel, who are simply bought and sold like goods, Salander's body is only commodified in the sense that these rumours of her sexuality are used to sell newspapers. However, she is considered to be 'a whore at the bottom of the social scale' (2009b: 35). This is depicted as rapist Advokat Bjurman's way of rationalizing the crime: Lisbeth's status makes this a risk-free act from his point of view. The sexual history of rape victims is rarely discussed in contemporary Swedish crime fiction, with the striking exception of Lisbeth Salander. This can be contrasted with Sjöwall and Wahlöö's novel *Roseanna* from 1965, a time when the women's sexual liberation movement was growing (Brodén 2008: 197). The majority of the interrogations with former lovers or friends in the novel concern the sexual history, behaviour, and preferences of the raped and murdered woman. The police require details of sexual intercourse from the victim's former lover, and during the interview this witness says that he first thought that she was 'an ordinary, cheap tramp' and perhaps a 'nymphomaniac' (Sjöwall and Wahlöö 2006: 82).

If in the 1960s it was a matter of whether or not a woman was sexually active, it is emphasized in the novels of the Millennium trilogy and *The Vault* that today it is about whether or not a woman is Swedish, and which class she belongs to. Lisbeth Salander is rapable because she is 'at the bottom of the social scale', and the victims of sex trafficking in both the Larsson novels and *The Vault* come from Russia and the Baltic states. Trafficking is also described as a business that does not threaten masculine power; rather, it enhances it, physically and economically. According to these authors, the women's nationality and class affiliation can also be the reason why the industry is growing. Stieg Larsson writes: 'Women disappear all the time. Nobody misses them. Immigrants. Whores from Russia' (2009a: 417), and in *The Vault* they are referred to as, for example, 'stupid whore[s] from Eastern Europe', or simply 'Baltic puss[ies]'(2008: 364). The Western world is basically depicted as using its economic superiority because it can, and, in the novels, the women's bodies are transformed into commodities.

In *The Vault* both the commodification of the women and the economic superiority of the West are represented by one of the customers, the 'man in the dark suit with the gold tiepin, who usually spat on the floor in front of her feet' (2008: 25). *The Vault* is the second novel by Roslund and Hellström, and it bears a strong resemblance to Lukas Moodyson's much discussed, globally successful 2002 Swedish film *Lilja 4-ever*, which follows a victim of trafficking, 16-year-old Lilja, a girl from Eastern Europe who is tricked into coming to Sweden, where she later ends her life by jumping off a bridge. The narrative focus in *The Vault* is split; it focuses, on the one hand, on the police investigation of the brutal beating of a young Lithuanian woman called Lydia Grajauskas and, on the other hand, it follows Lydia, providing insights into her thoughts and feelings and detailing how she ended up in Stockholm as a victim of trafficking. When she is brought to hospital she manages to escape and ends up in the hospital basement, holding many people hostage. She demands to see Bengt Nordwall, the police officer who was responsible for bringing her to Sweden. She kills him and then kills herself, as Lilja does in *Lilja 4-ever*, and Evert Grens and the other police inspectors soon realize that powerful people can be traced to the business of trafficking. However, they all choose to cover up this fact because they cannot deal with their own guilt and shame. The novel ends with new impoverished foreign girls arriving in Sweden, implying the hopelessness of the situation and suggesting that trafficking is an unstoppable crime.

Trafficking, in particular, in these novels is what gravely distorts globalization but also what links it with commodification: the free and global market includes sexual exploitation and the buying and selling of human bodies. Marx's term 'commodification' is useful in this context. Commodification, in short, is when something which was previously not considered sellable is now ascribed exchange value, and this can include, for example, both gender and bodies. In *The Vault*, one woman is given the order 'Clean up your cunt! New customer' (2008: 26), and this abrupt order sums up both the situation and status of these women. One police officer calls the trafficking business the 'slave trade' (340) and when he wonders 'how it was possible for a woman's body to be sold so that someone else could top up his bank account' (340), he simultaneously knows the answer to that question because he himself is part of a cover-up in order to protect another police officer. Chris Shilling writes on the subject of Marx and the body that '[Marx] viewed the body as a source of economic relations and developed a deep concern with the destructive bodily effects of capitalism' (2003: 208). Marx was concerned with the workers: the working class, and the body, as the source of economic value. However, if we view the women locked up in the apartment in *The Vault* as slaves, or at least as people who cannot themselves profit from the 'work' they perform, they are indeed symbolic of the 'destructive bodily effects of capitalism'.

Stieg Larsson adds a feminist perspective to trafficking and the commodification of bodies. In the second novel in his trilogy, *The Girl Who Played with Fire*, a couple who are investigating the trafficking industry in Sweden are found murdered. Earlier, one of them has spoken on the topic, saying that:

> [...] there is a sort of gender perspective to my thesis. It's not often that a researcher can establish roles along gender lines so clearly. Girls – the victims; boys – the organisers. Apart from a handful of women working on their own who profit from the sex trade, there is no other form of criminality in which the sex roles themselves are a precondition for the crime. Nor is there any other form of criminality in which social acceptance is so great, or which society does so little to prevent. (2009b: 98–99)

With a few exceptions – there is one woman involved in running the trafficking in *The Vault* – it is the men who profit from the trade in bodies, and the men who buy the goods. Larsson's critique of the 'social acceptance' of this crime is more overt than that of Roslund and Hellström in *The Vault*. In *The Girl Who Played with Fire*, a list of clients – or consumers – shows that men in government and other high places buy women's bodies. To acknowledge the existence of these women would therefore jeopardize their own good names and, in the end, shake the very foundation of the state. Nestingen and Arvas assert that, 'While many features of the welfare state continue to enjoy broad support, the consumer has displaced the citizen as the privileged figuration of political action' (2011: 8). This is something which is echoed in the equally cynical and realistic statement found in *The Girl With the Dragon Tattoo*: 'It's all about the money and it makes no difference if the Social Democrats or the moderates appoint the ministers' (2009a: 22). In Sweden, the Social Democrats, despite being the party behind the idea and development of the welfare state, has 'increasingly come to be seen as favouring the interests and markets' (Nestingen 2008: 7), and that is why Larsson can make the comment that it is 'all about the money': the neo-liberal parties and the Social Democrats have a similar take on the welfare state; the Social Democrats have 'forsaken their base', as Nestingen puts it (7).

In *The Vault*, the police are called to an apartment where they find an abused woman, beaten almost to death – it is hard to tell where the red bedspread ends and her bloody body begins (2008: 78). They soon discover that this woman is a Lithuanian prostitute. In the apartment building the police can read the occupants' names 'Palm, Nygren, Johansson, Löfgren. Couldn't be more Swedish. Only to be expected, given the kind of place it was' (75). The business of prostitution in a building such as this signals class and nationality. The victims of trafficking have become sexual slaves – the most severe form of commodification of the human body – because of their female gender but also because of their national origins and class affiliation. They come from poor countries and belong to the lower classes in those countries. The women – girls, in some cases – are victimized because of their gender, but their ethnicity doubles the victimization and places them below Lisbeth Salander on the social scale; they are not even human anymore. This is a transformation that the capitalist can easily produce, according to Marx. The capitalist 'is able to make something out of nothing. In doing so, of course, the capitalist also turns something into nothing [...]' (Marx cited in Tanner 1994: 96).

In *The Vault*, such nothingness is accentuated when Roslund and Hellström write that: 'These girls did not really exist, they had no identity, no work permit, no life of their own' (2008: 82). This is emphasized further by the women's own accounts of their experiences: one of the women states that she doesn't have a body, only a head, in order to endure the sexual meetings with the customers (twelve each day). They are efficiently turned from 'something into nothing', from somebody into nobody, as is graphically demonstrated when one woman has to eat spit from the floor before being forced into sexual intercourse (19–20).

The hopelessness–nostalgia motif

In their novels *Roseanna* (1965) and *The Man on the Balcony* (1967), Maj Sjöwall and Per Wahlöö address the topics of sexual violence against women and child molestation respectively. The novels are concerned with local, not global, issues, which is typical of the decade, with a welfare state that even in the 1960s was, according to the authors, developing in the wrong direction, *away* from a primary concern with both individual and larger social groups (and the welfare of both), and accordingly failing the very people it was created to help. The novels provide bleak images of a society in which poverty, drug abuse, and violence form an ironic contrast to the surrounding natural setting. For instance, we have the picturesque setting of *Roseanna*, where an unknown woman is found raped and murdered during the summer vacation period by a lake feted by Swedish and international tourists for its beauty and serenity. In *The Man on the Balcony*, also set in the summertime, where the hunt is for an unknown perpetrator who rapes and kills children, the authors write: 'All that the police really succeeded in doing was to stir up the dregs – the homeless, the alcoholics, the drug addicts, those who had lost all hope, those who could not even crawl away when the welfare state turned the stone over' (2007: 135). Sjöwall and Wahlöö here indicate that the state is responsible for the initial creation of the lower classes, the outcasts. When the anonymous 'welfare state' turns the stone over, it is much too late.

Roslund's and Hellström's novels about policeman Ewert Grens, who is bitter and constantly irritated or angry, is a recent echo of the hopelessness of 'those who had lost all hope' in the Swedish society Sjöwall and Wahlöö examine (Sjöwall and Wahlöö 2007: 135). In contemporary crime fiction, hopelessness is frequently expressed by way of the policemen or investigators looking into the crimes in which they have in some way been implicated. Ewert Grens is a nostalgic man who is reluctant to let go of the past, and according to his world view, everything is heading for the worse. This mind-set is best seen in his adoration of the female Swedish singer, Siw Malmkvist, who was at the top of her career in the 1960s, and Ewert's name is an attempt by the authors to stress his nostalgia even more: Ewert Grens is another version of Evergreens, which refers to a particular nostalgic style of Swedish music. His colleague, Fredrik Stefansson, is described as more realistic, and the Swedish singer that Grens adores is shown to disgust him. In *The Beast*, a novel about the brutal rapes and murders of young children, Fredrik Stefansson reacts strongly to Ewert's taste in music:

> Fredrik shuddered. The text was so stupid, and Siw's […] voice belonged to the past, the '50s and early '60s, to a less knowing, more naïve Sweden with high hopes for the future. Or maybe the lost innocence was just a growing myth. For him at least those years had meant his father and his beatings and his mother smoking her eternal Camels, while she looked the other way. No Siw then, to help *sing the sorrows away*, and she was no good now either; her world was all lies and escapism. It was on his tongue to ask the old Siw fan next to him what he was escaping from, and what stone he had been living under all this time. (2006: 306)

In comparison to Ewert Grens, who in the eyes of his colleague is 'less knowing' and 'more naïve', Fredrik illustrates a more nuanced view of times past. In a sense this quotation shows two sides of the same coin that is the welfare state. To have 'high hopes for the future' means to close at least one eye to the actual reality, which in this case implies child abuse and parental neglect, and to be nostalgic about the time of the naïve Sweden means that Ewert Grens is closing his eyes to the present.

Many other Swedish rape narratives also share the hopelessness–nostalgia motif. In Mons Kallentoft's *Midwinter Sacrifice* (2011) there are two victims of rape. The first one is the social worker Maria Murvall, who becomes an institutionalized, traumatized mute as a result. The other victim is a woman, Rakel, who lives outside of 'civilized' society's borders with the rest of her outlaw family. We learn that she was violently raped by a man in 1958 at a dance (315–319); Rakel never tells the police. Similarly to the foreign victims of trafficking in *The Vault*, with little or no knowledge of Swedish she can never verbalize what has happened to her, owing to her status and social situation. Instead she ends up hating and abusing the child who is the result of the rape, and when the child grows up he himself becomes a murderer.

The discussion about people like Rakel that Kallentoft incorporates in the narrative adds to the expressed hopelessness:

> You know, they were the ones who everyone knew would never turn into anything, but who rage and rebel against the system. You know, the ones who are sort of on the periphery from the start. Who are, I don't know, maybe doomed always to be outside normal society, knocking to get in. They were branded, somehow. (163)

Despite the displayed cynicism and the mentioned list of powerful people who buy prostitutes, there is, nevertheless, no sense of hopelessness or nostalgia for past times in Larsson's trilogy about Lisbeth Salander and Mikael Blomkvist, and this is what distinguishes these novels from other contemporary Swedish crime fiction. In the Millennium trilogy, the pasts that are described – mainly those of Lisbeth Salander and the Vanger family – are filled with murder, sexism, governmental conspiracies, extreme capitalism, racism, Nazism, rape, violence, general abuse of power, and abusive bureaucracy, and therefore – obviously – there was never a time when everything was 'better'. There cannot be any nostalgia for past times, since, for instance, the extreme governmental abuse of Lisbeth Salander started in her childhood. Larsson does not engage in a nostalgic discussion about whether or not things were better 'before'; instead he lets the characters be situated in the present, despite their often gruesome pasts. In addition, *The Girl With the Dragon Tattoo* is framed by statistics such as '46 % of the women in Sweden have been subjected to violence by a man' (2009a: 119), '13 % of the women in Sweden have been subjected to aggravated sexual assault outside of a sexual relationship' (255), and '92 % of women in Sweden who have been subjected to sexual assault have not reported the most recent violent incident to the police' (415). These statistics are a means for the author to situate the trilogy in a realist literary tradition, despite its often fantastic elements.

While most critics point out the fantastical elements of her character, it is important to note that in the characterization of Lisbeth Salander we find a rather down-to-earth view of life, society, and the men and women who inhabit it, despite the events that frame her life. She expresses a far from lamenting attitude when she thinks: 'Unfortunately society is not very smart or understanding; [I have] to protect [myself] from social authorities, child welfare authorities, guardianship authorities, tax authorities, police, curators, psychologists, psychiatrists, teachers, and bouncers [...]' (367). At the same time as criticism is directed towards all levels of society and state representatives, she thinks that this is merely unfortunate. This is also part of what makes her a (victimized) female character with agency. Compared to the victims of trafficking in *The Vault* and Mons Kallentoft's victims in *Midwinter Sacrifice*, and despite the fact that Lisbeth is on the bottom of the social scale, she is given a voice. Although important decisions are made in the 'men's sauna' (2009b: 602), Lisbeth can rather matter-of-factly say *'Dear Government...I'm going to have a serious talk with you if I ever find anyone to talk to'* (564).

Lisbeth Salander first refuses to speak of what has happened to her, a strategy she feels is best given her past experiences. She leaves traces of her voice, however, by tattooing Advokat Bjurman with the words: 'I AM A SADISTIC PIG, A PERVERT, AND A RAPIST' (2009a: 246). This is part of the revenge act, but rather than a statement about her own experiences she uses this message in order to save other women in the future. In the final novel in the trilogy, and using her own words, she is allowed to reconstruct her own rapes and therefore take charge of them. The story she tells gives a much more detailed version than was presented in the first novel when she was actually raped, when the narrator described the act only briefly:

> Then there were several lines of text where she identified the implements he had used during the rape, which included a short whip, an anal plug, a rough dildo, and clamps which he attached to her nipples. She frowned and studied the text. At last she raised the stylus and tapped out a few more lines of text. On one occasion when I still had my mouth taped shut, Bjurman commented on the fact that I had several tattoos and piercings, including a ring in my left nipple. He asked if I liked being pierced and then left the room. He came back with a needle which he pushed through my right nipple. (2010: 427)

This rape narrative notably lacks adjectives; Lisbeth's actual emotions and pain are not part of it, because they are not essential in her mind. Yet, for the reader the rape seems brutal and sadistic, and even though, in a sense, Lisbeth is raped again from the reader's point of view, this is what gives her agency. To be able to write up the 'autobiography' of the sexual violence gives her control of her own life because it is finally her own story, and it can finally be told to the authorities, here re-presented in the space of the court room.

Two ways of investigating trafficking

Andrew Nestingen writes that:

> Within the welfare state, the source of crime has conventionally been thought to be alcoholism, poverty, and tense family relations. Better understanding the causes of alcoholism, poverty, and domestic violence could lead to policy initiatives that would deploy resources to ameliorate these problems. (2008: 6)

Traditionally this view has been reflected in the crime fiction produced, but as the welfare state is in transformation, the themes of crime fiction are also changing. A recent theme is trafficking, and it is a topic emphasized in the work of both Larsson and Roslund and Hellström, who discuss and problematize the transformation of the welfare state. As has been shown in this chapter, however, the manner in which these authors examine sexual violence and trafficking differs. This chapter does not argue that one way of criticizing the globalization of the People's Home is more effective than the other, but, rather, has attempted to demonstrate how the difference in approaches crucially derives from the deployment of the motifs of nostalgia and hopelessness. The authors show, through carefully plotted narratives, that capital comes before people, and that a globalized economy can lead to the commodification of the body. In *The Vault*, as well as in the Millennium trilogy, gender, class, and ethnicity are depicted as factors which determine who can be bought and who can be raped. Nestingen and Arvas write that Scandinavian novels 'often articulate social criticism, critiquing national institutions and gender politics in particular. And they are frequently gloomy, pensive and pessimistic in tone' (2011: 2). *The Vault* openly suggests that there is no end to trafficking, since the free market seems to be in charge, which corresponds well with Nestingen and Arvas' description of Scandinavian novels. To the question of how many women are smuggled into Sweden, the answer is: 'As many as the market demands' (Nestingen 2008: 82). *The Vault* in particular indicates hopelessness in this situation, and the apparent impossibility of addressing it owing to this, which is enhanced by the protagonist Ewert Grens's inability to live in the present and the subsequent nostalgia expressed for the past. The characters are tired and can see no solution to the problem. A final ironic remark is made towards the end of the novel when new girls arrive at Stockholm Arlanda Airport, are met by one of the individuals who will lock them up in a new apartment, and are greeted with the words: 'Welcome to Sweden! I hope you'll enjoy your stay' (2008: 394). The apartment where Lydia was held captive has been exchanged for a new one, as have the girls. The welfare state does not care for these victims; in fact, it does not even acknowledge their existence. Roslund and Hellström present an important contribution to the debate on trafficking by giving one of the victims a name, Lydia, and by offering her side of the story to the reader. Even though the other characters do not really get to hear or to understand the full story, the authors give full knowledge of her fate to the reader, and this is an attempt to de-commodify her; she is transformed from an object into a subject. Larsson more unambiguously links the problem of trafficking to both patriarchy and globalization, and creates a feminist heroine, who despite being referred to as an ideal victim due to her appearance, background, and social status, still manages to beat the system. Via the character of Salander, Larsson openly links government and bureaucracy to capitalist powers and patriarchy and provides a feminist critique of power and institutions. Despite their underdog positions in society, the central protagonists in the Millennium trilogy *can* make a change. While *The Vault* provides its readers with a darker and much less hopeful vision than the Millennium trilogy, both Roslund and Hellström and Stieg Larsson offer a powerful critique of the commodification of the body and the problematics of the Swedish welfare state, and it is the strength of this critique that makes their respective works stand out as powerful exposés of sex trafficking in a globalized economy.

Works cited

Brodén, D. (2008) *Folkhemmets skuggbilder* [Shadow Images of the People's Home]. Stockholm: Ekholm & Tegebjer.
Burstein D., A. de Keijzser, and J. Holmberg (eds) (2011) *The Tattooed Girl: The Enigma of Stieg Larsson and the Secrets Behind the Most Compelling Thrillers of Our Time*. New York: St. Martin's Griffin.
Edwardson, Å. (2007) *Frozen Tracks*. Transl. L. Thompson. London: Vintage Books.
Forshaw, B. (2012) *Death in a Cold Climate: A Guide to Scandinavian Crime Fiction*. Basingstoke: Palgrave Macmillan.
Kallentoft, M. (2011) *Midwinter Sacrifice*. Transl. N. Smith. London: Hodder and Stoughton.
Larsson, S. (2009a). *The Girl with the Dragon Tattoo*. Transl. R. Keeland. London: Quercus.
Larsson, S. (2009b). *The Girl Who Played with Fire*. Transl. R. Keeland. London: Quercus.
Larsson, S. (2010) *The Girl Who Kicked the Hornets' Nest*. Transl. R. Keeland. London: Quercus.

Lundin, B. (1981) *The Swedish Crime Story*. Transl. A-L. Ringarp. Sundbyberg: Tidskriften Jury.
Nestingen, A. (2008) *Crime and Fantasy in Scandinavia*. Seattle and London: University of Washington Press.
Nestingen, A. and P. Arvas (ed.) (2011) *Scandinavian Crime Fiction*. Cardiff: University of Wales Press.
Roslund, A. and B. Hellström . (2006) *The Beast*. Transl. A. Paterson. London: Abacus.
Roslund, A. and B. Hellström (2008) *The Vault*. Transl. Unknown. London: Abacus.
Shilling, C. (2003 [1993]) *The Body and Social Theory*. London: Sage Publications.
Sjöwall, M. and P. Wahlöö . (2006 [1965]) *Roseanna*. Transl. L. Roth. London: Harper Perennial.
Sjöwall, M. and P. Wahlöö (2007 [1967]) *The Man on the Balcony*. Transl. A. Blair. London: Harper Perennial.
Tanner, L. E. (1994) *Intimate Violence: Reading Rape and Torture in Twentieth-century Fiction*. Bloomington: Indiana University Press.
Tapper, M. (2011a) 'Dirty Harry in the Swedish Welfare State' in A. Nestingen and P. Arvas (eds) *Scandinavian Crime Fiction*. Cardiff: University of Wales Press. 21–33.
Tapper, M. (2011b) *Snuten i skymningslandet. Svenska polisberättelser i roman och film 1965–2010* ['Cop in Twilight Country. Swedish Police Narratives in Novels and on Film']. Lund: Nordic Academic Press.

6
Over Her Dismembered Body: The Crime Fiction of Mo Hayder and Jo Nesbø

Berit Åström

Images of dismembered women can affect crime fiction readers in a number of ways: they may shock, enrage, disgust, or titillate them. In her novel *Birdman*, British author Mo Hayder presents a woman whose 'scalp had been peeled from the skull…folded over so the hair and face hung like a wet rubber mask, inside out, covering the mouth and neck, pooling on the clavicle' (2000: 24). In *The Snowman*, Norwegian author Jo Nesbø describes the body of a woman, so mutilated that it 'was only thanks to a naked breast that they had been able to determine gender' (2010: 54). Claims have been made that crime fiction is ramping up the violence towards female victims as a sales ploy (Hill 2009), yet I argue that in Nesbø and Hayder, the representation of violence is central to their attempt to examine critically society's contempt for women and their bodies. In this chapter I demonstrate, through close readings of Mo Hayder's *Birdman* and Jo Nesbø's *The Snowman*, how these two authors not only resist the powerful trope of the eroticized female corpse, but also use images of violence and dismemberment to criticize the way society reduces women to their sexual and reproductive functions and destroys them when they are surplus to requirements.

Both Hayder and Nesbø have been criticized for writing disconcertingly violent crime fiction. What critics have particularly focused on is a perceived sexual aspect to their writing, or as author Matt Beynon Rees refers to it, the 'perverse sexual element of much of the violence in today's crime fiction' (Rees 2011). As an example Rees gives a scene from Jo Nesbø's *The Leopard*, in which a woman's cheeks are pierced from the inside by long needles, a scene which he interprets as evoking 'gang-bang blow jobs'. Calling such writing 'crime fiction porn', he argues that it is 'reflective of a juvenile masturbatory quality in the writer' (2011). Similarly, Hayder's novels have been labelled as 'hard-boiled sexual horror stories' displaying a 'pornographic imagination' (Gerrard 2000). However, the critical dismissal of the violence in Hayder and Nesbø's work as 'perverse' or 'pornographic' ignores the way in which these two authors use violence to raise questions about society's objectification of women.

Disturbing as their imagery may be, what makes Hayder and Nesbø different from many other serial killer writers is not only their deployment of violence as a means of expressing social criticism, but also their use of the serial killer narrative, where they show the serial killer, not as a freak aberration easily contained and disposed of, but as a spokesperson acting out the desires and needs of society. It is often stated that the function of the serial killer is to concretize vague societal fears into something manageable, 'to personify free-floating fears... into a specific, potentially confinable, yet still ultimately evil, threat' (Simpson 2000: 2). In this way, the serial killer provides 'contemporary society with a refreshingly unambiguous villain against which nearly everyone can agree to unite' (7). The genesis of the serial killer is located, not in any systemic failure of society, but in a 'decontextualized family romance separable from the social order'; that is, the serial killer's evil stems from a discrete, individual situation, often an overprotective and/or nagging mother, and not from wider, societal problems (Freccero 1997: 48). In this way, the threat the serial killer poses is easy to exorcize: 'kill the serial killer and your problem goes away' (48). Because the pathology of the serial killer is so neatly contained, the threat is easily dispelled. In a way, Hayder's and Nesbø's serial killers also originate within the family romance. In *Birdman*, the mother's voluptuous body, unrestrained sensuality, and borderline incestuous behaviour seemingly drive her son, one of a pair of killers working together, to necrophilia. In *The Snowman*, the mother's infidelity motivates her son to kill other adulterous mothers. However, I argue that these killers are also functioning as agents of society, writing its misogynist contempt on the women's flesh. The two killers in *Birdman* treat women as disposable, anonymous sex toys, different from blow-up dolls only in that they decompose. The killer in *The Snowman* illustrates Western society's patriarchal obsession with paternity, and the concomitant need to control women's sexuality. In other words, on the surface the women in these novels fall prey to 'men who hate women', to borrow a phrase from Stieg Larsson, and the individual actions of the serial killers are shown to be horrifically disturbing and seemingly at odds with what is acceptable in contemporary society. Yet, what Hayder and Nesbø reveal, I argue, is that the actions of these serial killers are, in fact, society's attitudes and concerns writ large, taken to their logical conclusion. They are the actions of a society that hates women.

Although Jo Nesbø and Mo Hayder both use violence to criticize societal attitudes towards women, the quotations at the beginning of the chapter also highlight a crucial difference between the strategies the authors employ to achieve their aim. Hayder appeals to sensations of disgust and abjection, describing the dead women's bodies in relentless detail, making it very difficult to perceive them as erotic. Instead, I argue, her in-depth scrutiny of the defiled bodies criticizes society's destruction of women. Nesbø, on the other hand, withholds the details, thus, in a manner of speaking, protecting the reader from seeing too much of the gruesomeness and also too much of the potentially erotic body. The women's bodies in Nesbø's text are more important as signifiers of the killer's, and ultimately society's, obsession with controlling female sexuality.

British and Scandinavian violence

There are many similarities between Hayder and Nesbø, in terms of their writing as well as their public personae. They are both presented by the media as unconventional rebels who, as teenagers, were uninterested in schoolwork. Hayder's chequered past as barmaid, security guard, and hostess in a Tokyo club is often referenced, and her police record at 14, as well as her move to London at 16, is presented as a guarantee that her novels are grounded in reality (Upson 2000). One reviewer signals her rebellious character through the epithet 'tattooed "rock chick"' (Smith 2005: 24). Nesbø's past as a stockbroker and journalist is perhaps more conventional, but journalists and critics often focus on the fact that he used to play football in the Norwegian premier league, topped the music charts with his rock band in the 1990s, and still plays in a band. His athletic abilities are also brought up, and one interviewer makes the fact that he goes rock climbing a central point of his article (Robinson 2011). Evidently, the authors must appear to be, like their detectives, hard-boiled mavericks.

Yet, as regards violence, the authors are treated differently. Although Nesbø's writing features 'severed heads, serial killers, torture, corrupt policemen, rapists, assassins, drug addicts and religious perverts' (Oliver 2011), most reviewers and critics stay off that topic, focusing instead on characterization and political criticism (Meyhoff 2011: 62–73).

Hayder's political criticism goes unnoticed, for the most part but, on the other hand, she is often asked to defend the violence in her novels, confirming an observation made by Val McDermid (2009) that it is seen as inappropriate for women to write about violence towards women. On several occasions Hayder has stated that her use of detailed violence is a conscious decision, stemming from her dissatisfaction with other crime writers who 'used violent acts to springboard a story and yet never dealt in detail with the real horror of that violence' (Foster 2008: 137). Thus, her writing does not originate from a 'pornographic imagination', but from a desire to make the reader aware that the violence is not simply a plot device easily dismissed and forgotten.

A possible, additional reason why Hayder receives criticism for her descriptions of violence when Nesbø does not is the way her narratives relate to the violence. In Nesbø's texts, the protagonists and the narrative take a moral stance, condemning the violence. Hayder has chosen not to do so (Foster 2008: 137), leaving it to the reader 'to interject moral values' into the text (Young 1992: 100). As Elizabeth Young has noted, this strategy forces the reader to 'scrutinize his own values and beliefs, rather than those being provided for him within a Good-Evil fictive universe' (100). Just as critics took Bret Easton Ellis' refusal to condemn Patrick Bates' behaviour in *American Psycho* as proof of Ellis' misogyny (100), some critics interpret Hayder's lack of moralizing as an endorsement of violence. Yet one might argue that leaving the reader to make up her own mind about moral judgements, forcing her to engage with the text in a more hands-on manner, increases the impact of the writing. It is simply more difficult to forget and to move on.

In terms of genre, Nesbø and Hayder can both be categorized as writing hard-boiled crime fiction. Because of his nationality, Nesbø is often grouped together with other Scandinavian authors and he is marketed in the UK and the US as 'the new Stieg Larsson', despite the fact that he published his first novel eight years before Larsson. Nesbø, however, regards himself as writing more in the tradition of 'the American hard-boiled crime novel' (Foster 2010: 94). This allegiance is also picked up by some reviewers. One reviewer of *The Snowman* says about his writing: 'This isn't Norwegian. It's full-blooded American' (Curtis 2011: 82). Another reviewer links Nesbø with British crime writing when he writes that 'Harry Hole is so Rebus it hurts' (East 2009) Like so many other Scandinavian writers, Nesbø exemplifies the close connections between Anglophone and Scandinavian crime writing.

As novels within the hard-boiled genre, *The Snowman* and *Birdman*, despite superficial dissimilarities, draw on similar stereotypes, particularly in terms of their detectives. Hayder's Detective Inspector Jack Caffery is plagued by his brother's disappearance during their childhood and his mother's subsequent withdrawal from him, and at the beginning of *Birdman* he finds himself unable to break up with a girlfriend he has long since stopped caring for. Nesbø's Harry Hole lost his mother to cancer in his twenties, has a difficult relationship with his father, and has problems with girlfriends. Hole is an alcoholic struggling to stay sober, whereas alcohol is such a constant presence in Caffery's life, both at work and at home, that it is beginning to be disruptive. Furthermore, despite their personal problems, and in Hole's case a rather well-worn appearance, both men are presented as mavericks, attractive to women, and much better detectives than any of their colleagues.

Hayder's *Birdman* opens with the discovery of the mutilated corpse of a woman. Her breasts have been mutilated, her forehead displays curious marks, and a live bird has been sewn into her chest cavity. Other corpses soon follow, and before long five women have been found. During the course of the novel it is revealed that the women – prostitutes, exotic dancers, and drug addicts – are preyed upon by two men: Toby Harteveld, who kills them, in a fairly humane way, to satisfy his necrophiliac desires and Malcolm Bliss, who, as a sadist, is not really that much into necrophilia, but who will make do with what he can get. Bliss selects the victims and brings them to Harteveld. When he has finished with them, Bliss takes over the women's bodies. He mutilates them in order to make them look like a woman he is obsessed with and treats them as if they were living victims, subjecting them to verbal and sexual abuse. Halfway through the novel Harteveld commits suicide from remorse, and Bliss, who only becomes a killer towards the end of the novel, turns to preying on living women, on whom he performs breast reductions. The novel ends with Bliss raping and almost killing Caffery's new girlfriend, before being killed by Caffery. Harteveld and Bliss treat the women they prey on with utter contempt – they are chosen at random, used for sex, and then discarded, in a large-scale version of the way contemporary society treats women as disposable.

In *Birdman*, Hayder deals mainly with women at the bottom of the social scale. Nesbø, in *The Snowman*, chooses women in the most sacred position in Western society, that of the mother. The serial killer, Mathias Lund-Helgesen, traumatized by the realization that not only did his mother have an extramarital affair, but that he is the son of her lover, not the man he thought was his father, sets out to kill adulterous mothers who have deceived their husbands about the paternity of their children, leaving a snowman for every kill. Throughout the novel there are references, not only to the killer's obsession with paternity, but also to society's paternity obsession in general. The narrative suggests that most men worry about the genetic identity of their children, and hints that the actions of Lund-Helgesen are different in terms of degree rather than in kind.

The eroticized corpse

The corpse has always assumed a central place in crime writing, but despite – or perhaps because of – this centrality, it produces a number of anxieties. Gill Plain notes the contradictory nature of the dead body that forms 'the end point of a life that simultaneously signifies the beginning of a narrative' (2001: 12). The corpse as the simultaneous beginning and end presents a problem for the narrative. It is a *memento mori*, a reminder to the reader that she or he will also die – an image that is terrifying. Yet, without a dead body there would be no story to tell. As Plain states, 'The necessity of a body, while underpinning the whole textual project, is nonetheless unwelcome, bringing with it, as it does, uncomfortable resonances of wider social signification' (38). The reader's attitude towards the corpse is thus one of ambivalence. This ambivalence allows the corpse to fulfil a number of functions within the crime narrative. As a symbol of abjection, the dead body can signify a realization of the frailty of identity and bodily integrity, 'a fragile physical reification of the idea that human subjectivity is no more than a fragmentable construct' (Knight 2010: 209). But the corpse can also be interpreted as a symbol of social decay, as in James Ellroy's *The Black Dahlia*, where the 'naked, disfigured, eviscerated and cut in half' body of Elizabeth Short comes to symbolize urban disintegration (210). The dead body also fulfils other, more utilitarian, functions. In his strong criticism of the classic whodunit, 'The Simple Art of Murder', Raymond Chandler argues that in such novels corpses are simply produced for cerebral purposes, as a mental exercise for 'detectives of exquisite and impossible gentility' (Malmgren 1997: 116). It has also been suggested that the torture and death of female victims is a selling point, a clever strategy employed by female writers to prove that they are as tough as male authors, and thus boost their sales (Hill 2009).

However, whether the dead body is a symbol of the disintegration of society, a psychoanalytical signifier of the instability of the subject, or an excuse for the detective to show off his or her intellectual powers, it is, when female, clearly also linked to sex and the gazes of the detective and the reader. Admittedly, Katherine Gregory Klein has argued persuasively that from a structural point of view, the victimized body is always gendered female, regardless of biology (1995: 173), and Joy Palmer states that 'the process of detection' is at the same time 'a process of "feminization"', during which the body is turned into 'an object of the scientific gaze' (2001: 56). In other words, regardless of biological sex, because the victim is placed in a defenceless position, looked at, and analysed, he or she is read as female. Yet, I would argue that the gender of the victim is not as free-floating, as separate from its biological sex, as Klein and Palmer seem to suggest. After all, Klein also maintains that 'the Woman is the body in the library on whom the criminal writes his narrative of murder', which points at a societal and systemic designation of women as natural victims (1995: 173). Certainly, when the dead body is treated as an erotic object it is generally a female body. Thus, the body under scrutiny, be it in the library, in a skip in a back street, or in the autopsy suite, may be gendered female regardless of sex, but it is the biological female who is eroticized. By presenting their victims as dehumanized body parts, Nesbø and Hayder avoid this eroticization.

The erotic appeal of the female corpse has long been a part of Western literature, as Daniel A. Cohen discusses in his study of 'the beautiful female murder victim', a theme he traces back to English 'early modern court romances, murder ballads, sentimental novels and trial reports' (1997: 277). One particularly telling example which he quotes is an 1836 US newspaper article by James Gordon Bennett, where he narrates a visit to the morgue to see the body of a murdered prostitute. In his text, Bennett lovingly describes the attractiveness of her figure, face, limbs and bust, and sums her up as a 'beautiful female corpse' (277). As Cohen notes, the narratives of the 'beautiful female murder victim' often included 'graphic (and occasionally erotic or pornographic) descriptions of the victim's corpse' (278).

The eroticization evident in the texts Cohen has analysed continues in contemporary crime writing as well, in particular in serial killer narratives, where women often become 'eroticised victims of violence' (Walton and Jones 1999: 233), but also in other types of crime writing, where readers routinely encounter dead women in a state of undress arranged for their and the detective's gaze. Added to this is the clinical gaze of medical examiners and forensic pathologists. With the advent of the scientist as sleuth, the opportunity arrived for a closer engagement with the dead body. No longer does the encounter with the dead body end with its discovery. Now the reader also gains access to the autopsy suite and takes part when the body is opened and analysed – a situation that could invite further violation and eroticization, since the body is not only subjected to the gaze of the reader and the detective, but also the scientific gaze. Many of the medical examiners and forensic pathologists of contemporary crime fiction are women, however, and Joy Palmer has discussed whether the 'gaze of the female doctor may signal a potential subversion or shift' in the 'gendered viewing paradigms' established by the 'empiricist, investigative gaze' (2001: 55). Certainly the protagonists of authors such as Kathy Reichs and Patricia Cornwell express the notion that the forensic pathologist (or, in the case of Reichs, forensic anthropologist) is the defender of and spokesperson for the victim, a sympathetic ear for the 'speaking body', giving it subjectivity (Dauncey 2010: 172). According to Sarah Dauncey, Cornwell presents the morgue, not 'as a clinical environment for the objective study of bodies' but 'as a site of sympathetic understanding and communion' (172). However, other critics have taken a less benevolent view of this subgenre of crime fiction, and of Cornwell's novels in particular. Palmer, analysing *From Potter's Field*, claims that 'the clinical gaze effectively eroticises this body as feminine, natural terrain, territory to be discovered and marked' (2001: 65). That Cornwell's attempts at subverting the clinical, eroticizing gaze are at times frustrated serves to demonstrate the resilience of the trope of the 'beautiful female murder victim'. It is in this context that the novels of Mo Hayder and Jo Nesbø become so important, as attempts at resisting this very powerful trope.

Resisting the erotic and criticizing the societal

Hayder's novel *Birdman* opens with the discovery of the bodies of five women that have been buried on a construction site. When DI Jack Caffery comes to the scene, the first woman, later identified as Shellene Craw, is presented as an unrecognizable object: '*That? That's a body?* He'd thought it was a piece of expanding foam, the type fired from an aerosol, so distended and yellow and shiny it was' (2008: 14). This is not a 'beautiful female murder victim' arranged for the reader to admire, but a woman who has been reduced to an object. She is referred to as 'it' and 'that', drawing the reader's attention to how the killer's actions have dehumanized her, reduced her from a person to a thing. Caffery's reaction is a recognition of her dehumanized status, but it is also a reminder of how society objectifies women – their only value lies in an attractive appearance. This woman is no longer pretty, and he thus has difficulty recognizing her as human even though he has just been told that he is looking at a woman.

The dehumanization of the women continues at a later scene in the autopsy suite. Four more bodies have been found, and these five women are taken apart, analysed, and investigated. They are later identified by name, but at this stage the narrator refers to them as 'bodies', 'corpses', and 'carcasses', and the language used to describe them is reminiscent of butchered animals:

> five bodies, unseamed from pubis to shoulders, skin peeled away like hides, revealing raw ribs marbled with fat and muscle. Juices leaked into the pans beneath them... The corpse's scalp had been peeled from the skull down to the squamous cleft of the nose, and folded over so the hair and face hung like a wet rubber mask, inside out, covering the mouth and neck, pooling on the clavicle. (24)

The references to the ribs, 'marbled with fat and muscle', and 'juices' are reminiscent of food writing. Caffery also remarks to himself 'how like a side of hung meat the skinned human body is' (26). This is a reminder of how society consumes women, spitting out the leftovers. When alive the women worked as prostitutes and strippers, their bodies commodities to be consumed by men. This consumption is completed by the murderers, who use the women as so much meat, and when the meat goes off, literally, they are thrown out as rubbish.

Peeling down the woman's face, reducing it to a mask that can be taken off, also stresses how these women have lost their individuality and been transformed into generic victims by the killers. They are faceless and interchangeable, chosen more or less at random, the only requirement being that they are female so that the heterosexual killers can act out their sexual desires upon them. One of the killers literally puts a mask on them, painting on garish make-up and stitching a blonde wig to their heads, in order to transform them into his ideal woman. It can be argued that Hayder references, as a gruesome parody, advertisements for make-up and hair-colouring products. In such adverts, individuality is presented as inferior – a woman is not good enough as she is, she is unfinished. Similarly the killer views his victims as unfinished, in need of extra work. Just as society requires that women must be transformed in order to be acceptable, so does the killer.

There is a clear link between the actions of the killers and the actions of the authorities, the police officers, and the medical practitioners. The women are subjected to the full blow of the scientific, male gaze. Although there is at least one woman present (24), the principal actors are men – Caffery, Detective Superintendent Steve Maddox, and the forensic pathologist, Harsha Krishnamurthi – and they treat the bodies with professional detachment. When Caffery views the fourth body – later identified as Kayleigh Hatch but at this stage presented as 'a large white carcass…cracked down the centre and unfurled', and with her throat opened up, 'revealing a glimpse of a milky chord' (29) – his reaction is to note approvingly that she has a tattoo on her ankle, which will make her easier to identify. Here, it is not a question of speaking for the dead. Instead the dead are taken apart in order to find traces of the killer. The atrocity of what has been done, and is being done, to these women is not commented on by the men present or by the narrative. Instead, by exposing these women like butchered animals, Hayder leaves it to the reader to feel the humiliation of what the killer has done to them, and what further indignities this leads to. By showing the full horror of the women's mutilated bodies, Hayder removes any vestiges of the 'beautiful female victim' and instead invites the reader to consider how society victimizes women.

Most of the victims in Hayder's novel are dead at the outset, and she makes the point that most of them were not cared for, or much missed. DSI Maddox, a senior police officer, dismisses them as 'toms': prostitutes (26). Shellene Craw's boyfriend, who has lived very comfortably on her earnings as a stripper and prostitute, has not bothered to report her missing. When asked about it, he quips 'Missing? Missing what? A conscience?' (40). When Craw's employer is told that she is dead, her only reaction is to comment that she will now not recoup the money Craw owed her: 'Ho hum, two hundred quid. I'm going to guess she didn't leave it to me in her will' (46). Craw's mother sums her daughter up as *a right little prossie*' (61). No one cares for these women, Hayder seems to suggest, not lovers, parents, employers, or representatives of the government – society has abandoned them.

Although Nesbø' victims are respectable in a way that Hayder's are not, they have all committed the one crime patriarchy fears the most: they have cuckolded their husbands, tricked them into raising other men's children. Like those of Hayder, Nesbø's victims are cut into pieces, with one of them also being sewn back together again. Unlike Hayder's victims, however, the majority of the dismemberments are not carried out in order to bring pleasure to the killer, but for logistical reasons – to make it easier to transport the bodies. When the bodies are described, the descriptions are short, as is the description of the only murder where the killer is not in emotional control. It is described in a flashback to a murder that has taken place many years before the main events of the novel. Like the woman Caffery encounters at the construction site in *Birdman*, this corpse is difficult to identify: 'The body lying in the snow had been cut into so many pieces that it was only thanks to a naked breast that they had been able to determine the gender' (2010: 54). However, this reference to the female breast is not in any way eroticized. This body is not there to be gazed at, but to testify to the atrocity of the act – to the level of this killer's insanity. It is there as a witness to the killer's pathology. Nesbø also makes the point that this was a person who mattered to others, not just an object, when the investigating officer takes a junior officer to task for his indifference: 'Someone has or will soon report this woman missing' (57).

As in *Birdman*, there is a scene in *The Snowman* which features dead bodies in a clinical environment. In this case it is the Anatomy Department of Gaustad Hospital, where bodies are dissected by medical students. Harry Hole goes there to try to track down the missing body of a dead woman – only her head has been found at the murder scene. Unlike the bodies in Hayder's autopsy suite, these bodies are not murder victims; they have been donated to the hospital. Viewed from a distance, they are referred to as 'pale dolls' (464) and they are only sketchily described; for example, it is not mentioned whether they are male or female. When Hole finds what he seeks, Nesbø is also sparing with the details, adopting a clinical tone and distancing the reader from the corpse. The body is 'cold' and 'the consistency unnaturally firm because of the fixative' (465). The whole event takes less than two pages. These corpses, although they have been donated to science, are not there to be gazed at, in either a scientific or an erotic sense. Instead, the reader is reminded that the body they find is that of a woman, and she is identified by name, Sylvia Ottersen. She is a person, not an interchangeable piece of meat intended to titillate or scare the reader.

Another of the murderer's victims, Eli Kvale, has been cut into parts and then sewn back together again, 'reassembled' as Hole terms it (453). The body is on display on top of a snowman. Here too the description is short, with little detail. Although the text twice refers to the woman's body as naked and makes one reference to her breasts, the narrative attempts to steer clear of any eroticism, instead focusing on the ill ease of those present. Hole and the other crime scene investigators experience a numbing sense of dread, which is communicated to the reader. What 'scare[s] the living daylights' out of Hole, however, is not the fact that he is looking at a dead woman, since she does 'not seem to have been brutally mutilated', but the way her body is displayed, 'the cold-blooded nature of the arrangement' (452). It is not her body itself that is important, but the message it conveys. The killer has intended the woman to be a sign for Hole to read, and Hole reads her primarily as a sign of the killer's disregard for human life.

Where Hayder criticizes society's destruction of women by mapping it onto the bodies of those considered most expendable, Nesbø questions patriarchy's obsession with paternity. Early on in the novel, there is a reference to supposed Swedish research on paternity uncertainty, claiming that 15–20 per cent of children have a different father from the one they think they have (12).[1] This research is brought up in a radio programme presenting the alleged behaviour of one seal species, the Berhaus seal, where males are said to kill females to prevent them from mating with other males and producing offspring that will compete with their own. The seals' behaviour is anthropomorphized; the female seals are linked to human females, and it is intimated that both groups of females are promiscuous. Since the male seals' response is presented as biologically and evolutionarily sound, this would suggest that a similar response from human males is also sound. This research on paternity uncertainty and male seals killing females as a deliberate strategy comes back at several points throughout the novel, referred to both by Hole (179–80, 308) and by the killer (488, 535).

Questions of paternity form a counterpoint throughout the novel: there are constant references to fathers, fatherhood and men who are duped into raising other men's children as their own. It is even revealed that Hole's former girlfriend, Rakel, has lied about the identity of her son's father. Paternity and adulterous mothers are also linked to inherited disease. Through conceiving by their lovers rather than their husbands, several of the mothers have exposed their children to hereditary, sometimes deadly, illnesses.[2] One of these children is the killer himself, who has inherited scleroderma from his mother's lover, a disease that will lead to a painful, lingering death. The narrative thus conveys a sense of paranoia and distrust running through society – can any woman be trusted? – and the actions of the killer can be interpreted as the final stage of this societal paranoia. When the killer, Mathias Lund-Helgesen, realizes as a teenager that not only has his mother betrayed the man he believes to be his father, but also that he is the bastard offspring of her lover, he kills her. As an adult, he re-enacts this murder, setting out to punish and kill other unfaithful women. As a carrier of patriarchal concerns, it is symptomatic that he only punishes the women. He does not kill his mother's lover, nor does he kill the celebrity who indiscriminately fathers children with other men's wives, knowingly spreading his disease. Towards the end of the novel, Lund-Helgesen invokes the societal paranoia regarding paternity when he suggests to Hole that he too is illegitimate (535). Because no woman can be trusted, no man can be certain of who his father is. Lund-Helgesen also voices the notion that, just like Hole, he is only doing what society requires of him: 'we're in the same business, Harry. Fighting disease' (536). Adulterous mothers are not only a moral problem for society, they are also transmitters of disease, and they need to be stopped. When society and its agents, such as Hole, fail to act, Lund-Helgesen performs the task himself.[3]

Nesbø's and Hayder's differing approaches to violence towards women are noticeable, not only in how they treat bodies that are already dead, but also in their description of the mutilation of living bodies. In *Birdman*, Hayder includes two scenes where women have their breasts cut open, without anaesthetic, by the second perpetrator, Malcolm Bliss. In the first scene, Hayder builds up the tension by devoting several pages to the fear and distress of the woman, Susan Lister. Having been abducted, she tries to convince herself that she can cope with the rape she expects will follow. All she has to do, she thinks, is to give in: '*you'll survive if you don't fight, comply with everything he tells you*' (2008: 271). Later on, she thinks '*Pray that he only rapes you, Susan, pray it won't be more*' (274). Bliss, who finds her breasts too big to be attractive, mocks and abuses her, before taking out the scalpel to start the butchery. The cutting and stitching up is not described in this scene. Lister apparently loses consciousness almost immediately, but it is revealed afterwards, through the narration of the police officers, and through descriptions of photographs Bliss has taken, just how he has mutilated and humiliated her: 'Bliss had photographed himself ejaculating over Susan Lister's broken face' (362). Lister is presented as a tragic example of the 'good girl' – she thinks that if she only does what the man says, he will not harm her beyond raping her, rape in this context becoming something almost mundane that any woman should be able to cope with. In a society where all women are rapable, potential victims, all a woman can hope for is 'only' rape. Yet, as Hayder suggests, no amount of compliance will appease a society that hates women.

Joni Marsh, the second victim, has her breast implants removed whilst completely awake. Like Lister, she is bound and gagged, but she is fully conscious of what is happening to her. In this scene, the knife cutting in to Marsh's breast is described: 'the soft flesh bloomed up over the blade like cheese, strained, then relented and split long, like a heavy fruit' (339). The pain she feels is telegraphed mainly through descriptions of how her body thrashes and jerks in response to the cut and Bliss' fingers pulling out the breast implants. These scenes are relentless in the way they communicate the fear and suffering Lister and

Marsh feel, as well as the details of what is done to their bodies, but it is difficult to see how they could be interpreted as 'lurching into pornography' as one reviewer has claimed (Gerrard 2000). Instead, by showing Bliss attacking what is perhaps the foremost symbol of femininity, the breast, Hayder comments on contemporary society's view of women's bodies as never finished, never good enough. No matter what women do, they will be adversely judged. In a fashion climate where women are told that large breasts are a necessity, and where breast implants are commonplace, Susan Lister and Joni Marsh are brutalized for not having small breasts. Susan Lister tries to be a good girl and comply with men's desires. Marsh has had breast implants in an effort to comply with societal demands. Yet, they are not rewarded for their efforts. Instead Bliss, as a symptom of patriarchal society, destroys them.

Nesbø also includes two women who are cut up – Sylvia Ottersen and Eli Kvale. He devotes an entire chapter (eight pages) to Sylvia Ottersen's frenzied attempts to outrun a murderer who has explained to her that he is going to cut her up whilst alive using a looped electrical filament, a tool vets use to cut up stillborn calves while they are still in the womb. The focus, as in Hayder's description of Lister's suffering, is on the fear and distress Ottersen feels. Like Hayder, Nesbø also makes a comment on women's bodies as objects for male desire. In the midst of fleeing from the killer, she notes to herself that she is quite fit, the result of having followed an exercise routine intended to make her lose weight and become more attractive to men (2010: 92). Yet this fitness does not help her. In the end, the killer catches up with her. The actual dismemberment is not depicted, however. The chapter ends with the killer saying: 'Shall we begin?' (98), and the next time Ottersen appears it is as a severed head on top of a snowman. Unlike Hayder's after-the-fact descriptions of Lister's suffering, nothing more is revealed of how Ottersen died.

The second dismembered woman is Eli Kvale. Like the other women, she suffers from fear. In her case, it stems from a rape many years ago, a rape that resulted in her beloved son, but which has also had a debilitating impact on her life. Brief references to how this fear cripples her, as well as to how the killer exploits that fear, are sprinkled throughout the novel (146, 163, 173, 243, and 277, for example), but when she is finally killed it happens offstage. All that is revealed to the reader is that after her husband reports her missing, her dress is found cut in such a way as to suggest that she has been cut up with the same tool as was used on Sylvia Ottersen. Next time Kvale appears, it is as a reassembled corpse sitting on top of a snowman and there is no further information about how she died, or how she felt. Like Hayder, Nesbø shows the women's fear and how they are hunted by the killer. However, by keeping the violence at a distance, effectively protecting the reader, it also becomes less immediate and thus the social criticism becomes less effective. These victims are more easily dismissed as collateral in the intellectual struggle between the detective and the murderer.

Because of the detailed descriptions of dead and dying bodies, violence and suffering, Hayder's texts are sometimes difficult to read, as some readers attest in otherwise very positive online comments, and it often seems as if the text requires 'a kind of reading with eyes closed', as Vicky Lebeau has suggested of *American Psycho* (1995: 129). Yet at the same time it is this difficulty that forces the reader to engage with the causes of that violence, and what that violence says about the society within which it exists. Although Nesbø also includes violence and torture in his novels, it is kept at arm's length, allowing the reader an escape route. The violence is as much a part of social criticism in his texts as it is in Hayder's, but at times there is the risk that the dead women simply become symbols of the murderer's pathology, clues to the puzzle that Hole must solve in order to win the contest with the murderer. Nesbø counteracts this by making the victims more well-rounded than Hayder's characters, but that strategy is not always successful. The death of Eli Kvale, for example, becomes simply a stepping stone towards the solution, providing one of the final clues. Considering her life spent in fear, her final moments when encountering the murderer must have been horrific, but when her body, and her death, are revealed in the novel, they are treated in an almost offhand manner.

Both Mo Hayder and Jo Nesbø choose to depict women as victims, not because female victims boost sales, but as a means of criticizing the way society treats women. Through the use of disturbing imagery of violence, the narratives focus on the horror of what is done to the women, rather than dwelling on the eroticism of the female body displayed for titillation. Both authors employ the serial killer as a spokesperson for contemporary society and how it relates to women. By focusing on the killing, sexual exploitation, and mutilation of prostitutes and drug addicts, Hayder critiques how society treats women as worthless and interchangeable, useful only for sex. Nesbø discusses how society regards women as breeders, whose sexuality must be controlled at any cost. Whereas Hayder's female victims are interchangeable, in that they do not matter to the murderers, Nesbø's women are important individuals, who matter very much to their murderer. Yet despite this seeming contradiction, they exemplify the same societal mechanism – women's bodies are for the control and consumption of men and if they do not live up to expectations, they can be discarded.

Notes

1. Research suggests that the actual figure, in the UK and probably in other countries, lies somewhere between 1 and 3 per cent (Gilding 2009: 153).
2. A case in point is the disease Fahr's syndrome, which three of the illegitimate children in the novel may have inherited. Because Fahr sounds like the Norwegian word for father, several characters mishear the name of the illness as 'father's syndrome'.
3. The cultural paranoia regarding the uncertainty of paternity is made even more noticeable through the translator's choice of words in this scene. In the original Norwegian, Hole calls the killer 'jævel' (devil), but the translator uses 'bastard' (2010: 536).

Works cited

Cohen, D. (1997) 'The Beautiful Female Murder Victim, Literary Genres and Courtship Practices in the Origins of a Cultural Motif, 1590–1850', *Journal of Social History* 31.2, 277–306.

Curtis, B. (2011) 'Scandinavian Thriller Obsession', *Newsweek* 157.21/22, 82.

Dauncey, S. (2010) 'Crime, Forensics, and Modern Science' in C. Rzepka and L. Horsley (eds) *A Companion to Crime Fiction*. Oxford: Blackwell Publishing. 164–174.

East, B. (2009) 'The Redeemer by Jo Nesbø', *The Observer*, 25 Oct, http://www.guardian.co.uk/books/2009/oct/25/the-redeemer-jo-nesbo-review?INTCMP=SRCH, accessed 22 Feb 2012.

Foster, J. (2008) 'Diving into Darkness', *Publishers Weekly* 255.29, 137.

Foster, J. (2010) 'Norwegian Noir', *Publishers Weekly* 257.4, 94.

Freccero, C. (1997) 'Historical Violence, Censorship, and the Serial Killer: The Case of *American Psycho*', *Diacritics* 27.2, 44–58.

Gerrard, N. (2000) 'Sex With Dead People? Even Hannibal Lecter Likes to Have His Victims Served Hot', *The Observer*, 23 Jan, http://www.guardian.co.uk/books/2000/jan/23/fiction.reviews1?INTCMP=SRCH, accessed 22 Feb 2012.

Gilding, M. (2009) 'Paternity Uncertainty and Evolutionary Psychology: How a Seemingly Capricious Occurrence Fails to Follow Laws of Greater Generality', *Sociology* 43.1, 140–57.

Hayder, M. (2008 [2000]) *Birdman*. London: Bantam.

Hill, A. (2009) 'Sexist violence sickens crime critic', *The Observer*, 25 Oct, http://www.guardian.co.uk/books/2009/oct/25/jessica-mann-crime-novels-anti-women, accessed 22 Feb 2012.

Klein, K. G. (1995) 'Habeas Corpus: Feminist and Detective Fiction' in G. Irons (ed.) *Feminism in Women's Detective Fiction*. Toronto: Toronto University Press. 171–89.

Knight, S. (2010 [2004]) *Crime Fiction since 1800: Detection, Death, Diversity*. London: Palgrave.

Lebeau, V. (1995) *Lost Angels: Psychoanalysis and Cinema*. London: Routledge.
Malmgren, C. (1997) 'Anatomy of Murder: Mystery, Detective and Crime Fiction', *Journal of Popular Culture* 30.4, 115–135.
Mann, J. (2009) 'Crimes Against Fiction', *Standpoint*, 9 Sep, http://www.standpointmag.co.uk/crimes-against-fiction-counterpoints-september-09-crime-fiction, accessed 22 Feb 2012.
McDermid, V. (2009) 'Complaints about Women Writing Misogynist Crime Fiction Are a Red Herring', *The Guardian*, 29 Oct, http://www.guardian.co.uk/books/booksblog/2009/oct/29/misogynist-crime-fiction-val-mcdermid, accessed 22 Feb 2012.
Meyhoff, K. W. (2011) 'Digging into the Secrets of the Past: Rewriting History in the Modern Scandinavian Police Procedural' in A. Nestingen and P. Arvas (eds) *Scandinavian Crime Fiction*. Cardiff: University of Cardiff Press. 62–73.
Nesbø, J. (2010) *The Snowman*. Transl. D. Bartlett. London: Vintage.
Oliver, B. (2011) 'When Writers are Confronted by a National Trauma' *The Guardian*, 31 July, http://www.guardian.co.uk/books/2011/jul/31/norway-crime-fiction-scandinavia?INTCMP=SRCH, accessed 22 Feb 2012.
Palmer, J. (2001) 'Tracing Bodies: Gender, Genre, and Forensic Detective Fiction', *South Central Review* 18.3–4, 55–71.
Plain, G. (2001) *Twentieth-Century Crime Fiction: Gender, Sexuality and the Body*. Chicago: Fitzroy Dearborn.
Rees, M. B. (2011) 'Sicko Writing: Is Crime Fiction Too Gory?', *The Man of Twists and Turns*, 4 Aug, http://www.themanoftwistsandturns.com/2011/08/04/sicko-writing-is-crime-fiction-too-gory/, accessed 22 Feb 2012.
Robinson D. (2011) 'Interview: Jo Nesbø, musician and author', *New Scotsman*, 28 Feb, http://www.scotsman.com/news/interview_jo_nesbo_musician_and_author_1_1494862, accessed 7 March 2012.
Simpson, P. L. (2000) *Psycho Paths: Tracking the Serial Killer Through Contemporary American Film and Fiction*. Carbondale: Southern Illinois University Press.
Smith, W. (2005) 'Kafka's Chick', *Publishers Weekly* 252.22, 24–5.
Upson, N. (2000), 'Crime Waves', *New Statesman*, 7 Feb, http://www.newstatesman.com/200002070056, accessed 7 March 2012.
Walton, P. and M. Jones . (1999) *Detective Agency: Women Rewriting the Hard-Boiled Tradition*. Berkeley: University of California Press.
Young, E. (1992) 'The Beast in the Jungle, the Figure in the Carpet' in E. Young and G. Caveney (eds) *Shopping in Space: Essays on American 'Blank Generation' Fiction*. London: Serpent's Tail. 85–122.

Part III

Rewriting Scripts: Language, Gender, and Violence in Contemporary Crime Fiction

7
Disarticulated Figures: Language and Sexual Violence in Contemporary Crime Fiction

Meghan A. Freeman

Our job is to speak for the victim. This statement, or one very similar to it, has been used in numerous crime procedurals as a statement-of-purpose for those tasked with investigating acts of violence. Yet, how can the investigator truly speak for the victim if one aspect of victimhood is voicelessness – not physical muteness, but rather the condition of being institutionally deprived of the right to testify to one's own violation? In *The Differend,* Jean-François Lyotard argues that 'it is in the nature of a victim not to be able to prove that one has been done a wrong' (1988: 8). This chapter investigates problems of language as they pertain to one specific wrong – the act of rape – as represented in contemporary Anglophone and Swedish crime fiction. In particular, I explore how novels by Swedish author Stieg Larsson, Scottish author Val McDermid, and American author Susanna Moore struggle to *speak to* the voicelessness that is an important dimension of the rape victim's violation without *speaking for* that victim. I trace the trope of disarticulation in their works as it pertains to what, in current crime fiction, is often treated subtly and figuratively: the silencing of the rape victim through the workings of complex social dynamics which facilitate acts of rape and which render the experience of it partially or fully inarticulable after the fact, dynamics oftentimes repressed in political, legal, and criminological discourses.

The three novels considered in this chapter foreground the double-bind of the differend as it impacts the rape victim, in the process drawing attention to the ways in which the violation of the physical body is often reproduced in the textual body, generating narrative aporias in which the violent act that demands articulation creates a situation that makes articulation impossible. Beginning with a comparative analysis of Val

McDermid's *The Mermaids Singing* (1995) and Stieg Larsson's *The Girl with the Dragon Tattoo* (2008), I will examine how both authors do the work of 'bear[ing] witness to differends' through their narrative efforts to represent the processes by which rape victims are denied the opportunity to be recognized as victims – to use Lyotard's language, their violation and victimization '"asks" to be put into phrases, and suffers from the wrong of not being able to be put into phrases right away' or in the right way (1988: 13). The allusions to *The Mermaids Singing* in Larsson's novel create a bridge that spans temporal and cultural distances, foregrounding McDermid's and Larsson's shared preoccupation with reading what Shakespeare in *Titus Andronicus* called the 'map of woe' – that is, the rape victim's disarticulated body – in order to find a way back to the site of violation and thereby to reveal the institutional and ideological forces that allow for acts of sexual violence to occur unseen, unheard, and unpunished (2002: 3.2.12). From there, I will conclude with a discussion of a literary crime novel that was published in the same year as *The Mermaids Singing* but which approaches the problem of representing rape from a socio-linguistic as opposed to sociocultural angle: Susanna Moore's *In the Cut* (1995). While the novels of Larsson and McDermid testify to various discursive frameworks that deprive the rape victim of a voice, Moore's novel, I argue, concerns itself with creating a 'phrase regimen' that speaks to the condition of voicelessness, articulating the disarticulated, as it were.[1] It does this by shifting the focus from the objective act of sexual violence to the subjective experience of making sense of it. Focalized through a female professor studying urban slang, *In the Cut* makes strange the language used to describe acts of sexual violence and thus highlights the violence of language itself. In this way, Moore's literary thriller can be read as a meta-analysis of the stakes involved when graphic scenes of sexualized torture and torment are put into words, thereby calling attention to a central problematic in the crime fiction genre within which McDermid and Larsson are more properly situated, and which makes them both, at times, unwilling participants in the rhetorical disarticulation of the victims whose silent suffering their fictions attempt to bring to light.

'Stop the voice. Analyse': voiceless bodies and disembodied voices

Midway through Stieg Larsson's *The Girl with the Dragon Tattoo*, journalist Mikael Blomkvist, deep in the throes of an investigation into the disappearance of one woman and the murders of several others, finds himself alone on Midsummer's Eve. With a kind of journalistic precision befitting Blomkvist himself, Larsson details the events of that evening:

> At 6:00 [Blomkvist] took a shower. He boiled some potatoes and had open sandwiches of pickled herring in mustard sauce...He poured himself a shot of aquavit and drank a toast to himself. After that he opened a crime novel by Val McDermid entitled *The Mermaids Singing*. (2009: 383)

After that night, Blomkvist's reading material is not mentioned until several days later, when – again after dinner – he 'went to bed to read the denouement of Val McDermid's novel' (396). Blomkvist's only recorded impression of this conclusion: 'it was grisly'. For a novel involving the rapes, murders, and horrifying mutilations of numerous women, this terse judgement of another work of crime fiction should raise a few eyebrows, and, I would argue, that is Larsson's intention. Larsson's intertextual references to *The Mermaids Singing* work to establish a vital and specific connection to McDermid's crime procedural, one that begs further consideration.

At first glance, there seem to be more differences than similarities between the two texts. For one thing, the victimology of the killers is different. While Larsson's novel is preoccupied with violence against women, McDermid's novel concerns the abduction and murder of men. Yet, what *The Mermaids Singing* foregrounds – and *The Girl with the Dragon Tattoo* develops upon – is that gender is only one of a number of social integers at play in the private act of, and public response to, sexual violence, especially when the continuance of the killer's agenda is dependent on the institutionalized denial of the chosen victims' personhood and their right to justice. In McDermid's novel, the fact that the victims are men is less important than the fact that they are assumed to be closeted homosexuals. The disposal of their bodies in Temple Fields, an area associated with the gay sex trade, is enough to generate a kind of wilful deafness on the part of the authorities, who refuse to listen to the possibility that the murders are the work of one perpetrator. As the Superintendent in charge of the investigation says, 'How many times do I have to tell you? We've not got a serial killer loose in Bradfield. We've just got a nasty bunch of copycat queers' (1995: 34). The Superintendent's denial of the seriality of these murders constitutes a two-fold act of rhetorical disarticulation. First he separates the victims from the general population and conflates them with their killer (as they are all 'poofters'), and then he ignores the links between the murders, the ways in which they together form a pattern. The violence inflicted upon these men is instead grouped in with what he sees as the more generally aberrant behaviour of the gay community, and thus the suspected sexuality of the victims becomes, in a way, a justification for what has been done to them. That the Superintendent's attitude makes him complicit in the murders is recognized by one of his subordinates, Detective Inspector Carol Jordan, who interprets her boss's inaction as a reaction against the decriminalization of homosexuality: 'If you couldn't get them off the streets any longer by arresting them, let a killer remove them' (9).

The Girl with the Dragon Tattoo also strives to reveal how victims of sexual violence are often created *prior* to their violation by the social institutions that are supposed to protect and serve them. Larsson's focus, though, is broader than the criminal justice system. His novel aims to expose the connection between individual acts of violence against women and the network of global capital that infiltrates and influences almost every aspect of public life in modern Sweden. This goal is made explicit in the very layout of the novel. Divided into sections, each section is preceded by a title page, the subtitle of which is a key term taken from the discourse of finance – incentive, consequence analyses, merger, hostile takeover, final audit – below which is placed a single contemporary statistic concerning assaults on women. The typographical juxtaposition of these disparate discursive registers implies a linkage between them, a linkage that is finally embodied in the figure of Martin Vanger, captain of industry and serial rapist and murderer of women. When questioned by an imprisoned Blomkvist as to why he kills, Vanger points a finger at globalization for making it 'so easy… Women disappear all the time. Nobody misses them. Immigrants. Whores from Russia. Thousands of people pass through Sweden every year' (2009: 487). The position of these women vis-à-vis dominant culture denies their disappearance an outlet for being vocalized and registered. They were already among the 'disappeared'; as lower class, immigrant women, they were not legally recognized to begin with, and thus their absence goes unspoken and uninvestigated.

In McDermid's and Larsson's novels, it requires the murder of a so-called 'ordinary citizen' for the pattern of victimization, the very seriality of the killings, to be acknowledged by the authorities (245). The killer in *The Mermaids Singing* has to abduct a fellow policeman ('one of ours') before the murders are taken seriously, while Blomkvist's investigation into Martin Vanger's crimes has its genesis in the interest and financial backing of the Vanger family patriarch, who desires to know the fate of Martin's long-vanished sister, Harriet. That the perceived threat presented by the killer is fully legitimated only when it extends to cultural insiders is a point that both authors use to denaturalize the processes by which individuals are both included within and excluded from legal, social, and political categories that enforce their status and rights as citizens. In *The Girl with the Dragon Tattoo,* Larsson uses the compromised legal status of his heroine, Lisbeth Salander, to highlight the vagaries of these processes, the great 'infringements that a democracy can impose' simply through the deployment of official genres of discourse (246). Salander, having been declared 'legally incompetent' in adolescence, has had her control over her life and finances placed under the aegis of a guardian. Stripped of her right to self-management, she is vulnerable to exploitation, both at the hands of her guardian (the sadist Nils Bjurman) and by society more generally. Her legal status deprives her of the protections that come from being deemed 'ordinary' (etymologically, belonging to the order), and moreover, it denies her, and others like her, the means of making the abuses against them known. As Larsson observes, the paucity of complaints against the Guardianship Agency created to oversee cases like Salander's could indicate their satisfactory performance of duties, but how can we know, as 'the clients have no opportunity to complain and in a credible way make themselves heard by the media or by the authorities' (247)? In this way, the system works to create a class of 'victims' in Lyotard's sense of the word – not just individuals who have suffered a wrong, but individuals who have been dispossessed of the ability to speak of it. This form of victimhood is what Salander shares with Vanger's victims and other women not belonging to 'the sheltered middle class from the suburbs' (249). In Salander's world, to be 'forced to perform some sort of sexual act against her will' is not something to be reported to the police, as 'this was the natural order of things'; 'As a girl she was legal prey, especially if she was dressed in a worn black leather jacket and had pierced eyebrows, tattoos, and zero social status' (249). What is more, Larsson's suggestion here that Salander's 'zero social status' is as recognizable to others as her sex, and her affiliation with Goth subculture reinforces the idea that outsiders are not invisible so much as deliberately disregarded by cultural insiders who implicitly condone the inequalities of the system.

Yet, as the novel demonstrates, there is nothing 'natural' about being 'legal' prey – in fact, it is the persistent and widespread conflation of these discourse genres that enables some of the most horrific abuses of power, particularly Salander's violent rape at the hands of her guardian, Bjurman. Bjurman's position as Salander's 'advokat' (a term that can be traced back to *vocem*, or voice) skews their relationship as his actions are implicitly authorized by the institution he represents. As he tells her, in a chillingly unbalanced parallel construction, 'If you're nice to me, I'll be nice to you…If you make trouble, I can put you away in an institution for the rest of your life' (243). That any problems in their interpersonal dynamics can result in the intrusion of a legal system that is disproportionally favourable to Bjurman allows what might have been 'a matter of coercion and degradation' to become 'systematic brutality' (276). His words 'carry more weight' than hers, making his sadistic abuse almost state-sanctioned, for her legal status as *non compos mentis* renders everything that she might say suspect (244). Nils Bjurman's crimes are on a different scale from Martin Vanger's, but together they serve to undermine the comfortable fiction that an enemy of the social order is always an outsider of that order. Instead, they respectively illustrate how the disarticulation of any population creates opportunities for exploitation from those placed in positions of power. Industrialist and public servant, both are monsters created by systemic inequalities in the modern institutions they serve. Moreover, their strength is largely drawn from the institutional ground on which they stand. Their unfettered access to the information relentlessly collected and archived in the public sphere (such as psychiatric records, bank account information, family history, and immigration status) provides them with the tools to silence their past victims while seeking out new ones.

There is another danger, though, that attends the silencing of a vulnerable population, as McDermid's novel demonstrates. If Martin Vanger is the incarnation of the oppressive and abusive aspects of global capitalism, the killer at work in *The Mermaids Singing* is the return of the repressed in terms of those voices systematically silenced. Called the 'Queer Killer' by the police and press (a name that says less about the killer and more about the denigrative attitude of the public towards the victims), this shadowy figure is given two different names by criminal profiler Tony Hill: 'Handy Andy' and 'The Voice'. Hill does not realize until the story's conclusion that these two identities are but facets of the same person, as Handy Andy is the name he gives to the individual who handcrafts historical torture devices for use on his victims, and The Voice is an unknown woman who persistently tries to engage Hill in phone sex. Still, the disconnect between these two differently gendered personas is integral to understanding the killer's pathology and the social conditions that brought it into being. Handy Andy and The Voice are both parts of Angelica, a post-operative transsexual, who ensnares her prospective victims with raunchy telephone calls, only to 'punish' them for betraying her when they enter into relationships with women they have met in their public lives. As her chosen name suggests, she sees herself as a kind of avenging angel, dispensing justice to all the faithless men who choose the 'safe, pathetic option' of a conventional heteronormative relationship over 'the marriage of true minds and bodies' that she sees herself as being uniquely capable of providing (1995: 104–5).

Considered in relation to the trope of disarticulation, Angelica's murderous *modus operandi* could be seen as a twisted attempt to give voice to the unspeakable. As The Voice, she is the cruel mirror-inverse of the rape victim's voicelessness, a Siren whose song lures her listeners to their deaths. Unlike other telephone sex workers that Hill has previously interviewed, all of whom were united in feeling 'violated and degraded' by the work they were paid to perform, Hill's mystery caller is voracious, sexually predatory, and relentless in objectifying the men to fit them within *her* fantasy (49). Yet, it is only the fact that her voice is electronically severed from her body that allows her this power – in her own body, her transsexuality puts her beyond the pale of conventional and accepted romantic relationships with heterosexual men. And this is where Handy Andy comes in. Angelica murders and mutilates in order to avenge her own psychological disarticulation at the hands of a society by which she feels disregarded, unrecognized, and unheard. Moreover, in artfully delivering her messages via the broken bodies of her victims, Angelica insists that the individuals tasked with capturing her give her the authorizing focus of their attention while visually consuming the bloody tableau that is meant to symbolize their own culpability in her actions. Tony Hill, at least, recognizes the role he indirectly plays as a member of the mental health establishment when he catches himself thinking about the articles and books he might produce from the 'raw material' Angelica has provided. As he says to a plant on a windowsill, 'I'm a cannibal...Sometimes I disgust myself' (88).

Tony Hill and Larsson's Mikael Blomkvist both inhabit professions that make violators of them, at least metaphorically. Hill, a psychologist specializing in the criminally insane, is haunted by the thought that his therapeutic methods are merely 'tricks in [his] magic bag, designed to legitimize [his] prurient curiosity, tailored to unleash the twisted minds of the fuck-ups who are driven to act on their fantasies in a way society can't accommodate' (212). Blomkvist, a journalist, is not initially cognizant of his own culpability, but even he must come to terms with the fact that the publication of a rapist's crimes, even with the admirable goal of exposing the truth, can be seen as a kind of abuse. When he nominates himself to be that *'somebody* [who] has to say *something* about the women who died in Martin's basement', Lisbeth Salander undercuts his sense of ethical righteousness with a brutal question: 'which is worse – the fact that Martin Vanger raped [Harriet Vanger] in the cabin or that you're going to do it in print?' (2009: 559–60) For Salander, the public exposure of the recently deceased Martin Vanger is worthless because it does nothing to repair the injuries done to his victims. In fact, in assuming the obligation to 'speak up on their behalf', Blomkvist is, in her eyes, perpetuating their victimhood by substituting his voice for theirs. That these victims can no longer speak is not the point; to speak *for* them is still a violation in that it serves to obscure the negation of their voices, to cover up the fact that their subjective experiences of their own rape and murder 'must be put into phrases yet cannot be' (Lyotard 1988: 13).

Yet, if only the voiceless victim has the right to testify to the violation suffered, how do the individuals tasked with proving the existence of these violations do so without imitating the initial perpetrator? McDermid and Larsson use an identical strategy to get around this problem: they remove their protagonists from positions of authority and make them (temporarily, at least) victims. Before expanding on this point, though, it is worth mentioning certain parallels between the detecting teams at the centre of each novel. Profiler and policewoman (Tony Hill and Carol Jordan), and journalist and informations analyst/hacker (Mikael Blomkvist and Lisbeth Salander): both are male/female pairings in which both partners somehow fall outside accepted gender norms. The men have been semi-disenfranchised and emasculated professionally – Hill by the contemptuous attitude of the police force with whom he is liaising, who resent the involvement of 'some poncey bloody doctor', 'this wanker of a shrink' (1995: 197), and Blomkvist by a humiliating libel verdict that has harmed his reputation within the media community. On the other hand, the two women have successfully infiltrated masculine work environments, and both are distinguished by similar cognitive peculiarities: Salander possesses an eidetic, or photographic, memory, capable of retaining all visually-processed information, while Jordan has almost perfect auditory recall, giving her the ability to repeat, word for word, almost anything she hears. With neither member of either pair fitting easily into conventional gender roles, the cement bonding them is their outsider status, the fact that they occupy liminal positions within the institutions they serve.

This shared outsider status plays a crucial role in the *denouements* of the serial killer storyline in both texts, and again, the resemblance between these respective conclusions suggests that Larsson's reference to the 'grisly' ending of *The Mermaids Singing* requires further explication. Each of these plotlines ends with the male protagonists occupying the role of Bluebeard's final wife, trapped within the terrifying walls of the bloody chamber. Physically immobilized, with their hands cuffed behind their backs, Blomkvist and Hill come to identical realizations. Blomkvist concludes that 'he [is] defenceless. All he [has is] his voice' (2009: 481), while Hill tells himself, 'Never mind singing for your supper, talk for your life' (1995: 324). Though both men were already masters of the authoritative discursive genres associated with their work (able to analyse, to diagnose, to report), their tête-à-têtes with their captors reveal a more fundamental truth: that language itself is mastery, that the reality of a given situation depends on 'the state of the referent (that about which one speaks)' (Lyotard 1988: 4). Survival requires that they sacrifice their ethical commitment to using language *denotatively* (to describe the reality or truth of the thing) and instead utilize it *performatively* (to create an alternate reality or truth that gives them some measure of control over their captors). Thus, they each perform a desperate parody of their professional phrase regimen, with Mikael Blomkvist peppering Martin Vanger with questions to stave off the hangman, and Tony Hill deliberately playing to the narcissism of Angelica by giving her a heavily romanticized profile of herself. They gain the rhetorical upper hand, until their voices are temporarily silenced in a ghastly prelude to their permanent silencing, as both killers stop their mouths with a kiss.

Though the specifics differ, it is at the moment of physical contact between killer and victim that the arrival of a crucial third figure prevents the progression of the conventional rape narrative from moving towards its seemingly inevitable conclusion. Salander and Jordan, respectively, burst onto the scene as avengers, but also – and I would argue more importantly – as witnesses. The soundproof isolation required by the rapist/killer is shattered in this moment, and with that, Blomkvist and Hill are spared the fate of becoming like *Titus Andronicus'* Lavinia, 'speechless complainers' to their own violation (2002: 3.2.39). That said, as previously mentioned, in neither story does the full extent of the killer's crime ever come to light, nor do Hill or Blomkvist ever get their day in court. Both novels have shown themselves to be too sceptical of social institutions to find legal testimony a sufficient medium for the satisfactory recording and resolution of events. But what we get in its place is a different, more complicated fantasy, one that has its root in the authors' desire to continue to bear witness to forms of violation that find no outlet for expression within official modes of discourse. So, in these two novels, we have victims of sexual violence who live to tell the tale, yet choose not to because the deceased killers are no longer a threat to public safety, and also because the scene of their violation has been witnessed and preserved with pinpoint accuracy in the archival memories of their partners. Lisbeth Salander, who looks over Martin Vanger's chamber of horrors, and Carol Jordan, who listens to all of the taped conversations between Angelica and her victims, serve as human receptacles for the dehumanizing experiences suffered by their partners and the other victims. As such, Salander and Jordan do not speak for them. They do something far more valuable: they hold everything in their perfect memories and, thus, bear witness to what cannot be put into phrases in public circulation without being translated, corrupted, and manipulated. Larsson and McDermid insist on the necessity of listening to the silence, where it darkly resounds in the chambers of memory.

Plotting a murder-scape: the secret language of sexual violence

Frannie, the protagonist of Susanna Moore's literary thriller *In the Cut*, shares with Carol Jordan and Lisbeth Salander the responsibility of preserving a record of sexualized violence and victimization. In Frannie's case, though, she is not a viewer or listener tasked with remembering the crimes of one particular perpetrator so much as a general amanuensis, a transcriber whose hand is responsible for recording what Moore represents as countless acts of violence, all of them perpetrated against the English language. Dispersed throughout *In the Cut* are excerpts from her protagonist's dictionary of New York slang, a growing list of colloquialisms she amasses by listening to people talking informally and unselfconsciously, using those words and phrases that crop up like weeds in the cracks of 'proper' language. Slang words are 'thrilling' to Frannie, a philologist, for some of the same reasons that they are often excluded from official lexicons: for 'their wit, exuberance, mistakenness, and violence' (1995: 54). The manifestations of specific times, places, and situations, slang terms rupture the smooth fabric of a standardized language and expose certain weaknesses with regards to what that language cannot or will not fully represent. Frannie's lists show the proliferation of slang around two such taboo topics, with which the novel itself is intimately concerned: sex and violence. Teeming with synonyms for both weapons and body parts, her lists work within the context of the larger narrative as would a legend on a map – a key that translates for the traveller all the linguistic symbols that stand in for real objects in the landscape that the map represents. The apparent problem with this analogy, though, is that so many of the words Frannie transcribes translate to the same few things: for example, 'virginia', 'snapper', 'brasole', and 'gash' all are slang for 'vagina' (54). However, rather than assuming that these words are all simply reducible to the anatomically correct term, another way of looking at it would be to see them as unsanctioned expansions of it, idiolectic elaborations that work to figuratively reinvest the object being signified with some aspect of a particular speaker's perspective on it. Using the abovementioned example, then, we can see that the slang terms for vagina that Frannie has collected bear the impressions of many longstanding and contradictory cultural ideas about female sexuality. With 'virginia', we have an ironic substitution that gestures towards the fetishizing of female virginity; with 'snapper', there is both a crude olfactory connotation as well as a potential allusion to that tired, old workhorse of masculine fears, the *vagina dentata*; with 'brasole', as Frannie notes, the reference seems to be to deli meat, evoking here the visual and gustatory; and, finally, we have 'gash' (and the related 'cut', from which the title is taken), a term most disturbing in terms of the violence that it linguistically enacts on the female sex organ.

Yet, if more explicitly brutal than its idiomatic brethren, along with those other terms 'gash' also perpetuates a more subtle violence. They all work to rhetorically dislocate the signified object from the physical body of its possessor by reorienting it in relation to the larger social body, by which it is desired and despised in seemingly equal measure. Moreover, the sheer number of slang variants for this one contested site on the female body goes a long way towards illustrating Lyotard's claim that the 'body "proper" is a name for a family of idiolects' as well as 'the referent of phrases obeying various regimens' (1988: 83). In other words, the vulnerability of the physical body is that the individual's subjective experience of it can only be communicated in a language so personalized as to be incomprehensible to others. On the flip side, that same body is open to the endless discursive framings of those it comes in contact with, creating a cacophony of objective phrases that mask the enforced silence of the subjectivity inhabiting that body. Indeed, the representation of this cacophony is the function of Frannie's lexicon – grouped together, these slang expressions highlight the vulnerability of the body in language, the endless ways in which it can be used, co-opted, appropriated, violated, damaged, and destroyed. And, thus, these inset lists act as corollaries to Frannie's own experiences, as she attempts to put into words the condition of voicelessness that attends objectification in language, transforming the desiring subject into a mute object or the vocal plaintiff into a silent victim.

In the Cut begins with Frannie witnessing a graphic sexual encounter in the basement of a bar called *The Red Turtle*, the staging of which, she soon realizes, makes her unintentionally complicit in transforming what was initially a consensual activity into a form of violation. Making a wrong turn in search of the bathroom, Frannie encounters a man on a sofa, his face in darkness but with a distinctive wrist tattoo, being fellated by a redheaded woman leaning between his knees. Catching sight of Frannie, the man keeps his partner focused on the task at hand while subtly repositioning her so that Frannie can watch the woman bring him to orgasm. After it is over, Frannie admits, 'I backed out of the room like a thief and he still did not turn away, his hands in her hair, holding her there so she could not see me, so it was just the two of us' (1995: 9). The strange intimacy forged between Frannie and the faceless man depends upon the redheaded woman, who, upon Frannie's entrance, is no longer a knowing participant, but an instrument, an unwitting proxy facilitating an erotically charged stare-down between the other two. That Frannie flees the scene feeling 'like a thief' implies her awareness that she has contributed to what is, on some level, a rape. Rape being, etymologically at least, a form of seizure or theft, Frannie has helped to take from the woman her privacy, her awareness and control of the situation, and her agency.

In the midst of a novel preoccupied with the language of sex and violence, the scene in the basement of *The Red Turtle* is all the more striking for its near unbroken silence. The redheaded woman cannot speak, Frannie does not speak, and the faceless man will not speak; even his orgasm, Frannie observes, is marked only by 'a barely audible intake of breath as if he weren't going to give away any more than he had to, not even his breath, especially not his breath' (9). Still, the lack of speech in this encounter should not be confused with the absence of things needing to be said. Rather, the situation that Moore creates here accords closely to Lyotard's theorization of silence, which is as 'a negative phrase' associated closely with the differend, that 'unstable state and instant of language' in which what must be said is not put into words (1998: 13). All three participants, in not speaking, contribute to a pressurized atmosphere, a phrase universe characterized by withholding and restriction, by voicelessness in its defenceless, passive, and defensive postures. When the woman is later found murdered, Frannie is approached by a police detective with an identical tattoo, and in his description of how the woman was killed, this professor of language and literature is inadvertently provided with the perfect term to punctuate the scene in the basement of *The Red Turtle* and its aftermath:

> 'How was she killed?'
> 'Her throat was cut'. He paused. 'And then she was disarticulated'.
> What a good word, I thought. Disarticulated. (1995: 19)

If seemingly cold-blooded, Frannie's unspoken response is also indicative of her belief in the ability of words to establish the reality of an event. Here, the word 'disarticulated' catches her attention because of the double violence it implies: both the post-mortem dismembering of the victim's body and the earlier silencing of her voice. Moreover, in its morphology – the affixing of the prefix dis- (meaning 'apart' or asunder') to articulate (meaning both to speak distinctly but also to attach at the joints) – the word anticipates the performance it describes: a coming together of a prefix and a root morpheme that results in the inversion of what the root morpheme once meant; disarticulation is the breaking down of what was once joined, a severing of the integrity of the originary body, a fundamentally destructive act of union.

Later on, when Frannie enters into a sexual relationship with the detective and possible murderer James Malloy, the trope of disarticulation recurs at various narrative junctures, continuously strengthening and complicating the parallel it reveals between bodily violation and vocal suppression. Yet, because for much of the story it exists between them only as a concept, the idea of 'the disarticulated' comes to represent all those things between them of which they are aware, but of which they do not speak; or, as Malloy describes it, that 'something missing. A piece. Something I know that I don't know yet' (42). The strange courtship between Frannie and Malloy is, in fact, carried on almost entirely using rhetorical tactics that are meant to restrict or withhold access to sensitive information about themselves that the other seeks. Malloy is skilled in a kind of obfuscatory, anecdotal patter that discloses nothing personal; Frannie notes that 'he talked a lot, but he only told me what he wanted me to know. Which wasn't much' (47). Frannie, on the other hand, when faced with Malloy's questions, adopts 'some old, stubborn resistance-fighter tactic', which causes her both to lie and to refuse to speak (48). In a similar vein, the two also 'perform' disarticulation in the context of seduction. The first time, in a bar, Malloy strives to prove the killer's knowledge of bodies by demonstrating on her body the process by which an arm is popped out of its socket:

> He took my arm and held it away from my side, putting a hand between my breast and arm. I felt as if I'd been branded.
> 'The humerus here', he said. 'And this joint at the shoulder. Very difficult. You got to know what you're doing'.
> Like you, I thought. (49)

Frannie's (again) unspoken observation makes explicit an uncomfortable similarity between good killers, good investigators, and good lovers: they all know what they are doing with the bodies of others. And, as the affair between Frannie and Malloy progresses, it becomes equally clear that many of the moves are the same; only the emphasis and the end result differ. In fact, the prelude to the two of them going to bed together is a re-enactment of a recent attack on Frannie, in which she takes Malloy's 'right arm, bending it at the elbow, and laid it across [her] neck' (78). Her directives – 'Like this … like this' – that initially are meant to help him stage what her attacker did to her shade imperceptibly into suggestions as to what she would like him to do to her. A later liaison at Malloy's station house employs a different script of victimization, this one based on a fairly conventional narrative of police brutality: Frannie is handcuffed, bent over a desk, and anally penetrated, all the while being told by Malloy to 'give it up' (120). As unsettling as they are, what Frannie finds most difficult in these scenarios is, indeed, 'giving it up' – that is, avowing her own desire, specifically her desire to be 'fixed, to be held down. Opened' (120). And her problem here, one could argue, is not wholly of her own making, but is also one of language. How does one vocalize a wish to play at being a victim, even within the sphere of consensual sexual encounters, if a condition of true victimization is voicelessness? And what are the stakes of making such an avowal – does it evacuate the fantasy of its erotic charge or, more dangerously, does it work as a performative utterance, creating a real victim where before there wasn't one?

Ultimately, as a mostly unrepentant 'word casuist', Frannie knows better than most that 'you don't play around with language' (Lyotard 1988: 137). Her dictionary is a testament to the high stakes involved in its usage and misusage, especially in relation to the body. Thus, her attraction to scenarios of sexual and verbal violence must be considered in relation to the larger project with which she is engaged: idiomatic lexicography. For Frannie, slang language is fascinating precisely because it is language at its most personal, revelatory, and unstable. As she points out, her dictionary 'is a fluid list as the words are sometimes only in use for only a month or two, the meaning of the word varying in different parts of the city, signifying one thing in Brooklyn and something else in the Bronx' (54). To record these words, to attribute them to a specific population, to ferret out their private meanings, to trace their evolution, all of these actions give Frannie a modicum of control, a means of gaining temporary ascendancy over the language that, as a woman, so often effects her own disarticulation, reducing her to 'two tits, a hole, and a heartbeat' (51). In Moore's novel, a lexicographer is hardly, as Samuel Johnson cheekily defined it, 'a harmless drudge'; she is an investigator, continually returning to the scene of the crime – that point at which various cultural pressures create a tear in an existing language system, out of which emerges a new term that brings to light something formerly secret, taboo, inexpressible, and unsayable. That so many of these terms emerge out of the interstices of sex and violence attests to Moore's belief in how deeply intertwined they are within the human psyche and, moreover, how desperate we all are to understand the origins of our own desirous and destructive impulses.

Sex is the focal point for Frannie's investigations because it is, in her view, 'a conspiracy of improvised myths. Very effective in evoking forbidden or hidden wishes' (125). Her attraction to Detective Malloy might therefore be understood as an effort to uncover her own unconscious motivations through improvisations of the mythic story of Philomela, whose brother-in-law rapes her and cuts out her tongue to prevent her from testifying to her own violation, that myth representing 'the hidden part' of Frannie's story, 'the region that is still unexplored because there are as yet no words to enable us to get there' (Calvino 1986: 18). That a story about disarticulation would resonate so strongly with a student of language makes an intuitive kind of sense, for what is to be feared more by those whose power resides in words than the deprivation of speech? However, that explanation does not fully account for the allure that these dangerous encounters hold for her or for why she actively seeks out situations in which she will be rendered, for all intents and purposes, mute. If, as she insists, she 'is not a masochist', then what is she seeking when she affirms her belief that one must demystify the forbidden and hidden, even if it means 'surrendering to the soul's transformation, however terrifying it may be' (1995: 125)? For Frannie to be a masochist, victimization – and the unspoken pain and humiliation that attend it – would be an end in itself. Frannie, though, does not want to be a victim; rather, she wants to experience and understand what lies beyond that moment of trauma that precedes victimization, a subjective state outside language or, to put it another way, subjectivity disarticulated from language. In other words, she is courting what Lyotard calls the 'nothingness that "separates" one phrase from the "following"', the blank space that opens up before a victim is created through the total silencing of her voice (138).

In the Cut ends with Frannie in the killing room of the man she saw in the basement of *The Red Turtle,* a man who turns out to be not her lover but his partner, Detective Rodriguez, with whom Malloy shares the same three of spades tattoo. Unlike in *The Mermaids Singing* and *The Girl with the Dragon Tattoo*, though, there is no last minute salvation, no witness to what is being done to Frannie's body but Frannie herself. Faced with her own imminent demise and suffering through a slow and torturous mutilation by the killer, Frannie's narrational perspective becomes increasingly distant but also sharper and more precise. To take in all of the details becomes her obsession, because, as she says, 'I just knew this, that it would make a difference. I didn't try to understand it. I kept it simple. Malloy would have been proud' (174–75).

Of course, when it comes to giving evidence in a court of law, being able to recount the event objectively can make all the difference, but Frannie is not destined to be a claimant; she is going to be made a victim. The 'difference' it will make for her, then, is personal, having to do with her experience of the event itself. When Rodriguez makes the first cut – slicing across her throat, an act wedding physical and symbolic disarticulation – the effect is to dislocate her thoughts from their centre of self. She adopts the perspectival frame of the investigator, filtering out her subjective response to the violence so that (as Malloy once told her), 'Your whole world at that moment comes down to that body' (176). As Rodriguez continues, she considers her own violated body dispassionately, clinically, and yet still in the first-person. It isn't until he takes her nipple for a 'souvenir', though, that the full effect of disarticulation is manifested in her inner monologue:

> He grabbed me by the back of my neck, pressing the razor against my breast, just under the nipple, the nipple resting on the edge of the blade, the razor cutting smoothly, easily, through the taut cloth, through the skin, the delicate blue skein of netted veins in flood, the nipple cut round, then the breast opening, the dark blood running like a dark river, the Indian river, the sycamore, my body so vivid that I was blinded. My breast. My breastesses. (176)

In an earlier discussion, Malloy describes the souvenir taken by the killer as that crucial 'something missing', a synecdoche for the body that serves to call up in the killer's memory the crime itself, allowing him the fantasy of 'do[ing] it all over again' (77). For his victim, though, without the 'rose nipple' to give her breast 'weight, to give it meaning', her body becomes an overwhelming locus of sensation, blindingly vivid, open to the elements. Lacking now a clear sense of the division between physical being and the world beyond, Frannie can only cognitively process the trauma in a figurative register, substituting for the mutilated real body a symbolic landscape or, to reapply an idiomatic term used by one of her students, a 'murder-scape', a territory explored and mapped through an act of sexual violence. That Frannie increasingly describes the experience of sexual abuse in terms of signs and slang highlights the dismantling of subjectivity that accompanies violation, as the individual becomes overmastered, penetrated, effaced by the actions of another. At the same time, the disturbingly beautiful images and idiomatic expressions she uses in these last moments also work against this obliterating violence, by giving her a means of retreat into the intricacies of language at its most mysterious and secret. Reflecting on one final idiomatic expression, 'in the cut' – gambler's argot which Frannie defines as 'a place to hide. To hedge your bet. But someplace safe, someplace free from harm' (179) – Moore's protagonist shifts her focus away from the subjective experience of sexual violence to what comes next. In an uncompromisingly bleak final two sentences, Frannie narrates her own extinction as a subject, the vanishing point where one's voice is silenced in victimization and death. She recites a lyric she read on the subway and then states: 'I know the poem. She knows the poem'. The shift from first-person to third-person makes manifest her crossing over the unbridgeable divide of the differend, affirming her lingering existence, in her fading voice, with her dying breath.

Conclusion

She knows the poem. In Frannie's narrational fade-to-black, Susanna Moore eloquently gestures not only to the extinction of (first-)personhood suffered by the victim of sexual violence through an act that reduces her to something less than the sum of her parts, but also to one of the challenges faced by those who would attempt to document this process. As the novels of McDermid, Larsson, and Moore all demonstrate, *knowing* is one thing – *reciting* is another. To inhabit the role of the rape victim is to occupy a position vis-à-vis dominant culture where one's testimony is de-legitimated by the very experience about which one would testify. A parallel might here be drawn to the situation of the writer of crime fiction who endeavours to represent the scene of sexual violence – to narrativize this scene is, in the minds of many readers, the same thing as sensationalizing it. To record all of the 'grisly' details of a rape or other forms of sexualized violence is often enough, it seems, to render the motivations of the author suspect and to elicit accusations of voyeurism and prurience. Moreover, the silencing of the rape victim so carefully explored by McDermid, Larsson, and Moore is strangely reproduced in contemporary reviews of their novels that both elide and misrepresent the novelists' depictions of sexual violence. Thus, for *The Mermaids Singing,* McDermid is rather sarcastically applauded by one reviewer for 'find[ing] new ways to shock and revolt us in her account of a sadistic madman who captures sexually ambivalent men' (Stasio 1996) while the brutal rape of Lisbeth Salander in Larsson's novel is euphemistically and erroneously described as 'a nasty plot detour involving a lawyer foolish enough to try to take advantage of her' (Berenson 2008). In the case of *In the Cut*, an uncharacteristically sloppy review by Michiko Kakutani in *The New York Times* lambasts Moore for 'insist[ing] on sensationalizing those adventures with highly graphic descriptions of violence and sex, as if she were trying to translate the work of Joe Eszterhas and Paul Verhoeven to the page' (1995). That Kakutani has not read closely enough to know that Moore's protagonist is not an 'unnamed narrator' only adds insult to the more serious injury of comparing Frannie to the cartoonish female sexual predators at the centre of contemporaneous Eszterhas/Verhoeven films such as *Basic Instinct* (US 1992) and *Showgirls* (US 1995). Yet, her prim chastising of Moore for 'trying to startle the reader with gratuitously violent descriptions' gestures towards a more fundamental and pervasive squeamishness about what is being described – moments of violence that are 'gratuitous' insofar as they exceed the boundaries of what can be psychologically, socially, politically, and even linguistically accommodated. That said, the problem in these instances lies not with language, but with what a given culture is comfortable with expressing. As Lyotard observes, 'no one doubts that language is capable of admitting these new phrase families or new genres of discourse. Every wrong ought to be able to be put into phrases. A new competence (or "prudence") must be found' (1988: 13). If there is not yet a way to fictionalize acts of sexual violence that does not seem gratuitous or over-the-top, all that means is that we must find new phrases and create new genres that are capable of doing this work. And if Moore, McDermid, and Larsson all fall a bit short of this goal, their fictions nevertheless underscore the absolute necessity of the effort.

Note

1. Each phrase, Lyotard argues, 'is constituted according to a set of rules', which pertain to the function or purpose of a particular phrase regimen, be it 'reasoning, knowing, describing, recounting, questioning, showing, ordering, etc' (xii). Since they are heterogeneous, phrases from different phrase regimens 'cannot be translated from one into the other'; they can only be linked together within the context of a particular 'genre of discourse'. That said, as a single phrase could conceivably be linked to any number of different phrases, the act of linkage through which a phrase is actualized within language also constitutes the severing of that phrase from other potential regimens and genres. Articulation is thus also disarticulation; something is put into language through the carving away of other potential somethings. At this site of dis/articulation is what Lyotard calls the *differend*, a fundamental, irresolvable conflict or dispute in which there is no 'rule of judgment' capable of encompassing and reconciling the contrary claims of the opposing sides (1988: xi).

Works cited

Berenson, A. (2008) 'Vanished', *The New York Times*, 14 Sep, http://www.nytimes.com/2008/09/14/books/review/Berenson-t.html?_r=1&scp=1&sq=berenson%20dragons%20tattoo&st=cse, accessed 4 Nov 2011.
Calvino, I. (1986) *The Uses of Literature*. Transl. P. Creagh. New York: Mariner Books.
Kakutani, M. (1995) 'She has an ear for slang and an eye for trouble', *The New York Times*, 31 Oct, http://www.nytimes.com/1995/10/31/books/books-of-the-times-she-has-an-ear-for-slang-and-an-eye-for-trouble.html?ref=susannamoore, accessed 4 Nov 2011.
Larsson, S. (2009) *The Girl with the Dragon Tattoo*. Transl. R. Keeland. New York: Vintage Crime/ Black Lizard.
Lyotard, J. (1988) *The Differend: Phrases in Dispute*. Transl. G. Van Den Abbeele Minneapolis: University of Minnesota Press.
McDermid, V. (1995) *The Mermaids Singing*. New York: St Martin's Press.
Moore, S. (1995) *In the Cut*. New York: Alfred A. Knopf.
Shakespeare, W . (2002) *Titus Andronicus*. Oxford: Oxford University Press.
Stasio, M. (1996) 'Crime', *The New York Times*, Dec 22, http://www.nytimes.com/1996/12/22/books/crime-725340.html, accessed 4 Nov 2011.

8
Male Fantasy, Sexual Exploitation, and the *Femme Fatale*: Reframing Scripts of Power and Gender in Neo-*noir* Novels by Sara Paretsky, Megan Abbott and Stieg Larsson

Zoë Brigley Thompson

In the classic retro-*noir* movie, *Chinatown*, the private eye, Jake Gittes, makes a significant statement regarding the dynamics of power between men and women in hard-boiled narratives. Ostensibly trying to reassure the mysterious Evelyn Mulwray, Gittes's comment is extremely revealing about his attitude to the *femme fatale*:

> Just tell me the truth. I'm not the police. I don't care what you've done. I'm not going to hurt you, but one way or another I'm going to know. (*Chinatown*, Polanski and Towne 1974)

In conventional *noir* plots and the post-*noirs* that follow, the private eye seeks to break open the mystery of the *femme fatale* with supposedly benevolent violence. In addition, as the following analysis illustrates, post-*noir* narratives often portray their *femme fatales* as victims of brutality and abuse, like Evelyn Mulwray in *Chinatown* who was abused by her father. What this chapter focuses on, however, is new *noir* novels that subvert the victimization of the *femme fatale* and the scripts of power between the detective and the object of his or her scrutiny. These *femme fatales* may be victims of abuse, but by refusing the interrogative gaze of the private 'eye', they retain their dignity, privacy, and power. As the *femme fatale* in Sara Paretsky's *Body Work* asserts, '*You can get this close, as close as my skin, but you can't get inside me. I control the boundaries*'

(2010: 142). Paretsky's *femme fatale* promises that though the detective can be 'as close as my skin', physical contact is not enough to penetrate her, and there are 'boundaries' beyond which the investigator cannot reach (Paretsky 2010: 142). Such a statement takes on great significance in the context of survivors of sexual violence, and the *femme fatale* remains a mysterious and impenetrable figure: a fatal woman who is what Mary Ann Doane calls 'a figure of certain discursive unease, a potential epistemological trauma' (1991: 1).

The modern *femme fatale* emerged during the beginning of the *noir* genre in the sexy sadism of pulp fiction in magazines like *Black Mask*, and consequently in the novels of Raymond Chandler, Dashiell Hammett, and James M. Cain. Classic *noir* fiction was often subversive in its gender roles, offering vulnerable heroes and powerful heroines who represented post-war male anxiety about women's new political and social freedoms (Abbott 2002: 2; Biesen 2005; Chopra-Grant 2006; Fay and Nieland 2010; Spicer 2005). The Hollywood treatment of such stories, however, sought to re-establish retroactive gender norms, and Sheri Chinen Biesen suggests that, in classic *noir* films, there was a tendency for women to be sexually exploited, citing the example of *Gilda* (Vidor, US, 1946), where the *femme fatale* is revealed to be 'a victim of the misogynistic, violent men around her' and 'a virtual prisoner of her twisted heterosexual relationships' (2004: 70). Wager warns too that in post-*noir* films the complexity of the original *noir* genre is often reduced to 'a fantasy [...] of violent and repressive white male power and female passivity' (2005: 22). Wager categorizes this conservative type of post-*noir* as a 'retro-*noir*', a genre that 'provides an ideologically safe site for the portrayal of reactionary representations of gender, of muscular, violent, and successful white masculinity, and of passive and objectified femininity' (2005: 76). In contrast to the retro-*noir*, however, Wager poses the 'neo-*noir*', which is revisionist 'especially with regard to gender' (22).

Though Wager poses the term 'neo-*noir*' in the context of films, the analysis here applies it to three recent novels by authors Sara Paretsky, Megan Abbott, and Stieg Larsson.[1] Paretsky and Abbott are both female American crime writers, while Larsson is a male Swedish crime author, but all three use the *noir* genre to subvert retrograde scripts of gender and sexual power. These three writers also represent three different approaches to using the *noir* genre. Paretsky creates a female version of the hard-boiled detective for a modern, feminist age, while Abbott is preoccupied with rewriting the gender scripts of 1930s and 1940s heroines, revealing the sexual appetite beneath a sanitized vision of women's sexuality. Larsson is perhaps the least obvious in his employment of *noir* iconography, and while his indebtedness to English crime fiction is often noted, the influence of American *noir* fiction has not been discussed in as much detail.[2] Indeed, part of the mass appeal of the Millennium trilogy is the mysterious girl, a familiar *noir* plot device, but Larsson complicates the traditional vision of the *femme fatale*. Paretsky, Abbott, and Larsson have this strategy in common, since all three are concerned with scrutinizing and subverting the gender dynamic of the probing detective and the fatal woman.

The retro-*noir*, as defined by Wager, inculcates gendered scripts of power and violation with a new power, while the neo-*noir* seeks to subvert the gender conventions of the genre. Though *Chinatown* (Polanski, US, 1974) is a film not a novel, it is useful to briefly consider its narrative conventions as characteristic of a retro-*noir*, especially as it was pioneering in its treatment of *noir* and sexual violence. In *Chinatown*, Gittes is determined to uncover both the enigma of Evelyn's husband's murder and of Evelyn herself. What emerges is that Evelyn was abused by her father, Noah Cross, who is also the murderer of her husband. This overt connection between sexual violence and the *femme fatale* is not untypical, according to Jack Boozer, who explains that from the 1970s onwards, the *femme fatale* was not so much a 'criminally depraved and castrating' character but 'an object of ongoing social and personal abuse' (1999: 21, 24). Though *Chinatown* works to 'unveil [society's] brutish aspects' through the uncovering of the *femme fatale*'s 'personal disasters', the breaking open of the *femme*'s privacy forces her into an ambiguous position of victimhood and denies her any sense of autonomy (24). *Chinatown* perpetuates gendered sexual scripts where men are powerful, dominant, and commanding, and women remain passive, vulnerable, and rapable, even if they give an initial impression of power. Retro-*noir* narratives, like that of *Chinatown*, also promote the idea that women are complicit in their own suffering and sexual slavery, since, as James F. Maxfield notes, *Chinatown* is ambiguous with regard to whether 'the incest occurred as the result of a rape rather than a seduction to which Evelyn at least half-willingly succumbed' (1996: 127). The *femme fatale* is just another in a long line of mythological and allegorical women punished for their own cunning: a Pandora or an Eve.

In her study, *The Street was Mine*, crime author Abbott suggests that the problem with retro-*noirs* such as *Chinatown* is the detective's inability to see that, when it comes to the *femme fatale*, 'both sides of the binary are true, undercutting all convention, expectation, sense of coherent order' (2002: 195). This undercutting of passive/active binaries is exhibited in the neo-*noir* crime narratives of Paretsky's *Body Work* (2010), Abbott's *Bury Me Deep* (2009), and Larsson's *The Girl with the Dragon Tattoo* (2005). All three novels subvert classic hard-boiled stories and their key moment where the *femme fatale* is 'broken open'. As Virginia M. Allen points out, male anxiety about changing gender roles after World War II is embodied by the *femme fatale* in the *noir* genre, as she represents women's independence and ambitions. As a consequence, the *femme fatale* is often associated with other foci of male anxiety such as racial and colonial otherness or animal others (Doane 1991: 209; Flory 2010; Orr 2010). For Doane, the femme fatale is, to quote Freud, 'a dark continent' (1991: 209). Like a colonial explorer, the *noir* detective needs to 'conquer woman – to objectify her as a "thing" to be dominated and possessed, since only through domination can one conquer the fear' (Allen 1983: 7). This domination is often achieved through the use of supposedly benevolent violence, when the detective uncovers the truth behind the *femme fatale*'s duplicitous appearance. This is the power dynamic at the heart of the *noir* genre: the macho detective breaking down the *femme fatale*'s defences, breaking open the mystery that she presents, and consequently shoring up his own masculine pride. Paretsky, Abbott, and Larsson subvert this dynamic and seek to manipulate or reverse the terms of the binary that opposes detective and *femme fatale*, violator and violated. It is unsurprising, then, that all three novels use the association of the *femme fatale* with non-white or colonial subjects and with animalistic imagery to draw attention to her disturbing otherness. The novels highlight how the *femme fatale* is employed by men as a blank canvas upon which fantasies of sexual power and exploitation can be projected. In this scenario, it is impossible to truly 'break open' the mystery of the *femme fatale* because, as Doane hints, she 'never really is what she seems to be', or rather, she is never the fantasy figure that men imagine her to be (1991:1).

In each of these three novels, the *femme fatales* suffer sexual exploitation and violence, but all three novels seek to undermine representations of these women as solely passive without belittling the devastating consequences of sexual violation. The *femme fatale* often suffers from a similar power dynamic as the rape survivor, as 'a means for the satisfaction of [man's] desires for sexualized power' (Cahill 2001: 193–194). Paretsky, Abbott, and Larsson, however, contest the positioning of women's bodies as inherently 'rapable' and hence culpable, a myth that explains *Chinatown*'s dubious attitude to the sexual abuse of Evelyn.

The writers also emphasize that the explanation for sexual crimes does not lie in the survivor's behaviour; blame is placed solely on the rapist, who is framed as the *femme fatale*'s deadly opposite: the *homme fatale*. With his origins in 'Gothic noirs' such as Alfred Hitchcock's 1941 film *Suspicion*, the *homme fatale* often appears at first to be a stolid, reliable husband or suitor, but he is actually a version of the fairy-tale Bluebeard who uses his charms to satisfy a 'deep-rooted sexual sadism' (Spicer 2002: 89). His appetites for money, power, and sex are voracious. The *homme fatale* is normally a pillar of society, a status that masks his brutality and violence towards women. In Paretsky's *Body Work*, the *homme fatale* is represented by corporation executives who are complicit in rape and murder. Abbott conjures a specific character in *Bury Me Deep*, the respected drugstore owner Joe Lannigan, who is also the sexual exploiter and murderer of young women. Finally, Larsson reveals that a number of socially respectable men maintain a secret desire to brutalize women, including Lisbeth Salander's guardian Advokat Nils Bjurman, and head of the Vanger Corporation, Martin Vanger. Each novel emphasizes that sexual violence is staged and orchestrated through 'the strange, baffling or malevolent behaviour of the *homme fatale*' (Spicer 2002: 93).

Beyond the reach of the *homme fatale*, however, there are possibilities for healing, and space for resistance and recuperation. The novels express this complexity by subverting the traditional *femme fatale*, synthesizing the fatal spider woman with more humanized models of womanhood. As versions of the 'good-bad girl', the heroines can initially seem to be 'cynical', 'wilful', or 'obsessed with money' but, as Spicer notes, 'this stems from disillusionment with men' (92). Paretsky's Artist, Abbott's Marion Seeley, and Larsson's Lisbeth Salander are all represented with ambivalence, and even appear selfish at times, but they are also heroic. Wager describes this subversive model of the *femme fatale* as one who 'fights against male economic and social domination, usually at the cost of her life or her freedom' (2005:4). The analysis that follows will show how these neo-*noir* novels subvert the role of the *femme fatale* as spider woman to convey sympathetic narratives about sexual exploitation that offer possibilities of healing. As Abbott confirms, 'The visual power of the femme fatale and the dominance of her image […] may carry more potency than all the male-centred, male-identified, and male-narrated stories that sought to contain her' (2002: 138). Rather than being an enigma to be broken open and violated, the neo-*noir*'s *femme fatale* represents the complexity of a world where men and women not only act on others, but are acted upon.

Body Work

Spanning a period from the 1980s to the present day, Paretsky's hard-boiled VI Warshawski series paralleled the '[w]oman-centered *neo-noir* films of the 1980s and 90s' which began to 'showcase tough women cops and detectives operating with action, clarity, and decisiveness in a male-centered world' (Corey 1999: 311). Set in contemporary Chicago, VI lives 'in a place of indifference, greed, corruption – a jungle, a monster', but she is anything but a victim (Kinsman 1995: 16). According to Paretsky, the mystery genre is 'ideally suited for addressing social issues', and VI is an unconventional harbinger of justice, uncovering all manner of crimes, including sexual violence (cited in James 1998: 288). Often this plotting involves sexual abuse (for example, the mistreatment of Louisa Djiak in *Blood Shot*), but rarely is VI ever subjected to sexual violence, the exception being *Hard Time*, in which she is sexually assaulted in prison. While Abbott and Larsson allow their *femme fatales* to be avengers in a spin on the rape-revenge plot, Paretsky finds the two roles incompatible. Like the traditional *noir* detective, VI scrutinizes the *femme fatale* with mistrust in *Body Work*. Though the *femme* is created out of a legacy of sexual violence, VI regards her as dangerous because she employs her sexuality and beauty as power, a retrograde strategy in Paretsky's view, since it makes oneself an object of the male gaze and consequently a victim. This projection of male fantasies onto women's bodies is key in the sexual domination and exploitation of two characters: the Body Artist and Nadia Guaman, who were lovers and who are both subjected to sexual violence.

The Body Artist's act involves performing naked onstage at Club Gouge, inviting the audience to paint on her stripped body. This act recalls Marina Abramoviç's 1974 installation *Rhythm 0,* during which an audience were invited to make whatever use of her body they saw fit; the incident ended in a near rape (Green 2001: 165). The Artist forces VI to evaluate her provocative naked performance as both powerful and futile, forcing the question: 'Who was the exploiter, who was exploited?' (Paretsky 2010: 25). This enigma reverberates throughout the book as VI learns more about the Artist. This trail is signified by the Artist's many names, which VI uncovers; she is the Artist, she is the prosaic Karen Buckley, and finally she is Francine Pindero, who was abused as a teenager at gangster 'sex parties'.

As in most classic hard-boiled stories, Paretsky's *femme fatale* does not represent herself, but is presented through VI's first-person narration. Commenting on the use of voice-over in *noir* films, Karen Hollinger points out that *femme fatale*s are often trapped within male readings that 'try to interpret the meaning of femaleness by male standards' (1996: 245). Quoting Doane, Hollinger emphasizes that the act of 'embedding her words within a case history' is a means to 'control the woman's access to language and the narrative of agency' (Doane 1987: 54). *Body Work* does not reverse this trend, but VI does not objectify or vilify the *femme fatale*. The exotic paintings on the Artist's website display '[a] face painted like a tiger', and 'a jungle scene', images that employ a colonial imaginary, while, in her act, the Artist employs the most contemporary other in Western binaries – the Islamic religion – as 'two figures clad in burkas gyrated in time to the music' (Paretsky 2010: 12). The pictures and dancers create an association between the Artist and symbols of racial otherness recalling the *femme fatale*'s association with other sources of anxiety for white men. Being covered up, the dancers (who are really men) remain – like the *femme fatale* of male fantasy – 'a symbol of the unknowable' (Abbott 2002: 197).

Just as the dancers in burkas remain anonymous to the audience, so the Artist is difficult to read. Paretsky expresses this feeling poetically when VI visits the Artist's apartment, only to find 'several large Rorschachs of blood [that] stained the ice on the porch and stairs' (Paretsky 2010: 280). The ink blots of the Rorschach Test are interpreted according to the viewer's desires and needs, just as the Artist becomes a projection of personal fantasies. During her act, the Artist tells the audience, 'I'm your canvas, your – bare – canvas' (13). Paretsky emphasizes, however, that the Artist's nakedness on stage does not guarantee penetration of her identity or history. VI's artist friend, Tessa, comments that the Artist is 'exposing herself, but not her *self*', and the Artist's lover, Allie Guaman, writes in her diary that '*I get no real glimpse of her, only the many masks she wears in public*' (72, 380). The Artist's anonymity means that she is 'a blank canvas where people imagined whatever they wanted' (429). The projection is 'Usually an erotic fantasy' but VI discovers that the gangster Anton Kystarnik uses the Artist 'as a message board', painting codes on her body to communicate his illegal deals (429). When Kystarnik's man, Rodney, paints the codes on the Artist's buttocks, VI describes the act as 'so aggressive that his painting looked like a sexual assault' (118). The painting of the codes is a symbolic violation that serves to remind how Kystarnik (a Bluebeard who murdered his wife) forced the Artist 'to help entertain his friends', and how she became a drug user 'to get through the night' (490). The Artist, however, refuses to be broken open like Evelyn in *Chinatown*, and her brief, dispassionate comment on Kystarnik's 'sex parties' never positions her as a victim. Warshawski describes her instead as a complex and difficult woman: 'a black hole: she drew emotions in, but reflected nothing out' (428–429).

The second strand of the narrative in *Body Work* revolves around the rape and murder of Allie Guaman, a young woman in the employ of a contractor in Iraq, the Tintrey Corporation. Paretsky's story echoes allegations in the late 2000s that female employees of American contractors in Iraq had been raped by fellow workers and the crimes covered up by their corporate employers (Roberts 2007). In *Body Work*, Allie's murder is covered up by Tintrey, and they employ Kystarnik's gangsters to murder her artist sister Nadia, who knows too much. Allie is another kind of *femme fatale*, though an unwitting one; as a lesbian, she refuses the advances of her male co-workers in Iraq, but her reserve only heightens her desirability as a canvas for projected male fantasies. Reading Allie's diary, VI discovers that Allie becomes associated with the racial and religious otherness represented by the dancers in burkas, as she cultivates a relationship with an Iraqi woman, Amani. The diary describes how on meeting her boss, Mr Mossbach, who supposedly wants to give her some advice on her job, Allie has to fend off an assault: 'A drink led to attempted sex; she fought him off, and then her life became hell indeed' (Paretsky 2010: 386). Ultimately, Allie is 'raped, murdered, and then set on fire and left in a public place so that everyone would assume she had been victim of an Iraqi assault' (427).

Paretsky cleverly juxtaposes the Artist, who intentionally takes on the persona of *femme fatale*, and Allie, who unwittingly becomes a source of male fantasy. Ultimately, however, Paretsky directs the blame at the Tintrey executives, who are ostensibly respectable, but who emerge as devious and calculating *homme fatale*s. Complicit with the positioning of women as rapable, the Tintrey executives hold little regard for women's bodies except as commodities pliable to their ready cash. After viewing the Artist's act, one executive admits that he 'thought about sticking a twenty up that girl's sunshine' (120). When the Tintrey executives frame the Iraq veteran Chad Vishneski for the shooting of Allie's sister, Nadia, it is of huge symbolic significance that they use the date-rape drug Rohypnol in their murder attempt. Their complicity with sexual violence is matched by their voracious appetite for monetary satisfaction as they knowingly supply the US Army with faulty body armour. When VI challenges the executives, they reveal a sinister yearning for domination and she describes their insatiable 'need to be in power over others' (221–222).

Though VI is never a victim of Kystarnik or the Tintrey executives, she symbolically explores a loss of autonomy when she poses as the

Body Artist at the end of the novel in order to draw out the real Artist. Sitting naked onstage, VI describes herself as 'exposed, powerless', and she imagines herself objectified by the audience as 'a giant doll, really, not a woman at all' (468, 469). VI's sense of vulnerability and exposure is described powerfully: 'My naked body under the spotlight, a perfect target' (475). This insight into the experience of posing naked onstage is a surprising counterpoint to the Artist's impenetrable blankness, and emphasizes the *femme fatale*'s status as a complex and difficult woman, one who undermines the binaries of victim versus vamp.

Bury Me Deep

While *Body Work* focuses on the female PI's investigation of the *femme fatale*, Abbott's *Bury Me Deep* presents a subversive twist on a different kind of hard-boiled hero. Abbott's protagonist Marion Seeley is a version of the hapless 'sap driven to crime', most famously presented in novels by James M. Cain, such as *Double Indemnity* (Abbott 2002: 7). Marion is led astray by a *homme fatale*, Joe Lannigan, who wants to create a fatal woman to satisfy his perverse sexual appetites. The novel's third-person subjective narrative makes *Bury Me Deep* different in approach to *Body Work*. Abbott privileges Marion's story in a way that is normally only allowed for *noir* detectives and, foregrounding Seeley's inner monologue, she offers illuminating insights into how and why the *femme fatale* is constructed. Abbott offers a pastiche of classic *noir* fiction by Chandler, Hammett, and Cain, but she also offers a female point of view, subverting conventions so that the male hero becomes fatal and the *femme fatale* is humanized, likeable, and sympathetic. As Hollinger asserts, *noir* stories are often told to the reader or audience in order 'to grant a kind of absolution and to act as a curative force' (1996: 244). Similarly, Marion's version of the story is presented as a means of finding absolution for her sexual exploitation at the hands of 'Gentleman' Joe.

Set in 1930s small-town America, *Bury Me Deep* presents Marion in an unhappy marriage. While her husband, Dr Seeley, goes to Mexico to beat his drug addiction, Marion meets the voluptuous, red-headed Louise at the clinic where they work. Through Louise, Marion encounters 'Gentleman' Joe Lannigan, the owner of a chain of pharmacies, and, after some resistance, they begin a sexual relationship. However, once Joe has had intercourse with Marion he becomes bored and seeks more perverse interactions. What Marion does not know (but which emerges later) is that Louise has been blackmailing Joe for drug-dealing and abusing his wife. Feeding Louise's lover, Ginny, with drugs, Joe is directly responsible for Ginny's accidental death when she threatens Louise with a pistol, and he takes advantage of the confusion to shoot Louise too. Marion only comes to realize the full implications of his actions when he has put her on a train to Los Angeles with the bodies in a trunk. Marion is the 'fall guy' for the killings and is only saved from prison by Dr Seeley, who commits suicide leaving a note which claims that he is the murderer. Marion is free to expose Joe to the community as a *homme fatale*.

The plot of *Bury Me Deep* is as sensational as any Cain novel, but, in a serious way, it also engages with sexual exploitation and the objectification of women in male fantasy. The short prologue at the beginning of the novel describes one of Louise's parties, presenting an image of female sexual submission: 'They lay there on their daybed, men all standing over round' (Abbott 2009: 3). Such women are objects for male manipulation and pleasure, and sexual exploitation of women is a recurrent theme of the novel. Marion recalls her church friend Evangeline who describes sex as being '*riven in two*', '*like a hot poker stuck*', or '*wire sticking in me*' (34). Louise confesses to Marion that she was raped as a young girl, commenting: '*You haven't had to scrub with horsehair brush the soft flesh on the inside of your thighs, rubbing away things left behind by three gentlemen in pale suits who caught you practicing dance steps behind the church on a summer night*' (173). Marion herself becomes a victim of sexual violation, when she encounters her Gothic *homme fatale* or Bluebeard, 'Gentleman' Joe.

At the beginning of *Bury Me Deep*, Marion bears more resemblance to the *femme attrapée*, 'the passive, domestic antithesis to the femme fatale' (Wager 2005: 4). Frustrated with her asexual role as 'a very good homemaker', Marion discovers a more erotic self at the parties of Louise and Ginny (Abbott 2009: 8). Singing for the male visitors, Marion conjures the *femme fatale* as torch singer, such as Rita Hayworth singing 'Put the Blame on Mame' in the notorious scene from the movie *Gilda* (Vidor, US, 1946). One of the guests compares her to the actress Sylvia Sidney, famous for playing gangster's molls, and another tells her that she could be 'making Scarface Capone cry into his beer' (17–18). By the end of the novel, after the murders, Marion is regarded as 'a stranger, an alien thing', a 'beast or witch', 'a madwoman', and 'a tigress', recalling the exotic, colonial imaginary that signified the unknowable qualities of the Artist in *Body Work* (159, 159, 203).

Marion becomes a *femme fatale* because of sexual violation and degradation at the hands of 'Gentleman' Joe. To the community at large, Joe is respectable: 'Beloved husband and father. Man about town. Friar. Knight of Columbus Member' (62). Repeatedly described as a knight, Joe promises to save Marion from her loveless marriage, telling her: 'Were you my wife, I'd not lose my way from you. I'd not abandon you to the world' (37). However, ambiguous descriptions of Joe reveal his hidden appetites for sex and power. His smile is 'like a swinging gate' and he smells of 'wind and travel and far-off places', while his hair is blindingly 'blond and bright' (23–24). Joe's smile might easily swing to a frown, but he has an exotic, erotic appeal for Marion which blinds her to his faults. He describes Marion as a 'peach', signalling his sexual appetites, and she is rendered passive when Louise comments: 'We haven't wrapped her for you yet', an image echoed again when Marion describes herself as an object in 'a game of Pass the Parcel' (24, 42). Recalling Paretsky's use of doll imagery to describe the *femme fatale*, Marion pictures herself as 'a baby doll rocking in the corner', signalling both her objectification and a sense of inconsolable trauma in the 'rocking' movement (28).

Joe's obvious desire for Marion is tantalizing at first, and his gaze feels to Marion like 'the tip of his finger [...] tickling the lace bristles on her underthings' (34). There is no such delicacy, however, once their sexual relationship begins in earnest; instead, Marion is 'rubbed to roughness, to blood-pocked, flushy ruin' (64). Joe uses the language of a conqueror, telling Marion, '*you are mine*', and he states, unabashedly, 'I have made you a whore' (49, 64). The gender script of male penetration and female opening-up is obvious when Joe describes Marion as a '*Pandora*': 'the little black box I had to, had to open' (65). Once 'opened', however, Marion has little appeal, so she remakes herself as a *femme fatale*, dyeing her hair platinum blonde. In her new guise, Marion regains her mystery and glamour 'like a swirling puff of cotton edged in bright silver' or a 'twisting silver pinwheel' (71). Marion's transformation into a blonde *femme fatale* recalls Abbott's discussion of the 'ostentatious blonde-banged wig' worn by Barbara Stanwyck in *Double Indemnity* (Wilder, US, 1944) (2002: 141). The blonde wig 'embodies such falseness, such artifice that [Stanwyck] points to her role as the projection [...] of male fantasies and fear' (141). The remaking of Marion represents her desperate attempt to become a male fantasy, which is recognized by Joe when he comments on her new appearance: 'I like all Marions, old and new [...] And I like how many Marions there are. And how many there are to give' (Abbott 2009: 72).

When Marion is no longer enough for Joe, she furnishes him with a young nurse, Elsie, hoping that her actions might allow 'months of love unfettered by deviance' (104). During this low point of Marion's experiences, she *is* a traditional *femme fatale*: amoral, dubious, and complicit. After the murders, Joe certainly imagines Marion as a 'cunning witch' onto whom he can displace his guilt and desire. Regarding Marion, he states, 'all I see is death [...] dead girls and sorrow', and reversing Marion's impression of Joe's blindingly blonde hair, he adds: 'Your beauty is blinding but behind it I see death' (169). Ironically, Joe projects his own violence and amorality onto Marion's *femme fatale*, leaving her to take the blame for his crimes. He retreats behind his respectability boasting: 'There are levers and switches and keys and I know which way they all go' (168).

In contrast to Joe, Marion is never truly fatal because she feels tremendous guilt about her role in the exploitation of Elsie, and the killings of Louise and Ginny. For example, Marion is horrified by Elsie's expression after she has sex with Joe, 'like a hook caught in her mouth and dragged round' (104). Marion realizes that she has passed on a legacy of violence and sexual humiliation, sacrificing the women around her, who she has 'wrapped [...] with a fat ribbon' (113). Marion is victimized and manipulated for much of the novel, and in some ways, she recalls the victimized *femme fatale* of the retro-*noir*. In contrast to Evelyn in *Chinatown*, however, Marion is not rendered totally passive, as she rediscovers her own power by avenging herself on Joe. Using her manipulative powers, Marion becomes a genuine *femme fatale,* and the 'shuddering' *femme attrapée* is 'gone forever' (185). Being a *femme attrapée*, however, is what created Marion's 'doom' to begin with, and by the end of the novel she rediscovers her power, exposing Joe's illegal dealings, and shooting him in the knee in the final scene. More than a match for Joe's *homme fatale*, Marion's fatal woman is an avenging figure who repeats back to him his earlier boast: 'There are levers, switches, keys, and I know which way they all go' (230).

The Girl with the Dragon Tattoo

While Larsson's *The Girl with the Dragon Tattoo* is not generally thought of in relation to *noir*, a number of self-conscious references link the novel to the reinvention of *noir* traditions, particularly in relation to gender. The journalist-hero, Mikael Blomkvist, reads a number of neo-*noirs* including books by Val McDermid (Larsson 2008: 314) and Paretsky (356). Like McDermid and Paretksy, Larsson revises the traditional mystery plot with regard to gender, and his Millennium trilogy is devoted to understanding Lisbeth Salander, though this does not represent a breaking open, as in the traditional *noir* narrative. Indeed,

Larsson implies that in many *noir* plots violence against women is a breeding ground for misogyny, since in the cabin of the psychotic rapist Gottfried Vanger, Mikael Blomkvist finds novels by 'Mickey Spillane with titles like *Kiss Me Deadly*' (261). Larsson's story does overlap with *noir*, however, especially in relation to the genre's links to psychodrama, which JP Telotte defines as a narrative 'locating and mapping the source of trauma' (2004: 140). Similar to *noir* films like *The Snake Pit* (Litvak, US, 1948) or *The Three Faces of Eve* (Johnson, US, 1957), *The Girl with the Dragon Tattoo* focuses on 'psychotic crimes, desires and violence' (146). Larsson, however, reinvents *noir* tropes by creating a politically subversive narrative around the mysterious Lisbeth Salander, described by Povlsen and Waade as being 'as aggressive as a hardboiled masculine character' (2009: 65).

Like VI Warshawski, Lisbeth Salander can be as tough as a traditional *noir* detective, but she differs because she is subjected to gruelling sexual violence, while VI is never that vulnerable. Lisbeth has similarities, though, with the Artist in *Body Work* and Marion in *Bury Me Deep*, because she is the subject of male fantasies, and Larsson's use of third-person narration is particularly effective in revealing the disparity between men's impressions of Lisbeth and her motivations. As in *Bury Me Deep*, the narrative voice often takes up Lisbeth's point of view, explaining her actions and revealing her in all her complexity. Larsson reveals, however, that because Lisbeth is inscrutable in appearance and behaviour, men often project their fantasies onto her. Men's impressions express anxiety about her lack of emotion – an 'astonishing lack of emotional involvement' (2008: 33) – which is viewed as a fatal quality rather than a symptom of her Asperger's Syndrome. Lisbeth certainly proves to be a fatal woman to 'Men Who Hate Women': her legal guardian Advokat Bjurman, who rapes her; the serial murderer Martin Vanger; and the industrialist Hans-Erik Wennerström, who terrorizes an old lover into having an abortion. Like the executives of Tintrey in *Body Work* or Joe Lannigan in *Bury Me Deep*, the villains of *The Girl with the Dragon Tattoo* are versions of the *homme fatale* who 'get away with their crimes because they are unassailable public figures' (Dipaolo 2011: 120). Lisbeth's role, however, as a fatal arbiter of justice suggests that the *femme fatale* is no longer a token to be exchanged and fought over by men, but a complex creation writing her own narratives of lawfulness and healing.

Whether Lisbeth is a victim or not is a subject of debate throughout the novel. Dragan Armansky, Lisbeth's employer at a security firm, views her as a vulnerable *femme fatale* in the mould of *Chinatown's*

Evelyn, describing her as a 'perfect victim' (Larsson 2008: 50, 367). The reality is far more complex, as Lisbeth is both acted upon and acts upon the world around her. Lisbeth does recognize, however, that as a subject within a system of institutions, she cannot escape being acted on. After being raped by her legal guardian Bjurman, Lisbeth reads that 'The sadist specialised in people who were in a position of dependence', and she recognizes that because of her history of mental health issues and consequent vulnerability, Bjurman 'had chosen her as a victim' (227). This victimhood, however, is something that is projected onto Lisbeth's inscrutable exterior and it tells her 'something about the way she was viewed by other people' (227).

Like the Artist in *Body Work*, Lisbeth is often described as being a blank canvas from which investigators try to extract answers. Teachers and psychiatrists who try to elicit a response from Lisbeth or force her to open up are met, 'to their great frustration, with a sullen silence' (141). Unlike the traditional *noir* plot, Lisbeth is never broken open by these detectives, and so they project onto her their theories about her psychological and sexual motivations. Lisbeth bears comparison with Allie in *Body Work*, since both engage in lesbian relationships and unwittingly attract male sexual fantasies through their distanced, inscrutable personae. Lisbeth is seen by men as 'a foreign creature' (38) and, like Paretsky's Artist, she is associated with racialized otherness in the 'high cheekbones that gave her an almost Asian look' (34). Armansky's questioning of his desire for Lisbeth makes the link to the *femme fatale* explicit; she is not the type he is 'usually attracted to', a type that resembles the classic *femme fatale*: 'blonde and curvaceous, with full lips that aroused his fantasies' (38). Though Lisbeth Salander is not a traditional *femme fatale*, her blankness and inscrutability make her subject to male sexual fantasies. Even the lover with whom she is closest, Mikael Blomkvist, describes her as 'more and more of an enigma' (351) finding himself 'baffled' (357), and it is precisely this mysterious quality which creates her appeal for Blomkvist, who describes her 'like nagging itch, repellent and at the same time tempting' (307).

While Blomkvist is content to be patient and allow Lisbeth to reveal herself in time, the seemingly respectable Advokat Bjurman seeks to break her open symbolically and physically in a power dynamic common for *noir* novels. In his interview with Lisbeth, Bjurman begins by asking questions which become more and more intrusive, ranging from '*Who do you spend time with?*' to '*Have you ever had anal sex?*' (147, 180). Even while he is sexually assaulting her, Bjurman cannot help asking 'You've done this before, haven't you?' (199). What frustrates

Bjurman the most, however, is Lisbeth's silence (200), and her lack of responsiveness only heightens Bjurman's sadistic desire to uncover her through dominating, brutalizing, and raping her.

Martin Vanger, another *homme fatale*, has similar preoccupations to Bjurman. Superficially friendly and helpful in Salander's and Blomkvist's investigations, Martin resembles the Bluebeards Kystarnik in *Body Work* and Joe in *Bury Me Deep*, as he imprisons Blomkvist in his 'private torture chamber' to be violated and murdered (394). Martin explains that he has to 'identify my prey, map out her life, who is she', and his questioning of women's lives and identities is penetrating and sinister: '*Is she married or single? Does she have children and a family? Where does she work? Where does she live?*' (403, 417). Later, Martin's 'death book' is found, which records the details of every woman 'he had ever come into contact with' (417). Just as Bjurman seeks to break open Lisbeth, Martin describes his need to expose and humiliate his victims, taking overwhelming control of their bodies and autonomies.

For men with insatiable appetites for sex, violation, and power like Advokat Bjurman and Martin Vanger, Lisbeth Salander proves to be a fatal spider woman. Her mannerisms are described as being 'quick and spidery' (34), and when she saves Blomkvist from Martin's torture chamber she is described moving 'with the lightning speed of the tarantula' (409). Lisbeth is compared to a witch (504), and is posed in similar animalistic terms to Marion and the Artist in *Body Work*: a tigress who goes 'on the attack' with 'Her teeth bared like a beast of prey' (409). Exposed to such ferocity, Bjurman is tattooed with his true status as a rapist and sadist beneath the respectable mask of the *homme fatale*. When it comes to Wennerström, Lisbeth attacks his appetite for money, using her hacking skills and a *femme fatale*'s disguise of a blonde wig, manicure, make-up, and fake breasts in order to deplete his bank accounts (504–505). Lisbeth's transformation into the blonde figment of Armansky's imagination echoes Marion's remaking of herself with the platinum blonde hair dye in *Bury Me Deep*. In contrast to Marion, however, Lisbeth's disguise is not designed to pander to male fantasy, but to exploit it, cementing her connection to the lethalness of the *femme fatale* as spider woman.

By the end of *The Girl with the Dragon Tattoo*, Lisbeth Salander is revealed as a complex character, both victimized by male brutality and driven to powerfully avenge crimes against women. Some critics have complained that 'All bestial crimes actually committed against women in the novel are suppressed and never brought to public awareness or trial' (Stenport and Alm 2009: 161). The *homme fatale*s are never actually tried for their misogynistic crimes, but maintain their public face of respectability. Lisbeth's desire to maintain secrecy surrounding these events, however, represents a justified resistance to narratives which frame survivors of sexual violence as victims, irretrievably broken open for public spectacle. As Ananya Jahanara Kabir argues, opening up rape narratives can sometimes constitute a 'double violation' (2010: 148). Lisbeth expresses this view to Blomkvist when she asks, 'which is worse – the fact that Martin Vanger raped [Harriet] out in the cabin or that you're going to do it in print?' (Larsson 2008: 461).

Ultimately, in the neo-*noir* secrecy is preferable to the exposure and penetration of vulnerable and brutalized women in the retro-*noir* narratives. The *femme fatale*s in *Body Work*, *Bury Me Deep*, and *The Girl with the Dragon Tattoo* are complex characters, because although they become fatal after experiencing sexual violence, they also find power in their status as spider women. By the end of all three novels, the *femme*s are never truly fathomed, and escape further scrutiny as they disappear. VI allows the Artist to 'vanish into whatever shadows she chose' (Paretsky 2010: 499). *Bury Me Deep* ends with Marion Seeley leaving on a train for an unknown destination (Abbott 2009: 231). Lisbeth Salander ends her story by rejecting intimacy with Blomkvist and disappearing into the snow (2008: 533). All three characters flout traditional *noir* scripts of gender and power, because although they are acted upon as canvases for male fantasies of power and sadism, they also act upon others, to different extents. Most vulnerable is Paretsky's Artist, who never manages to expose her abuse by Kystarnik, while Marion Seeley, though victimized for much of her story, manages finally to employ the *femme fatale*'s wiles to exact revenge. Lisbeth Salander, however, is the most powerful, performing her revenge without punishment or retribution for breaking and bending the law, and, as a character that is neither wholly victimized nor invincible, she remakes herself as a truly subversive fatal woman.

Notes

1. Though the representational conventions of film and fiction are different, in *noir*, the two genres have had a kind of symbiotic relationship throughout the genre's development. The author Raymond Chandler could be a case study for this relationship. Chandler created the archetypal *noir* hero, Philip Marlowe, in fiction, but also worked as a screenwriter, adapting the works of other crime writers for the big screen, such as James M. Cain's *Double Indemnity* and Patricia Highsmith's *Strangers on a Train*. He also wrote an

original screenplay, *The Blue Dahlia*. One can say with certainty that *noir* films and books have been intertwined from the beginning – in their narratives, their characters, and their representations of gender.
2. In his essay 'The Man Who Inhaled Crime Fiction', John-Henri Holmberg (2011) briefly discusses the influence of a hard-boiled American tradition on Larsson.

Works cited

Abbott, M. (2002) *The Street was Mine: White Masculinity in Hardboiled Fiction and Film Noir.* New York: Palgrave Macmillan.

Abbott, M. (2009) *Bury Me Deep.* New York: Simon and Schuster.

Allen, V. M. (1983) *The Femme Fatale: Erotic Icon.* New York: The Whitson Publishing Company.

Biesen, S. C. (2004) 'Manufacturing Heroines: Gothic Victims and Working Women in Clasic Noir Films' in A. Silver and J. Ursini (eds) *Film Noir Reader 4: The Crucial Films and Themes.* New Jersey: Limelight. 161–173.

Biesen, S. C. (2005) *Blackout: World War Two and the Origins of Film Noir.* Baltimore: John Hopkins University Press.

Boozer, J. (1999) 'The Lethal *Femme Fatale* in the *Noir* Tradition', *Journal of Film and Video* 51.3/4, 20–35.

Cahill, A. J. (2001) *Rethinking Rape.* Ithaca NY: Cornell University Press.

Chopra-Grant, M. (2006) *Hollywood Genres and Postwar America: Masculinity, Family and Nation in Popular Film and Film Noir.* London and New York: IB Tauris.

Corey, W. (1999) 'Girl Power: Female Centered Neo-*Noir*' in A. Silver and J. Ursini (eds) *Film Noir Reader 2.* New York: Limelight. 311–327.

Dipaolo, M. (2011) *War, Politics and Superheroes: Ethics and Propaganda in Comics and Film.* Jefferson: McFarland.

Doane, M. A. (1987) *The Desire to Desire: The Woman's Film of the 1940s.* Bloomington and Indianapolis: Indiana University Press.

Doane, M. A. (1991) *Femme Fatales: Feminism, Film Theory, Psychoanalysis.* London and New York: Routledge.

Fay, J . and J. Nieland (2010) *Film Noir: Hard Boiled Modernity and the Cultures of Globalization.* London and New York: Routledge.

Flory, D. (2010) *Philosophy, Black Film, Film Noir.* University Park: Pennsylvania State University Press.

Green, C. (2001) *The Third Hand: Collaboration in Art from Conceptualism to Postmodernism.* Minneapolis: University of Minnesota Press.

Hollinger, K. (1996) '*Film Noir*, Voice-over, and the Femme Fatale' in A. Silver and J. Ursini (eds) *Film Noir Reader.* New York: Limelight. 243–260.

Holmberg, J. (2011) 'The Man Who Inhaled Crime Fiction' in D. Burstein, A. Keijzer and J. Holmberg (eds) *The Tattooed Girl: The Enigma of Stieg Larsson and the Secrets Behind the Most Compelling Thrillers of Our Time.* New York: St. Martin's Griffin. 99–105.

James, D. (1998) 'Interview with Sara Paretsky' in J. Grape, D. James and E. Nehr (eds) *Deadly Women: The Woman Mystery Reader's Indispensable Companion.* New York: Connell and Graf Publisher. 287–290.

Kabir, A. J. (2010) 'Double Violation? (Not) Talking about Sexual Violence in Contemporary South Asia' in S. Gunne and Z. B. Thompson (eds) *Feminism, Literature and Rape Narratives: Violence and Violation*. London and New York: Routledge. 146–163.

Kinsman, M. (1995) 'A Question of Visibility: Paretsky and Chicago' in K. G. Klein (ed.) *Women Times Three: Writers, Detectives, Readers*. Bowling Green: Bowling Green State University Popular Press. 15–28.

Larsson, S. (2008) *The Girl with the Dragon Tattoo*. Transl. R. Keeland. London: MacLehose/Quercus.

Maxfield, J. F. (1996) *The Fatal Woman: Sources of Male Anxiety in American Film Noir, 1941–1991*. Madison/Teaneck: Farleigh Dickenson University Press.

Orr, S. (2010) *Darkly Perfect World: Colonial Adventure, Postmodernism, and American Noir*. Columbus: Ohio State University Press.

Paretsky, S. (2010) *Body Work*. New York: Penguin.

Polanski, R. and R. Towne (1974) *Chinatown*. Dir. R. Polanski, prod. C.O. Erikson and R. Evans. Paramount Home Entertainment.

Povlsen, K. K. and A. M.Waade (2009) 'The Girl with the Dragon Tattoo: Adapting Embodied Gender from Novel to Movie in Stieg Larsson's Crime Fiction', *p.o.v.: A Danish Journal of Film Studies* 28, 64–74.

Roberts, Y. (2007) 'Gang rape Green Zone?', *The Guardian*, 23 Dec, http://www.guardian.co.uk/commentisfree/2007/dec/23/gangbanggreenzone?INTCMP=SRCH, accessed 13 Feb 2012.

Spicer, A. (2002) *Film Noir*. Harlow: Longman.

Stenport, A. W. and C. O. Alm (2009) 'Corporations, Crime, and Gender Construction in Stieg Larsson's *The Girl with the Dragon Tattoo*: Exploring Twenty-first Century Neoliberalism in Swedish Culture', *Scandinavian Studies* 81.2, 157–178.

Telotte, J. P. (2004) 'Voices from the Deep: Film Noir as Psychodrama' in A. Silver and J. Ursini (eds) *Film Noir Reader 4: The Crucial Films and Themes*. New Jersey: Limelight. 145–159.

Wager, J. B. (2005) *Dames in the Driver's Seat: Rereading Film Noir*. (Austin: University of Texas Press.

Part IV
Ethics, Violence, and Adaptation

9
Rape and Replay in Stieg Larsson, Liza Marklund, and Val McDermid: On Affect, Ethics, and Feeling Bad

Tanya Horeck

David Fincher's long-awaited adaptation of Stieg Larsson's *The Girl with the Dragon Tattoo* (US, 2011) (the first of the three films in the trilogy to be produced by Sony), came with the tantalizing tagline that it was to be the 'feel bad movie of Christmas'. It is a tagline that seeks to capitalize on the cultural familiarity with the 'dark' subject matter of Larsson's novels, and which also plays on David Fincher's status as an auteur interested in the adult topics of crime and violence. But, more crucially for my purposes, the tagline is important for the way in which it focuses attention on affect, and its presumption of how we will *respond* to the explicit violence on display in this film. Feel-bad films, according to film scholar Nikolaj Lübecker in his discussion of the work of controversial Danish director Lars von Trier, are those that refuse to give us any form of satisfying release and instead put a 'deadlock on catharsis', turning the 'cinematic experience into a visceral practice that pushes the spectator towards ethical reflection' (2011: 167). Based on this definition, I would argue that Fincher's Hollywood film version of *The Girl with the Dragon Tattoo* does not actually make good on the intriguing promise of its trailer to make its spectators 'feel bad'. Rather, the film's graphic scenes of rape, followed swiftly by scenes of brutal retaliation, work according to well-worn genre expectations so that when Lisbeth Salander's vengeance against her rapist comes, we can only feel immense satisfaction. I would argue that there is no ethical questioning of our position or of how we may be implicated in the scene of violence. The visceral rush of adrenaline that may be felt during the vengeance scene comes from the thrill of seeing the rapist tortured and punished for his crimes. This is about pleasure, not unpleasure: in other words, there is a kind of pleasure to be had here which is fully in keeping with longstanding genre conventions that function according to clear-cut oppositions between good and bad, heroes and villains, rape and revenge.

The violence in Fincher's film is what Asjbørn Grønstad has elsewhere described as 'classical Hollywood violence, a form that is designed to please rather than to appal and that is frequently too formulaic and insipid to cause much unease in the audience' (2011: 195). To be sure, the rape scene in Fincher's version did make me feel uneasy, but not in ways that challenged or forced me to confront my own relationship to violence. It made me feel uneasy largely because I was troubled by how Fincher's particular style of filmmaking, which Ignatiy Vishnevetsky has recently referred to as his *'bam-bam-bam* construction' of events, portrays the scene of sexual violence largely from the point of view of the rapist (2010). In Fincher's film, which has also been described as 'a montage-based cinema of this happened and then this happened and then this' (Kasman in Vishnevetsky 2010), the event of rape is swiftly followed by the event of revenge (*bam*, the rape happened and then, *bam*, the revenge happened); the uncomfortable rape scene is made uncomfortable only so that any troubled feelings we may be experiencing at being party to such a grubby scene of sexually violent exploitation (ooh, this is *so* unpleasant) can be swiftly dissipated with the cathartic revenge scene (yes! she got him!).

I open this chapter with my reflections on this 'feel bad film' that does not make us feel nearly bad enough, in order to introduce the issue of affect into a discussion about sexual violence and crime fiction. So far, much of the debate over the so-called 'grotesque' violence of the Millennium trilogy has centred on its representational significance and questions of moral judgement regarding Lisbeth Salander: is she a 'good', feminist character or she is a 'bad' misogynist fantasy come to life? Or, as the headline to one *Guardian* blog bluntly puts it: 'The Girl with the Dragon Tattoo, feminist or not?' (Groskop 2010). While the focus in such discussions is on the Millennium trilogy's qualities as a representation, what is perhaps more interesting to explore is the matter of how we are invited to viscerally respond to the figure of Lisbeth Salander and the Millennium trilogy's 'epochal tale' about the 'pervasiveness of violence and abuse against women, especially young and vulnerable women' (Burstein 2011: xvi). For critic Dan Burstein, as for many others, the fascinating question is why Lisbeth Salander so 'captivated reader attention and seemed to enter not just our heads or our hearts but to get into our very bloodstream' (xvi). In other words, it is the sheer affective impact of 'the girl', and the way she gets under our skin, that comes across most strikingly in the visceral responses to the various cultural manifestations of her story of rape and vengeance, whether in the books or the films (and indeed, it is increasingly difficult to separate these cultural texts).

Though it is not necessarily always explicitly acknowledged, the strong responses to the figure of Lisbeth Salander are inextricably bound up with the role that rape plays in her story and, more precisely, the ways in which scenes of rape are used to affectively engage the reader/viewer. More generally, too, it is also the case that in the burgeoning scholarship on the question of the affective impact of film experiences, rape occupies a central role in discussions about the 'ethical relation by which the viewer and the film are both enveloped' (Grønstad 2011: 193). In many European art house 'feel-bad' films, there is a tendency to use explicit rape scenes as a means of challenging the spectator to think critically about their own relationship to images of pain and suffering. What is interesting, though, is how this idea of a 'feel-bad film' and the notion of images that 'inflict violence upon the viewer' (195) has begun to move into the mainstream, where there is often less of an emphasis on ethical reflection and more of a focus on violence and sensation as part of the moral lessons of the film's narrative.[1]

While most of the discussion around rape and its relationship to questions of ethics and affect has taken place in relation to cinema, in this chapter I want to consider the affective charge of sexualized violence in contemporary popular crime fiction. Taking on board theorist Marco Abel's point that 'the real question violent images raise is not whether violence is good or bad but what it does' (2007: 39), I want to ask: what does the scene of sexual violence 'do' in the contemporary crime blockbuster? And, perhaps more crucially, what is the nature of our affective encounter with such sexualized violence? In what follows, I will open up these questions through a discussion of the work of two bestselling female crime authors: Swedish writer Liza Marklund and Scottish writer Val McDermid. Both Marklund and McDermid write crime series that can be situated, along with the Millennium trilogy, in the context of a so-called new wave of 'feel bad' crime fiction that is seen as violent and disturbing. Marklund's Annika Bengtzon series and McDermid's Tony Hill/Carol Jordan series feature female protagonists who, like Lisbeth Salander, are raped and sexually victimized but who survive and who fight back. As with Larsson and the Millennium trilogy, Marklund and McDermid's work is framed within a broader feminist awareness of the social and cultural underpinnings of violence against women. In this regard, it is telling, as McDermid has noted, that it 'took a male writer' to bring the issue of misogyny and violence against women to public attention, when she and other female writers 'have been writing edgy, conflicted, complex and strong female characters for quite some time – often with a feminist slant' (cited in Forshaw 2011: 299). We might also add that where Larsson's work has attained extraordinary amounts of cultural attention (and praise) for its brand of 'male feminism', however controversial, female writers such as McDermid are often criticized and called to account for the violence in their work, largely because of their gender (and sometimes because of their sexuality).[2] But, as McDermid argues, rather than dwelling on such gender politics, it is time for us to 'address the really interesting question of why we are so fascinated by the threat, the fact and the consequences of violence' (2009). I agree with McDermid that what is necessary, and what is actually not dealt with in the context of media debates about graphic 'feel bad' violence in crime narratives, is an interrogation of the category of violence itself, its affective uses, and the work it is called upon to do in terms of fashioning ideas about selfhood, ethics, and agency.

I want to argue that what is especially salient about the blockbusters written by these three authors – the Millennium trilogy, the Annika Bengtzon series, and the Tony Hill/Carol Jordan series – is that the subject of sexual violence and its aftermath is developed over the course of several novels, thus enabling a continual re-evaluation and reworking of the question of violence and its relationship to notions of victimhood. If, as I have suggested, the 'bam-bam-bam' style of filmmaking of a director like Fincher is problematic due to the ways in which it closes down the potential power and force behind sensation and affect, what is interesting about these novels is how they take their time with violence, and how they are able to linger longer over uncertainties regarding the event of violence and our engagement with it. Following feminist theorist Carine Mardorossian's argument that it is absolutely imperative for feminism to scrutinize 'the very term *victim* and what it encompasses' in discussions of rape, I want to suggest that contemporary crime fiction is an important site for tracking how the 'opposition between victimization and agency' gets negotiated – and renegotiated – in popular culture (2002: 767). Thinking through the categories of violence, victimhood, and agency, and how they relate to conceptions of self and other, is, in large part, what all three of the crime series under consideration in this chapter are at pains to explore. Finally, though rape scenes have long been major sites of cultural controversy, I will argue that in these contemporary crime blockbusters it is not the rape scenes themselves that are of the most interest but, rather, the ways in which they are replayed and redeployed across a series of novels (and in the case of the Millennium trilogy, a series of films as well). How this replay affects the reader, and how it solicits our visceral engagement with violence, is the subject of this chapter.

Affect and ethics

In Larsson's trilogy and its many adaptations, the use of violence as a means of establishing the agency of the heroine is amplified to an extraordinary degree. What seems difficult to reconcile is that this agency goes hand in hand with, and indeed appears to be unimaginable without, a traumatic backstory of violence and sexual victimization. While acknowledging that 'crime novels do have an overwhelming number of female victims', crime author Tess Gerritsen has nonetheless recently suggested that we need to move beyond quick moral judgement and condemnation of such storylines in order to consider just why it is that female in jeopardy (fem-jep) storylines are so incredibly popular, especially amongst female readers, who constitute the primary audience for contemporary crime novels.[3] According to Gerritsen, women need not feel guilty about enjoying such scenarios as they are not necessarily about misogyny or self-loathing, but rather about 'confronting our fears' (2010). This notion of the scene of female victimization as a fantasy via which women readers are able to work through common fears and anxieties is a compelling one. But, as Alison Young has recently argued, 'there is much more at stake than simply pointing out that popular culture helps people deal with a common fear through storytelling' (2010: 2). Exploring the affectivity of violent images, outside of commonly held paradigms regarding truth and representation (Abel 2007: 47–48), enables us to ask more productively unsettling questions about the 'use of binaries between victim and perpetrator, passivity and agency' (Brigley Thompson 2010: 11) and our own relationship to such categories.

Critics such as Marco Abel have begun to question the limits of a representational approach to the problem of violence. According to Abel, what is called for is a form of criticism that pays attention to the 'violence of sensation' and the 'production of effects', rather than putting the emphasis on deciding what an image means. As Abel puts it, 'a critical encounter with violent images would therefore have to attend to these images' *affective* intensities – their effects rather than their representational "meanings"' (10–11). The term 'affect', as it is being used here, is not interchangeable with that of 'emotion'. As Abel notes, 'Sensation – affect – is presubjective: it is what constitutes the subject rather than being a synonym for an already constituted subject's emotions and feelings' (6). Thinking in affective terms enables us to open up important questions about the ethics of violence. As Abel suggests, 'The question of ethics is raised at and through the very moment when the audience can sense the violence of sensation' (10) and therefore 'the question of the ethics of violence...emerges prior to any representation of violence' (11). Such a view of the ethics of violence is very different from that of moral judgement, which occurs when we take a position on the 'rightness' or 'wrongness' of a representation and comment upon it. As Abel sees it:

> The affective or intensive forces inhering in the violence of sensation...produce effects *prior* to their inevitable narrativization, their eventual territorialization onto the plane of representation – and because these forces affect me before the narrative apparatus captures them for me – I am always already response-able. (10)

One of the reasons why this affective approach is so significant, then, is that it forces us to think through the constitutive nature of our (ethical) encounters with violence. This is important for examining depictions of rape, which are too often viewed in relation to questions about their 'realism'. As Young observes:

> it is no answer to state that sexual violence exists and that films must therefore depict it with forensic authenticity. Such a claim constructs cinema as separate from the 'real', as offering a window through which we can look at the world and understand it better, an understanding which comes close to positing that the experience of viewing rape can teach us all something about the experience of being raped. (2010: 73)

Young's point about how cinema should be viewed in terms of its own material reality is similar to Abel's suggestion, noted above, that we need to encounter violent images, be it in literature, film or indeed in any cultural art form, on 'the level of their own reality rather than their meaning' (2007: 3). Keeping this crucial notion in mind, I now want to turn to a consideration of Liza Marklund's crime series in order to examine what kind of affect emerges from our encounters with violence in her work, and how this relates to her broader critical attempt to expose the problem of violence against women.

Exposing violence: Liza Marklund

In the wake of the success of Larsson's Millennium trilogy, there has been a particular interest in finding not only the next big Scandinavian crime-writing sensation, but in particular the new female 'star' of Nordic crime. While many female crime writers, including Camilla Läckberg, Camilla Ceder, and Karin Fossum, are seen to vie for the (marketing) title of 'Queen of Scandinavian Crime Fiction' (Kärrholm 2011), in terms of sheer commercial success Liza Marklund emerges as the 'undisputed' leader, as her promotional website announces. Her crime thrillers have sold over 13 million copies worldwide and have been translated into 30 languages (www.lizamarklund.com). Furthermore, thanks to the recent publication of *Postcard Killers* (2011), which she co-wrote with American blockbuster writer James Patterson, Marklund has earned the following kudos: she is now the second Swedish writer in history, after Stieg Larsson, to reach number one on the New York Times bestseller list.

That Larsson's success has paved the way for other Scandinavian writers is openly acknowledged by Marklund, who has expressed admiration (and gratitude) for his books.[4] It is interesting to note the similarities between these two bestselling Swedish thriller writers, who share common ground beyond their astonishing commercial success.[5] Both writers were raised in remote locations in the north of Sweden, and both also come from a background of crusading journalism. Most important, for this anthology, though, is the fact that Larsson and Marklund share a serious interest in the topic of violence against women. As Marklund is quoted as saying in an interview with *The Guardian* (in rhetoric that calls to mind Larsson's polemical stance on male violence in the Millennium trilogy):

> We don't have a long tradition of protecting women in this country. What happens at home is your own business in Sweden. Yet every 10 days a woman is beaten to death by her partner. It's a subject I was angry about when I was a journalist – and I'm still angry. My bosses used to say: "You and your fucking women. No one is interested, no one cares." (France 2005)

In her successful series featuring crime reporter Annika Bengtzon, Marklund restages this moment of callous indifference when her heroine's boss informs her that he is 'not interested in domestics' (2011: 18). Marklund's heroine is outraged by this attitude; like Marklund herself, Annika is determined to tell the stories of violated and abused women. Importantly, Annika – whom Marklund has described as a 'larger-than-life' protagonist on a par with Larsson's Lisbeth Salander (cited in Burke 2011) – has her own past experience of abuse, which makes her empathize with the abused female characters she encounters, and which critically shapes her actions as a protagonist.

To date, there are nine books in the Annika Bengtzon series, and it is important for an understanding of how violence operates in Marklund's work to note that these were not published – or, even more significantly, written – in chronological order. The first novel, *The Bomber*, was published in Sweden in 1998, seven years before *The Girl with the Dragon Tattoo*. This novel introduces us to Annika, who struggles with the tensions between her home life as a wife and mother of two children and her work as an intrepid crime reporter. The second novel in the series, *Exposed* (1999), takes place several years before the events in *The Bomber* and details Annika's life as a 24-year-old reporter before she has met her husband or had her children. Chronologically, this book is the first in the series and of particular significance for the purposes of this chapter is the fact that this novel, written after Annika Bengtzon was already established as a character, provides us with a backstory of sexual violence.

The fact that the novels are written out of sequence – with *Exposed* going back in time to stage an 'origin story' of rape and retaliation, which later novels in the Annika Bengtzon series such as *Paradise* (2000) then make reference to and revisit – makes explicit what is apparent in other successful crime series, including Larsson's Millennium trilogy and McDermid's Tony Hill/Carol Jordan novels: that, for many contemporary crime writers, sexual violence is absolutely key to the character development of the female protagonist. What I find most interesting, though, is the issue of how we encounter the violence in these series – our mode of engagement with it. In *Exposed*, for example, it is important to note that the story of Annika's sexual victimization is not made immediately apparent, and indeed is not presented to us at all in the context of the main narrative. Rather, it is conveyed to the reader affectively through scenes of violence, not initially attached to Annika, which are interspersed throughout the main narrative.

The novel begins with the discovery of a dead, raped girl in the park. Annika is sent to cover the story and soon finds herself caught up in the life of the victim's young flatmate, Patricia, who works as an exotic dancer in a sleazy nightclub. As the investigation goes on, Annika learns details of the victim's life, including the fact that she had a violent and possessive boyfriend who used to rape her. After a hundred or so pages of this main narrative, short chapters begin to appear, without any introduction or explanation, which are written in the first person and presented in italics. These sections are written anonymously in the form of a diary entry, with the age of the girl writing them given to us at the heading of each entry (beginning with *'Seventeen years, four months and sixteen days'*). These diary entries give an increasingly graphic and violent account of the deterioration of a love affair, including descriptions of the sexual violence suffered by the young woman. The big revelation at the end of Marklund's thriller is that these diary entries are written not by the raped and murdered girl whose body was found in the park, nor by Patricia, the friend of the murdered girl whose thoughts and feelings we are privy to throughout the novel, but by Annika herself, who, as we subsequently realize, has been in a sexually violent relationship since she was 'seventeen years, four months and sixteen days old'.

The graphic scenes of violence found in the diary entries are alternated with scenes from the main narrative where personal relationships, such as that between Annika and her fiancé Sven, are low on detail and are kept enigmatic. While violent happenings are referred to in the main narrative, there is not much gory detail about these events, which are filtered through Annika's reactions and responses. By contrast, the first-person diary entries are written in a cruder, more direct language:

> *I sit on top of him, feeling him deep within me as he slaps me hard on the face with the palm of his hand. I stop, my eyes filling with tears. I ask him why he'd do something like that. He strokes my cheek, and pushes in hard and deep. It's to help you, he says, and hits me again, then thrusts in hard until he comes.* (214)

The fact that the man and the woman in these scenes are not named or identified until the very end of the novel is significant in terms of Marklund's overall argument about violence, which is that it is a terrible but mundane part of domestic everyday life and is something that happens to most women at the hands of men they know and love. 'A woman is being beaten' is the primal scenario at work in these diary entries that draw the reader in affectively through their confessional, first-person, presentation. Before we relate to these events in representational or narrative terms, then, we are invited to experience them affectively, as primal scenes and situations of violence, in which a woman is being hurt by a man. These scenes provoke sensations of uneasiness because they are not immediately accounted for within a 'representational framework' (Abel 2007: 7); the narrative, in other words, does not come along to explain the violence or help us to dispel any uncomfortable feelings we may have about being implicated in the scenes. In calling on our affective response to violence, the question of ethics – of the kind discussed by Abel – emerges, whereby we are 'always already response-able' for the violent images before us (10). If, broadly speaking, as Libby Saxton and Lisa Downing suggest, 'ethics can be thought of as the encounter that occurs between a reader or viewer and a text or work of visual art' (2010: 1), then what is most interesting about the scenarios of first-person violence found in Marklund's text is how they make us think through the terms of our encounter with violent images, and, following on from that, how they also encourage us to interrogate the relationship between passivity and agency.

That we find out about Annika's victimization at the very moment she commits her greatest act of violence – the murder of her abuser, Sven – underlines the point that she is victim and agent, perpetrator and victim, all at once and inseparably. In *Exposed*, the violence of the past is moved into the present moment and put on dramatic display for the benefit of the reader, who affectively processes the horror of Annika's abuse before it is identified as such. This temporal relocation of the event of violence means that we viscerally experience the abuse before it is tied to Annika – and to her narrative. With the revelation that Annika is the woman in the diary entries, we then have to revisit our experience of violence, recasting our thoughts about the status of the 'victim' in the text.

Spectacularizing violence: Val McDermid

The use of violence as a means of viscerally engaging the reader is a strategy also used by Scottish writer Val McDermid, a writer who is known for her 'penchant for gore' (Simhon 2004). Describing McDermid as 'The Woman Behind the Man Behind the *Girl with the Dragon Tattoo*', Barry Forshaw has noted that her influence can be seen in Larsson's work, 'notably in the beleaguered-but-capable female protagonist obliged to confront the darkest extremes of human behaviour, and graphically described scenes of sexuality and violence' (2011: 298). Of all the novels discussed in this chapter, McDermid's books featuring Tony Hill and Carol Jordan are undoubtedly the most violent. It is not only that the images are the most explicit of the novels under discussion, but that the experience of reading them arouses feelings of disgust and displeasure in a way that Larsson's and Marklund's books do not. One need not look further than Larsson's *The Girl with the Dragon Tattoo* to get an example of the experience of reading one of McDermid's novels. Mikael Blomkvist, Larsson's male protagonist, is pictured reading McDermid's *The Mermaids Singing* at several key moments in the investigation into the disappearance of Harriet Vanger. He finishes reading the novel just as he and Lisbeth Salander are coming close to uncovering the grotesque serial murders of vulnerable women over a 37-year period. Blomkvist has his dinner and then 'went to bed to read the denouement of Val McDermid's novel. It was grisly' (2008: 325).

McDermid, who has spoken out at length about her thoughts on violence and crime writing, has argued that the graphic scenes she creates are central to the territory of the serial killer novel and are necessary in the context of her books, which are about a male profiler of serial killers and a high-ranking policewoman. Against continual claims that she 'glorifies' violence, McDermid emphatically insists that she does no such thing, and that, in fact, she is concerned with 'showing what violence is and what it does' (2011 interview). One of the most remarkable things about McDermid's response to charges regarding the violence in her work is her refusal to even acknowledge that her work is violent. While this may strike some as disingenuous, I would argue that what McDermid is actually objecting to is the very notion of violence that is being put forward by her interrogators, namely as something to be revelled in, and as something that is readily knowable and identifiable as 'gratuitous'. For although much has been written about the violence in McDermid's work, less – if anything – has been written about the affective experience of reading this violence and how that affective experience relates to the overall pacing and construction of the narrative.

Given her reputation for extreme violence, it is important to note that the rape of her heroine Carol Jordan in *The Last Temptation* (2002) is not described at all. The chapter in which the rape occurs ends with the sentence 'Then he was on top of her and she wanted to die' (2002: 531). When the narrative next picks up with Carol, there are detailed descriptions of the aftermath of the trauma:

> Her face was a streaked mess of blood, saliva, mucus and tears. Her nose was swollen and angled improbably. Her eyes were invisible in the puffy purpling of bruised flesh. Smudged trails of blood and shit were visible on her thighs. (542)

The next book in the series, *The Torment of Others*, is about Carol's emotional recovery from the event of violence, at the same time as it also, curiously, replays a rape scenario for the reader in the context of another storyline.

The Torment of Others spends a great deal of time giving us the reactions of her colleagues to Carol post rape, many of whom repeatedly voice the concern that she is not capable of the same professionalism as she once was: 'maybe she's lost her nerve', as one colleague thinks (2005: 190). In an effort to contextualize Carol's psychical recovery from rape, there is a reference made to novelist Alice Sebold's highly praised rape memoir, *Lucky* (1999), which is given to Carol by her fleeting love interest, Jonathan France, who tells her 'It's not schlocky or sensationalist or sentimental' (230). This comment acknowledges the pitfalls of writing rape and also hints at readers' responses to such depictions. Carol reads the book, which 'seemed to speak to her at a level nothing and no one had touched before. After forty pages, she had to put the book down. Her hands were trembling and she felt on the verge of tears' (243). Such a visceral, bodily response to this story of rape and recovery is significant in a novel which so self-consciously stages gorily violent encounters for its readers, in an attempt to deliberately provoke sensation. Indeed, what is interesting to consider further is how this sensitive depiction of a woman coming to terms with rape, and discovering a new inner strength and resolve, relates to the descriptions of sadistic violence found in the same novel, the central plot of which concerns a serial killer who murders female prostitutes. As with Marklund, but in even more dramatic and spectacularized fashion, our affective relationship to the narrative of rape and recovery in McDermid is routed through violence.

In effect, *The Torment of Others* repeats the scenario found in *The Last Temptation*, where Carol was sent on a botched undercover operation which resulted in her rape. This time, it is Paula, one of the young female police officers on Carol's team, who goes on an undercover operation that fails, resulting in her rape and near murder. Here is one of the novel's more graphic moments, from the serial killer's third-person point of view, shortly after Paula is kidnapped:

> *He turns away, ignoring the mewling noises coming through the gag. He takes out the dildo he prepared earlier. The bright light gleams on the sharp edges of the razor blades. It's fucking wicked, this death machine. He swivels on the balls of his feet, spinning round to face her. When she sees the dildo, the colour drains from her face, leaving her chest blotchy and ugly. He steps forward, pushes up her skirt and rips her pants away. He waves the dildo in her face and grins. That's when she pisses herself. Which annoys him, because it's going to make the room smell, and that's not very nice.* (309–310)

There is no question that such descriptions of the killer's sadistic violence in *The Torment of Others* can be hard to take; it would seem, on the face of it, to give credence to Jessica Mann's claim that too much crime writing features 'male perpetrators and female victims in situations of "sadistic misogyny"' (cited in Hill 2009).[6] Certainly, it is the descriptions of sexualized violence that have led to McDermid's writing being labelled as 'torture porn' (Pheas 2011), a term which, while initially used to refer to a new breed of horror films, including the *Saw* franchise (2004–2010) and others films such as *Hostel* (Roth, US, 2005), is now also used more broadly to refer to works that stage violence as an explicit spectacle. Torture porn can be defined as a film (or in this case, a novel) which 'constructs scenes of torture as elaborate set pieces, or "numbers", intended to serve as focal points for the viewer's visual pleasure, and (in some critics' view) for which the narrative is merely a flimsy pretext' (Middleton 2010: 2). This is certainly how some reviewers receive the scenes of violence in McDermid, with many claiming that their brutal explicitness and insight into the mind of the killer is simply 'unnecessary' (this is a word that is used repeatedly in criticisms of McDermid's use of violence).[7] And yet, I would argue that the set-piece scenes of violence can, in fact, be seen as central to the wider narrative exploration of rape and recovery in McDermid's crime series, especially when we view these scenes in terms of affective response and the kind of reader engagement they elicit.

There is a constant shifting between perpetrator and victim throughout *The Torment of Others*, a shift that is played out in an affective register, where the queasy feelings generated by the spectacles of violence, which are inserted at regular intervals, and which seek to implicate us through their direct and visceral mode of address, alternate with the main narrative and its focus on the aftermath of rape. For the serial killer, who stages grand displays of violence through media technologies (a common trope of torture porn), and watches the violence through the medium of the screen, it is about the pleasure to be gleaned from violence as spectacle. However, the disturbing scenes of violence, which, as Geoff King has noted, are 'part of the expected and anticipated repertoire' in horror and the 'serial killer format' (2004: 129), do not simply translate into 'pleasure' for the reader, which seems to be the assumption of much of the criticism of violence in McDermid. Rather, the cumulative build-up of such scenes creates strong sensations of disgust, leaving the reader feeling uncomfortable and slightly grubby for having read them, especially as we shift between the extreme violence of the perpetrator(s) and the narrative account of the after-effects of violence on the female protagonist of the series. While it is true that the return to the main narrative after the gross scenes of violence may come as a kind of relief or comfort, it is also the case that we are then made to engage with

Carol Jordan's post-traumatic syndrome via the immediate sensations generated by our experience of violence and vice versa.

Towards the end of the novel the spectacle of violence moves into the space of the main narrative, in the rape of the character Paula. Where, in *The Last Temptation*, Carol's rape is withheld from the reader, in this later novel about aftermath and recovery, the rape of Paula is staged in uncomfortably graphic detail:

> She tried to dissociate herself from what was happening to her body, but it didn't work. Mercifully, it was over quickly. He hammered his hand into her, his hips forcing her thigh deep into the mattress as he speeded up... Then he collapsed on top of her, his fingers slithering out of her bruised vagina. (2005: 329)

In contrast to the other violent images in the novel, this scene is not presented to us within the italicized serial killer sections. Rather, it appears in the context of the main narrative, and is presented to us from the victim's third-person perspective (329). In Marklund's work, as already discussed, there is a temporal relocation of the event of (past) violence into the present; in this instance, we are made to revisit Carol Jordan's (past) rape by confronting the bloody violence done to other female bodies. This, in part, is so we can *feel* the horror of what Carol has gone through, beyond merely processing it intellectually. Notably, Paula's rape is only presented to the reader after Carol has started to move 'beyond' the rape and 'her body was hers again' (295). While it may seem problematic to replay rape in such a way, with the violation of another female body, I would argue that it is repeated with a critical difference: we are only shown the scene of sexual violence (which was withheld from us in the previous novel) once Carol is in recovery. In other words, the violence in this text is tied to Carol and her process of recovery, and we are asked to respond to it in this context. It is important that we are only given the scene of rape once Carol has made it through the other side and once she has regained her agency. Indeed, we are made to engage with the scene of victimization through Carol's agency, as it were.

Writing on serial killer narratives, Richard Dyer has noted that:

> if you just told the story of the victim *as* victim then there'd be next to no story and it'd be over too soon. And we cannot dwell on any individual victim too much anyway, because the point is the repetition, the next episode/victim, in short, the seriality. (cited in Hills 2005: 140)

For Dyer, such repetition is the pleasure of narrative, but in the crime series I have been discussing, in which violence is played out over the course of several novels, the repetition of the event of violence also becomes the crucial moment for opening up, and provoking questions around, the very status of victimhood and the relationship between passivity and agency. This is because in these crime series the repetition of violence, and our affective experience of it, is so closely wedded to the female protagonist's reflections on its aftermath. In the final analysis, one of the most compelling things about the Millennium trilogy is how it continually returns to, and restages, rape across all three novels, redefining the female protagonist's relationship to violence, as well as our understanding of it. Thus, for example, the scene of Lisbeth Salander's brutal violation at the hands of Bjurman is returned to in the final novel of the trilogy, *The Girl Who Kicked The Hornets' Nest* (2009), when she writes her account of the rape for her 'autobiography' to be circulated as a court document. Here, the heroine replays the rape on her own terms, and takes the reader through her account of 'how Advokat Bjurman had violently and sadistically raped her. That was the part she had spent the most time on, and one of the few she had rewritten several times before she was satisfied' (343). In the same novel, the event of violence is also replayed in the courtroom as visual spectacle and, crucially, as 'evidence'. As with Marklund and McDermid, there is a relocation of the event of violence, from the past into the present, which encourages an (ethical) review of our response-ability.

In this chapter I have demonstrated how violence operates as an affective encounter in three contemporary crime series that are recognized for their participation in a so-called violent new wave of crime fiction. The crime serial is one of the few locations in popular culture where the story of sexual violence has the space – and the time – to be told in this way, where commonly held ideas about the relationship between passivity and agency can be revisited and reviewed in temporal terms, over the course of several novels and across different time periods, and where the reader's affective experience relates to the development of the female character in such an intimate and complex way. While feminist discussions of rape have tended to organize themselves around identity politics, with a focus on images and representations, much is to be gained from factoring the issue of affect into the debate, as this opens up difficult new questions about sensation, ethics, and the nature of our involvement with violence. Standing outside of a representation and deciding what 'meanings' it holds forecloses the productive potential of our engagement with violence. To think through the affective resonance of our encounters with violence is to raise questions about the relations between victim and perpetrator, subject and object, actor and acted upon, in a space where we register sensation – and 'sensation as violence' – but before we are asked to pass judgement on the event (Abel 2007: 184–187). Something of this ethical moment – a moment where we are not quite sure of the exact relationship between victim and agent, abused and abuser, self and other – is captured in the replay of rape found in the crime series of Liza Marklund, Val McDermid, and Stieg Larsson, which, at their most challenging, ask us to reflect on our own embeddedness in violence. This, in the end, might go some way towards accounting for what makes Lisbeth Salander such a culturally compelling figure: she embodies something about the problem of violence, or violence as a problem, which emerges not only in the 'meanings' ascribed to her but in our affective encounters with her.

Notes

1. Thanks to Tina Kendall for this observation.
2. See Lea (2007) for a description of the controversy that broke out when Scottish crime writer Ian Rankin allegedly remarked that the most violent crime fiction is written by lesbians.
3. Sisters in Crime commissioned a market research study by Bowker, which found that 68 per cent of 'mysteries' purchased in the US in 2009 and the first half of 2010 were purchased by women. As Barbara Fister has pointed out to me in email correspondence, there are some problems with the data, in so far as Bowker treats 'mystery' (a word used for crime novels in certain publishing circles) as a separate category from 'espionage and thrillers' and it is not clear that readers make sharp distinctions between those categories, but it is nonetheless revealing on the gender differential in crime readership. For the data, please see http://sistersincrime.org/associations/10614/files/ConsumerBuyingBookReport.pdf.
4. See Burke's interview with Marklund (2011).
5. Marklund's novels are also currently being filmed by the same production company (Yellow Bird) that made the successful Swedish film versions of Larsson's books, and a Hollywood production company has recently bought the distribution rights to the Swedish film version of her Annika Bengzton crime novel, *Nobel's Last Will* (2006).
6. One of the problems with grand pronouncements against male violence/female victimhood in crime fiction is that the more complex rendering of violence that often occurs in contemporary crime novels is overlooked. For example, in *The Torment of Others* the serial killer who is pulling the strings, and finding young men to do her dirty work for her, is a woman and a lesbian. While this may pose its own set of problems, Val McDermid has jokingly counted up the tally of corpses in her writing and concluded that it is definitely 'equal opportunities', with '12 men, 12 women and one transsexual' (Bindel 2007).

7. It says something about McDermid's reputation for depicting violence and torture to find that the online Collins dictionary, under the usages for the word 'torture', includes a reference to one of her novels, *Kick Back* (2002): 'According to the DI at the scene, he had a proper little torture chamber in his wardrobe'.

Works cited

Abel, M. (2007) *Violent Affect: Literature, Cinema and Critique After Representation*. Lincoln: Nebraska.
Bindel, J. (2007) 'I start my day in a condition of rage', *The Guardian*, 17 Aug, http://www.guardian.co.uk/books/2007/aug/17/crime.gender, accessed 23 Feb 2012.
Burke, D. (2011) 'The Gospel According to Marklund', *Crime Always Pays*, 2 Sep, http://crimealwayspays.blogspot.com/2011/09/gospel-according-to-marklund.html, accessed 6 Feb 2012.
Burstein, D. (2011) 'Introduction' in D. Burstein, A. de Keijzer, and J. Holmberg (eds) *The Tattooed Girl: The Enigma of Stieg Larsson and the Secrets Behind The Most Compelling Thrillers of Our Time*. New York: St. Martin's Griffin: xv-xxii.
Downing, L. and L . Saxton (2010) *Film and Ethics: Foreclosed Encounters*. Oxford and New York: Routledge.
Forshaw, B. (2011) *The Man Who Left Too Soon: The Life and Works of Stieg Larsson*. London: John Blake.
France, L. (2005) 'Murder They Wrote', *The Guardian*, 12 June, http://www.guardian.co.uk/books/2005/jun/12/crimebooks.features, accessed 14 Feb 2012.
Gerritsen, T. (2010) 'Why Dead Women Sell Books', *Murderati*, 10 Aug, http://www.murderati.com/blog/2010/8/10/why-dead-women-sell-books.html, accessed 19 Jan 2012.
Grønstad, A. (2011) 'On the Unwatchable' in T. Horeck and T. Kendall (eds) *The New Extremism in Cinema: From France to Europe*. Edinburgh: Edinburgh University Press. 192–205.
Groskop, V. (2010) 'The Girl with the Dragon Tattoo: feminist or not?', *The Guardian*, 15 March, http://www.guardian.co.uk/books/booksblog/2010/mar/15/girl-with-the-dragon-tattoo, accessed 13 Feb 2012.
Hill, A. (2009) 'Sexist violence sickens crime critic', *The Guardian*, 25 Oct, http://www.guardian.co.uk/books/2009/oct/25/jessica-mann-crime-novels-anti-women, accessed 25 Jan 2012.
Hills, M. (2005) *The Pleasures of Horror*. London and New York: Continuum.
Kärrholm, S. (2011) 'Swedish Queens of Crime: the Art of Self-Promotion and the Notion of Feminine Agency – Liza Marklund and Camilla Läckberg' in A. Nestingen and Paula Arvas (eds) *Scandinavian Crime Fiction*. Cardiff: University of Wales Press: 131–147.
King, G. (2004) '"Killingly Funny": Mixing Modalities in New Hollywood's Comedy-with-Violence' in S. J. Schneider (ed.) *New Hollywood Violence*. Manchester: Manchester University Press: 126–143.
Larsson, S. (2008) *The Girl With the Dragon Tattoo*. Transl. R. Keeland. London: MacLehose/Quercus.

Larsson, S. (2009) *The Girl Who Kicked the Hornets' Nest*. Transl. R. Keeland. London: MacLehose/Quercus.

Lea, R. (2007) 'Rankin Accused of Insulting Female Crime Writers', *The Guardian*, 16 Aug, http://www.guardian.co.uk/books/2007/aug/16/ianrankin, accessed 7 Feb 2012.

Lübecker, N. (2011) 'Lars von Trier's *Dogville*: A Feel-Bad Film' in T. Horeck and T. Kendall (eds) *The New Extremism in Cinema: From France to Europe*. Edinburgh: Edinburgh University Press.

Mardorossian, C. (2002) 'Toward a new feminist theory of rape', *Signs: Journal of Women in Culture and Society* 27.3, 743–75.

Marklund, L. (2002 [1998]) *The Bomber*. Transl. K. Von Hofsten. London: Simon & Schuster.

Marklund, L. (2004 [2000]) *Paradise*. Transl. I. Eng-Rundlow. London: Simon & Schuster.

Marklund, L. (2011 [1999]) *Exposed*. Transl. N. Smith. London: Random House/A Corgi Book.

McDermid, V. (2002) *The Last Temptation*. London: HarperCollins

McDermid, V. (2005) *The Torment of Others*. London: HarperCollins.

McDermid, V. (2006 [1995]) *The Mermaids Singing*. London: HarperCollins.

McDermid, V. (2009) 'Complaints about women writing misogynist crime fiction are a red herring'. *The Guardian*, Oct 29, http://www.guardian.co.uk/books/booksblog/2009/oct/29/misogynist-crime-fiction-val-mcdermid, accessed 13 Feb 2012.

McDermid, V. (2011) Interviewed by: Sackur, S. *HardTalk*. BBC iPlayer. http://www.bbc.co.uk/iplayer/episode/b016djqp/HARDtalk_Val_McDermid_Crime_Writer/, accessed 1 Feb 2012.

Middleton, J. (2010) 'Torture and the Pain of Americans in *Hostel*', in *Cinema Journal: The Journal of the Society For Cinema & Media Studies* 49.4, 1–24.

Patterson, J. and L. Marklund (2011) *Postcard Killers*. London: Arrow Books.

Pheas, N. (2011) 'Fever of the Bone', 1 May, http://readpheasntthroughout.blogspot.com/2011/05/fever-of-bone.html, accessed 3 March 2012.

Simhon, R. (2004) 'Thoroughly Modern Brutality', *The Daily Telegraph*, 13 June, http://www.telegraph.co.uk/culture/books/3618855/Thoroughly-modern-brutality.html, accessed 24 Jan 2012.

Thompson, Z. B. and S. Gunne (2010) 'Introduction' in S. Gunne and Z. B. Thompson (eds) *Feminism and Rape Narratives*. London/New York: Routledge. 1–20.

Vishnevetsky, I. (2010) 'Obsessive/Compulsive: "The Social Network" (David Fincher, USA)', *Notebook*, 21 Sep, http://mubi.com/notebook/posts/obsessive-compulsive-the-social-network-david-fincher-usa, accessed 1 Feb 2012.

Young, A. (2010) *The Scene of Violence: Cinema, Crime, Affect*. Oxford: Routledge.

10
The Girl with the Dragon Tattoo: Rape, Revenge, and Victimhood in Cinematic Translation

Claire Henry

Towards the end of the Swedish film adaptation of *The Girl with the Dragon Tattoo* (Oplev, Sweden, 2009), Harriet Vanger is reunited with her great-uncle Henrik and the loose threads of her mysterious disappearance 40 years earlier are tied up. She tells the story of how her father and brother raped her from the age of 14, and how one day she knocked her drunken father into the water with an oar and held him under until he drowned. This classic rape-revenge scene is presented in an overexposed slow-motion flashback. The teenage Harriet flees from the cabin with blood on her face and bruises on her arms, and is chased down to the jetty by her topless, lumbering father. A close-up shot of the swinging oar anticipates the vengeful act of violence Harriet now confesses to. As she holds Gottfried under the water with the oar, the reverse shot shows her distressed yet determined expression and her wild blonde hair backlit by the sun. This flashback is the text's originary scene in two ways: narratively, as the event which initiates the primary mystery of Harriet's disappearance; and generically, in terms of locating it within cinema's rape-revenge genre. *The Girl with the Dragon Tattoo* pays retro-tribute to the genre with Harriet's backstory, but also presents a contemporary alternative to this rape-avenger figure in Lisbeth Salander – Stieg Larsson's vision of the ultimate victim/avenger in a corrupt welfare state.

Larsson's Millennium trilogy brings into focus some of the tensions surrounding the cultural politics of the place of the victim in contemporary rape-revenge narratives, particularly through the figure of Salander. Director Niels Arden Oplev's Swedish film adaptation of the first novel, *The Girl with the Dragon Tattoo*, further highlights these tensions through its exploration of affective experience and ethical spectatorship. This chapter explores how the Swedish film adaptation works to create a series of contradictory experiences for spectators – we are invited to ethical reflection, but also encouraged to develop 'perverse allegiances' with the avenging protagonist. The film calls for a re-thinking of the relation between affect, ethics, and moral action in the rape-revenge genre, and it points to how contemporary film theory can – and must – move beyond examples from the narrow sets of experimental and art house films typically used to discuss questions of materiality, affect, and ethics.[1] I will primarily be exploring these fields through a close examination of the film's rape and revenge scenes. Although the two rapes committed by Salander's new guardian, Advokat Nils Erik Bjurman, and Salander's violent revenge upon him take up only a small mid-section of the first novel (2008: 197–236) and approximately 13 minutes of screen time, they are key in constructing Salander's character and conveying some key themes of the trilogy, including victimhood, individualism, and responsibility. Before I delve into the ambivalent ethics, affects, and politics of these scenes, I will give a brief overview of three key contexts – theoretical, generic, and political – into which the film can be placed to reveal its workings: contemporary film theory discourses on ethical spectatorship; the broader genre location of 'medium-concept' films, which tempers the deployment of rape-revenge and the ambiguous uses of intense affective or sensory experiences; and finally, contemporary anti-victimism discourse, a discourse linked to the individualism promoted by post-feminist and neo-liberal ideologies.

The rape and revenge scenes draw on models of ethical spectatorship in interesting ways, encouraging empathetic engagement with Salander, while also steering particular responses to the rape scenes through Salander's example in the post-rape scenes. I suggest that although ethical engagement with Salander is encouraged, ethical spectatorship is limited because the moral and political meanings of rape and revenge are tightly controlled and kept within particular ideological and generic strictures. In other words, we are not challenged to reflect upon or question the moral frameworks that inform the text – such as the vigilantism of the rape-revenge genre – a requirement of ethical spectatorship (Aaron 2007: 114). Michele Aaron's model of ethical spectatorship, which I draw on in this chapter, focuses on notions of response and responsibility and posits ethics as being 'all about thinking through one's relationship to morality rather than just adhering to it' (109). Key to the distinction of ethics from morality is the 'prioritisation of (ethical) recognition, realisation, reflection – the stuff of agency – over (moral) prescription, proclamation and punishment – the stuff of ideology' (109). There is a tension between the moral and ethical responses to rape and revenge in the film, with Salander's rape calling on an *ethical engagement*, while Bjurman's rape (by Salander) calls on a particular *moral response*, one which is in line with neo-liberal individualism (which here seeks a heroic overthrowing of the corrupt welfare state, as represented by the guardianship system) and the demands of the rape-revenge genre (aligned with the moral precept of 'eye for an eye'). Reading the rape scenes against the revenge scene helps to articulate the contrast between ethics and morality in spectatorship, with the latter scene providing moral reassurance against the difficult ethical questions and uncomfortable spectatorial positioning of the former. While the rape scenes in the Swedish film version display trappings of ethical spectatorship – such as that developed by 'new extremism' films[2] – ultimately *The Girl with the Dragon Tattoo* cannot follow through with this to fully confront or implicate the spectator. Rather, it uses these trappings only to the degree that they fit within, and contribute to, the moral framework, genre conventions, and mainstream audiences of the text.

These tensions may be partly symptomatic of the film's 'medium-concept' position. *Dragon Tattoo* can be located within what Andrew Nestingen conceptualizes as Nordic 'medium-concept' cinema, a marriage of genre narratives and art-film aesthetics which inflects crime narratives with 'philosophical and cultural-political questions and demands' (2008: 48). The film adaptation of the Millennium trilogy marks the culmination of the development in Swedish cinema which Nestingen traces, where the increasing number of adaptations of Scandinavian police procedurals and spy novels in the 1990s produced a prevalent form 'with the aim of merging popular cinema and social critique, even when the latter is confined to a few gestures required by the genre' (49). *Dragon Tattoo* epitomizes the way that 'these films use genre form and its conduciveness to marketing to raise political questions and instigate debate and attract large audiences' (49). Oplev's film uses the rape-revenge genre to explore questions of response and responsibility around issues of rape and victimization. The rape-revenge genre is an appropriate template for the tensions in the text, with its conventions employed to synthesize the contradictions between the film's ethical call (to acknowledge the serious negative impact of rape on the victim, for example), its rejection of victimhood, and its advocation of violent response. Individualism is a key site of debate in medium-concept crime films (Nestingen 2008: 97), a concept that I argue similarly permeates the politics of rape and revenge in *Dragon Tattoo*. The use of Hollywood-esque goal-oriented protagonists to represent social struggles means such issues play out in the realm of 'individualism and the personal resolution of complex socio-economic and moral problems' (15). *Dragon Tattoo* follows this pattern, using the individualist attitudes and actions of its heroine to explore rape and the appropriate responses to it.

In the Millennium trilogy, Larsson goes further than suggesting that revenge is the desirable and justifiable response to rape, as many other rape-revenge texts before him have done. He advocates the idea of revenge as the *responsibility* of the rape victim, a notion that resonates with the threads of anti-victimism and individualism in post-feminist and neo-liberal cultures. The two rape scenes I discuss are just two examples of the constant victimization of Salander. Repeat victimization is key to Salander's character, and the epic trilogy has the space to keep returning to and elaborating upon those rapes, often with pulpy and salacious descriptions. Larsson describes how Salander suffers under and is *created by* systematic injustices (including domestic violence and the guardianship system) and sexual assault, which by definition makes her a victim, and yet there is a strong rejection of the label:

> Even though she was well aware of what a women's crisis centre was for, it never occurred to her to turn to one herself. Crisis centres existed, in her eyes, for *victims*, and she had never regarded herself as a victim. Consequently, her only remaining option was to do what she had always done – take matters in her own hands and solve her problems on her own. (2008: 213)

Alyson M. Cole argues that the linguistic disavowal of victimhood is 'the best evidence of the success of the crusade to shame victims' (2007: 2). Cole identifies an 'anti-victimism' discourse in contemporary American culture and politics, and argues that anti-victimists have constructed a notion of 'true victimhood' in opposition to 'victimism' (5). Salander reflects the figure of the True Victim, particularly the characteristics of responsibility (commanding her fate and rejecting the victim label) and individuality (not engaging in 'victim politics' or being a victim by affiliation) (5). Larsson distances Salander from 'victim feminism', a label used by post-feminist authors in the 1990s and related to the broader anti-victimism campaign. Rape statistics and anti-rape literature are particularly contested terrain for post-feminist authors such as Katie

Roiphe, Camille Paglia, and Christine Hoff Sommers, who promote the idea that 'Victims in fact owe their victimization not to the experience of rape but to a feminist propaganda that has brain-washed women into thinking of themselves as victims' (Mardorossian 2002: 748). Salander is also distanced from the Nordic concept of 'state feminism', a label given to the women's movements of the 1970s, which were collective, consensus-based, and cooperated with the state (Stenport and Alm 2009: 169). Salander's personal revenge, although positioned by Larsson as a feminist response, might be more accurately described as an individualist post-feminist response, as it forecloses broader social critique and the possibility of the type of collective response characteristic of second-wave feminisms.

The rape-revenge narrative, characters, attitude, and aesthetic in this film strongly reflect an anti-victimism perspective. For anti-victimists, 'blaming, whining, complaining, and other public displays of weakness are considered aesthetically repulsive and socially harmful' (Cole 2007: 130–31). Salander's attitude to the commonplace nature of her and other girls she knew being forced to perform sexual acts is that 'There was no point whimpering about it' (2008: 204). Her attitude towards Harriet's story is fiercely anti-victimist, bordering on victim blaming, as she demonstrates in a conversation with Blomkvist where she accepts no excuses for Harriet running away in 1966, referring to her as a 'bitch' and as 'Harriet Fucking Vanger' (448).

Salander's attitude supports Melanie Newman's argument that the ass-kicking babes in crime novels by authors such as James Patterson, Stieg Larsson, and Dean Koontz reveal misogynistic beliefs such as 'if only females would stop acting as "victims" and discover their own capacity for violence, the aggression visited on them by men would disappear' (2009). In the anti-victimist view, as in the rape-revenge genre, 'Victimhood is a transitory state from which the victimized are expected to ascend' (Cole 2007: 138). Salander does this through avenging her own rape, and becoming a vigilante against other injustices. The affective drive I will now outline in the analysis of the rape scenes is underpinned by – and at the service of – anti-victimist politics, and the pay-off for both of these affective and political motivators is the brutal revenge which matches her brutal victimization.

The first rape scene: power, control, disgust

There is a strong fidelity to the novel in the Swedish film adaptation of *Dragon Tattoo*, as might be expected due to the popularity of

Larsson's work. However, in the shift between the mediums there are subtle yet significant shifts in the tone, graphicness, and structure of the rape scenes. These small schisms, created in translation, illuminate the meaning attributed to rape, and how rape and its responses are constructed in fiction/film representations. In the novel, Larsson explicitly outlines the exploitative and illegal nature of what occurs between Bjurman and Salander:

> The initial sexual assault – which in legal terms would be defined as sexual molestation and the exploitation of an individual in a position of dependence, and could in theory get Bjurman up to two years in prison – lasted only a few seconds. But it was enough to irrevocably cross a boundary. (2008: 198)

The action of the scene, a ten-minute ordeal in which Salander is forced to perform oral sex on Bjurman, is described in just a few sentences, about the same number of words given to her cleaning her face, mouth, and sweater in the bathroom in the following paragraph (199). The film adaptation is faithful to the action of the scene, but uses a specific film grammar to construct the meaning of rape and its impact on Salander and the viewer. Larsson takes a legalistic, educational tone in the account of the first rape, as shown in the above-quoted passage, and makes clear what can be defined as rape and what evidence could be used in this case to prove it:

> The bruises on her neck, as well as the DNA signature of his semen staining her body and clothing, would have nailed him. Even if the lawyer had claimed that *she wanted to do it* or *she seduced me* or any other excuse that rapists routinely used, he would have been guilty of so many breaches of the guardianship regulations that he would instantly have been stripped of his control over her. (201)

Larsson continues in an educational tone as he elaborates on the welfare system in Sweden and the differences between trustee and guardianship, making clear his position that the guardianship system is a great infringement of democracy (2008: 201–202). Larsson's narration explores the affective and fantasy responses to misogyny through Salander's character while also adding political commentary about appropriate real world responses to sexual violence and other injustices. His political and educational commentary, and the insights into the thoughts of Salander and Bjurman during the rape scene, are more difficult to convey in narrative film, and are further limited by genre conventions. The film emphasizes not the legalities or the institutionally oppressed position Salander is in, but the more affective elements such as power, control and disgust.

The dynamics between the two characters and the significance of what occurs between them are expressed through film grammar, particularly camera angles: the breakdown of the shot/reverse-shot exchange, and the contrasting of a clinical wide shot with close-ups that emphasize unpleasant sensory experiences. The scene opens like a continuation of Bjurman and Salander's earlier conversation in his office; they are seated in the same positions either side of his desk and the film conventionally shot/reverse-shots between them as he again asks prurient personal questions. Bjurman closes the blinds and moves around to her side of his desk. He slaps her and threatens her – a more violent beginning to this incident than described in the novel, and one which helps establish alignment with Salander because we experience the cinematic shock as she experiences the physical shock. The violence of the scene and the powerlessness of Salander's position cannot be commented on by Larsson's narration in the film, so this slap functions as a shortcut. It also marks a power shift in the scene; now the camera is held level, square on, in the shots of her, and at a slight low angle in the shots of him, indicating he is increasingly asserting his power. The alternating shots of them are no longer shot/reverse-shots, which emphasizes the different experiences of the characters and their 'disconnect'. Salander directs several expressionless glances direct to camera while Bjurman threatens her and gropes her breasts. These glances seem to say directly to the spectator, 'Look what's happening to me' (even perhaps a 'Help me'), seeking to draw us into a response to the rape scenes which acknowledges the fear and harm experienced by Salander.

A further power shift, an amping up, is indicated by a shot of Salander looking up at him when he turns her around to face him, her face filling the frame. The rape is then depicted mainly between two alternating shots: a wide shot of the whole office from behind Bjurman, his body blocking Salander, and a close-up shot of the back of Salander's head with Bjurman's hand gripping her hair and controlling her. This pairing shows the action and gives it (feminist) meaning – it removes any doubt as to what is happening (by documenting it in a wide shot) while also removing the sexual nature of oral sex in this instance, indicating through the close-up that it is forced, that it is about power and control. Both shots block the spectator's view of the 'action', minimizing the scene's potential to be exploitative or sexy. A low angle shot of Bjurman's sweaty face (aligned with Salander's position, although not from her point-of-view), and his dialogue, 'If you're nice to me, I'll always be nice to you,' adds disgust to the scene. Disgust is a useful rhetorical device in vengeance narratives; physical and socio-moral disgust are wedded and exaggerated to justify the execution of the criminal (Plantinga 2009: 213). Here, the use of disgust points to the way in which the film increasingly falls back on a moral rather than an ethical approach to what occurs between Salander and Bjurman.

The scene then cuts abruptly to a close-up of Salander in the bathroom vigorously scrubbing her mouth out with three fingers, as if to make herself vomit. Truncating Salander's ten-minute ordeal and omitting Bjurman's climax curtails the potential spectatorial enjoyment, exploitation, and pornographicness of the scene. Depicting vigorous washing rather than the dirty act itself directs a particular response to the rape scene; it mirrors, prompts, or encourages feeling dirty or disgusted. This construction forecloses a variety of responses which the rape scene (if made longer, or shot differently) may have evoked, responses which are opposed to Salander's response and the politics of the text. Again, disgust is being used to direct a more normative *moral* response, as opposed to allowing the spectator agency to recognize and reflect on the issues raised by the scene in their own *ethical* response. Salander's action of washing the evidence away points to her individualist approach, which is condoned in the text through Harriet's and Salander's private ways of dealing with their rapists, and the covering up of Gottfried and Martin's rapes and murders at the end. Affectively and ethically, the response to rape is channelled into the desire and imperative for individual revenge outside of the law. In constructing an intense experience of rape for spectators, inviting us to share the affects it produces (such as disgust and rage), the film implicates us through embodiment. By incorporating the spectator in this way, the film is able to advise us on how to react to the difficult spectacles of violence it is presenting. The use of the videotape after the second rape plays a similar role in guiding spectatorial response.

The second rape scene: victimization, affect, and emotion

The film's second rape scene uses similar filmic techniques to the first, emphasizing Salander's victimization through repetition and increasing the affective motivation to see revenge against Bjurman. In a three minute scene set in Bjurman's bedroom, Bjurman strikes Salander, handcuffs her to the bed, gags her, hits her again, ties her feet to the end of the bed, pulls down her underwear and his own, and then rapes her. The cinematographic grammar, numerous close-ups, the use of sound, and the replaying of Salander's videotape are techniques which affectively underscore the repeat victimization of Salander. The film is driven by a rejection of victimhood, but it relies on an affective presentation of the constant victimization of its protagonist to highlight its cinematic thrills and its story of individual heroic triumph over misogyny and the corrupt welfare state.

The scene packs an immediate affective punch, but it is not as graphic as in the novels, in the sense of not including – or returning to – salacious details such as the nipple piercing, a list of Bjurman's torture implements, and his attempt to strangle her with her t-shirt (*Hornets' Nest* 2009: 343). The difference in the reading and viewing experience is not in the representation's *graphicness*, understood as representational explicitness, but in its *affectiveness*, understood as the ability to move the spectator using 'visceral forces' (Seigworth and Gregg 2010: 1), which is achieved through certain film techniques such as slow motion, distorted sound, and colour. Graphicness alone can be exploitative and/or unaffecting, but affectiveness conveys to the spectator what rape trauma feels like and creates a space for affective, reflective, and ethical engagement. The relative restraint in terms of graphicness (in contrast to many new extremism and exploitation films, for example, and also in contrast to the detail described in the book) does not detract from conveying the violence or trauma of rape. Indeed, the filmic grammar used here limits the potential for exploitation or voyeurism inherent in a rape scene. Salander's body is not sexualized in this rape scene – she is fully clothed for most of it, with only brief shots of both Bjurman and Salander's naked buttocks. Spatially, there is no intimate, involved perspective: the two-shot economy positions the spectator at either an uncomfortable distance from the action in a long shot, or an uncomfortable proximity to Salander's experience in the facial close-ups, as I will detail further below. For the rape scenes in *Dragon Tattoo* the affect derives from the effect of rape, its aftermath, rather than from film techniques that merely sensationalize the act itself. This approach may be considered part of the film's ethical address, in that it leaves the spectator wondering how to dispose of those affective charges. In other words, how does affect convert into (moral) action? The easiest answer, for both film and spectator, is to allow genre formula to step in, converting anger and disgust into revenge through the rape-revenge narrative.

The repetition and escalation of violence between Bjurman and Salander is shown by connecting the first three scenes between them (initial conversation, first rape, second rape) through visual mirroring. For example, the wide shot of the office from behind Bjurman during the first rape matches the wide shot of Bjurman on the bed raping Salander again in terms of framing, distance, and the positioning of the characters. In both scenes, the wide shot alternates with a 180-degree reverse close-up shot of Salander. This contrast depicts the dichotomies of power/powerlessness, control/loss of control; the meaning of rape is constructed as being about this switch, and emphasizing the contrast makes the spectator *feel* Salander's loss of power and control. As in the first rape scene, the film grammar changes with the power shift when the rape begins. After a conventional shot/reverse-shot construction during their conversation when Salander arrives, the commencement of violence is marked by a new two-shot construction: a close-up of Salander's face in the foreground (with a shallow depth of field leaving Bjurman's face out of focus in the background), which ends as she turns around and is surprised by a punch to the face from Bjurman; this is followed by a match-on-action edit to a wide shot, which shows her falling onto the bed from the force of the punch. A surprise blow to the face denotes the beginning of the physical violence against Salander in both rape scenes. Such repetition emphasizes the ongoing victimization of Salander. Like the slap in the first scene, this punch also functions as a 'cinematic shock' to the spectator (Hanich 2010: 133). This cinematic technique snaps us into affective alignment with Salander, with both Salander and the viewer experiencing a shock to the senses and being violently put in her/our place by Bjurman.

Affective alignment with Salander is also forcefully achieved in the film adaptation through close-ups of Salander's face. Her pained, frightened, and panicked facial expressions are deeply affecting, particularly her final harrowing silent scream, which emphasizes these affects by using film techniques such as camera distance and angle (close-up, level with the bed), distorted sound, and slow motion. Salander's close-ups reflect Carl Plantinga's argument that 'facial expressions in film not only communicate emotion, but also elicit, clarify, and strengthen affective response – especially empathetic response' (1999: 240). The climactic silent scream close-up marks the scene as an example of what Plantinga terms a 'scene of empathy', where narrative pace slows and attention becomes focused on a character's emotional experience (239). Since the most powerful scenes of empathy are reserved for 'a kind of emotional and cognitive summation of the ideological project of the film' (253), Salander's scream can be understood as a summation of the film's cycles of victimization and vengeance.

When Salander arrives home in the scene after the rape, she takes the hidden video camera out of her bag and plays back the tape while smoking a cigarette. There is no shot of the video footage; instead we see close-ups of her shaking hands and her bloody face while listening to the audio of the rape along with her. Salander listening to her rape via video, outside of the experience itself, mirrors our experience while watching the previous scene. This pair of scenes (rape and playback) take us through an affect to emotion transition, developing our immediate sensory response into reflections upon these responses and emotions, such as anger and disgust. This transition is key to the rape-revenge connection, preparing the viewer to become ready and keen for Salander's response of revenge (which the tape plays a key role in enacting). We initially experience the rape scene affectively – perhaps ourselves needing to cover our eyes, turn down the sound, have a cigarette, feel shaky or sick – because of the powerful visuals and sound. Then Salander experiences it as a spectator and her post-traumatic and affective reaction takes the film's spectators to another level of processing the event. Immediately after the rape scene, the film directs the spectator to respond in a certain way by depicting how Salander herself responds to it. The spectator is affectively and narratively led to support Salander's individualist and violent revenge on Bjurman and her covering up of his and her crimes, even if this conflicts with the spectator's political or ethical views on how to respond to sexual violence. Hence, a more complex or challenging ethical engagement may be abandoned because the film reassuringly offers a guide to responding in ways that are in keeping with its standard moral and genre frameworks.

Salander's post-rape playback in the film is a kind of response correction, analogous to the way that Larsson tightly controls the meaning of what happens to her in the novel. For example, the chapter after the second rape begins:

> Salander spent the week in bed with pain in her abdomen, bleeding from her rectum, and less visible wounds that would take longer to heal. What she had gone through was very different from the first rape in his office; it was no longer a matter of coercion and degradation. This was systematic brutality. (2008: 226)

These opening sentences highlight the different tools available to book and film in conveying the physical and other traumas Salander experiences (with the film using sound to represent the pain of these internal wounds that Larsson can identify more explicitly), but it also highlights how authorial voice is foregrounded in the book's narration. The book tells the reader that the rape is a case of punishment, coercion, degradation, and systematic brutality, whereas the film encourages the viewer to discover the meaning of the act (and the imperative for revenge) through the direction of response led by Salander's demonstration. For the film, affectively responding in the 'correct' way is important to lead the spectator into the revenge scenes. Like *Strange Days* (Bigelow, US, 1995), and other heavily self-reflexive mainstream films discussed by Michele Aaron, *Dragon Tattoo* incorporates both the spectator and the spectator's response in order to present 'very clear (moral) guidelines of how to react to these difficult spectacles' (2007: 96). However, while Aaron's examples implicate their spectators by simultaneously 'heavily restricting the reassurances on offer' (93), *Dragon Tattoo* eases the spectator's sense of ethical responsibility and implication by offering reassurances, such as meeting genre expectations and pleasures when Salander becomes a vigilante in the revenge scenes.

The man with the avenger's tattoo

The film visually emphasizes Salander's choice to respond to her rape with an act of revenge which mirrors the second rape. She returns to Bjurman's apartment, Tasers him in order to tie him up, anally rapes him with the same dildo he used on her, and then forces him to watch the videotape of him raping her. She threatens to release the video to the media and police if he does not give her back control of her money and arrange the termination of her guardianship. She then tattoos 'I am a sadistic pig and a rapist' on his abdomen. The duration, setting, action, and cinematography all mirror the previous rape scene: there are distanced high angle shots taking in the whole scene, including Bjurman tied up naked on his bedroom floor; there are level close-ups of his frightened face with a gagged mouth; and a low angle shot showing Salander above him, shoving the dildo in his anus, then kicking his kidneys twice. After raping him, Salander puts on the DVD of her rape and leaves the room. Bjurman is left to this uncomfortable audio-visual experience alone, while the spectator keeps Salander company outside of the room as she smokes and waits for it to finish. We are face-to-face with Salander in a close-up as she smokes, with her gaze just off camera as though her eyes could flicker to look directly at you at any moment. This facial close-up, the act of smoking, and the close-up of her hand as she butts out her cigarette, all echo the post-rape playback scene.

This works to remind viewers of Salander's (and their own) embodied response to the event, and keeps us aligned with the perspective of the traumatized victim hungry for revenge, even in the face of her ethically dubious choice to respond with a rape for a rape.

Salander's revenge is effective, yet ethically problematic, precisely because it mirrors her own rape. Naomi Wolf writes that 'Rape activists have found that one of the most effective – and punishing – therapies for convicted rapists is to have victims of rape tell them in person the damage the assault did to them' (1994: 118). The existence of the DVD keeps Bjurman under control, preventing him from committing further violence because its release would ruin him, but its replaying is also about forcing him to relive the rape from the victim's perspective, which he is now in a position to empathize with since he is tied up, raped, and still vulnerable. The tattoo Salander gives Bjurman is another method of making him understand the damage he did to her and of enacting retributive justice. The tattoo is a metaphor for rape which can be graphically portrayed – the tattoo represents injury, bodily trauma, penetration, and resultant bleeding, and its depiction in close-up makes it the most graphic, climactic act of violence between them. There is more build-up than there was to the rape as she sets up her kit, then there are close-ups of the tattooing and a slow-motion close-up of Bjurman raising his head to look at her, his eyes wild and rage-filled and his nostrils flaring. The slow-motion technique suggests that Bjurman is experiencing the same pain that Salander did at the moment of her slow-motion scream in the second rape scene. Slow motion is an effective technique for conveying pain, as Jane Stadler writes: 'As a cinematic technique, slow motion can enunciate the experience of being in a situation of extreme stress when every second and every moment through space holds magnified significance' (2008: 166 n10). Does this effect similarly create empathy for Bjurman? To the contrary, it seems to be working here as a reminder of *Salander's* pain when she was raped. Since Salander is constantly victimized and the spectator is led to empathize with her and stay with her in the post-rape scenes, we can only see her as a victim – she remains the True Victim despite her brutality against him here. In the revenge scene, when the ethical face-to-face relationship has fully disintegrated, we can stay on Salander's side, even as a perpetrator of rape and disfigurement.

Spectatorial alignment is subtly manipulated through point-of-view conventions, with the earlier part of the scene presenting Bjurman's point-of-view of Salander (such as the out-of-focus shot of her entering the room) but not vice versa, whereas the later part of the scene, after we have joined Salander outside for a cigarette, shifts to present more of Salander's point-of-view shots of Bjurman's face. The novel describes how 'His eyes were burning with hatred' (2008: 234), which mirrors the end of the second rape scene when Bjurman 'almost recoiled when he met her eyes. Never in his life had he seen such naked, smouldering hatred' (225). The role reversal between rapist and rape victim is common in contemporary rape-revenge films, for example, the way the prey becomes predator in *Hard Candy* (Slade, US, 2005), and how rape is used as revenge upon a rapist in *Straightheads* (Reed, UK, 2007) and *Descent* (Lugacy, US, 2007). Violently rejecting the role of victim, these protagonists regain control and satisfy their need for revenge, albeit at the price of landing in an ethically problematic position. The repetition and role reversal bring up questions about the ethics and effectiveness of vengeance, and narrativize the issue of victims becoming perpetrators. However, *Dragon Tattoo* does not problematize Salander's revenge to the same degree as these other films, instead allowing the spectator a more morally righteous satisfaction in her eye-for-an-eye revenge. The Swedish film adaptations of the next two books in the trilogy, both directed by Daniel Alfredson and released in 2009, also increasingly present Salander's brand of justice as both clever and justified, potentially excusing the unethical nature of some of her actions.

Despite the fact that the revenge scene mirrors the rape scene quite closely, we do not have the same empathy and ethical engagement with the victim in the revenge scene, nor are we positioned to morally judge or be disgusted by Salander's violence as we were with Bjurman's. How can this double standard of ethics be accounted for? Drawing on a cognitive theory of character identification, I suggest that our engagement with Salander (and other rape-avenger protagonists in the genre) is one of what Murray Smith calls 'perverse allegiance' (1999: 221). In Smith's account, allegiance is often based on traits that we desire to possess, ones which may be socially or morally proscribed, and 'indeed, the desire, and the pleasure arising from an imaginary experience of fulfilling it, may arise as a resistance to such social and moral constraints' (221). These desirous characteristics may include various transgressive aspects of Salander's character, from her goth/punk appearance, to her rude behaviour with Milton Security clients, to her computer hacking abilities, but as a revenge film, her trait of taking justice into her own hands is the one we experience vicariously. Genre films, including rape-revenge, may particularly lend themselves to such perverse allegiances, as Rick Altman argues that a committed genre film spectator must be 'sufficiently committed to generic values to tolerate and even enjoy in genre films capricious, violent, or licentious behaviour which they might disapprove of in "real life"' (1996: 279). We turn away from the face-to-face ethical encounter with Bjurman, the film's monster but also its current victim, in order to enjoy the pleasures of the genre, including the violent spectacle of revenge. While the revenge scene conveys Bjurman's pain and offers some degree of a face-to-face ethical encounter (in the slow-motion moment, for example), it is not sufficient to override the strong, perverse allegiance the spectator has with Salander throughout the trilogy. The *moral* structure of character allegiance takes precedence over the more challenging *ethical* engagement the spectator can be invited to make when the roles of victim and perpetrator are reversed. Since ethical questioning can bring moral frameworks into doubt, ethical spectatorship may be experienced as uncomfortable spectatorship. By maintaining clear distinctions between victim and perpetrator, good guys and bad guys, *Dragon Tattoo* allows the spectator to remain in a more comfortable realm of morality, where answers are provided and required actions are clear. We do not question our avenging protagonist or sympathize with her rape victim too much because perverse allegiance with Salander is supported by the text as a whole, and even the genre as a whole, as well as the moral codes upon which both draw. This type of engagement becomes more about the pursuit of pleasure than ethics; it is the pleasure of reassuring moral law being exacted. Such pleasures, typical of genre films from Westerns to action films, contrast with the displeasures of what Nikolaj Lübecker terms the 'feel-bad' film, in which the spectator is denied catharsis or punished for it (2011: 165–67).

Conclusion

As a case study, *Dragon Tattoo* points to the many and complex influences which shape representations of rape and the response to rape, from socio-political contexts to various genre conventions. This chapter has explored the politics, ethics, and affects in the filmic construction of rape and its revenge. This popular, medium-concept text is a rich site for exploring these fields because it negotiates various tensions and captures slippages between the source novel and the film adaptation. These tensions play out around the key themes of victimhood and individualism, and particularly through the character of Salander and her rape-revenge narrative.

In both the novel and its Swedish film adaptation, personal revenge is positioned as a political and ethical imperative, with the rape and revenge of Lisbeth Salander highlighting the Millennium trilogy's advocation of individualist revenge as a response to social injustice. In line with post-feminist and anti-victimist rhetoric, the text constructs an idea of revenge as responsibility, particularly for the erasure of female victimhood and victimization. Revenge becomes an aesthetic and moral imperative in the face of systematic injustice, and Salander becomes an exemplar of the victim-avenger figure for the novel's politics and for cinema's rape-revenge genre. The novel presents a collective oppression solvable by individual responsibility, while the film concentrates this individualism by crystallizing cycles of victimization and vengeance in a goal-oriented protagonist who resonates with audiences affectively and generically.

The film draws on models of ethical spectatorship, but the revenge narrative and the demands of the genre cause this to be abandoned, or at least overridden, by our 'perverse allegiance' with Salander as she pursues her righteous vengeance. This is a consequence of frictions in the medium-concept marriage of genre narratives and art-film aesthetics; the scenes of rape and revenge point to the contradictions and dilutions that medium-concept crime films are susceptible to. This compromise – the abandoning of the ethical for the sake of revenge – is one reason why the film is both satisfying and popular: it embroils the spectator in an affecting, compelling ethical engagement, but steers away from implication, letting the spectator off the hook with the reassurance of moral hard lines in the revenge scenes. The rape-revenge of Lisbeth Salander treads a fine line in order to avoid being voyeuristic and exploitative, yet contradictorily, aims to be thoroughly watchable and thrilling. By detailing the rape, post-rape, and revenge scenes, I have sought to show how ethical spectatorship is both constructed and compromised through tensions with political, affective, and generic drives. Limitations are placed on ethical spectatorship because the moral and political codes – as well as the genre expectations for a revenge film – demand individual responsibility and insist that righteous, violent vengeance is enacted.

Notes

1. Theories of sensation and affect in film studies have been developed through analysis of experimental films, 'intercultural cinema', and new extremism films by scholars such Martine Beugnet (2007), Laura U. Marks (2000), and Jennifer M. Barker (2009). Similarly, ethics in film theory, once confined primarily to the study of documentary, has more recently been applied to popular Hollywood cinema as well by, for example, Fred Botting and Scott Wilson (2001), and Lisa Downing and Libby Saxton (2010).

2. The new extremism refers to a diverse body of contemporary films directed by European auteurs such as Catherine Breillat, Gaspar Noé, Lars von Trier, and Michael Haneke, which feature 'contentious subject matter' and an 'emphasis on shock effects and unpleasurable sensations' (Horeck and Kendall 2011: 6). Tanya Horeck and Tina Kendall note that: 'Beyond the collective emphasis in these films on explicit and brutal sex, and on graphic or sadistic violence ... it is first and foremost the uncompromising and highly self-reflexive appeal to the spectator that marks out the specificity of these films' (2011: 1).

Works cited

Aaron, M. (2007) *Spectatorship: The Power of Looking On*. London: Wallflower Press.
Altman, R. (1996) 'Cinema and Genre' in G. Nowell-Smith (ed.) *The Oxford History of World Cinema*. Oxford: Oxford University Press. 276–85.
Barker, J. M. (2009) *The Tactile Eye: Touch and the Cinematic Experience*. Berkeley and Los Angeles: University of California Press.
Beugnet, M. (2007) *Cinema and Sensation: French Film and the Art of Transgression*. Edinburgh: Edinburgh University Press.
Botting, F. and S. Wilson (2001) *The Tarantinian Ethics*. London: SAGE Publications.
Cole, A. M. (2007) *The Cult of True Victimhood: From the War on Welfare to the War on Terror*. Stanford: Stanford University Press.
Downing, L. and L. Saxton (2010) *Film and Ethics: Foreclosed Encounters*. London: Routledge.
Hanich, J. (2010) *Cinematic Emotion in Horror Films and Thrillers: The Paradox of Pleasurable Fear*. New York and London: Routledge.
Horeck, T. and T. Kendall (2011) (eds) *The New Extremism in Cinema: From France to Europe*. Edinburgh: Edinburgh University Press.
Larsson, S. (2008) *The Girl With the Dragon Tattoo*. Transl. R. Keeland. London: MacLehose Press.
Larsson, S. (2009) *The Girl Who Kicked the Hornets' Nest*. Transl. R. Keeland. London: MacLehose Press.
Lübecker, N. (2011) 'Lars von Trier's *Dogville*: A Feel-Bad Film' in T. Horeck and T. Kendall (eds) *The New Extremism in Cinema: From France to Europe*. Edinburgh: Edinburgh University Press. 157–68.
Mardorossian, C. M . (2002) 'Toward a New Feminist Theory of Rape', *Signs: A Journal of Women in Culture and Society* 27. 3, 743–75.
Marks, L. U. (2000) *The Skin of the Film: Intercultural Cinema, Embodiment, and the Senses*. Durham and London: Duke University Press.
Nestingen, A. (2008) *Crime and Fantasy in Scandinavia: Fiction, Film and Social Change*. Seattle: University of Washington Press.
Newman, M . (2009) 'Feminist or Misogynist?' *The F Word*. 4 Sep, http://www.thefword.org.uk/reviews/2009/09/larrson_review, accessed 13 Feb 2012.
Plantinga, C. (1999) 'The Scene of Empathy and the Human Face on Film' in C. Plantinga and G. M. Smith (ed.) *Passionate Views: Film, Cognition, and Emotion*. Baltimore: The Johns Hopkins University Press. 239–55.
Plantinga, C. (2009) *Moving Viewers: American Film and the Spectator's Experience*. Berkeley: University of California Press.

Seigworth, G. J. and M. Gregg (2010) 'An Inventory of Shimmers' in M. Gregg and G. J. Seigworth (eds) *The Affect Theory Reader*. Durham and London: Duke University Press. 1–25.

Smith, M. (1999) 'Gangsters, Cannibals, Aesthetes, or Apparently Perverse Allegiances' in C. Plantinga and G. M. Smith (eds) *Passionate Views: Film, Cognition, and Emotion*. Baltimore: The Johns Hopkins University Press. 217–38.

Stadler, J. (2008) *Pulling Focus: Intersubjective Experience, Narrative Film, and Ethics*. London: Continuum.

Stenport, A. W. and C. O. Alm (2009) 'Corporations, Crime, and Gender Construction in Stieg Larsson's *The Girl with the Dragon Tattoo*: Exploring Twenty-First Century Neoliberalism in Swedish Culture', *Scandinavian Studies* 81. 2, 157–78.

Wolf, N. (1994) *Fire with Fire: The New Female and How It Will Change The 21st Century*. London: Vintage.

11
'Hidden in the Snow': Female Violence against the Men Who Hate Women in the Millennium Adaptations

Philippa Gates

The incredible success of Stieg Larsson's Millennium trilogy saw its adaption for the big screen with a series of Swedish films – *The Girl with the Dragon Tattoo* (Oplev, 2009), *The Girl Who Played with Fire* (Alfredson, 2009), and *The Girl Who Kicked the Hornets' Nest* (Alfredson, 2009). Just as the novels saw their translation and publication into several languages, the film series was produced with an international audience in mind.[1] As Anna Westerståhl Stenport and Cecilia Ovesdotter Alm note, Larsson's *The Girl with the Dragon Tattoo* had become 'a global cultural artefact translated to thirty-five languages and with translation rights pending in more' (2009: 157). Certainly Scandinavian crime stories have, in general, become popular with Anglophone audiences over the past decade, with many novels translated into English and others transformed for the screen (large and small), including the British TV series 'Wallander' (2008–10) starring Kenneth Branagh.[2] Indeed, Hollywood deemed the stories worthy of a reboot and released an English-language remake of *The Girl with the Dragon Tattoo* (2011), directed by David Fincher of *Fight Club* (1999) and *The Social Network* (2010) fame, and a remake of *The Girl Who Played with Fire* is rumoured to be in development. A related universalizing – or even 'Americanizing' – of the conventions and themes of Scandinavian crime fiction occurs with their adaptation to the screen for an international audience, as this chapter will discuss.

Martha Woodroof described *Dragon Tattoo* as an 'unlikely best-seller' because it was written by a previously unknown Swedish journalist who died before the book was published; however, due to an innovative marketing campaign, American publisher Knopf saw its product debut at No. 4 on *The New York Times* bestseller list (2011). Indeed, Stenport and Alm suggest that *Dragon Tattoo* 'is one of literary Sweden's largest international commercial successes since Astrid Lindgren's Pippi Longstocking series' (2009: 158). The marketing of Larsson's novels was successful, and this widespread awareness of the novels meant that North American audiences were primed for the Swedish film adaptations when they were released in 2010, a year after their release in Scandinavian theatres. While novels can appeal to niche markets, films – with their large budgets – need to appeal to as broad an audience as possible in order to recoup their costs and make a profit. *Dragon Tattoo* reportedly cost $13 million to produce, which is very little when compared to the average Hollywood film budget of around $60 million, and equates to only about 10 per cent of the estimated budget for Fincher's American remake.[3] In terms of North American box office, the Swedish films did respectably for foreign-language films, but they were by no means huge hits.[4] The translation of Larsson's novels to the screen for a cinematic and international audience capitalized on the theme of foreign criminals operating in isolated spaces. As one of the taglines for the American remake suggests, 'What is hidden in the snow, comes forth in the thaw', suggesting that Sweden's desolate, winter landscape conceals mysteries waiting to be revealed. The adaptations of the novels, however, included some key alterations to make Larsson's themes more palatable to a broader, mainstream audience –significantly, reducing Blomkvist's sexual escapades and moralizing the heroes' relationship to the law.

In his overview of Swedish crime fiction, G. J. Demko identifies two 'very distinctive traits': first, 'the use of the mystery as a very important mirror of the political, social, and economic policies and processes in a welfare oriented state', as pioneered by Maj Sjöwall and Per Wahlöö in their novels from the 1960s and 1970s; and, second, a 'strong sense of place', as exemplified in the work of Stieg Trenter from the mid-1940s to the late 1960s (2011: 8–10). Larsson's novels and their Swedish film adaptations firmly embody both of these trends: the novels place social and political issues squarely at the centre of the narrative – from Salander's personal battles with psychiatric care and legal guardianship to the underhanded dealings of the Secret Police to the fall of 'consensual corporatism' represented by the Vanger Group, and within Sweden-specific locations – from urban Stockholm condos to remote island cabins to country farmhouses. What Larsson's novels have in common is the investigations by reporter Mikael Blomkvist and hacker

Lisbeth Salander into criminal activities that involve the systematic victimization of women: the disappearance of Harriet Vanger and the serial murders of women in *Dragon Tattoo* (2008); the sex-trafficking trade in *Played with Fire* (2009a); and the illegal operations of a government organization in *Hornets' Nest* (2009b).

In the first part of this chapter I discuss how Larsson identifies the villains as foreign to, and hiding out in the fringes of, Swedish society. The villains represent the intersection of political corruption (in terms of the government) with patriarchal corruption (in terms of the family). Salander embodies both of these themes in terms of female victimization: as a teenager she took revenge on her father for his abuse of her mother; as punishment, she was made a ward of the state and was further victimized by male authority figures including her psychiatrist and later a state-appointed guardian. It is the nature of these villainous 'men who hate women' that then sparks – and goes some way towards justifying – Salander's vengeance as she seeks justice for their female victims (including herself), which is the focus of the second part of the chapter. While the second part explores which aspects of Larsson's themes were altered, or lost, in translation to the screen in the Swedish adaptations, the third part discusses this in relation to the American remake of *Dragon Tattoo*. The aim of this chapter is to explore the shift from Larsson's novels to their film adaptations in terms of how and whether female violence committed against the men who hate women is justified: while Larsson's novels and the Swedish films question Salander's vengeance, the American film channels Larsson's characters and themes into a recognizably Hollywood formula – heteronormativizing Salander and presenting her as an American action hero.

I Larsson's Men Who Hate Women

From the fringes

Immigration has been a hotly contested point in Sweden over the last few decades and, recently, the anti-immigration Sweden Democrats party – which has been described as racist and neo-Nazi – has been gaining greater public and political support.[5] The main villains in Larsson's novels are not Swedish: Salander's wife-beating father, Alexander Zalachenko, is rumoured to be Polish, Serbian, Czech, or Yugoslavian, and is eventually confirmed to be Russian, and his monstrous son, Ronald Niedermann, is the product of a liaison with a German woman. Although Larsson's villains tend to be foreigners his novels are not necessarily anti-immigration, a subtext of several Swedish crime novels. In Kjell Eriksson's *The Princess of Burundi* (Swedish Crime Academy Award winner for 'Best Crime Novel' in 2002), two police detectives discuss the issue. One argues, 'Sweden isn't how it was.[...] There's a lot of new folk now, that's bound to lead to trouble'. The other retorts, 'I know you don't like immigrants, but both Little John [the victim] and Vincent Hahn [the murderer] are products of Swedish social democratic policy, our so-called People's Home' (2006: 228). Eriksson suggests that while immigration may bring bad men like Hahn, it can also bring hard-working citizens like John. Similarly, Larsson offers many positive characters who are immigrants: Dragan Armansky, Salander's employer, is Armenian; Annika Giannini, Blomkvist's sister, is married to an Italian; Harriet Vanger marries an Australian; Detective Bublanski, the lead investigator in *Played with Fire*, is Polish and Jewish; and Dr. Sivarnandan is Sri Lankan but raised by a Finnish couple. In fact, as Stenport and Alm suggest, Larsson presents 'non-Western male immigrants and women with an international connection' as highly successful and as alternatives to the demise of the traditional corporate structure, as represented by the Vanger Group (2009: 166–167). Nor are all of Larsson's immigrants necessarily criminals; when female, they are also victims. Martin Vanger's victims in *Dragon Tattoo* and the women in the sex-trafficking trade in *Played with Fire* and *Hornets' Nest* are also foreigners, mainly from Eastern Europe. Salander is aligned with these women, not only as a victim of male violence, but because of her marginal position in society as a ward of the state. Like an illegal immigrant, Salander lacks her full citizen rights; her life is micro-managed by her guardian – from her finances to her sexual relations.

It is significant that Zalachenko and Niedermann – along with the trilogy's minor villains such as Atho and Harry Ranta (Finnish citizens from an Estonian family) and Tomi and Miro Nicolich (Serbian) – are not naturalized Swedish citizens, nor do they contribute to society through gainful employment and taxes. Instead, they engage in criminal activities against the state: Zalachenko was a top Soviet spy who was granted asylum by Säpo (the Swedish Secret Police) in exchange for information, and Niedermann came from Germany to help his father run his criminal activities, including sex and drug trafficking. Notably, Larsson's villains do not reside in the major, urban centres of Sweden (for example, Stockholm, Göteborg, Malmö, or Uppsala) but hide out – undetected – in rural locations. Slavoj Žižek has argued, in reference to Mankell's Wallander novels, 'The main effect of globalisation on the detective fiction is discernible in its dialectical counterpart: the powerful reemergence of a specific *locale* as the story's setting – a particular provincial environment' (2011: 2). Critics have noted the common depiction of what Žižek describes as the 'Scandinavian bleak countryside with its windy rain, oppressive grey clouds and mist, dark winter days' in Ingmar Bergman's films to Mankell's novels – dubbing the latter 'police procedurals in Bergmanland' (2011: 5).[6] Stenport and Alm suggest that only English-language critics focus on the Swedish landscape and argue that *Dragon Tattoo* actually marks a departure from the local to 'a delocalized and dehumanized world order' (2009: 160–161). I agree with Stenport and Alm that the issues raised in the novel are identified as global ones; however, I would also point out that the novels and their adaptations firmly link their core themes with Swedish spaces and present the Swedish countryside in ways similar to the novels of other contemporary authors including Henning Mankell, Kjell Eriksson, Åke Edwardson, Inger Frimansson, and Åsa Larsson. Indeed, the covers for their novels (at least the English translations) invariably offer scenes of remote, winter landscapes – trees in the snow, footprints in the snow, a lone individual walking in the snow, and a remote farmhouse…in the snow. In *Dragon Tattoo*, those isolated, fringe spaces include Hedeby island where the Vanger clan have homes and Martin has his torture chamber.

Larsson by no means identifies all rustic or remote locations as evil. Interestingly, isolated spaces can make characters 'happy' and 'strangely content', as is the case with Blomkvist's cabin on Sandön island (2008: 770), and can also be the place where the truth is discovered, as with the Vanger's small cottage on Hedeby where Blomkvist resides while researching Harriet's disappearance. In contrast, Martin's dungeon, where he holds his victims prisoner and tortures them, is in the basement of his ultra-modern home. As Martin later informs Blomkvist, he had a girl from Belarus locked up in a cage in the dungeon while Blomkvist dined with him upstairs. 'It was a pleasant evening as I remember, no?' Martin asks (640). In the Swedish film adaptation, Martin's home may be contemporary and stylish, and his dungeon looks more like an antiseptic hospital operating room than how we might imagine a torture chamber to look, but they are located far from urban civilization on the small island of Hedeby, a few hours north of Stockholm. Similarly, *Played with Fire* and *Hornets' Nest* offer remote locations for the sites where evil is planned, enacted, and/or concealed: Björck's summer cabin on Smådalarö, where Blomkvist tracks him down for an interrogation; the Svavelsjö Motorcycle Club, where Niedermann conspires with bikers to kill Salander; the warehouse near Lake Yngern, where Niedermann attacks Salander's friends, Miriam Wu and Paolo Roberto; Bjurman's summer cabin near Stallarholmen, where he hides Salander's damaging reports; Zalachenko's abandoned brickyard outside Norrtälje, where Niedermann hides out from the police; and Zalachenko's farmhouse at Gosseberga (a fictional place), where Salander confronts her father. In *Played with Fire*, Salander ponders her father's choice of hideout:

> She was surprised that Zalachenko would have chosen to live in such an isolated place. It was not like the man she remembered. She would never have expected to find him out in the country in a little white farmhouse. In some anonymous villa community, maybe, or in a vacation spot abroad. He must have made more enemies even than Salander herself. (2009a: 684)

As Salander's thoughts confirm, these villains do not necessarily choose to be isolated; it is often as a by-product of needing to conceal themselves and/or their crimes that they reside on the fringe.

Patriarchal corruption

A central focus of Swedish crime fiction since the 1960s has been the interrogation of Sweden's political and social landscape, and this is perhaps a key reason for the popularity of Scandinavian crime fiction translations with Anglophone audiences.[7] The criminal activities explored in Larsson's three novels and the films see the intersection of political corruption in terms of the government with patriarchal corruption in terms of the family. As Stenport and Alm confirm, in *Dragon Tattoo*, 'Gender and business are consistently intertwined', notably through the novel's section headings, which juxtapose corporate terminology with statistics on the abuse of women in Sweden (2009: 159). In Hollywood films the linking of these types of corruption is often reserved for *noir*, a corpus of films known for their dark tone and socially critical themes. For example, *Chinatown* (Polanski, US, 1974) famously links Noah Cross's (John Huston) political corruption – a plot with water officials to buy up land to which city water can be diverted to develop it – and his paternal corruption – his committing incest with his daughter when she was a teenager. Similarly, in *Devil in a Blue Dress* (Franklin, US, 1995), mayoral candidate Mathew Terrell (Maury Chaykin) blackmails his rival over his relationship with his bi-racial girlfriend, and is later revealed to be a paedophile who abuses his own adopted son.

Larsson's 'men who hate women', then, are familiar *noir* villains – if somewhat rare in the sadistic level of their violence. In Larsson's *Dragon*

Tattoo, Salander is the victim of rape by the lawyer Nils Bjurman who abuses his position of authority as her guardian. Similarly, Harriet Vanger is the victim of incestuous rape by her father, Gottfried Vanger, a key player on the board of the powerful Vanger Group and also a fervent Nazi who murdered Jewish women. In *Played with Fire* and *Hornets' Nest* it is revealed that Salander witnessed the abuse of her mother by her father as a child, and then was mistreated by the psychiatrist, Dr. Peter Teleborian, who was supposed to help her deal with her trauma. Salander is just another chapter in the history of heretical women: she is declared incompetent by the state not because she is mentally ill, but because she refuses to cooperate with male authorities (that is, doctors and lawmen), rebelling against the social roles prescribed her as a woman, a victim, and a patient. Although not the victim of incest at the hands of her father as Harriet was in *Dragon Tattoo*, Salander is the victim of attempted murder in *Played with Fire* as her father, Zalachenko, tries to bury his political secrets along with his daughter. In contemporary detective narratives in fiction, film, and TV, the violence committed is almost always committed against women: or, as Jane Caputi and Diana Russell define it, 'femicide': 'the murder of women by men motivated by hatred, contempt, pleasure, or a sense of ownership of women' (1990: 34). Indeed, by its very title, Larsson's *Män som hatar kvinnor* (*Men Who Hate Women*) connects the violence against women to male hatred of them.

II Adapting Salander's revenge

Detecting the female

Karen Klitgaard Povlsen and Anne Marit Waade argue that in the Swedish film version of *Dragon Tattoo* the protagonists are presented in simple gender terms, albeit in reverse: Blomkvist (Michael Nyqvist) is presented as feminized and Salander (Noomi Rapace) as masculinized (2009: 65). Indeed, Salander's body is portrayed as hard in comparison to Blomkvist's 'soft' body and, even in scenes when Salander's naked body is put on display, the camera offers not feminine breasts, legs, or buttocks 'to-be-looked at', to use Laura Mulvey's term (2000: 487), but Salander's thin and muscled back – or, more accurately – the dragon tattoo on her back. And, in the end, it is Blomkvist who is the victim of male violence at the hands of Martin Vanger and Salander who must come to his rescue. Povlsen and Waade argue that the gender inversion of the protagonists 'corresponds to the genre-specific and media-specific conditions' of film, and they connect the representation of Salander to the increasing presence of female action heroines in Hollywood films – notably, *not* the Scandinavian crime narrative tradition of which gender equality and ambiguity are characteristic (2009: 65–67).[8] In the 1990s American films saw the rise of the female detective following the popularity of Clarice Starling in *The Silence of the Lambs* (Demme US 1991); in the early 2000s, she was joined by the 'chick flick' heroines of crime-comedies like Elle Woods in *Legally Blonde* (Luketic US 2001) and 'action babes' Lara Croft and Charlie's Angels.[9] Salander is at once both a sleuth like Starling *and* a woman of action like Croft, wielding guns, axes, and golf clubs with the same dexterity as she handles her motorcycle and laptop keyboard; however, unlike Hollywood's action babes, in the Swedish film adaptation she is not presented as a fantasy of female physicality. Hollywood's action babes are clad in spectacular outfits that cling to and highlight their femininity – curvaceous breasts, hips, and buttocks – and presented as distinctly heterosexual, politically conservative, and socially desirable; in contrast, Salander is presented as androgynous, bisexual, subversive, and an outcast.

Rather than be celebrated for her 'girl power', as are her Hollywood post-feminist counterparts, Salander – and the violence she perpetrates – cannot be so readily embraced: she is a complex and potentially problematic heroine. As Linda Mizejewski comments, 'the messiness of the crime film – its gendered violence, haunted masculinities, and obsession with the body – resists declaring feminism a closed case' (2005: 126). Salander's presence in *Dragon Tattoo* makes things messy – embodying all three protagonists of the crime narrative triangle as alternately 1) a detective on a case (investigating Harriet's disappearance), 2) the victim of a crime (raped by Bjurman), and 3) a criminal (her rape of Bjurman and attack on Martin). Notably, Salander is a successful detective due to her knowledge of information technology and her computer-like brain (with photographic memory), skills that are contrasted with, and arguably complement, Blomkvist's humanity and his ability to interact with, and to read, people. In Larsson's *Dragon Tattoo*, their investigative achievements are paralleled: Blomkvist and Salander figure out, at the same time and independently of each other, that Martin was the man that Harriet saw at the parade the day she disappeared. In Oplev's film, however, it is only Salander who figures out the killer's identity in time to stop him, while Blomkvist confides in Martin all of the investigation's facts and theories, and Martin is able to take Blomkvist prisoner.

Despite Salander's success as a detective, all three Swedish films struggle with her role as a violent avenger, opting for a more conservative set of moral values in terms of presenting Salander as heroic.[10] Larsson's first novel concludes with Martin choosing suicide over incarceration and humiliation as he steers his car into the path of an on-coming truck. Conversely, in the film, his SUV is clipped by the logging truck and spins out of control only because his broken arm – care of Salander's golf swing – impairs his ability to steer and shift gears at the same time. Importantly, Salander has the opportunity to save Martin before his SUV bursts into flames, but she does not: she stands aside and watches him burn while he extends his hand and begs for her help. Blomkvist tells Salander that he would not have done what she chose to do – but he does understand why she did it. According to the film, Salander's machine-like mind and anti-social personality are regarded as superior in terms of tracking down and bringing evil to justice. Salander is recast from being an exceptional hacker and researcher (that is, detective) to being a vengeful action woman (that is, avenger), *à la* Hollywood. On the one hand, the Swedish film seems to be progressive in offering a fringe female detective as the investigative superior; on the other, however, the message is clear that Salander is damaged and will not be cured until she becomes more human/e (a lesson she can learn from Blomkvist). And, whereas the novel – at Salander's insistence – saw Martin's dungeon and evil secrets die with him, the film – at Blomkvist's insistence – sees the police called in to investigate. In the end, the Swedish film offers a much more conventional and law-abiding conclusion in keeping with mainstream (American) crime film conventions – namely, seeing justice served *within* the bounds of the law.

Gendered crime

Stenport and Alm argue that Larsson's *Dragon Tattoo* tends to suppress the horrific crimes committed against women: instead, it is the corporate crimes that are exposed and brought to the public's awareness by trial and/or the media. Indeed, in the first novel, the crimes committed by Gottfried and Martin Vanger are never brought to light, but those of corrupt businessman Hans-Erik Wennerström are (2008: 161).[11] The Swedish film version alters this as part of its more traditional ending, with the exposure of both the corporate and femicide criminals. Stenport and Alm note that the 'gendered crimes are generally overlooked by reviewers and readers' discussions despite the fact that the novel's original title in Swedish (*Män som hatar kvinnor* [*Men Who Hate Women*]) makes clear that gender relations are central to the plot' (2009: 159). However, I would point out that title of Larsson's novel is *not* 'The Women Whom Men Hate'. Just as the focus of Dag Svensson's exposé in *Played with Fire* is on the 'johns' and pimps who abuse women in the sex-trafficking trade (while the focus of his girlfriend's thesis is on the female victims of the trade), so too the focus of Larsson's novel is the bringing to justice of 'The Men Who Hate Women'. Salander's victimization at the hands of various authority figures functions less as the main focus of the novels and adaptations and more as a means to fuel her desire to see these men punished for the crimes they commit against other vulnerable women.

In the first half of Oplev's *Dragon Tattoo*, Salander is the victim of male violence on three occasions. In the first instance, she bumps into a man by accident in a subway station and he forces her into a choke-hold so that his friend can pour beer on her; she frees herself by biting him, but the man and his friend punch and kick her. In the end she is able to chase off her attackers only when she slices one of them with a broken beer bottle. This scene prompts the second instance of male violence, because during the first attack Salander's laptop is damaged and she must request funds for its replacement from her newly appointed guardian. Bjurman closes the blinds in his office before he suggests to Salander that the only way he will release her own money to her is if she 'earns' it – in other words, completes a sexual favour for him. He slaps her, then stands behind her with his arm down the front of her shirt and unbuckles his trousers to masturbate. He assures her, 'If you're nice to me, I'll always be nice to you' before he forces her to perform fellatio on him. Her 'reward' for compliance is a cheque for 7,000 kronor (but not the 20,000 kronor she requested). This forced oral rape triggers the third instance of male violence as Salander plots to record Bjurman's abuse of power with a hidden camera in her backpack. First, she attempts to talk him out of abusing her: she says firmly, 'I won't give you a blow job every time I need money'. He replies, 'Do you want me to call the probate department and say you've trespassed and you're threatening me? Then we'll see how quickly you're back in the psychiatric ward'. Unfortunately, this time Bjurman wants more than a blow job and Salander is subjected to an extended and brutal rape. He punches her hard; as she lies unconscious, face-down on his bed, Bjurman handcuffs her to the headboard. When she returns to consciousness and cries out, he gags her – muffling her cries into panicked moans and animal-like howls. She tries to kick herself free, but he binds her feet with cords to the end of the bed. He asks, 'Are you a good girl now?', and removes her underwear and then his trousers before grabbing her by the hair and anally raping her. At this point, the soundtrack of the scene becomes muted, and her final scream is muffled. The camera then cuts abruptly to a long shot of her hobbling home along a bridge: she is unable to walk comfortably, or later sit down in her kitchen, because of the pain. She does, however, reveal the security camera she had concealed in her backpack and confirms that she has the entirety of the terrible attack recorded. Only two minutes of the two-hour rape are shown, but its brutality sears the incident into the viewer's mind.

The brutality of the scene is important to the plot as it aligns audience sympathy firmly with Salander, a character with whom viewers might struggle to identify, with her impassive face beneath thick gothic make-up and her stony silences. Indeed, it is because of her rape by Bjurman that viewers – male and female, Scandinavian and Anglophone – are invited to excuse the violence she then exacts on Larsson's male villains. At the beginning of *Dragon Tattoo*, Salander begins the narrative as a twenty-first century Robin Hood operating solely in cyberspace who can, to an extent, be excused because her crimes are (mostly) committed against criminals who deserve exposure; however, her rape by Bjurman sees her transform into a woman of action in the physical world as well. Her first act of retribution is on Bjurman. With no sense of how much time has passed since her rape, Salander appears again at Bjurman's front door. She forces her way past him as he accuses her of misunderstanding 'the rules' (his rules). She then uses a Taser to incapacitate him; when he returns to consciousness, he finds himself naked (except for his socks) on the floor, bound, and tied to the foot of his bed. Salander then secures tape over his mouth, retrieves his dildo from the drawer where he kept his handcuffs, and rapes him anally. The scene of Salander's rape by Bjurman felt claustrophobic because the viewer was often confined to a shot of Salander's face and, like Salander, was unable to see what Bjurman was doing behind her, capitalizing on the effect of witnessing Salander's fear. The corresponding scene of Bjurman's rape by Salander offers a world off kilter, with the camera tilting to a canted angle and then alternating between a shot of Bjurman's face full of pain, and Salander's face full of hatred. When done, she explains to him about the recording she has of her rape and how she will leak it to the media unless he plays by the new rules – *her* rules – which include giving her control over her money and the information about her he provides in his monthly reports. She leaves him tied up, with the video playing. Like the scene of her rape, Bjurman's also lasts two minutes of screen time, but she makes him watch all two hours of the recording. In addition to raping Bjurman, Salander has one more act of revenge planned: she tattoos a message on his abdomen 'I am a sadistic pig and a rapist' (in the novel, she adds 'a pervert' in between) to warn potential victims and to deter willing lovers.

As a victim of male violence, a detective, and a crime-fighter, consecutively, Salander has precursors in America's Blaxploitation heroines of the 1970s, especially Pam Grier's *Coffy* (Hill, US, 1973) and *Foxy Brown* (Hill, US, 1974). These African American women were inspired to turn detective when violence was committed against their loved ones. On the one hand, they were empowered by their sex – infiltrating criminal organizations as lovers or prostitutes; on the other, their sex made them vulnerable to male violence and both Foxy and Coffy are victims of rape. Importantly, the punishment for the villains in these films (even if not rapists) was a metaphorical, and sometimes literal, castration. At the end of *Coffy*, the heroine shoots her boyfriend in the groin with a shotgun when she discovers that he has betrayed her; similarly, *Foxy Brown*'s heroine has her revenge on Miss Katherine, the head of the drug-dealing organization, by presenting her with her lover's genitalia in a pickle jar. The ultimate revenge for these heroines is that both men survived these attacks and have to live with their castration.

Parallel to these female Blaxploitation films was a cycle of B-level 'rape-and-revenge' films such as *I Spit on Your Grave* (Zarchi, US, 1978) and *The Last House on the Left* (Craven, US, 1972), in which violence is regarded as the appropriate punishment for rapists. Salander's story follows the three-act structure of the rape-and-revenge film: she is savagely raped, survives and plans her revenge, and then takes out her revenge on her rapist. In the case of *Dragon Tattoo*, however, the three-acts are condensed into one sequence and Salander's revenge on Bjurman is carried out in the scene following her rape. Bjurman's rape of Salander – in both novel and film – can be inferred as justifying the female victim's retaliation and revenge upon her own victimizer (namely, her rape of Bjurman), but also that exacted on Harriet's victimizer when Salander chases Martin (Harriet's brother and rapist) to his death. Similarly, the brutality of Bjurman's rape of Salander can be construed as justification for the viciousness of her own – perhaps otherwise indefensible – acts of revenge against Bjurman and Martin in the first film, the journalist Per-Åke Sandström and her father Zalachenko in the second, and her half-brother, Niedermann, in the third.

I would argue, however, that the films are sophisticated in that they leave audiences wondering if the rape *does* indeed justify the level of Salander's revenge. As noted earlier, Salander is faced with a choice at the end of Oplev's *Dragon Tattoo*: to save Martin or to let him die. She chooses to watch him burn alive – an act of revenge that she also committed as a 12-year-old girl in order to punish her abusive father. In *Played with Fire*, Salander wants information out of Sandström, who is also one of the johns in a sex-trafficking case: she incapacitates him using a Taser and then strings him up with a noose around his neck (just as Martin did to Blomkvist in *Dragon Tattoo*). Salander threatens Sandström: if he does not tell the truth, she will use her Taser and he will asphyxiate himself on the noose. It is only in this scene in the second film that Salander dons her gothic 'war paint', and she does it to a far greater extreme than she did in *Dragon Tattoo*: her face is painted white with blackened eyes and lips, and a jagged red lightning bolt (evoking a blood trail) is drawn from one eye to the opposite corner of her mouth. Salander terrorizes the journalist, and when his teenaged daughter walks in to find him strung up in the noose, one cannot help but feel that Salander has crossed a line: she has become as bad as the bad guys.

In both *Dragon Tattoo* and *Played with Fire*, violence is presented as questionable no matter who exacts it. Salander, it would seem, may not have fallen far from the tree in terms of her capacity to commit violence – something that Salander herself suggests when Zalachenko reveals to her that Niedermann is her half-brother. In Larsson's novel, she thinks to herself 'bitterly', *'There are all sorts of genetic defects in the Zalachenko family'* (2009a: 696). Indeed, in the third of the Swedish films, parallels are drawn *not* between Salander and Blomkvist, but between Salander and Zalachenko as they both lie in the hospital with bandages wrapped around their heads, each plotting the other's demise. Salander's humanization is never fully achieved in the Swedish series and the final scene of the last film shows Salander closing her door to Blomkvist – and the world outside her window (the last shot as the credits roll). Whereas in Larsson's third novel, Salander 'opened the door wide and let [Blomkvist] into her life again' (2009b: 563), in the film, like America's Western gunslinger or Dirty Harry, Salander must remain machine-like, anti-social, and isolated in order to remain an effective weapon against the men who hate women. It makes sense, then, that Fincher's 2011 remake of *Dragon Tattoo* would confirm this alignment with American heroism; however, the valorization of vigilantism is taken one step further as Blomkvist condones Salander's attempted murder of Martin, and the questioning of that violence from Larsson's novel is, indeed, lost in the translation to an Anglophone version.

III Americanizing Salander

In both Larsson's *Dragon Tattoo* and Oplev's 2009 film, there is a sense that, in order to survive the cruel millennial world, the two protagonists can and must learn from each other – as is standard in a buddy narrative. Blomkvist must learn to bend the rules, as villains like Hans-Erik Wennerström do, and Salander must learn to deal with the real world (human beings) as well as she does the virtual world (computers): in other words, Blomkvist humanizes Salander and Salander, in turn, demonstrates the necessity of bending the rules. In Fincher's film, Blomkvist (Daniel Craig) initially complains that Salander (Rooney Mara) relies on methods that are both 'illegal and immoral'. By the end of the film, however – notably, following his victimization by Martin Vanger (Stellan Skarsgård) – Blomkvist embraces Salander's methods because they mean that Wennerström's financial crimes will be exposed. And, while Larsson and Oplev's reporter-hero questions Salander's vigilantism (exacting justice outside of the bounds of the law) and also her vengeance (letting Martin burn to death when she could have saved him), Fincher's Blomkvist wholeheartedly approves. As Martin stumbles out of the torture chamber and escapes, Blomkvist encourages Salander to take a gun and go after him. When she pauses to ask with innocent frankness, 'May I kill him?', Blomkvist nods emphatically in the affirmative. Just as Salander desired vengeance on Bjurman for raping her, so too does Fincher's Blomkvist desire the same after experiencing his own victimization. Interestingly, rather than make Martin's car crash an act of suicide (as did Larsson) or an accident (as did Oplev), Fincher punishes Martin for trying to run Salander and her bike off the bridge by seeing him lose control and crash as a result. While Oplev's film saw Blomkvist question Salander's allowing Martin to burn to death, Fincher's rejects a moral debate: Salander poses with the gun cocked, ready to shoot Martin, but she is denied her vengeance when his vehicle bursts into flames. The camera offers a close-up of her legs as she uncocks the phallic gun resting against her thigh, and the film invites us to be disappointed, as is Salander, that she is denied the chance to mete out a killer's just punishment.

The shift in the moralizing tone of *Dragon Tattoo* is tied to the recasting of Salander; indeed, most North American reviewers noted that the one aspect of Fincher's film that deviated most from the Swedish version was Salander herself. In a review of Fincher's film for *The New York Times*, A. O. Scott describes Salander as 'more complex than the average superhero' (2011). Yes, but the American remake also *reduces* her to the role of superhero. Indeed, when Salander has her revenge on Bjurman, she sports a superhero-like mask of make-up with her eyes blackened like a raccoon's. She may not leap tall buildings in a single bound, but Salander is an 'American' action hero, leaping between subway escalators to retrieve her computer bag from a thief and swinging a golf club hard enough to break Martin's jaw and send his teeth flying across the room. Noomi Rapace received much critical acclaim for her near-silent and highly effective performance in the Swedish films – so much acclaim, in fact, that Hollywood cast the Swedish actor in the big-budget *Sherlock Holmes: A Game of Shadows* (Ritchie 2011), notably released at the same time as Fincher's *Dragon Tattoo*. Some reviewers argued that Mara's portrayal of Salander is superior (Howell 2011; Lacey 2011), or is certainly the best part of Fincher's film; as J. Hoberman of *The Village Voice* suggests, it is Mara's 'pale flame that illuminates the movie' (2011). However, the praise for Mara was not unanimous: Kenneth Turan of the *Los Angeles Times* says Fincher's film is 'too frigid' and 'betrays a misunderstanding of what's at the heart of the phenomenal international success of the Millennium trilogy books [...] the character of Lisbeth Salander' (2011). Turan argues that while Rapace's heroine was 'savage', 'there was always a sense of an actual person inside those fierce defences that enabled audiences to connect on screen'; Mara's version, on the other hand, he describes as 'robotic' (2011). Whether Mara's Salander is an *improvement* over Rapace's is of less importance than the fact that she is *different*. Rapace's heroine was tough and defiant, muscled and insubordinate; Mara's, on the other hand, is small, slight, waif-like, and, rather than offering a challenging stare, Mara's big blue eyes (made larger by their contrast with black bangs and bleached eyebrows) tend to be directed off to the side or fixed on the floor – and often close to tears.

As Monika Bartyzel asks, 'does the American characterization of Salander really invoke the spirit of Larsson's creation, or does it fall prey to the pitfalls that plague Hollywood's artistic output?' (2011). Certainly the earliest trailer for Fincher's film (released in summer 2011) suggested a more violent film: a montage of images set to Trent Reznor's version of Led Zeppelin's 'Immigrant Song' (featuring Karen O), with its angry guitar and high-pitched vocal wails. As I have noted earlier, immigration and the anxieties arising from it are a key issue in Scandinavian crime fiction in general and Larsson's novels in particular. Despite the use of 'Immigrant Song' for the first trailer and the final film's opening credit sequence, immigration is not a key theme: in fact, it is mentioned only once, when Martin describes his last prisoner as an 'immigrant whore'. Instead, the song is most likely used because of its pounding rock rhythms and lyrics which link the film – and Salander – to Scandinavia's Viking past: 'We come from the land of the ice and snow/From the midnight sun where the hot springs flow'. The original poster tagline, 'Evil shall with evil be expelled', suggested that Salander is somehow as evil as the villains she and Blomkvist seek, and the poster offered a topless Mara with only Craig's arm and the film's release date covering her breasts. The combined impact of the 'Immigrant Song' trailer, 'Evil' tagline, and 'naked' poster led North American audiences to believe that Fincher's version of *Dragon Tattoo* would be more violent, sexual, and edgy – more like his 1995 film *Seven* (even the credit sequence recalls Fincher's *Seven*, which also featured a rapidly-edited montage of shocking images set to a Reznor-produced soundtrack). Indeed, Bartyzel blames, in part, the early 'teaser' publicity for sexualizing Salander:

> Rapace's fully clothed Salander was replaced with Mara's sexy Lisbeth – baring her cleavage for the camera, baring her ass for a tattoo, standing in front of a wintry landscape topless, straddling a bike in underwear and tights, or posing in a tutu. The woman fighting against objectification had become a sexual commodity to the public at large. Eventually, the marketing material changed focus, but it was too late – Salander was already made into the sex object. She had become another female ass-kicker swathed in sexy, revealing clothing, balancing tough smarts with alluring sexiness. (2011)

All three of these marketing tools, however, were replaced in the fall of 2011, recasting the film as a straightforward detective narrative. The tagline, 'What is hidden in the snow, comes forth in the thaw', was accompanied by a new trailer following a standard mystery, puzzle-plot format and a poster which presented a Mohawked-Mara in profile, with a smaller image of Craig placed inside her head. From the physical to the cerebral, Mara's Salander was re-presented in keeping with Larsson's Longstocking detective; however, the film itself did not necessarily support this re-branding of the heroine.

Certainly, in the film, there actually appeared to be a *reduction* in the degree of brutality – especially in the instances of violence against women. The first act of violence perpetrated against Salander in the subway is downgraded in Fincher's film from a sexual assault perpetrated against her because of her sex to a common – and non-sex related – robbery. Although Bjurman's rape of Salander is no less horrifying a crime, lost is some level of the brutality that Oplev's film explicitly showed and sometimes, and to more effect, kept just out of frame. The amount of screen time given to the rape scene is no less than in Oplev's film, nor are the atrocious acts committed by Bjurman altered or omitted; perhaps the difference is Oplev's noirish lighting, canted angles, and out-of-focus background, or perhaps the recasting of Bjurman from a sinister Peter Andersson to Yorick van Wageningen, 10 years his junior. During both rape scenes Oplev aligned the audience with the victim: first, with Bjurman's rape of Salander, the camera offers its uncomfortable close-up of Salander's face in focus and a blurred Bjurman moving in the background; then, with Salander's rape of Bjurman, the camera offers Bjurman's face in focus from a floor-level position and a blurred Salander moving menacingly in the background. In contrast, Fincher's film offers more shots of Bjurman's face in anticipation and pleasure during the rape, and only a few shots of Salander's, which is most often obscured by her hair. In Fincher's film, the matching shots are not those of the victim's point of view but of the victor's: in the first case, the camera is placed above Bjurman's head as he arches it back with pleasure from the blowjob he has forced Salander to perform; similarly, in the second instance, the camera is placed above Salander's head as she arches it back, delighting in her plan for revenge. The second major difference between the two rape scenes is the interruption: in Oplev's, the scene of Salander's rape is followed directly by that of her walking home and then the revelation that she recorded the whole incident with a hidden camera; in contrast, Fincher's cuts from the rape to Blomkvist conducting his research at the cottage before it cuts back to Salander after the rape is over. In doing this, some of the power of the previous scene and/or our identification with Salander is lost. The final key difference is that, while Oplev cuts abruptly from the rape in progress to Salander walking home in appalling pain, Fincher shows the aftermath of the rape in Bjurman's apartment: a defeated Salander dresses in the bedroom and then stands in the hallway, awaiting her cheque with tears in her eyes. Whatever the combination of factors, the end result is that Fincher's version of Salander's rape sets up a different thematic tack. While Larsson and Oplev question the morality of Salander's acts of revenge, Fincher does no such thing: Mara's Salander is presented as justified in – and, more importantly, celebrated for – her acts of violence against the men who hate women, and it is this aspect of the film that sees the full Americanization of Larsson's twenty-first century Longstocking into a two-dimensional superhero (not unlike the comic-book, child-vigilante, Hit-Girl of *Kick-Ass* (Vaughn 2010)) even down to the raccoon-like mask of make-up that Salander sports during her revenge attack on Bjurman.

While Larsson and Oplev suggest that Rapace's Salander might be mentally impaired, Fincher assures us that Mara's Salander is only emotionally damaged: the latter is a victim, through and through. Despite her own suggestion that she might be 'insane', we have no doubt that Mara's Salander is *not*; she is merely a victim of male violence and all it takes to cure her is her romantic relationship with Blomkvist. In Larsson's novels, we are led to believe that Salander has some form of Asperger's syndrome and will most likely never be fully socialized. More importantly, in the Swedish film we are left to wonder whether Rapace's Salander wants to be 'normal'; in contrast, in the American film, we see that Mara's Salander desperately does. While Oplev's film ends with a confident Salander in disguise walking along a palm-lined boardwalk far from the gloomy winter skies of Stockholm – alone and triumphant – Fincher's ends (as Larsson's novel does) with Salander feeling abandoned and hurt. In the course of her snooping through his computer files, Salander had found an old photo of Blomkvist from when he had a motorcycle, sporting a biker jacket. Perhaps hoping to mould him into a boyfriend more of her ilk, Salander has a copy of the jacket custom-made and heads to his Stockholm apartment to present it as a Christmas gift and cement their relationship. As she approaches, however, she sees a happy and laughing Blomkvist heading out for the evening with his business partner and lover, Erika Berger. Salander hurls the present into a dumpster in the alley and, as the couple leave in a taxi, Salander drives off on her bike in the opposite direction – alone and angry. As I noted earlier, the American hero becomes ineffective when accepted into society and must remain an outsider in order to pursue justice for that society: Salander remains an unfettered, anti-social, and effective hero…ready for a sequel.

Violent conclusions

Rather than suggesting that one version of *The Girl with the Dragon Tattoo* is better or more faithful to Larsson's novel than the other, the goal of this chapter has been to explore the various ways that Larsson's stories have been reimagined for different audiences – readers versus viewers, Swedish versus Anglophone, national versus international. While the Swedish films had begun the 'internationalization' process of the character of Salander by enacting many mainstream (that is, Hollywood) tropes – from the rape-and-revenge film to the solitary hero who walks off into the sunset (or sunshine, in Salander's case) – the American film pushed Salander firmly into the role of superhero and action babe. As Bartyzel suggests, 'Fincher removes the suffocating, repetitive sense that Lisbeth is prey.[...] Fincher's Lisbeth is not Larsson's. She is sexualized, softened, romanticized, and less empowered' (2011). A. O. Scott agrees, noting that the sexualization of Salander is 'perfectly conventional – the exploitation of female nudity is an axiom of modern cinema – but it also represents a failure of nerve and a betrayal of the sexual egalitarianism Lisbeth Salander argues for and represents' (2011). Gone is the equality established between Blomkvist and Salander in Larsson's novel and the gender inversion Povlsen and Waade identify in the Swedish film, with Blomkvist feminized and Salander masculinized; instead, in the American film we see gender relations re-polarized and Salander moulded after other Hollywood heroines of recent years.

The most important shift with Fincher's film, however, is the questioning of revenge – or the lack thereof. Larsson's novel and Oplev's film posed a question to their respective audiences regarding whether Salander's revenge was justifiable, placing readers/viewers in the uncomfortable position of questioning their identification with Salander and the vicarious pleasure they might find in the violence on offer. The moral dilemma for Larsson's Blomkvist is whether to call the police and expose the truth about Martin Vanger; for Oplev's Blomkvist, the dilemma is to understand and accept that Salander did nothing to save Martin; in contrast, Fincher's Blomkvist suffers no dilemma and gratefully sends Salander after Martin to exact the revenge (that he cannot) for his own victimization. Ultimately, what was hidden in Sweden's snow was an American superhero waiting to be unleashed.

Acknowledgements

The author would like to thank Dr Tanis MacDonald and Dr Madelaine Hron for sharing and reflecting upon the Larsson experience with her.

Notes

1. I will refer to the films as Swedish; technically, however, they are Swedish/Danish/German/Norwegian co-productions.
2. Krister Henriksson starred in the Swedish TV series, 'Wallander' (2005–06), and a direct-to-video series (2009–10). There was also a 'Wallander' series of Swedish films starring Rolf Lassgård (1994–2007).
3. All budget and box office statistics are from *Box Office Mojo*, www.boxofficemojo.com, accessed 20 Jun 2011.

4. *Dragon Tattoo* made $105m worldwide ($11m in North America); *Played with Fire* $67m worldwide ($7.6m in North America); and *Hornets' Nest* $44m worldwide ($5.2m in North America). *Dragon Tattoo* ranks #24 of foreign-language film releases.
5. See Traynor (2010) and Castle (2010).
6. See Nolan (2009).
7. The American remake (aired on AMC in 2011) of the Danish TV series 'The Killing' ('Forbrydelsen' 2007), also links political ambition to corrupted morality: a mayoral candidate is arrested for killing a young woman.
8. Povlsen and Waade imply the connection to Hollywood films by citing Rikke Schubart, *Super Bitches and Action Babes: The Female Hero in Popular Cinema, 1970–2006* (Jefferson, NC: McFarland, 2007), which focuses on Hollywood cinema.
9. *Charlie's Angels* (McG 2000) and *Charlie's Angels 2: Full Throttle* (McG 2003); *Lara Croft: Tomb Raider* (West 2001) and *Lara Croft Tomb Raider: The Cradle of Life* (De Bont 2003).
10. The novels also allowed their protagonists a greater degree of sexual freedom, while the films attempt to hetero-normativize them. In the novels, Salander is presented as unrestrained in her choice of partners, including girlfriend Miriam, investigative partner Blomkvist, teenager George, and married Dieter. In the novels, Blomkvist is presented as a womanizer, having sexual relationships with Erika Berger, Cecilia Vanger, Harriet Vanger, Salander, and Monica Figuerola. Just as Salander is reduced to two lovers in the films, so too is Blomkvist: only Salander and Berger. In the novels, Berger is a key character whose problems and desires are given narrative voice – including her wish to have a threesome with her husband and Blomkvist. In the Swedish films, Berger is recast as single and in love with Blomkvist; by the end of the third film, we are assured that they are in a committed – and monogamous – relationship.
11. I would like to point out that, while this may be true in the first novel, in the third, Blomkvist insists, 'When it comes down to it, this story is not primarily about spies and secret government agencies; it's about violence against women, and the men who enable it' (Larsson, 2009b: 514).

Works cited

Bartyzel, M. (2011) 'Girls on Film: Softening and Sexualizing Lisbeth Salander', *Movies.com*, 22 Dec, http://www.movies.com/movie-news/sexualizing-lisbeth-salander/5948, accessed 3 Jan 2012.

Caputi, J. and D. E. H. Russell . 'Femicide: Sexist Terrorism against Women' in J. Radford and D. E. H. Russell (eds) *Femicide: The Politics of Killing Women*. New York: Twayne Publishers. 1992. 410–26.

Castle, I. (2010) 'Swedish Anti-Immigration Party Claims Seats', *The New York Times*, 20 Sep, http://www.nytimes.com/2010/09/20/world/europe/20sweden.html, accessed 13 June 2010.

Demko, G. J. 'The Mystery in Sweden', *G.J. Demko's Landscapes of Crime,* http://www.dartmouth.edu/~gjdemko/swedish.htm, accessed 24 May 2011.

Eriksson, K. (2006) *The Princess of Burundi*. Transl. E. Segerberg. New York: Thomas Dunne Books.

Hoberman, J. (2011) 'The Girl with the Dragon Tattoo', *The Village Voice*, http://www.villagevoice.com/movies/the-girl-with-the-dragon-tattoo-2615197/, accessed 27 Dec 2011.

Howell, P. (2011) 'Rooney Mara squeezes fresh pulp in *The Girl with the Dragon Tattoo*', *The Toronto Star*, 19 Dec, http://www.thestar.com/entertainment/article/1104421 – review-rooney-mara-squeezes-fresh-pulp-in-the-girl-with-the-dragon-tattoo, accessed 27 Dec 2011.

Lacey, L. (2011) 'Efficiency trumps boldness in David Fincher's *The Girl with the Dragon Tattoo*', *The Globe and Mail*, 18 Dec, http://www.theglobeandmail.com/news/arts/movies/efficiency-trumps-boldness-in-the-girl-with-the-dragon-tattoo/article2274439/, accessed 27 Dec 2011.

Larsson, S. (2008), *The Girl With the Dragon Tattoo*. Transl. R. Keeland. Toronto: Penguin Canada.

Larsson, S. (2009a), *The Girl Who Played With Fire*. Transl. R. Keeland. Toronto: Penguin Canada.

Larsson, S. (2009b), *The Girl Who Kicked the Hornets' Nest*. Transl. R. Keeland. Toronto: Viking Canada.

Mizejewski, L. (2005) 'Dressed to Kill: Postfeminist Noir', *Cinema Journal* 44.2, 121–27.

Mulvey, L. (2000 [1975]) 'Visual Pleasure and Narrative Cinema' in Robert Stam and Toby Miller (eds) *Film and Theory: An Anthology*. Oxford: Blackwell. 483–494.

Nolan, T. (2009) 'Crime Novels in a Cold Place', *The Wall Street Journal*, 28 May, http://online.wsj.com/article/SB124347203128660835.html, accessed 20 May 2011.

Povlsen, K. K. and A. M.Waade (2009) '*The Girl with the Dragon Tattoo*, Adapting Embodied Gender from Novel to Movie in Stieg Larsson's Crime Fiction', *p.o.v.: A Danish Journal of Film Studies* 28, http://pov.imv.au.dk/Issue_28/section_2/artc7A.html, accessed 13 June 2011.

Scott, A. O. (2011) 'Tattooed Heroine Metes Out Slick, Punitive Violence', *The New York Times*, 20 Dec, http://www.nytimes.com/2011/12/20/movies/the-girl-with-the-dragon-tattoo-movie-review.html, accessed 27 Dec 2011.

Stenport A. W. and C. O. Alm (2009) 'Corporations, Crime, and Gender Construction in Stieg Larsson's *The Girl with the Dragon Tattoo*: Exploring Twenty-First Century Neoliberalism in Swedish culture', *Scandinavian Studies* 81.2, 157–78.

Traynor, I. (2010) 'Sweden joins Europe-wide backlash against immigration', *The Guardian*, 24 Sep, http://www.guardian.co.uk/world/2010/sep/24/sweden-immigration-far-right-asylum, accessed 13 June 2010.

Turan, K. (2011) 'The Girl with the Dragon Tattoo is too frigid', *The Los Angeles Times*, 20 Dec, http://www.latimes.com/entertainment/news/la-et-girl-with-the-dragon-tattoo-20111220,0,716278.story, accessed 27 Dec 2011.

Woodroof, M. (2008) 'The Making of a Posthumous Best-Seller', *National Public Radio*, 13 Nov, http://www.npr.org/templates/story/story.php?storyId=96539049, accessed 17 June 2011.

Žižek, S. (2011) 'Henning Mankell, the Artist of the Parallax View', http://www.lacan.com/zizekmankell.htm, accessed 13 June 2010.

Index

Aaron, Michele, 176
Abbott, Megan, 2, 11, 137–140, 144–147
Abel, Marco, 13, 161
The Accused (film), 12
action heroes, 13–14, 24, 29, 200, 206–211
affect, 161–166, 171–172, 176, 182–186
Aftermath (Robinson), 55
agency, 2, 13, 23, 31, 68, 70, 93, 128, 142, 160–161, 166, 170–171, 177
alcoholism, 84
Along Came a Spider (Patterson), 44–45
Alvi, Moniza, 67
American audiences, success of Millennium trilogy with, 7, 34–5, 47, 48–9
Anglophone crime fiction, 2, 62
Anglophone writers, 2
Annika Bengtzon (character), 163–166
Åström, Berit, 5
avengers, female, 7–8, 24–26, 31–32, 51–64, 75–77, 200–201

Baksi, Kurdo, 11–12, 74
Birdman (Hayder), 10, 97–112
The Black Dahlia (Ellroy), 102
Blaxploitation heroines, 204
Blyton, Enid, 39–40
bodies, 9, 10, 83–90
  dead, 10, 97–112
  dismembered, 97–112
  female, 103, 111–112, 127, 139–140, 170
body politic, 28, 83–90
Body Work (Paretsky), 11, 136–137, 139, 140, 141–144, 149, 151
The Bomber (Marklund), 164
Bowers, Elizabeth, 23
The Bride Wore Black (Woolrich), 69–70

Bryant, Kobe, 21
Buffy the vampire slayer (character), 24
Bury Me Deep (Abott), 11, 139, 144–147, 151

Caedmon's Song (Robinson), 55–56
capitalism, 88–89, 92, 122
Chandler, Raymond, 40–41, 59
child molestation, 82, 90
Chinatown (film), 136, 139, 148–149
cinema, 13. *see also* film adaptations
citizenship, 9, 28, 58
clothing line, 6
Cohen, Daniel A., 103
commodification, 83–90
Cornwall, Patricia, 104
corpses, 10, 97–112
corruption, 195, 198–199, 201
Craig, Daniel, 1, 6, 206, 208
crime fiction
  Anglophone, 62
  conservative nature of genre, 10
  contemporary, 3–5
  detectives in, 52–55, 58–59, 139
  female avengers in, 51–64
  gender in, 10–11
  rape in, 15n4, 22–32, 110, 170–171
  Scandinavian/Swedish, 2, 8–10, 15n7, 62, 63–64, 81–90, 194–195, 198–199
  sexual violence in, 1–5, 15n5, 53–54, 140, 159–161
  violence against women in, 2–3, 35–38
  violence in, 8–9
crime writers, feminist, 22–25, 31–32, 40
cultural translation, 6
culture, popular, 21–22, 40, 48–49

dead bodies, 10, 97–112
Demko, G. J., 194

215

Denby, David, 5
detectives, 52–55, 58–59, 139, 200
disarticulation, 117–119, 122, 123, 129–133
dismembered bodies, 97–112
Dunant, Sarah, 24
Dyer, Richard, 170–171

Edwardson, Åke, 82
Ellis, Bret Easton, 100
Ellison, J. T., 35–36
Ellroy, James, 59, 102
emotion, 182–186
empowerment, 3, 5, 14, 23
Eriksson, Kjell, 196
ethical spectatorship, 176–190
ethics of violence, 12–13, 161–162, 176
evil, 46–47, 49, 208
Exposed (Marklund), 164–166

female action heroes, 13–14, 24, 29, 200, 206–211
female avengers, 7–8, 24–26, 31–32, 51–64, 75–77, 200–201
female body, 103, 111–112, 127, 139–140, 170
female characters, traumatic backgrounds of, 35–36, 161
female corpses, 10, 97–112
female detectives, 59, 200
female killers, 57–58
female sexuality, 127
female victims, 3–5, 24, 71, 109–112, 161, 195
femicide, 199
feminism, 3, 6, 22, 40, 68, 76–78, 160, 178–179
feminist crime writers, 22–25, 31–32, 40, 74, 76
femme fatale, 11, 70, 136–152
film adaptations, 12–13, 193
  Hollywood, 13–14, 14n1, 157–158, 193, 206–211
  rape-revenge narrative in, 175–190
  Swedish, 13, 61, 175–190, 194, 197–198, 199–205
Fincher, David, 1, 14n1, 157–158, 160, 193, 206, 211

forensic crime shows, 8
Frozen Tracks (Edwardson), 82

Gabrielsson, Eva, 12
Gates, Philippa, 6
gender roles, 3, 10–11, 63, 139
gendered crime, 201–205
George, Elizabeth, 53
Gerritsen, Tess, 161
The Girl Who Kicked the Hornet's Nest (Larsson), 28–29, 58. *see also* Millennium trilogy
The Girl Who Played with Fire (Larsson), 28, 58, 88–89, 198, 205. *see also* Millennium trilogy
The Girl with the Dragon Tattoo (Larsson), 58, 67, 89, 92, 118, 139. *see also* Millennium trilogy
  film adaptations, 1, 6, 13–14, 157–158, 175–190, 193, 197–211
  message of, 38–39
  as *noir* novel, 147–151
  rape scene in, 36–38, 175–190
  success of, 193–194
  violence in, 1
  voicelessness in, 118–126
globalization, 83, 95, 196–197
Gregersdotter, Katarina, 9
Gunne, Sorcha, 3

H&M, 6
Harriet Vanger (character), 27, 42, 47, 120–121, 124, 167, 175, 179, 195, 196, 199
Harris, Thomas, 7, 35, 44–45, 175, 199
Hayder, Mo, 10, 97–112
Hellström, Börge, 9–10, 81–82
Hollywood film adaptations, 13–14, 14n1, 157–158, 193, 206–211
homme fatale, 11, 140, 150
hopelessness, 10, 82, 90–93, 94
Horeck, Tanya, 5, 23
Hostel (film), 169

idealism, 40–41
images, of violence, 12–13
immigration, 195–196
In the Cut (Moore), 11, 118, 126–133, 134

individualism, 177–178
The Inspector and Silence (Nesser), 9, 69–73, 76

judicial system, 30–31

Kallentoft, Mons, 84, 91, 93
Karneef, Natalie, 6
Kurt Wallander (character), 68, 82–83, 84

Läckberg, Camilla, 53–54
Ladies Night (Bowers), 23
language, 11, 126–133
Lara Croft (character), 24, 200
Larsson, Åsa, 53–54
Larsson, Stieg, 2, 4, 137–138
   death of, 68
   influences on, 39–40
   witness of rape by, 11–12
The Last Temptation (McDermid), 167
The Leopard (Nesbø), 97
Lilja 4-ever (film), 87
Lindell, Unni, 56–57, 62
Lisbeth Salander (character), 5–8, 41–42, 73–74, 92–93
   as action hero, 13–14, 29, 200, 206–211
   body of, 85–86
   as female avenger, 7–8, 51–64, 75–76, 200–201
   as feminist heroine, 22, 24–25, 61–62, 67–68
   as *femme fatale*, 148–151
   hypersexualization of, 6
   as investigator, 58–59, 200
   media treatment of, 29
   rape of, 36–38, 67, 74–75, 93, 121–122, 179–186, 202–203
   resistance by, 75–76
   response to, 14, 158–159, 172
   revenge by, 186–189, 203–211
   social status of, 121
   as victim, 25–26, 29, 32, 77–78, 178–179, 199
Little Red Riding Hood (Lindell), 56–57, 62
locale, 197–198

Lyotard, Jean-François, 11, 117, 118, 134, 135n1

male detectives, 36
The Man on the Balcony (Wahlöö), 90
Mankell, Henning, 82–83, 84
Mann, Jessica, 3–4
Mara, Rooney, 5, 6
Mardorossian, Carine, 160, 179
Maria Adler (character), 68–69, 70–73, 77–78
Marion Seeley (character), 144–147
Marklund, Liza, 2, 159–160, 162–166
Martin Vanger (character), 120–122, 124–126, 140, 150–151, 197, 201, 206, 211
Marx, Karl, 88, 89
materiality, 176
McCabe, Jess, 36
McDermid, Val, 2, 11, 32, 117–118, 134, 159–160, 166–172
McFadyen, Cody, 45
media
   rape in the, 27
   treatment of Lisbeth in, 29
Mehta, Sonny, 34
melodrama, 51, 52, 58, 60–61, 63
The Mermaids Singing (McDermid), 11, 117–126, 134, 167
Midwinter Sacrifice (Kallentoft), 91, 93
Mikael Blomkvist (character), 25–27, 32, 42–43, 47, 118–119, 123–125, 147, 149, 167
Millennium trilogy
   American audience and, 34–35, 48
   body politic in, 28, 85–86
   as feminist fiction, 74–78
   melodrama in, 58, 60–61
   message of, 38–40
   origin of, 11–12
   rape in, 6–9, 21–32, 36–38, 67–78, 92–93, 121–122, 159–160
   serial killer fiction and, 7, 43–49
   success of, 7, 193–194
   villains in, 195–199
   violence in, 1–2, 4
misery, 8
misogynist violence, 3–5, 160
Modesty Blaise (character), 40

Moore, Susanna, 11, 118, 126–133
morality, 176–177

neo-*noir* novels, 136–152
Nesbø, Jo, 2, 8, 10, 97–112
Nesser, Håkan, 2, 9, 54–56, 62, 68–73, 76–78
Nestingen, Andrew, 94, 177
Newman, Melanie, 4
Nils Bjurman (character), 26, 28–29, 37–38, 67, 74–75, 121–122, 149–150, 179–186, 199, 202–204, 206–210
noir genre, 11, 136–152
nostalgia, 10, 82–83, 90–94

O'Connell, Carol, 40
Oplev, Niels Orden, 13, 175–176, 201–202

Paretsky, Sara, 2, 11, 23–24, 32, 35, 59, 62, 136–138, 140–144
passivity, 13
paternity, 108–109
patriarchy, 95, 198–199
Patterson, James, 44–45
perpetrators, 3
Peter Teleborian (character), 26, 30, 60, 75, 85, 199
Pippi Longstocking (character), 39, 60
Plain, Gill, 10, 15n4
politics, 58, 81–82, 195, 198–199
popular culture, 21–22, 40, 48–49
The Princess of Burundi (Eriksson), 196
prostitution, 89, 92. *see also* sex trade
psychology, 44, 54
psychopath, 3, 7, 10, 52

rape. *see also* sexual violence
 in crime fiction, 1–3, 15n4, 22–32, 110, 170–171
 depicted in film, 175–190
 high profile cases, 21
 media treatment of, 27
 in Millennium trilogy, 6–9, 21–32, 36–38, 67–78, 92–93, 121–122, 159–160
 politics of, 9
 reparation for, 27–28

representations of, 12–13, 160–161
 revenge for, 51, 63–64, 75–76, 158, 175–190
 rhetorical meaning of, 47–49
 victims, 21–22, 117–126, 133–135
 witnessed by Larsson, 11–12
realism, 40–41
reparation, 27–28. *see also* revenge
resistance, 75–76
retro-*noir*, 136–139, 151
revenge, 31, 37, 51, 63–64, 75–77, 158, 175–190, 199–205
Robinson, Peter, 55
Roseanna (Sjöwall), 90
Roslund, Anders, 9, 81–82
Rushing, Andrea, 31–32

Saw (film), 169
Scandinavian crime fiction, 2, 8–10, 15n7, 51–64, 81–90, 198–199
Scandinavian writers, 2
Seltzer, Sarah, 38
serial killer narratives, 7, 35, 42, 43–49, 55, 62, 98–99, 124–125
sex trade, 28, 31, 86–95
sexism, 35, 41
sexual violence, 90. *see also* rape; violence against women
 affective responses to, 13, 161–166, 171–172, 176, 182–186
 in crime fiction, 1–5, 15n5, 35–38, 53–54, 140, 159–161
 language of, 126–133
 victims of, 120–126
Shadow Man (McFadyen), 45–46
The Silence of the Lambs (Harris), 35, 44–45, 200
Sisters on the Road (Wilson), 22–23
Sjöwall, Maj, 9, 40, 41, 52, 81, 83–4, 86–7, 90–1, 194
slang, 126–127, 131
Smith, William Kennedy, 21
Smoky Barrett (character), 45–47
The Snowman (Nesbø), 10, 97–112
social criticism, 40–43
social injustice, 40–41
society, 83–90, 98, 120, 121
speaking to/speaking for victims, 11, 117–118

Strauss-Kahn, Dominique, 21
Swedish film adaptation, 13, 61, 175–190, 194, 197–205
Swedish society, 60–61

Tapper, Michael, 85
television, 8
Thompson, Zoë Brigley, 3
Tony Hill (character), 123–125
The Torment of Others (McDermid), 167–171, 172n6
torture porn, 169
Transgressions (Dunant), 24
Turan, Kenneth, 1
Tyson, Mike, 21

Ulcer School, 84, 85

Van Veeteren (character), 69, 72–73
The Vault (Roslund and Hellström), 9–10, 81–95
V.I. Warshawski (character), 23–24, 59, 62
victimhood, 13, 23, 25–28, 77–78
victimization, 2, 3, 178–179, 182–186
victims, 3, 4–5
 as avengers, 54–57, 62–64
 female, 24, 71, 109–112, 161, 195
 rape, 21–22, 117–126, 133–135
 of sexual violence, 120–126
 speaking to/speaking for, 11, 117–118
 voiceless, 117–126

violence. *see also* rape; sexual violence
 affective responses to, 13, 157–158, 161–166, 171
 in crime fiction, 8–9
 ethics of, 12–13, 161–162, 176
 in film remake, 1
 specularizing, 166–172
 against women, 2–5, 35–38, 63, 68, 90, 109–110, 160, 162–172, 199
violent images, 12–13
voicelessness, 11, 117–126, 128

Wager, J. B., 137, 138, 140
Wahlöö, Per, 9, 40, 41, 52, 81, 83–4, 86–7, 90–1, 194
welfare state, 9, 10, 62–63, 81–83, 94–95
Williams, Linda, 4
Wilson, Barbara, 22–23
witnesses, 125–126
Woman with Birthmark (Nesser), 9, 56, 62, 68–69, 70–72, 74, 76, 77–78
women
 bodies of dead, 10, 97–112
 commodification of, 86–90
 violence against, 2–5, 35–38, 63, 68, 90, 109–110, 160, 162–172, 199
Woodroof, Martha, 193–194
Woolrich, Cornell, 69–70

Young, Alison, 161, 162